S0-AEN-628

halfi

HEB

FEEHA

Feehan, Christine, author
Leopard's rage
33410017192974   08-09-2021

DISCARD

DISCARD

LEOPARD'S RAGE

CHRISTINE FEEHAN

THORNDIKE PRESS
A part of Gale, a Cengage Company

Copyright © 2020 by Christine Feehan.
A Leopard Novel.
Thorndike Press, a part of Gale, a Cengage Company.

ALL RIGHTS RESERVED
This is a work of fiction. Names, characters, places, and incidents either are the product of the author's imagination or are used fictitiously, and any resemblance to actual persons, living or dead, business establishments, events, or locales is entirely coincidental.
Thorndike Press® Large Print Romance.
The text of this Large Print edition is unabridged.
Other aspects of the book may vary from the original edition.
Set in 16 pt. Plantin.

LIBRARY OF CONGRESS CIP DATA ON FILE.
CATALOGUING IN PUBLICATION FOR THIS BOOK
IS AVAILABLE FROM THE LIBRARY OF CONGRESS.

ISBN-13: 978-1-4328-8365-2 (hardcover alk. paper)

Published in 2021 by arrangement with Berkley, an imprint of Penguin Publishing Group, a division of Penguin Random House, LLC

Printed in Mexico
Print Number: 01   Print Year: 2021

For Adaiah, this one's for you.

FOR MY READERS

Be sure to go to http://www.christinefeehan.com/members/ to sign up for my private book announcement list and download the free ebook of *Dark Desserts.* Join my community and get firsthand news, enter the book discussions, ask your questions and chat with me. Please feel free to email me at Christine @christinefeehan.com. I would love to hear from you.

ACKNOWLEDGMENTS

Thanks to Brian for getting me through this one. It was a tough go, but we did it! Thank you, Domini, for always editing, no matter how many times I ask you to go over the same book before we send it for additional editing.

1

Sevastyan Amurov paced back and forth with long, angry strides, trying to rid his body of the dark, ugly, animalistic, moody edge his leopard brought along with his own bad temper. Over the years, he'd worked at staying in complete control. He'd succeeded in preventing that hot red volcano welling up inside him from showing itself to the outside world, but he'd never managed to eliminate the vile emotion. He knew he never would.

He was leopard. Not just any leopard. He was Amurov, born and bred in a brutal lair known for cruelty, for such savage practices that other lairs wanted nothing to do with them. He couldn't blame them. The men in his lair took women to be their mates — not the women who held the mate for the leopards — but women who would give them sons. If they produced females or after they gave them sons, to show their loyalty

11

to their lair, the men murdered their wives, usually in front of their sons. Often, they insisted their sons participate. Female children were either killed or given away or sold as brides to others who would later kill them after they produced sons for their husbands.

Sevastyan had been beaten most of his childhood, as had his leopard, in an attempt to make him stronger — a fighter for his lair. He was raised to be an "enforcer." One who would be a bodyguard to the *vor,* or the one who would interrogate a prisoner for information. As he had grown up, that horrendous anger inside of him had grown, fed by his leopard's rage.

His leopard was very strong and controlling him wasn't easy. As the years had passed, unlike his cousins, his need for sex and domination had grown, not diminished. His leopard prowled closer and closer to the surface, demanding more and more, and those needs had turned sexual for him. It was a vicious cycle and one Sevastyan feared he was going to lose eventually. He often visited the underground clubs to ease the needs he had, but that was always dangerous when his leopard was so brutal. He had to be very careful that he didn't allow any of the cruelty of his cat to spill over to his

12

games with the women he played with.

Glancing at his watch for the tenth time, he hissed his displeasure. The woman from the landscaping company had blown him off. *Again.* That was three times. The first two times, at least she'd had the courtesy to let him know she couldn't make it. It was an inconvenience, but she'd given him enough time that he hadn't left Mitya, his cousin and boss, without protection.

He was Mitya's bodyguard. Mitya had enough enemies that Sevastyan wasn't about to take chances with his life. Already he'd been shot more than once, and leaving his protection to others didn't sit well with Sevastyan.

Like always, when he was very upset, the anger in him translated to a deep sexual need that he despised. It rose up like a tidal wave, a hunger that took hold of him and wouldn't let go until he rode a woman hard — and what was the difference between him and the other men in the lair he'd left so long ago? He despised himself for using women, no matter that they were fully consenting. He might visit the clubs and spend hours there doing the things he needed to do, but he was never sated. Never. His leopard roared his rage and deep inside, he did as well.

13

The truth was, Sevastyan wanted a woman of his own. A partner. A woman to love. A woman who held the mate for his leopard. That same gift his cousins had. He doubted if that was going to ever happen for him. His father and Mitya's father both had seen to that with their torture and deviant training. His needs weren't going to go away because he willed them to. Long weeks of trying. Months. Nothing had stopped that terrible craving. Nor would his rage. He had watched his cousins to see if they were like him. None of them were. Mitya was dominant, but he wasn't in the least like Sevastyan. Still, his leopard deserved a mate.

He had one thing going for them. His leopard — and he — were in their first life cycle. That meant they could claim an unmated female shifter. They just had to find one.

Deep inside, his leopard snarled and raked at him with sharp claws, leaping suddenly in an attempt to take him by surprise and get out. It wasn't the first time and wouldn't be the last. Sometimes, Sevastyan thought his leopard, whom he affectionally called Shturm, meaning assault, would end his life by literally ripping him open and climbing out of him rather than shifting the normal way they exchanged forms.

14

"I'm having enough trouble staying in control without you adding to my problems," he hissed in displeasure at the cat, raking his fingers through his hair, uncaring that it went wild on him. He was normally groomed to perfection, as part of his intimidating look.

Sevastyan was built the way many shifters were, with roped muscles and no fat. He was taller than most with wide shoulders and a thick, defined chest, narrow hips and muscular legs. He kept his cat in fighting form, which meant he was as well. He ran every day and let his cat out to run. He practiced with weapons daily and trained in hand-to-hand combat. He left nothing to chance when it came to Mitya's safety.

The cat leapt again, clawing for freedom, and Sevastyan turned toward the door. Shturm was being a little too persistent, which could only mean they weren't alone. Maybe the landscaper hadn't blown him off entirely, maybe she was just late. Not a good start, but at least she'd managed to get her ass here. He'd make it very clear he didn't tolerate that kind of crap from those he employed unless there was a very good excuse, in which case she should have let him know immediately.

Sevastyan took his time getting to the

15

door, deliberately slowing his steps, breathing deep to find that calm place he maintained in front of all others. His weapons were close, as they always were, so many tucked into his boots, the holster under his arm, the slim sheath between his shoulder blades, the many loops inside the jacket he shrugged into as he paused just at the door.

A woman hurried up the walkway, looking surprisingly young for being the owner of a renowned landscaping business. Sevastyan knew Leland Carver had passed away several years earlier, leaving the business to his daughter. Flambé Carver had grown up working alongside her father, and some said she had surpassed him in brilliance for her designs in incorporating the natural topography, flora and fauna into beautiful and unique works of art.

Leland Carver was a shifter, and he had designed the woods with their arboreal highways for the leopards to travel quickly throughout Mitya's property. It was the same on their cousin Fyodor's property. Carver had also landscaped and planted that property with fast-growing trees. Sevastyan wanted the same on his property. Part of the land had already been planted, but he wanted his property connected to his cousin's so he could travel fast without a car to get to Mitya, should there be need.

The woman hurrying up the walkway had the smaller, curvy body of a shifter, although she was much smaller than many of the women, and she had shocking red hair. Sheets of bright red hair, which he'd never seen on a shifter before. It wasn't dyed red; it looked too natural for that. The sun shone on it, turning it into a fiery blaze that spilled in all directions. She had it pulled up into a simple ponytail, but in her haste, in spite of the thickness of shifter hair, it had come loose and was pulling free, giving her the appearance of looking wild.

Sevastyan found the dominant rising like a tidal wave, strong, taking over, needing to tame that out-of-control woman rushing up his walkway, late by nearly half an hour to a very important appointment she'd already cancelled twice. He let her get right to the door and push the doorbell not once, but twice, with several long moments between before he took his time leisurely opening the heavy oak door to stand framed there just looking at her.

There was a long silence. She was breathing hard as if she'd been running a long distance. Just because she came from a line of shifters didn't mean she had a leopard, or that she knew she was a shifter. Men had their leopards nearly from the time they were born, where as women often weren't aware of their leopards until the leopard and the woman both had the same hormone cycle. Sometimes that never happened and the leopard never emerged. Still, most shifters were in good shape, and she shouldn't be so out of breath.

He studied her deliberately, drawing out the silence. She had unusual eyes, green with golden flecks, and he recognized the eyes of a female leopard immediately. He also became aware of Shturm's reaction to the woman. It was an easing of tension out of the big cat. The claws seemed to retract slowly and he simply went quiet, almost as if, like Sevastyan, he was observing the woman instead of reacting negatively toward her.

Shturm hated all humans and let his human counterpart know at every opportunity. It was rare for him to go quiet, and that alone kept Sevastyan from saying anything to dispel the rising tension between the woman and himself — not that he wanted to. She needed to take responsibility for his time away from Mitya. His job as his cousin's bodyguard was important.

Looking down at her red-gold-tipped lashes that had swept down to veil the

18

expression in her green eyes, a curious emotion gripped him, one he couldn't recognize. She had a generous mouth, beautiful lips, very red, although there was a smudge of dirt near the corner on the left side he could barely keep from leaning down to wipe away with the pad of his thumb.

"I'm so sorry I'm late," she started. Her tone was soft. Pleasing. There was no remorse, but her voice did tremble the least little bit.

He frowned, his eyes on that little smudge. He took a step toward her, caught her chin in a firm grip and angled her face toward the sun. "What the hell happened? Did someone hit you?"

There was barely controlled fury in him, although his voice sounded the way it always did — calm. He *knew* someone had struck her. Recently. Within the last half hour. That was the reason she was late. While he'd been pacing up and down in his front room, furious at her, some asshole had *hit* her. Struck a woman. When he turned her face toward the sun, he caught sight of a large lump on the side of her head, up high in the hairline. Hidden, but it was there. He forced himself to let go of her.

She glanced over her shoulder as if it was possible she was being pursued. She hesi-

19

tated, as if she might not answer, or she might try to lie, but then she simply told him the truth. "Unfortunately, yes, I'm so sorry. I know we're getting off to such a bad start, and it's so unprofessional. Our company is really the best. We've just had bad timing with our scheduled meetings. I really tried to get here but . . ." She was babbling. The words stumbling over one another.

"Ms. Carver," Sevastyan interrupted, his voice a whip. He was used to giving commands and having them obeyed. He'd been trained from the time he was a young boy and as he had taken over the duties of head of security for his cousin, his natural dominant character had come out more and more. "Tell me what happened."

She stood blinking up at him. She was already more than a foot shorter than he was and with him standing a step above her, it only added to her diminutive stature. Once he realized what that smudge was and had seen that swelling on the side of her head, Sevastyan hadn't brought her fully into the house, where she might feel vulnerable alone with him. Still, he intended to take advantage to get the information he needed to hunt down whoever had struck her.

Flambé shrugged in an attempt to be

20

casual, but the movement hurt and she winced visibly. "There's a man who is very angry with me for a lot of different reasons. I refused to take his calls and he's been watching me. I called the police and reported him numerous times, but because he hasn't actually done anything, well, until now, they said there wasn't anything they could do."

"He's stalking you."

She made a face. "I hate using that word because it sounds like something everyone uses now, but yes. He turns up everywhere I go. He stands across the street from places I go to eat with my friends. I made him angry. I should have just kept quiet, but I got so sick of him always pushing at me. I confronted him and told him to keep the hell away from me."

Sevastyan detested that she thought she had to be the one to give in to her stalker's demands in order for her to have peace. That was what the women in their lair felt; in the end, all of them knew they would be murdered and yet they quietly accepted their fate. There was no rising up. No fighting back. Again, that place inside of him that roared with rage turned red with anger, threatening to erupt like an angry volcano, but on the outside, he appeared completely

21

calm. He had to. The last thing this woman needed was to fear him.

"Why do you think you should have to keep quiet? He's the one doing something wrong, not you. You had every right to tell him to stay away from you, although you shouldn't have been alone when you confronted him."

"I wasn't when I confronted him. But he waited until I was coming out here and he forced me off the road." Her entire body was shaking, whether she was aware of it or not.

Sevastyan was unprepared for Shturm's furious reaction. The leopard leapt at him, raking and clawing for freedom as if he would go hunting right then and find Flambé's stalker. Sevastyan remained absolutely expressionless but he couldn't stop himself from stepping in to her and circling her the way his leopard would, inhaling as he did so. The moment he did, his leopard went crazy. He felt a little insane himself. Her stalker was leopard. He wasn't Amurov. He wasn't from Russia, or from one of the lairs Sevastyan was familiar with, but none of that mattered, he was leopard and he was stalking Flambé for a reason.

"He struck you. Hit you. Did he do anything else to you?" Sevastyan forced

22

himself to take a step back when he wanted — no — *needed* — to yank her closer, spin her around and see for himself.

Flambé frowned and touched the swelling on the side of her head, her hand trembling. She looked confused. "The moment he tried to throw me against the car, I fought him. He punched me and I went down to the pavement and hit my head very hard."

Sevastyan wanted to pull her close to him, even on the pretense of just steadying her, but the attack had shaken her. Shturm was acting crazy, one minute rolling over and the next struggling to get out. He had to be careful with her.

"He straddled me, grabbing me by my hair, and I kneed him hard, managed to get to my feet and ran for your property. I'd been here a few times with my father so I knew approximately where the trees were the thickest. He'd planted them when I was really young."

Sevastyan swore to himself. "Is this man someone you know? Someone you were promised to by your father?"

She tilted her head and studied his face for a long moment before answering him. "No. He didn't know my father. Clearly, you're aware of what we are or you wouldn't have been so set on hiring our company."

"Before we go any further, if I ask you inside, will you be uncomfortable alone with me? There is no one else here. I didn't know how much you knew about shifters and I wanted a chance to tell you what I needed from you when it came to landscaping without anyone around, but I don't want you to be in the least uncomfortable. We can discuss this and then business on the outside patio if that is easier for you, but you need to sit down."

Flambé hesitated, faint color stealing up her neck into her face, surprising him. Sevastyan studied her averted face as she once again peered over her shoulder before looking back at him. He had the feeling this time her hesitation wasn't because she feared whoever it was that had struck her. She was avoiding looking at him.

"I'm not afraid of you. Your family has a certain reputation and there is honor and integrity involved."

There was the smallest hint of untruth in her voice. She wasn't afraid exactly, more like intimidated, and he was okay with that. Sevastyan had been intimidating people nearly his entire life.

"And criminal activity," he prompted.

For the first time a faint smile lit her face, doing extraordinary things to her eyes.

"That too."

He stepped back and held open the door. "Come in then. I've had a lot of work done to the interior, but it's by no means finished." He stayed where he was, forcing her to move past him. He took up a lot of space and that meant her smaller body would have to slide next to his, touching his briefly. He wanted to see what reaction his leopard would have. He already knew what reaction he had to her.

Again, there was that small hesitation. He caught the briefest hint of sexual interest flaring in her eyes before she managed to veil all expression with her lashes. She didn't want to be that close to him. She reacted to him just as he was reacting to her. She had courage though, he had to hand that to her. She slid past him, her small body whispering against his.

Shturm nearly rolled over, purring. *Purring.* The cat had never purred in his life. More, he felt her cat rising. The female moved fast, reaching for Shturm, calling to him, the scent of her filling the air so that Sevastyan had to fight his leopard to keep him under control. His own body went hot and hard with urgent need.

"I presume you did your research on me then?" Sevastyan said when he could

25

breathe properly, as he pulled the door closed, matching her steps nearly exactly, his silent.

She glanced over her shoulder and went pale when she saw him so close. "Yes. You're Amur leopard. Rare. From Russia. There are rumors about your kind. Very unfortunate rumors." She shivered and rubbed her arms as she made her way into the living room.

Sevastyan really loved the large, spacious room with the high ceilings and great stone fireplace. He waved Flambé toward the coziest chair. Most of his furniture had been purchased for a big man. His cousins were all large like he was and when they came to visit, he wanted them comfortable.

"Flambé," he said, when she stood by the chair. "Sit down. We have a lot to get through. You may as well be comfortable. If you're cold, I can get you a blanket or start the fire." He poured persuasion into his voice. He wasn't asking. He wanted to know who this man was and why he thought he had any right to her. She looked fragile, as if she might fall down at any moment. Her face was pale and the swelling on the side of her head was alarming to him. Her eyes were overbright, almost as if she was a little dazed.

Flambé sank into the chair. "Mr. Amurov, are the rumors around the Amur shifters true?"

"The lairs where my cousins and I grew up? Yes. Absolutely they are true and worse than anything you've heard. The worst criminals want nothing to do with the lairs, for good reasons. My cousins and I broke away and came here, and we have death sentences hanging over our heads." He shrugged his shoulders. "They've made their try a couple of times, but so far they haven't succeeded. Call me Sevastyan. Not Mr. Amurov. I prefer Sevastyan."

"Our shifters come from South Africa. We're strawberry leopards. There are so few of us that researchers believe we are mutations with recessive genes producing an overproduction of red pigments or an underproduction of dark pigments. Poachers go after us, hunting us relentlessly the moment one of our kind is spotted in leopard form. Researchers don't have a chance to actually find out we're our own subspecies, not a mutation."

Sevastyan sank onto the love seat across from her chair and leaned toward her. He had heard rumors, of course, of strawberry leopards. They all had, but no one had seen one. Most thought them a myth, or like the black leopard, a leopard born with an overproduction of red pigments like researchers believed.

He felt his heart accelerate and did his best to get it under control. For his sake. For Shturm's. There were fewer than a dozen strawberry leopards to his knowledge. At most, perhaps under twenty. Chances were good she was unmated. Her female had risen, responding to Shturm's presence. Sevastyan was attracted to her physically. In fact, the chemistry between them was extremely strong. He could make it work. He just had to proceed with care.

"Your father brought the shifters into the country and taught them his business and then when they could work on their own, he allowed them to move on and he brought in more." It was a guess — an educated one.

She nodded. "Yes. He sponsored them. When the first had their businesses set up, they brought in others and sponsored them. Most, of course, weren't strawberry leopards. It wasn't like we had very many. Our species is nearly extinct. Poachers love a strawberry coat. We were hunted nearly to death. Unfortunately, recently, as many as twelve leopards were spotted in various places at one time in South Africa and it was on the world news. We're trying to get

28

the females with babies out of there to safety, but it isn't easy. There are less than thirty of us left alive in the world that I am aware of. If we can't save the ones exposed in South Africa, we'll lose a third of that number."

"I presume that your father sponsored both male and female leopards of all different species here in the United States."

"Yes, of course he did. He tried to get as many as he could regardless of age or sex. They became citizens and owners of their own businesses. That way they can continue to help other shifters find safety. It wasn't only strawberry leopards he brought in — most weren't."

"Are there any other strawberry females here?"

She hesitated just for a moment, but he caught it. "Yes."

"Have the females gone into the Han Vol Dan?"

She frowned. "I don't know exactly what that is."

"The emerging of their leopard?"

"I believe my father said one or two have married. I don't know if they have a leopard or not. I would hope so." She rubbed her hand up and down her left thigh restlessly.

"When did you become aware of your

leopard?"

Her gaze jumped to his face. She moistened her lips. "About two weeks ago. She told me her name was Flamme. I can feel how restless she is." Again, she hesitated. "I've been restless as well. I wake up in the middle of the night and have to go running. I've been afraid ever since . . ." She trailed off.

"Who is he?" Sevastyan demanded.

"Sevastyan. It isn't a good idea to get mixed up in my problems. He comes with some big resources, which is why I think the cops don't want to do anything about him. They won't even talk to him."

"That is not what I asked you."

Silence stretched between them. She lifted her chin stubbornly. That little gesture got him right in the gut. To a man like Sevastyan, that was the same as issuing a challenge. She wasn't going to tell him for whatever reasons — or at least she didn't think she was. He wasn't going to allow her to get away with it.

"I actually came out here to discuss landscaping and what you wanted or needed on your property," Flambé said, looking very determined. "You said the project would be quite extensive." She rubbed her temple and winced. Swayed. She wasn't in

30

any condition to work.

Lulling her into a sense of security was always a good thing. He could mesmerize with just his voice. Control with it. Sound very gentle or equally as harsh. Any dominant worth his while could do so, and Sevastyan was particularly good with his voice. "That is very true. This property belonged to my sister-in-law's family, the Dover family. I own it now and need the trees planted all the way from the woods in back to Mitya's woods with the arboreal highway extended from my home to his. I want a clear path both on the ground and in the trees for me to get to him if he's in trouble. A good portion of the acreage was planted in grapes. I had a third of that pulled up. More will eventually be taken out as well."

She nodded and looked around her, looking a little helpless. Again, she lifted her hand to the lump on her head as if it hurt. "I usually have my notebook but I left my car out on the road some distance from here."

He rose at once and retrieved a pen and paper from a rolltop desk in the wide hallway. "We'll have to make do with this." He gave it to her and paced across the gleaming hardwood floor to the wide expanse of window. "I like to see what's com-

31

ing at me at all times. The house is sitting lower than I'd like. The road is just a little above it so any plants added for looks could take away from security. I had the gardener pull out the ornamental bushes that were planted up close to the house. He wasn't happy, but he did it."

"I noticed that there weren't any plants at all around the front of the house and it seemed very stark to me. I can come up with something pleasing that wouldn't take away from your need for security."

He kept a smile from showing on his face, his back to her as he continued to stare out the window. *Your need for security.* She had deliberately worded it that way to get to him. Needling him. She was restless because her leopard was. Both hands were rubbing her thighs now. She shifted in her seat more than once, her legs moving. She didn't understand that her female was driving her, making her edgy, moody.

Her leopard was pushing her hard, throwing off her scent to call the male to her, insistent, urgent, demanding, flirtatious. The closer she pressed to the surface, the more Sevastyan and Shturm were affected, unable to resist the lure of the females. Every movement Flambé made was blatantly sexual, although she didn't seem to be aware of it. She touched herself, her hands moving over her body, and her fragrance, filling the air so that he breathed it in with every lungful he took, was enough to put him over the edge.

Shturm came to attention, pressing forward, urging him to stake their claim. Flambé was in far more danger than she realized, not in a way that would ever harm her. She was the safest woman in the world from him. Not only had Sevastyan taken a real interest in her when he didn't in any woman, but so had his leopard.

"Are you paying attention to anything I'm saying to you?" Now there was a distinct bite to her voice.

"I would never be so rude as to not pay attention to you, Flambé." Sevastyan turned slowly toward her, deliberately allowing his gaze to run over her.

Flambé had drawn her legs up. Her body was flushed, aroused, the heat of her female leopard fully on her. She'd removed her jacket and her breath was coming in ragged pants. Beneath the blouse she wore, obviously her "power suit" when she met with her customers, her full breasts rose and fell as she tried to control her breathing. Her nipples were hard, pushing against her bra, which inflamed them more. She was suffering, just the way her leopard was, nearing the excruciating demands of the Han Vol Dan of their people and not realizing what was happening to her.

Sevastyan wanted her to belong to him with every breath he drew. His leopard leapt and raked, clawing for supremacy, demanding they claim her, but that wasn't Sevastyan's way. His woman was going to be his fully because she wanted him. Exclusively. Him. With every one of his flaws — and he had them in abundance.

He measured his steps, pacing in slow deliberate strides around her chair, very close so her leopard would feel his male. Feel the dominant fighter. Her little female was looking for her mate — desperate to find him after the assault on them. If it was her first cycle, she would want a strong mate who could care for his shifter family, protect them when they might not be able to protect themselves.

The strawberry leopard rose fast, seeking Shturm. She was so close Sevastyan could almost see her moving beneath Flambé's skin. That flawless skin glowed hot, as if her temperature had risen by several degrees. Without conscious thought Flambé reached up and undid the first two buttons of her blouse. Her red hair was damp, beginning to curl in wisps and tendrils around her face.

He inhaled her scent. Drew her into his lungs. This was an intelligent woman. He had done his own research on her when he had decided to hire her landscaping company to do the work on his property. Her father had a reputation among the shifters — he had for years. He had started the business as a very young man and didn't have children until he was in his late forties. His wife had died in childbirth and he had raised his daughter alone. She'd worked at his side almost since birth.

Sevastyan brushed up against Flambé's arm as he passed her chair, his skin sliding against hers. There were instant sparks, a chemistry arcing between them. He was far too experienced not to know she felt it, although she tried to hide it. She kept her face averted and took a deep breath, biting hard on her lower lip. He smiled and continued walking to the small refrigerator behind the bar to get himself a water.

"What type of plants were you thinking would look good around the front of the house? I like the way Mitya's home always looks, beautifully kept, but easily defendable."

She turned her head toward him. She was so beautiful to him for a moment he

35

couldn't control the way his blood pounded so hotly through his veins. He needed to stay in control. Shturm was useless, going from purring to roaring his demands. Flambé and her little hussy of a female were in such dire straits, they were throwing off enough hormones to call in every male leopard for a hundred miles.

Flambé was squirming in the chair and he was fairly certain if it kept up she would ask where his bathroom was just so she could try to find a little relief. That would only make it worse, but she didn't know that. She also seemed a little out of it, as if she couldn't quite follow along in their conversation. He didn't know if that was from the potent effects of the female heat or the blow to the head. He wanted to examine that knot in her hair a little closer.

One of them had to have a clear head. He breathed through the blood thundering in his ears and pounding hard in his cock. He wanted this woman to trust him. To give herself to him. To let him into her life. He needed that from her and taking her wasn't the way to get that even if in this moment she threw herself at him. If he really was going to have such an unexpected gift handed to him, he wasn't going to throw it away because he didn't have enough control to handle her with care.

She cleared her throat twice, frowning, obviously trying to follow the conversation. "There are so many beautiful plants native to this area that would look lovely in groupings around the front of the house. They're low enough that they wouldn't cover windows or in any way impede your ability to see anything coming at you."

Her voice was very low. Husky. It played along his nerve endings, slid down his spine and teased his cock as if she brushed her fingers and tongue over his sensitive shaft. There was no question this woman was the one for him. No one had ever affected him the way she did. Not with just the sound of her voice. He opened the water bottle, pausing there at the bar, taking the time to savor the genuine feeling she was gifting him with. For once his leopard wasn't demanding blood or violent sex and he could just enjoy the beauty of wanting his woman because she was extraordinary.

Flambé had her Bachelor of Arts, Masters and PhD in Landscape Architecture and Environmental Planning from UC Berkeley. She'd had so much experience from working with her father that she had excelled in the program. Her father only took jobs that allowed him to use local plants and designs that worked to sustain the environment and were pleasing to the eye as well. He was a genius with plants and it appeared his daughter followed in his footsteps.

"There are flowers that bloom at different times of the year and succulents that don't need as much water. I know of this lovely little star-like ground cover that once it takes root, takes very little water, can be walked on just like grass and yet doesn't need the care grass does." As she talked, enthusiasm crept into her voice. She definitely liked her job.

"Do you do the planting yourself, or do you work on getting new clients and let your crew do the actual work on the properties while you supervise?" He moved away from the bar, again very casually, coming to stand beside her chair, letting the heat of his body blend with hers.

Her cat went wild. Sevastyan knew because he was completely tuned to her now and he felt the animal in her respond to the animal in him. His male was big and mean. A fighter. A male in his prime. A perfect mate. Just what the female wanted and needed. Exactly what she was looking for in a mate. His leopard pushed hard toward the surface and Sevastyan let him come close, but held him at bay. The last thing he

38

needed was for the big male to get loose. The female leopard reacted, becoming more amorous, pushing toward the surface as well, demanding to be close to the male.

Flambé gasped and wrapped her arms around her middle, ducking her head, averting her flushed face from him. Her breasts were immediately pushed up beneath the thin silk of her blouse, nearly tumbling from her lacy bra. He could see she was fighting the feverish need crawling through her, the desperate cravings and urgent demands of her heat.

"Is it too warm in here?" Sevastyan asked in his most solicitous voice. He bent down and very gently pushed back the damp hair on her forehead and laid his palm there, as if checking her temperature.

The moment he touched Flambé, the two leopards went into a frenzy of need. His blood ran so hot he expected that at any moment he might burst into flame. He was used to controlling his brutal sexual hunger and nothing had ever been as bad as this. He couldn't imagine what it was like for her. She clearly didn't have the experience he had.

At his touch, her red-golden-tipped lashes fluttered and then lifted. Her gaze met his. The natural sensuality in her shook him.

39

He recognized several traits in her immediately — traits that guaranteed they would be compatible if he could win her trust. She was a natural submissive. He had been in that world too long not to recognize the trait when he saw it.

Submissive, to Sevastyan, didn't mean she was less than him, or giving in to him, it meant that she knew who she was and what she wanted. She would be able to give her trust and loyalty to those she believed in. She didn't fight unnecessarily just for the sake of fighting. Having complete control wasn't important to her.

Clearly, Flambé was able to be at the helm of a company. Her landscaping business was thriving. She was bringing in members of other leopard subspecies from other countries in a desperate attempt to save them from extinction. She helped them to become citizens, provided an education in whatever business they wanted to learn and then set them up for success. She had to be somewhat adventurous to do any of that, as well as highly intelligent.

"It is a little warm in here," she admitted, sounding distracted.

Again, her voice was husky, playing along his nerve endings. He found he wanted to spend time with her. Hours. All night.

Watching her just like this. Hungry. Needy. Bordering on desperate. Looking at him with those eyes of hers. Sensual beyond belief. Filled with desire. Turning a dark green with lust as her gaze moved over his body and settled on his cock. He felt the heat of her gaze right through the material of his jeans. He didn't attempt to hide his thick bulge from her. It was blatant. Nearly at mouth level. If she leaned forward and unzipped his trousers, she could wrap her lips around him. It would be a stretch, but just the idea of her trying sent more hot blood pounding through his veins and had his cock jerking and pulsing in anticipation. She looked as if she might just do it too, lean forward and unzip his jeans right there. She looked mesmerized, completely focused, her leopard so close she could barely function.

He pressed the bottle of cold water with the drops of condensation on it against her neck. "Try this while I get you a cold cloth. I'll turn on the air conditioner. I really hadn't noticed the heat, but I tend to not really pay attention to the outside temperature much."

He was used to keeping his expression absolutely calm at all times. He stayed in the background. He could disappear there

41

easily with his stillness. He often appeared to be more civilized than his other cousins, even sometimes seemed to have a bit of a sense of humor. He had learned, over the years, to hide the terrible pent-up rage inside of him, the rage in his leopard that refused to leave either of them and manifested itself in brutal ways — fighting or in sex clubs.

"Thank you. I'm afraid I'm not making a very good impression on you. I think my encounter this morning really shook me up more than I thought it did."

He was very aware that his touch shook her up. His closeness. She couldn't stop staring hungrily at the bulge in the front of his jeans. Her gaze narrowed, centered there, and she even leaned forward just a small scant inch or so without being aware of it. Her tongue touched her lip, moistened it. He couldn't move if he wanted to. His cock burned, was stretched so tight he thought he might burst.

She squirmed, trying to ease the terrible burning between her legs. He had the control thanks to years of being a dominant. She had none. Her cat was giving her fits, raging at her in desperate hunger at the close proximity of her chosen mate. Her skin was beginning to glow. Sevastyan began

42

to fear that her female was closer to the emergence than he first thought.

Normally, a female would come close to the surface and then retreat, only to reappear a few days to a week later. Often an appearance would be so brief and elusive that a male leopard would barely catch the scent of a female. This was a very advanced appearance. Flambé's leopard was close to emerging — too close to give him time for a real courtship.

Sevastyan regretted that. He would have to change his plans. She needed care, especially with the kind of lifestyle she would be entering into with him. He was Mitya's bodyguard and he always would be. They lived a dangerous life. There was no question about that. He would expect his wife, his mate, to live that life with him. He had no idea how being his wife would affect her business, and she obviously loved her business.

Then there was the fact that he needed his woman to give him sex any way he liked it. Anywhere he wanted it. He knew that was the result of his screwed-up upbringing in the lair from hell. Having a woman for his own didn't make that need go away as he'd hoped it might. He found the hunger grew deeper in him just being close to her.

43

That was something she would have to live with as well.

"You've made an impression on me, Flambé. More than any other woman I've ever met. I knew when I did the research on your company with you at the helm that I wanted you to continue where your father had left off here on the property. After having met you, I'm very interested in the woman."

He wanted to make that plain. No beating around the bush. His body was saying it for him, but he was determined that she understand he wanted her for who she was. "There is quite a lot about you on the internet and I read it all." He made his confession hoping he didn't sound worse than the man who had been stalking her.

Her gaze jumped back up to his. She licked her lips again and then her gaze drifted down to his groin, as if she couldn't help herself. One hand moved up to her hairline where the bump was hidden, as if it was hurting her.

"I tried to do research on you." She made it a confession, but her voice sounded a little vague, as if her mind was drifting along with her gaze. "There wasn't much to find. There was hardly anything in fact. A little more on your cousins than you. I think your name

44

was mentioned once."

Sevastyan forced himself to walk away from her, over to the switch that controlled the air conditioner. It was on the wall beside the bank of windows. As he crossed to the wall, just above their heads strobes went off along the upper corners of the room, letting him know that several people had tripped alarms set in the ground leading up to the house.

He stood at the window, his wide shoulders framed within the glass. "We're about to have company, *plamya.*" He glanced over his shoulder and then crooked his finger at her. "Come here. Tell me if this is your gentleman friend. He hasn't come alone."

45

2

Flambé rose slowly but without hesitation, although she seemed a little wobbly, and crossed to his side. He slid his arm around her, pulling her beneath his shoulder so she could fit snugly into the window frame with him. He could have easily moved over to give her room, but he wanted to see her reaction to his proprietary claim on her. She seemed to accept him, just the way her leopard accepted his close proximity.

The man coming toward the house was still a distance away and was striding boldly up the walkway, two men on either side of him. He acted as if he owned the property, and no one would ever think to oppose him.

"He has more men with him. They're hidden from view in the shrubbery on either side of the house. I've counted at least six, but most likely there are more." Sevastyan was matter-of-fact. Calm. He kept his arm around her.

46

A little shudder went through her body and she took an involuntary step back as if to get away from the window. At the same time, she tried to tug on his waist to take him with her. Her little leopard pushed very close to protect her. Shturm roared and clawed for freedom, raging to be set free to exact vengeance for the bruises and the injuries on Flambé.

"You're safe in here with me, honey," Sevastyan assured softly, although he agreed with his leopard and wanted to do a little hunting of his own. "They can't get in. Even if they did decide to shoot at us, the windows are bulletproof glass. I'll text my team if need be. I want to see what they do. Who is this joker, Flambé? Now that he's bent on attacking me as well, don't you think I have the right to know?"

Sevastyan could see it took effort, but Flambé pulled her gaze away from the big man coming up the walkway with his deliberate strides. She looked up at Sevastyan, meeting his eyes. Whatever she saw there reassured her.

She took a deep breath before answering him. "His name is Franco Matherson. He and his brothers say they're 'big game' hunters. They're very wealthy. They're really looking for female shifters. They ran across

47

one of the female strawberry leopards my father was sponsoring. She was taking one last run as a leopard before leaving the country. It was silly of her to chance it. Matherson spotted her and nearly shot her just for her unusual coat. No one knew about red leopards so it didn't occur to him that she could possibly be a shifter."

"So even though he's a shifter, a leopard, he thought it was appropriate to kill a beautiful and different leopard that he spotted just because he could." There was a wealth of disgust in him and it showed in his voice. What shifter would kill a leopard for its pelt? She was speaking the truth but it was also mixed with lies. He didn't call her on it.

"Right? He turns my stomach, just the fact that he would even admit that he was contemplating shooting a leopard because she had a strawberry coat. In any case, he tracked her to a cave. She went in as a leopard and emerged as a human. He knew immediately that she had to be a shifter. She just managed to escape him. He eventually tracked her here. Of course, she was gone and my father had died by the time he unraveled where she had gone to."

"But he found you and knows you're a shifter."

She nodded once more, turning her gaze back to the window and the approaching man. He was closer, looking more arrogant than ever. Sevastyan had seen so many men like him. They thought their money somehow entitled them to anything they wanted. They bought their way through life. They took from people and intimidated and stepped on others to get their way. Like his father and uncles, they brutalized and even killed, knowing they could get away with it.

Flambé had some knowledge of what and who Franco Matherson was. She was good at researching her clients and she most likely had done the same, researching the man stalking her. Still, there was something in her voice that told him something wasn't quite right. She was either omitting something or not telling him the exact truth. There was more to the story than she was willing to divulge.

Sevastyan assessed Matherson as he came toward them. He was definitely leopard. It was in the way he moved. The play of his muscles beneath his skin. And he let his leopard out to fight. Most likely he pitted his leopard against wild leopards and enjoyed the battles. He looked like a brutal man, and he wanted Flambé. There was no question about that.

Sevastyan slid his hand up to the nape of her neck, his fingers beginning a slow, soothing massage. "Do you know what he was going to do when he tried to throw you up against the car? Your leopard is close to emerging. She's rising and male leopards want to claim her. This is her first rising and she's looking for a mate. My leopard has confirmed that and he's willing to mate with her. When you're close to me, what does your female do?"

"She acts like an idiot," Flambé admitted, disgust in her voice. "She's rolling around like some little sex kitten." She pressed tighter against him, rubbing her body along his, mimicking her leopard but barely noticing she was doing so. She pulled away with a muttered apology, her face going red.

He smiled down at her. "Don't be embarrassed. The leopards can get us worked up. The chemistry between us without them is bad enough. With them, it's off the charts. Matherson would have forced your female to accept his male."

The color leached out of her face. "How could he do that?"

"If you were mine to claim, I would push the back of your shirt up so my leopard could coax your female to the surface. He would hold you still and they would touch

50

if she agrees to his claiming. Once that happens, Matherson's leopard would not be able to mate with her. He knows that. That's why he's tried so hard to keep you away from every other shifter. He doesn't want your female to run across any other she might accept."

Flambé turned her body toward his, her front to his side, rubbing her body against his like the little cat she was, amorous, so naturally sensuous and provocative he thought his control might actually shatter. One leg wound around his thigh while her hand caught at his shirt, fingers clutching.

Her little leopard was very close to the surface, calling continually for Shturm. The scent was so potent, filling Sevastyan's lungs, it was all he could do not to throw Flambé up against the wall and take what she was offering. Her hands burrowed under his shirt, hot, stroking caresses over his skin while her hips rocked against his thigh, pressing her sex against him.

"He scares the hell out of me," she admitted in a low voice. "I don't want his leopard anywhere near mine."

"Your leopard is in heat, and her heat will affect you," he said, keeping his voice low and soothing. "It may sound terrible and might be after, depending on how he treats you, but at the time, it might not be the end of the world. Although, once he claimed you, you would have to stay with him."

A little shudder went through her body. "Don't even say that. Don't even think it." Her gaze jumped to meet his. Daring him. Challenging him. "You said your leopard was willing to mate with mine." There was pure seduction in her voice.

"A claim isn't for just a heat, Flambé. You have to understand that. The shifter world has rules. We live by those rules."

"I'm aware of that. My father told me. I don't know about claiming, but I do know we are not human and we live by a different set of rules." She was becoming frantic, her body moving against his, hot, shaking with need.

"I wouldn't let you go. I'm not an easy man to live with. I'm dominant in and out of bed. I like sex and I need it often. Leopard sex can be rough." Even as he explained this to her, he kept his voice gentle, his fingers on the nape of her neck massaging the tension from her. One finger traced the lobe of her ear. He leaned down and nipped that same lobe with his teeth, watching goose bumps rise as endorphins rushed through her body.

Flambé's gaze continued to stray to the

man walking with such confidence up the walkway. Franco couldn't fail to see Sevastyan and Flambé framed in the window watching him.

She moaned low, the sound somewhere between sensual and desperate. "Do you want me?"

"Yes." He took her hand and blatantly, right there in front of the glass, curved her palm over his denim-covered cock. "You know I do."

"I mean *me.*"

"Yes."

"Does your leopard want my leopard?"

He turned her to face the window, pressed her against the glass so Matherson couldn't fail to see her small figure facing him with Sevastyan towering above her. Sevastyan's eyes met Franco's through the glass as he slowly began to push up the back of Flambé's top. Inch by inch he gathered the material in his hands, pulling it up to the nape of her neck, leaving her front fully covered, but exposing her back and shoulders to Sevastyan.

For the first time, Matherson's absolute confidence was shaken. It was a small stumble only. A brief strain on his face as he gave a barely imperceptible shake of his head. Sevastyan bent his head, his eyes go-

53

ing cat, banding with heat. He brushed kisses along the nape of Flambé's neck and then on the soft skin of her shoulder before he allowed Shturm to surface. Even then, it was a partial shifting, Sevastyan staying in control as his cat sank his teeth in a holding bite in Flambé's shoulder, drawing her female to the surface, injecting chemicals into her body.

The female rose fast, needy, a little desperate for her male, communicating with him, letting him know she feared the other male leopard's intentions. That she tried to hold back but she was close to emerging and she feared Flambé would have no choice but to accept Matherson. Shturm, to Sevastyan's astonishment, let the female know Sevastyan would never accept that outcome. It was a fierce denial. The images so savage Sevastyan thought they might upset the little female cat, but instead, they seemed to give her reassurance. She settled.

Sevastyan shifted back to his fully human form and pressed kisses to the bites. Blood trickled down her shoulder blade in a steady stream. He had expected a little blood, but not quite that much. His cat had licked at the bites and that should have helped to clot the blood, but it hadn't. He frowned.

"I don't want you to move. Matherson is

54

going to come to the door, or the window, and be very dramatic. Remember, he can't get in. He can threaten and posture, but he's like the Big Bad Wolf in the children's fairy tale. He can huff and puff for all he's worth. I'll get a first-aid kit and see to that bite. Your female accepted my male."

He caught her arms and turned her around to face him. Flambé kept her head down so he tipped her chin up. "Are you crying?" His heart stuttered unexpectedly at the dampness the pads of his fingers encountered when he touched her face. "Did Shturm hurt you? Surely he was careful." If he wasn't, Sevastyan was going to have a few choice words to say to his leopard.

"It just felt so permanent between them. Intimate. Everything is happening so fast. I always hoped if I ever got into a permanent relationship it would be about love. Not protection." Her lashes swept down to veil her expression. "I just thought I might have that someday." There was vulnerability in the red-gold tips of her lashes as well as in her tone.

Sevastyan leaned forward and brushed kisses over her lips and then sipped away the tears on her face. "It would be impossible to have the kind of relationship we're going to have and not be in love. I intend to love you with everything I am. What you do is up to you. I'm sorry I didn't have the chance to give you a proper courtship. You deserve one and we'll take every minute we can to get to know each other."

She blinked up at him, confusion swimming through the liquid in her eyes. "You're . . . unexpected."

He hoped he would always be unexpected to her. "Stay right here, baby. I've got a first-aid kit behind the bar. We stash them in all the rooms. Evangeline, my cousin Fyodor's wife, is the one who insisted we do that, and it has really come in handy."

"You have a lot of cousins."

That was true. He did. Sevastyan was halfway across the room but keeping an eye on Matherson. He had deliberately showed the man he was leopard and that he had claimed Flambé. He hoped that was enough to take the pressure off her and the idiot would go home and annoy someone else. Clearly, that wasn't the case. Franco Matherson was furious that his prize had been stolen out from under him.

"Evangeline has the bakery in San Antonio a few blocks from the huge building Jake Banniconni owns downtown. Her bakery is called The Sweet Shoppe," Flambé said. Her voice shook as she informed him she

56

knew of Evangeline's bakery.

Sevastyan made his way back to her and turned her around but put her hands on the windowsill to steady her. He wanted to take a look at the lump on her head as well. "Look at the floor, not at him."

Matherson had come straight to the window and was staring in, his eyes glowing with his cat's menacing presence. Sevastyan ignored him, once more pushing up Flambé's shirt in order to expose the leopard's bite. It was still bleeding. When he wiped the blood away, he could see that Shturm really had been careful to keep his bite shallow, just enough for holding to call to the female. That was shocking to Sevastyan.

Shturm was fierce, a rough, brutal leopard, honed from the many beatings Sevastyan's father and uncles had given him when the cat had tried to protect the boy. They'd let their larger adult cats loose on the young, immature leopard, tearing him nearly to pieces at times, until Sevastyan had forced a shifting in order to protect him, willing to let the leopards kill him rather than see Shturm suffer any further. Theirs had been an ugly childhood with little room for gentleness. He was thankful his leopard had shown that trait to Flambé.

Sevastyan applied pressure to the puncture

wounds until he was certain the bleeding had slowed to trickles. He smeared on the antibiotic cream, placed Band-Aids over the two puncture wounds before pulling down her top and turning her almost in one motion so she wouldn't see that Matherson was right at the window, the threat of death in his eyes. He pulled Flambé into his arms, tight against his chest.

"We'll find our way through this. I'm excited to see what you're going to do with the landscaping. I've been looking forward to hearing your ideas and seeing them drawn out since I made the call asking you to meet with me." He brushed a kiss on top of her head, his gaze meeting Franco's without hesitation.

There were cameras everywhere recording every threat the man might make. He might destroy one or two, but he wouldn't find them all. Sevastyan had every confidence that he wouldn't be able to breach the house, not as a man, and not as a leopard.

Matherson gestured toward the door. Sevastyan looked him up and down as if he were so far beneath his notice he couldn't be bothered. The man hadn't had the decency to go to the door before he peered through the window like some Peeping Tom. Worse, he'd actually run Flambé off the

58

road and then struck her. He'd be paying for that, just not at that moment, not when Flambé, or anyone else, would know Sevastyan had anything to do with retaliating.

"Tell me how you got your name. There must be a story behind it."

Sevastyan ignored Franco's pounding on the window and took Flambé's hand to walk her deeper into the living room, where he found a chair that kept her just out of Franco's sight. The man would be able to see her legs and lap, but not her face. The chair had wide arms and a deep cushion, meant for a big man like him.

Flambé sank into the chair and he immediately went to the floor and positioned himself between her legs, kneeling there, so his wider body kept her legs spread open for him. That would torment a man like Franco. Drive him absolutely insane. It would ensure that Matherson would come after him and not Flambé.

Flambé's eyes went wide when he dropped to his knees, his arms circling her waist, but she didn't protest. She moistened her lips, indicating she was nervous, but she reached out and pushed at his hair, touching him tentatively. When he didn't pull back, she stroked his hair away from his temples and gave him a little half smile. Her other hand

59

rubbed her thigh restlessly.

"My mother was a chef. She worked at a famous restaurant. Apparently, one of her most famous desserts included something where she poured alcohol over it and lit it."

When she smiled, even that little half smile, her eyes lit up and he found the experience extraordinary. Her eyes could be green or gold or light brown or amber. So many colors depending on her mood or what she might be wearing. With her leopard added to the mix, his woman's eyes could be any number of colors and he would have to learn what each of them meant. It would take a lifetime, maybe nine of them.

"Flambé. Of course."

"My father wanted children." Her voice had gone neutral. Almost as if she was retelling a story. "She had a multiple pregnancy, but lost two early on. I was the last, and at first the doctors thought she had lost me as well."

Her voice had gone soft and very sad. Sevastyan thought she might be reflecting her father's sorrow at the loss when he told her the story. She had a lot of empathy in her. That told him he would have to shield her. He would take care to do so without making her think he saw her as weak. He wished he had that quality. He never saw empathy

60

as a sign of weakness. Evangeline, his cousin's wife, had that trait in abundance. Sevastyan was drawn to Flambé because she had that characteristic in her nature.

"The pregnancy was very difficult on my mother and she was weak when she had me. There was a huge blood loss. Both my father and the doctor knew she wasn't going to live. My father insisted that she wanted me more than anything, that she considered me her greatest gift to him."

She gave him another smile, but this one was sad. "I'm not so certain of that. I really hate that she lost her life giving me mine."

"That wasn't your fault, Flambé," Sevastyan pointed out.

Matherson was at the door, pounding with his fist. It sounded like his men were taking a battering ram to it. He hoped so. He hoped the recording would show the damage so he could sue them. There might not be evidence against Matherson for his assault on Flambé, but everything he did at Sevastyan's house would be on the security tapes.

"Yes, I know. They say it is a myth that redheads are prone to bleeding, and maybe it is just our species, but apparently, we have lost many of our women in childbirth due to blood loss. That was what happened to my mother."

Sevastyan was taking note of that. Flambé had the thick hair that marked the leopard species, but it was as bright red as could be. There wasn't a doubt in his mind that she was a natural redhead and between her legs would be red curls. Her leopard would be strawberry. There was no taking chances with his woman. If they were going to have children, a surrogate could carry them, not Flambé. That would be a discussion for the far future, not for now.

"And your name?" He prompted again, because the door banging was really loud and twice her gaze had jumped in that direction. "How did you come by it?"

His hand moved on her thigh, fingers running up and down just as hers were doing, pressing deep, soothing the raw nerve endings. He stroked caresses upward, every now and then moving his fingers toward the inside of her thigh. Just one deep brush then another. Close to the heat and then back to the surface, distracting her from the door.

"My hair was thick and red and about an inch long. My father said I looked wild. Eyes too big for my face and hair as red as flames. My mother looked up at him and smiled. She said one word. *Flambé.* He told me he wasn't certain if she wanted me named that, but after she passed, he couldn't think of another name that meant fire or flame that would honor her as well. So Flambé was what it was."

"I like it," Sevastyan said. "It suits you." He touched her hair. It felt like silk. He was going to have to move back away from her. Fortunately for both of them, her leopard was subsiding, giving them a respite. He hoped that once her female retreated, Flambé wasn't going to try to change her mind.

"Stay here, *plamya,*" he said, calling her *flame.* He stood, towering over her, his body very close to her. Too close. The moment he stood he was all too aware of exactly the position of his cock and her mouth. Sometimes he detested that he was such a sexual dominant. It was stamped into his bones, so much a part of him.

Sevastyan stepped away from her and caught up his forgotten water bottle so he could make his way leisurely to the window. He angled himself so he was fully visible to Matherson and his men as he stood watching them as if they were circus animals and he was enjoying a show. He waited until they were fully aware of him and had stopped their furious pounding and battering on the door, which they clearly weren't going to get through. He opened the intercom.

"Gentlemen, I suggest you leave the property immediately."

"Before you call the police?" Franco sneered. "You coward."

Sevastyan smiled and took a long drink of the cool water. "I prefer not to involve the police. I think when grown men act like children throwing tantrums they need to be treated like children."

He reached down to the long row of buttons hidden just below the windowsill, activating several. Water gushed out in long pulsing streams like firemen's hoses, coming from the eaves of the house, blasting the men and driving them back and away. Within seconds they were soaked and on their butts, sliding in the puddles on the walkway.

Cursing, Franco tried to rise, only to fall several times. Sevastyan never cracked a smile. He simply watched dispassionately from his vantage point at the window. Behind him, Flambé jumped up and rushed toward him. He didn't turn around.

"Stop right there. I don't want him to see you looking afraid or alarmed. Back away from the window." He kept his voice low but commanding. "Now, Flambé."

She came to an abrupt halt, one hand going to her throat defensively. "You don't know him, Sevastyan. You haven't done any research on him like I have. He's vindictive. You've humiliated him in front of his men. He'll never stop until he kills you."

Her voice trembled and Sevastyan, in spite of his resolve to continue looking at Franco as if he were an ant, couldn't help but turn to look at his woman. She was genuinely upset. She wasn't a woman easily intimidated and yet Franco Matherson had really shaken her up. It wasn't the fact that he'd struck her. She knew Sevastyan came from a family of criminals and yet she was that shaken.

"Baby." He whispered the endearment softly.

She shook her head. "You don't understand. He's evil. He's truly evil. I spent a great deal of time finding out as much as I could about him when the cops wouldn't help me." Even though she was so distressed, she still backed away from the window, keeping out of Franco's line of vision. "There's a subspecies of leopards, of shifters, the Arabians he and his brothers first went after to find wives. They bartered with the elders and tried to get them to give them several females. The elders told them

65

it didn't work that way, but Matherson became angry the way he does and, in the end, tried to take the females."

Again, there was a mixture of truth and a lie. He couldn't quite put his finger on what it was to call her on it. "I can see him doing that. He doesn't like being thwarted in the least. If he can't have his toy, he'd rather break it so no one else can have it."

She nodded. "That's exactly what he did. He and his brothers began a systematic hunt, and they used the natives to help them stamp out the Arabian leopards by putting bounties on the leopards, poisoning them, capturing them for zoos, killing them for various body parts and their pelts. That's how vindictive they are."

"You're afraid he'll come after me."

She started to answer and then fell silent, studying his face. "You're deliberately angering him. You sized him up in five seconds and you're drawing his attention away from me and putting it onto you. On purpose." That was an accusation. "Sevastyan. You can't do that."

He quirked an eyebrow at her. "I can do anything I want, Flambé. I'm very familiar with evil. I grew up surrounded by it. I know the kind of man he is. I recognized what he was immediately. I want his attention centered on me, not you. Still, it's best if you stay close to me where I can protect you. Since you'll be working for me anyway, and you don't want to endanger your crew, that will work. We'll get whatever you need sent here."

She opened her mouth to protest.

"Your female is emerging anytime. You can't have her breaking free in front of anyone either," he pointed out, and turned back to the intercom and Matherson. He shut off the valve for the water. "I suggest you gentlemen leave my property immediately. I don't want to have to tell you again."

Matherson jerked his head toward the road and his two security people went with him, stalking down the walkway, looking more like wet, wretched hens than tough guys. Sevastyan didn't believe it was over for a moment. Franco wouldn't leave quietly. He wanted to show Sevastyan he wasn't in the least afraid of him. He had a larger force of men hiding in the brush and there was no doubt that he would leave instructions to retaliate in some manner. When, was the question. Franco didn't have a clue Sevastyan knew the men were out there.

Flambé threw herself into the wide chair again, drawing up her knees and wrapping her arms around her legs. "You shouldn't have done that, Sevastyan. I can't thank you enough, but you shouldn't have done that. He'll never stop coming after you. He's really a monster."

"I could see that. What are his brothers like? Have you seen them? Met them?" Sevastyan moved across the room from her, resting one hip against the bar, regarding her carefully. She looked strained, trying to cover it up. The smudge by her lips had darkened. She continually covered the swelling at the side of her head.

"I've seen them, but they always stay in the background. He's the one out in front at press conferences. He does the talking. He can be charming when he wants something. He's good at smiling for the cameras."

"You look tired. Are you getting hungry?"

"I need to deal with my car. It's off the road, but it's going to have to be towed." She put her head back and closed her eyes. "I don't know how I managed to get away from him. It was my female. Flamme. I ran faster than I've ever run in my life."

Sevastyan couldn't help it. He found himself smiling. He wasn't that given to the real thing. But Flambé? Flamme? It was possible there was a warning in those two names. Shturm and he had better take heed and listen to it.

"I'll have your car taken care of. Are the keys in it?"

"I threw them on the front seat. At least I think I did. I just hit the ground running. He was coming at me. He was on me so fast and I was so scared. I knew I couldn't let his leopard anywhere near Flamme."

"Why did you name her Flamme?"

"I didn't. She told me that was her name. I haven't seen her, but I presume she's strawberry like most of us." Flambé opened her eyes and regarded Sevastyan. "Your leopard is Amur?"

Sevastyan nodded. "He's big for any leopard. He can ride me pretty hard, Flambé. There are times I can be edgy. I won't ever use that as an excuse to mistreat you. If you don't like something I say or do, speak up." Pulling out his cell, he texted Mitya, his cousin. There were plenty of security personnel who could take care of towing Flambé's car to the garage and get it fixed for her.

Her smile was a thing of beauty. Fascinating to him. It came slow, a curve of her mouth and then lighting her eyes and then her face. "I have no problems whatsoever expressing myself when I don't like something, Sevastyan." She pointed to her red hair. "That is the warning signal, after all."

"My woman has a temper?"

"I prefer to say I have a sense of justice and when someone crosses it, it is at their peril."

He laughed. Actually laughed. It might have sounded a little rusty, but it was definitely a laugh. He liked her. He liked being with her.

"You don't have to take care of my car for me, Sevastyan. I can do it, although I appreciate you volunteering. I was procrastinating. You'll find I do that. Not anything to do with work. That's what will frustrate you the most about me. I tend to get everything done to the smallest detail with work and the people I'm trying to help, but once I come home and need to take care of my own things, I put it off all the time. You'll want to pull out your hair — or mine. I miss important appointments like doctor appointments all the time, and you know how hard it is to get in with a shifter doc."

He frowned down at her. "You miss doctor appointments?"

She nodded. "All the time. They even charge me for my missed appointments." She sighed. "Nothing helps. I just can't seem to be bothered to remember my own things once I get home after taking care of everyone else."

70

"That will change. I have my ways to make certain you do the things in our household that need to be done — especially those that pertain to your care."

Her eyes widened. "You do? You have your ways? You have *ways*?"

He nodded with deliberate slowness and paced around her chair with a leopard's prowling gait. The silence stretched between them, tension heightening suddenly, all raw sexuality.

"Are you going to tell me what those ways are?" She turned her head to follow him as he circled behind her.

"I prefer to let you find out when the time comes. According to what you just told me, you often neglect your important appointments. If that is true, it won't take long before you find out just how I deal with my errant woman when she doesn't take care of her health."

She laughed and drummed her fingers on the arm of the chair. "I guess I'll have to figure out inventive ways to take care of my errant man when he doesn't take care of his health. I'm fairly certain you don't even know what a doctor is."

Sevastyan laughed. "The women in my family are going to love you, Flambé. Let's go out and grab something for dinner. We

71

can stop on the way home and pick up whatever you need from your house and bring it back here."

For the first time she looked uncomfortable. A shadow moved across her face and she shifted slightly in the chair. "I shouldn't stay here, Sevastyan. I think it's like pouring salt into the wound. At least study Matherson before you make up your mind. I can forward all the research I've done on him to you. I'm very thorough and I've dug up quite a bit."

"Then you should know you aren't safe."

She looked down at her hands. "I honestly didn't think he would really make so blatant a move on me here in the States. I should have known better. The road out here isn't very well traveled. He must have been able to get into my phone to know I was on my way here."

"The two appointments you cancelled?" he prompted. "Did Franco have anything to do with them?"

The color crept up her neck and into her face. "My leopard introduced herself with a vengeance. I didn't dare walk out the door. One moment I was perfectly fine and the next I was all over the place. It was really terrifying being that out of control."

Sevastyan could hear the underlying fear

in her voice. She was struggling to maintain. As a rule, Flambé was a confident woman, but between Matherson and her newly emerging leopard, she was off-balance.

"That's understandable. A leopard in heat can be difficult for any female, even one expecting it. We'll get you through her emergence." He poured confidence into his voice. "But, baby, you know you have to stay close to me, not only in case Matherson tries again but in case your leopard rises. Shturm isn't going to stand for a separation any more than I am."

He crouched down in front of her, his hands on her knees. "I know you're nervous. This is the last thing you expected. I'm a stranger to you. I swear, Flambé, we'll go as slow as the leopards allow us. There are plenty of bedrooms. You can choose one a distance from mine and stick a gun under your pillow if you're worried I'm going to try to break down the door."

"I doubt a gun under my pillow would stop you, but okay, I'll stay here with you."

He cupped the side of her face gently with his palm and slid the pad of his thumb over the bruise at the side of her mouth. His gaze dwelled on the lump in her hair. "This looks bad."

"It gave me a headache is all."

73

"I hope that's all." He bent forward and brushed a light kiss over it, feeling her shiver in response. "Thank you, Flambé, for agreeing to stay. After Matherson, it can't be easy to give your trust to anyone, least of all a man like me."

"A man like you?"

Her lashes made her look so innocent, those red-gold tips turning up right at the ends. He loved them already and knew he could spend a lifetime looking at them and never get tired.

"Don't pretend you don't know what I am or where I came from. There might not be mention of me in the papers, but there is of Mitya and Fyodor."

Her eyes searched his. "I was holding out hope that the things they said in the papers weren't true. Everyone wants to accuse people from Russia of being in organized crime just like they do if you're Italian."

"They're true, Flambé. I was up front with you about what and who I am." It was very possible, with the leopard's heat on her so severely, she could barely understand a word he was saying.

"Leopards hear lies, Sevastyan, and that's the first lie you've told me." She tilted her head and studied his face. "Why would you want me to believe that you're in the mob?"

He swore to himself but never changed expression. Didn't blink. Didn't look away from her. "My father was a *vor*. He ruled a lair in a brutal and savage way and trained me to be that way. Mitya's father and Fyodor's father were the same. Gorya's father tried to get out and they killed him — his own brothers and sons. They would have killed Gorya — an infant — but Fyodor's father had plans for him. I come from a very long line of evil leopards, Flambé, all of whom were *bratya*. That is the Russian equivalent to the mob. Perhaps the interpretation is lost in the way I speak and I sound as if I am speaking an untruth."

Flambé searched his eyes. "Perhaps." There was pure skepticism in her voice.

He took her hand and pulled her to her feet. "Out of curiosity, do you have any of your mother's skills when it comes to cooking?"

"I hear pleading in your voice. Are you telling me you can't cook?"

"It depends. I might be able to cook when it matters to me. That's not when I'm hungry, only when it matters. I have no problem sharing the kitchen duties, in fact I like that idea, but it would be nice if you're good at it."

She put her hands on her hips. "I'm okay

being the modern, hear-me-roar, I-can-do-it-all kind of woman, but what exactly are you bringing to the table?" Her gaze swept him up and down. "Aside from the obvious really good looks. Okay, brutally good looks. Aside from that, what are you bringing to the table?"

He stepped close to her, letting her feel his raw heat. The hot blood pounding through his veins. He dropped his voice to that velvet whisper of sheer command. "Sex, Flambé, the way no one else can or ever will give it to you. You'll scream with pleasure, you'll beg me for my cock. You'll do anything I ask of you, just to feel that pleasure, knowing I'll take you there over and over."

He dropped a kiss on top of her head and put her hand in the crook of his arm when she continued to stare up at him looking shocked. "We're going out the back way. Matherson has men watching the house. We'll take the car in the underground garage. They don't know about that one yet. There's a tunnel that goes straight to Mitya's property and comes out on the other side of his drive. I've texted him we're using it and to alert his security people so they don't decide to treat us like we're the enemy."

76

"You have a secret underground garage?"

"*We* do. Technically, since we're going to be together and Shturm claimed Flamme, it's our tunnel. I didn't think of it first. The Dovers owned the property before me. They were all about cars and they had the underground tunnel put in. Ania, Mitya's wife, didn't even know about it until after her father died. We discovered it when we were clearing out the garage of all the cars the Dovers owned. We had to reinforce the tunnel with steel in a few places, but it's a nice escape route for us and for them. Dover had a few surprises for us."

She looked around. "I love the house."

"The best is upstairs. The entire floor is dedicated to a bedroom, sitting room and bathroom. That floor has a wraparound balcony. It wasn't the master bedroom. That's downstairs, but I prefer the upstairs room. I had that one remodeled before anything else. I'll show it to you sometime." Sooner than later, he was certain, going by her leopard's antics. In the meantime, he was going to do whatever he could to earn her trust.

3

"What do you know about the Matherson family?" Mitya Amurov asked Jake Bannaconni. He sat back and regarded the billionaire across the wide expanse of the cherrywood desk. "The bastard Franco Matherson went to Sevastyan's home and threatened my cousin after running Flambé Carver off the road, assaulting her by punching her in the face and then trying to force his leopard's claim on her. She got away and ran to Sevastyan's home. Who is this man that he dared do these things and think he is safe from the police?"

Mitya Amurov was a big man with flat, cold eyes that right now spoke volumes. He sat at the table with Jake Bannaconni, Fyodor Amurov and Drake Donovan. Standing in the shadows were Gorya, Timur Amurov and Sevastyan Amurov, all cousins, and another bodyguard by the name of Logan Shields.

"Franco Matherson is safe from the police," Jake said. "The evidence against him would simply disappear. That's why he's an arrogant prick. He gets away with murder. He always has, he's just more blatant about it now. His family has tried to get him to see reason, but he doesn't listen to them. There are five boys. Franco is the oldest. They come from old money, somewhere in the Congo area, I heard."

Drake Donovan nodded. He owned a small but trusted international security company, one that was made up of mainly shifters, although very few knew that. He was probably the leading authority on the shifters and various lairs around the world. "They're African leopards, big ones and fighters. They keep their leopards in combat shape."

"Sevastyan deliberately provoked him to get his attention off Flambé," Mitya continued. "She's very close to the emergence. She'll be staying with him until her leopard makes an appearance. Right now, Matherson has several men watching Sevastyan's home. They can't get in and if they try to burn him out, he's prepared for that as well. We're on a wait-and-see policy at the moment. We wanted to find out what you had on Franco," Mitya added. His voice was clipped. It was evident to everyone in the room, Jake included, that Mitya didn't want to wait at all. He wanted to take care of the problem and just go after Matherson right then.

"Let me find out how extensive his reach is into law enforcement," Jake said. "That shouldn't be difficult. Franco is relatively new to this area. He had to have reached out to someone to get in. He had to hire locals to help him. He brought leopards, but he can't have that many. His brothers travel with him, but they don't always stay if they think he's going to pull them into deep shit. Messing with the local mob might constitute deep shit to them."

"Did you not hear that he left his men on Sevastyan's property?" Fyodor snapped.

Sevastyan stirred, just the slightest of movements to remind his cousins that it really didn't matter what the decision was at the table. In the end, he was going to kill and burn the bodies of every leopard Franco Matherson left behind for whatever purpose. He would get his woman to sleep and then go hunting. His cousins would want to hunt with him, but he was the head of security and he was forbidding that. He had already contacted the team he wanted with him. They were on standby.

Drake Donovan glanced over his shoulder, more like flicked his gaze at him, but then turned his attention to Mitya. "We know. We heard. They can't get to him. This is really about Flambé. Matherson wants her and he can't have her so he's throwing one of his fits. It's what he does. He's dangerous when he's like this."

"I don't get it," Fyodor said. "Why isn't he going after the women in his lair? Or one of the lairs closer to his? He has the money. He had the opportunity. You said he's a fighter and so is his family. The chances of his mate being among the women there are so much greater."

Drake shrugged. "He still has to abide by the shifter laws within his lair. The elders refused to allow him to search. He has a reputation for cruelty and they fiercely protect their women and children. It didn't matter how much money the Matherson family had, the lair didn't care. They drove them out."

"Yet Franco didn't retaliate by hunting and killing the leopards in his lair," Mitya pointed out, "the way he seemed to do with the Arabians."

"There were too many of the African leopards. The lairs would have banded together and hunted Franco," Drake said.

81

"They have an enforcer team. I've tried to recruit members for my security team — they're that good — but so far I haven't been able to persuade them away from their home turf. I wouldn't be surprised, given Franco's reputation, if these boys don't come hunting him."

"They'll have to get in line," Mitya said, his voice grim.

"Unfortunately, if Franco disappears now, the cops will look at Sevastyan first. He's already gone to your house, Sevastyan, and he hit your woman."

"She didn't report it," Mitya said when Sevastyan didn't so much as stir in the shadows. "And she isn't going to."

"That will still come out if Franco disappears," Drake said. "You can bet there's footage of Franco assaulting her. His people would have taken it. They can twist these things to their advantage. That footage would be produced and questions would be asked. Sevastyan would be looked at long and hard. Their side would have video of Franco pounding on the front door and Sevastyan spraying him with water. These things look bad when a body has disappeared. Already, the Amurov family is under suspicion of being mobsters."

"That's because we are," Mitya said, leaning forward. "I'm so sick of having to let these pricks hurt our women and stomp on us because we want to look good for the cops. The cops come into our homes and put listening devices in our living rooms. It's bullshit, Jake. We're trying to be the good guys and they're acting worse than we ever did. Why aren't they going after Matherson? I'll tell you why. He's fucking bribing them. That's why."

"We can't bribe them," Fyodor pointed out. He glared at Drake. "Because we're somehow supposed to be the good guys. But we're still the bad guys. Makes perfect sense to me. Especially now when we've got some psycho trying to kill Sevastyan so he can steal his woman."

"Let me find out who the cops are that are backing Matherson," Jake said. "Eli can help me. He was in law enforcement and he's still got friends there. Give me a few days. Meantime, Sevastyan, keep Flambé close to you." He put his hands on the tabletop and pushed up. "I'm heading home. If there's anything else I can do for you, let me know."

Sevastyan didn't say a word. He was a bodyguard, not one of the men running one of the territories. Jake didn't run any territory. He was as clean as they came, but he shut down companies for them, took them apart or put them together, depending on what was most beneficial. He could tell within minutes of learning about a company how best to utilize it. How best to make money from it. Whether to keep it running and revamp it, or to sell it off piece by piece.

Drake Donovan stood up to go as well. He was the most trusted man of all of them. He ran the international security agency that had brought them all together, and he had been the one to conceive of the idea of removing the worst of the mobsters, especially shifters running the crime syndicates, and replacing them, hoping to slow down or even stop the worst of the traffickers. At the moment, those in the room were feeling very discouraged. It seemed that as fast as they removed one head, another took its place.

They were always in danger. Worse, their families were always in danger. No matter what they did to protect them, the women, and now their children, had to live surrounded by guards day and night. There was no way out for them. If they left the protection of their family, they wouldn't last alone and all of them knew it.

Sevastyan knew he would be bringing Flambé into that world. He didn't like it.

He didn't want that for her. On the other hand, he could protect her from the Mathersons of the world, the ones who thought they were above both human and shifter law. He waited until Drake and Jake and their bodyguards had left Mitya's home before he moved out of the shadows and toed a chair around to sit at the table with his cousins. Gorya and Timur, two more cousins, joined them.

"What's the plan?" Fyodor asked.

"The plan is, you and Mitya stay in your homes with your wives where you're supposed to be," Sevastyan said. "That's the plan."

"Don't be an ass," Mitya hissed. "I want to know what the hell you're up to, Sevastyan."

"What I'm up to is getting my woman home and putting her to bed before she falls asleep on her feet. She's nervous and uncertain. I want to reassure her. I hope tomorrow I can introduce her to Evangeline and Ashe. Get her feeling comfortable with our side of the family. She can start work on the property. Her crew is going to come in with the supplies she needs in a couple of days. I want to make certain it's safe for them before she brings them in."

He was careful not to give out too much

information, because Mitya would never buy it if he talked too much. He wasn't a talker. His family knew that. He had to say something. Put them off as if he were going to listen to Drake. Everyone listened to Drake. Ultimately, he called the shots in the roller coaster and dangerous game they played. Unfortunately for Drake, Sevastyan wasn't part of his crew. He wasn't a *vor.* He wasn't a don. He wasn't a territory holder. He wasn't anything at all but a bodyguard who loved his cousin. His sole loyalty belonged to his family.

Mitya sighed. "That sounds like a good plan. Ania was excited to meet her tonight. She has always been interested in how the trees and brush were developed on the properties."

"I'm particularly grateful for the underground tunnel her grandfather came up with," Sevastyan said, allowing tiredness to edge his voice. "I've been doing some exploring and found two other escape routes, Mitya. They need work. One has partially collapsed and needs to be reopened, but it leads to the main road. It comes out several miles above a neighbor's vineyard, very close to the exit leading to the freeway. At the time the escape tunnel was constructed, there was no way of know-

86

ing a major highway would be put in right there, but it worked out nearly perfectly."

"You have to be careful," Mitya said, narrowing his eyes at his cousin. "You take too many chances, Sevastyan. Those tunnels could collapse completely and you could be buried alive in them without any of us knowing you're down there."

Fyodor and Sevastyan exchanged an amused look with Gorya. "You sound like an old hen, Mitya," Fyodor cautioned. "Always worried."

Mitya glared at him. "The tunnel *did* collapse, you cretins. Someone has to think for you. None of you think in terms of safety. Those tunnels are fifty years old. Who knows how they were constructed? They need major renovations before they can be used."

Sevastyan hid a smile. "Mitya is right. I'm being careful. I've got someone I trust, an engineer, looking them over. We're shoring the tunnels up and then retrofitting them section by section. I have no intentions of being buried alive, but I think having ways for us to exit our homes without being seen, or traveling between the two properties without being seen, are major advantages for us."

"I have to agree," Mitya said. "But, for

now, I think you need to get your woman home. You look tired, Sevastyan, and that's a rare thing."

Fyodor nodded. "I have to agree. You're working too hard. Maybe you should take a little time off. Turn over Mitya's security to Gorya for a week or two. Let him handle it while you see to Flambé. You've been renovating your home and working long hours for some time now. Give yourself some time off."

Mitya nodded. "I think that would be a good idea."

Sevastyan pushed himself away from the table as he rose. "I'll think about it." He turned away from his cousins. The men in this room were his family — the ones he cared most about in the world — the ones he could count on. He could hear the affection in their voices, the genuine concern. He did his best to stay apart — emotion didn't work when one was a bodyguard — but it was difficult when these men were all he had.

Now, apart from Gorya, each of them had found a woman. Fyodor had Evangeline. She was amazing. Sevastyan had done his best to keep his distance, but it was difficult when she was so genuine. Then Timur had fallen hard for Ashe. That had been unex-

88

pected. Like Sevastyan, Timur was a body-guard, and he took protecting Fyodor seriously. Mitya had found Ania on the side of the road in a rainstorm. She had a flat tire and he had stopped to help her, against Sevastyan's advice. Mitya had ignored the head of his security as usual, and this time, it had turned out to be a very good thing. Ania was amazing for Mitya. She suited him perfectly. Sevastyan could only hope that Flambé would suit him just as well as the other women matched his cousins.

Ania and Flambé were in the drawing room, both seated beside the warmth of the evening fire. It was on low, and the two had their chairs close and were talking in soft voices when Sevastyan strode in. He saw Flambé's gaze jump to his face. He could see her instant relief in his presence. She was glad to see him, but there was wariness too, as if she was uncertain what to do.

He held out his hand to her. She rose and crossed the room to him, but she didn't take his hand. "Did Ania take good care of you?" He bent to brush a kiss across her temple. "I tried not to be too long."

Ania joined them as well. "I really enjoyed meeting Flambé," she said. "Thanks for bringing her over, Sevastyan. She knows so much about plants. Indoor and outdoor."

"I had a good time," Flambé added.

"Good. You look like a sleepy kitten." He wrapped his arm around her and brought her under his shoulder, up close to his body, a claiming move, a bit proprietary, waiting for her to stiffen or object. She did neither, but she didn't settle or relax against him either.

"Thanks, Ania. Flambé is important to me." Sevastyan wanted to make that very clear. "She had a traumatic day."

"That bastard hit her," Ania acknowledged. "She told me."

Before Flambé could protest the topic of conversation, Sevastyan tightened his arm around her, pressing her front to his side. "I don't want her thinking about him anymore. He's my problem now. She's going to be designing the landscaping for the property. I can't wait to see what she comes up with. Since she'll be staying with me, I'll get to see her process. She's going to be working hands-on. Maybe you'd like to come over and watch sometime, Ania?"

"Would you mind, Flambé?" Ania asked, excitement edging her voice. "I can bring your crew Evangeline's baked goods. Trust me, I won't make them myself. I nearly burned down her bakery trying to help her once and learned my lesson when it came

90

to that kind of baking crap. It isn't as easy as it looks. She even had the dough made up."

"Really?" Flambé tried to keep a straight face but couldn't. She burst into laughter.

Sevastyan didn't make the mistake even though both women were laughing. He'd seen his cousins fall for the same bullshit over and over and get into trouble. He just looked down at the two women impassively. Ania sobered up first, looked up at him and rolled her eyes.

"Don't be all judgy, Sevastyan. I know you want to laugh."

He didn't say a word. He simply turned toward the door, taking Flambé with him. At the last moment, he remembered to keep his strides shorter to allow her to keep up. They headed out to the small Jeep he had purchased so that it could fit in the tunnel he'd renovated, allowing him to drive between the two properties unseen.

"I like her. I'd never had a chance to meet Ania Dover. She was always working or taking care of her father. We only went out a couple of times when her father wanted more trees planted. That was before the accident and then the robbery."

He settled her in the Jeep. "You do know what happened with her mother and grandparents wasn't really an accident, right? Someone deliberately ran them off the road and killed them. The same people tried to murder her father and make it look like a robbery." He walked around the hood of the car to slide behind the wheel. He really detested telling her the truth, but mates didn't lie to each other. Even if some did, he wasn't built that way. He expected her to trust him. In order to do that, he had to tell her the truth, no matter how difficult it was.

By the silence, he could tell she hadn't known or even suspected. He glanced at her as he put the vehicle in motion and drove it straight toward the entrance to the underground passage.

"Is that true?" Flambé put one hand to her throat defensively. "Why would anyone target the Dover family, Sevastyan? They've been around for generations. That's not right. Was it because they're a shifter family?"

"Unfortunately, it's more complicated than that."

Flambé rubbed her temples as if she might have a headache. "I don't understand why people are so ugly to one another."

"I don't either, baby. Just put your head back and rest. I'll get us home and you can go to sleep." He kept his voice pitched low

92

and soothing.

"If I fall asleep and don't have a chance to tell you, thank you for dinner and stopping by my house to get my clothes and my own garden tools and laptop. Things like that are important to me."

"Naturally. If we couldn't have gone ourselves, I would have sent for them. It was just nicer for you to choose what you wanted to bring with you." He wanted the chance to see her home. To see how she lived and what she surrounded herself with. Whatever made Flambé comfortable was what he was going to provide.

"You're a very thoughtful man."

He glanced at her again. Those long red-gold-tipped lashes had fallen, leaving her looking young and vulnerable whenever the lights from the tunnel hit her as they flashed past. Her hair would briefly blaze to life and then darkness would settle around them like a cloak. He wasn't a thoughtful man — not as a rule — not for others unless it came down to security details. It was just that she mattered to him. He found it astonishing and disconcerting just how quickly she'd come to matter so much. How every little detail about her counted.

It wasn't just that she was going to be his leopard's mate and by default, his. He was already intrigued with her. More than intrigued. So much more. He wanted this woman the more time he spent with her. The pull between them grew stronger, and the chemistry hotter.

He knew the leopards had a lot to do with it, but it wasn't all about their leopards. He was far too disciplined and in control to allow himself to to be swayed to this extent by his cat. It was the promise of Flambé. The way she looked at him. The brush of her gaze moving over his body and then retreating. He knew women. He read them easily. He was a shifter and he had all of his cat's enhancements. He could smell her arousal. Her interest. Her submission. Her needs and demands.

Right now, she sat in the Jeep, seat belt tight around her, clad in the power suit she'd worn to his house earlier in the day. The silk blouse clung to her generous breasts, showing a hint of the darker bra beneath it. She had to have known, when she slid into the seat, that her blouse had come unbuttoned, those first three buttons, but she hadn't tidied them. She'd left them, so the upper curves of her breasts showed where the material was pulled apart.

He didn't need the lights in the tunnel to see her. His leopard was close, and he saw

94

every detail of her bone structure along with her satin skin and the fall of silky hair as he drove fast through the passageway. She was beautiful. He couldn't wait to see her laid out for him like a feast. In the meantime, he was looking forward to getting to know her, finding out all the things that pleased her, made her smile and laugh, that mattered to her.

Sevastyan drove the Jeep from the underground tunnel straight into the garage with no lights and parked it, turned it off and just sat there listening. He called Shturm close, wanting the cat to ensure no leopard or man was in the garage or close by. He hadn't perceived danger near, but he wasn't taking any chances with Flambé.

When Shturm assured him the garage was clear, he woke Flambé gently and gathered her suitcases. "Let's go, *malen'koye plamya*. Stay very quiet. I don't want any of Franco's men to hear us. They think we're inside."

"They're still out there?" She turned her face up toward him, the back of her head rubbing against his chest.

She was very tactile. As a rule, Sevastyan forbade touching. His leopard would never have stood for it. When he went to the clubs, the women didn't touch him unless he commanded them to do so. Most of the time, he didn't allow it. He looked forward to skin-to-skin touch with Flambé. He also knew it would be advantageous if she needed a continuous physical demonstration between them. It had bothered him that she hadn't taken his hand at Mitya's house when he'd offered it to her.

He bent to brush a reassuring kiss on the side of her cheek and skimmed one hand down her neck to the swell of her breasts, the sweet expanse of curves her open blouse revealed. He covered the satiny mounds with the heat of his palm and the wide expanse of his fingers. Her breasts were soft yet firm. He didn't make excuses for touching her. He didn't need to. She'd given him the invitation.

He rubbed the pad of his thumb back and forth over the curve of her breasts. "They're out there."

Her breath hitched. Flambé didn't pretend she didn't like what he was doing to her. She inched into his hand, not away from it. Her hips moved slightly in rhythm. She was very responsive to the chemistry happening between them. At the moment, her leopard wasn't involved. He was grateful she was responding to the man and not his leopard.

"What do they want?"

96

She wasn't thinking anymore, not about Franco Matherson. She was thinking about Sevastyan and he wanted to keep her that way. He didn't want to answer that question. Leopards could hear lies and he wasn't about to lie to her. He didn't want her to be afraid nor did he want her to know that he was going hunting the moment she fell asleep.

Deliberately he slid his hand deeper into her blouse, finding her left nipple through the thin lace of her bra. He tugged for a moment and then, watching her face, flicked with his thumb and finger. She gasped as he rolled and tugged again.

"I love that you're so responsive." He whispered it like praise and then bit gently on the lobe of her ear before letting her go and once more picking up her suitcases. "Come on, baby, we've got to get inside. I need you safe." He led the way fast, clearly expecting her to follow him.

She was silent when she walked, a true leopard. She'd been brought up in a lair. Trained as a leopard. Her father had definitely taught her the rules of their world. She knew they weren't entirely human and they weren't animal. Theirs was a strict society because it had to be secretive in order for them to have a chance at survival.

97

Sevastyan didn't understand, when there were such good men as Ania's father had been, why aberrations like his father and Matherson were born into an already dying species. Sevastyan couldn't claim he was a good man, although he tried to be. He wanted to be. He did his best when he knew he'd been fucked up since the day he'd been born. For the woman following him into the house, he would do his best to be a better man every day. For her.

He would find a way to make her life extraordinary. Fyodor managed to make Evangeline happy. But Evangeline was an angel. Sevastyan didn't want an angel. He couldn't afford to have one, not with the kind of man he was. He wanted a woman who would catch fire with him. Go up in fiery flames. Be fierce when she needed to be. Have no fear when she confronted him or with the kinds of things he would ask or demand of her.

He would be asking a lot of Flambé. He believed she had it all in her, just by the things he'd read about her and her father. She'd grown up beside her father, doing the things he'd done. Rescuing her people, giving them opportunities to make their way in life. She seemed to possess all the characteristics he admired and respected in a woman,

98

the ones he most looked for.

He was an extremely sexual man. There was no getting around that. The way she related to him already, he could tell she was as well. The sex wasn't going to be all about her cat; when the leopard subsided with her heat, Flambé's needs wouldn't just go away. She would match his nature, and hopefully be open to adventure.

"I thought this room would be a good one for you. It was the master bedroom and has a sitting room. You can use it for work until you move upstairs with me." He pushed open the door to the enormous suite of rooms.

The Dover manor was large and the downstairs master bedroom could have easily been a city apartment complete with kitchen, dining room and living room. It was open, with two stairs leading up to the actual bedroom, where a gas fireplace was on one wall. Chairs and a small table were down below the two stairs on a thick gray carpet facing another gas fireplace. One wall was accented a dark color while the rest matched the silvery gray of the carpet. Two tall lamps were slashes of dark color with oval-shaped shades over the dim bulbs standing on either side of the enormous bed.

"The bathroom is through those doors.

Has a shower and bathtub. Anything you need should already be in there for you, but if not, intercom me." He gestured toward the phone. "Anything at all, Flambé, if your leopard rises, or you get frightened, you call me." He walked over to the phone and showed her where to press the button. "That will call me. Don't come up the stairs. That could get you in trouble."

She quirked an eyebrow at him. "Trouble? What kind of trouble?"

"You know exactly what I'm talking about. I'm being as gentle with you as I can. The leopards aren't going to give us much time. I want to take what we have to get to know each other. Don't make it more difficult than it already is." He poured warning into his voice and hoped she heeded him.

She didn't look afraid, only intrigued. He opened the double closet doors. The closet could fit a small apartment into it as well. Hers. She lived in a little studio. It was on her father's property, but she didn't reside in the main house. He didn't know who stayed there and he didn't care. She liked small spaces, which was good to know that she didn't mind them.

"Wow. This is the master bedroom?"

He indicated the built-in walkways that looked as if they were shelves that artfully ran the length of all the rooms. They had been cleverly put throughout the house for the leopards to rest on, or use for prowling from one place to another.

She stroked her fingers along her throat. "It's a little intimidating. I'm used to my little studio. We always had so many people staying with us that the main house was crowded, so I had the studio apartment for my own. Thankfully, my father kept it for me even when I went away to college."

He took possession of her hand and brought it to his lips, biting on the ends of her fingers just hard enough to make them sting before sucking them into the heat of his mouth to take the edge of any pain off. Her eyes went wide. Again, she didn't pull her hand away from him, only stared at him a little uncertainly.

"You'll be safe here. Just take your shower and go to sleep. Don't wander around tonight. Once you're in bed, I'll check on you a couple of times unless you're a very light sleeper and you think that will bother you."

"I'll leave the door open." There was relief in her voice.

He found it interesting that she was more afraid of being alone in the large room with the door closed than with him coming in to check on her. Her leopard was still very quiet. Shturm was prowling close to the surface, eager to be on the hunt, but there was no evidence that Flambé trusted Sevastyan because of the leopards.

He cupped the side of her face, his thumb gently running over her soft skin. "You'll be safe here, Flambé. Matherson can't get to you. I'd never allow that. Neither would Shturm. Go to sleep and let yourself get a good night's rest."

Her dark green eyes searched his for a long time and then finally she nodded. He bent his head and brushed a kiss across her lips. A brief touch, no more. His heart nearly stopped at that touch. His stomach somersaulted. She was potent. He wanted to mesmerize her. To bring her under his spell. She was completely captivating him. Ensnaring him when he hadn't thought it was possible for anyone to do such a thing.

He dropped his hands abruptly and turned and stalked out without looking back. It was difficult to keep his hands off her. He'd promised himself he'd give her every reason to trust him, and at his first real test, he was already failing. He would fail. He knew it. She purred the moment she came into physical contact with him. That shouldn't matter. He should have enough discipline to stay in control, but he didn't. He couldn't stop his body's reaction — or his mind from turning to all kinds of erotic images.

He waited downstairs, not daring to go up to his bedroom. He'd first had the room painted, carpeted and tiled the way he wanted before he added the other renovations himself. He'd taken his time and added every single thing he might ever want or need and that was pleasing to his eye. He'd done the work himself. He had escape routes for himself, his leopard and especially his woman, should he ever find one.

He knew he couldn't allow Flambé anywhere near what was now the master bedroom. If he took her up to his room, he would want her to stay there for the rest of her life. There would be no period of waiting, no getting to know each other. His resolution would be over that fast.

Sevastyan turned off the lights in the house one by one, as if they were preparing for bed. He left the television on in the living room for a short while and then turned that off. His team would be arriving any minute, coming in through the same tunnel he'd driven the car in. He'd chosen carefully. He had picked men he knew well, those he personally could count on. It wouldn't have mattered to him before, but now that he had Flambé, that had changed. Before, it hadn't mattered whether he lived or died. Now he wanted to live a very long time. He had something unexpected to live for.

Kirill Chernov and Matvei Bykov had been unexpected in his life as well. Both men had been childhood friends when there were no such things. His father, Rolan Amurov, saw to that. If Sevastyan was ever careless enough to show he liked someone, which he often did as a very young child, his father made certain to beat the child in front of him, most times nearly to death. Sometimes to death, laughing the entire time. Sevastyan learned to stay away from other children. Rolan made certain his son couldn't form alliances or in any way have followers who might someday rise up to defeat him before he was ready to step down from his position as *vor*.

Kirill and Matvei had proven their loyalty to Sevastyan over and over, all the while making certain Rolan and his lieutenants never saw the boys talking. They developed their own code, although at first, Sevastyan was distrustful of the offer of friendship. It was Shturm who convinced him the boys and their leopards were sincere in their determination to become his friend. They

104

had witnessed time and again his father and his lieutenants beating Sevastyan and his leopard for trying to protect others in the lair. As they grew up, the friendship only got stronger, and when Sevastyan and his cousins left Russia with prices on their heads, Kirill and Matvei went with them, risking their lives as well.

Sevastyan knew both men had the same problem with their leopards, that fierce, savage nature that the Amur leopard trained from birth to fight and kill gave them. That made life so much more difficult, adding to the burden of their already edgy, challenging lives as shifters in a world not meant for men with animalistic traits.

He turned off all the lights and then unlocked the back door separating the garage from his home. The two men would enter the garage directly from the tunnel. The men Franco Matherson had left behind to watch him wouldn't be able to enter the garage. Even if they did manage to find an entry point, they would set off every hidden alarm and he would know.

He made his way down the wide hall to Flambé's room, hoping she had been exhausted enough to actually fall asleep. He didn't like the idea of her being afraid. He didn't mind a little fear — but only for the right reasons. Tonight, he wouldn't be there to comfort her. He could tell the room was too big for her. She had looked around her, liking the beauty of the master bedroom because she was an artist and could see the natural artistry of the space, but for her, it didn't work. He wasn't certain why, but those answers would come over time.

The door was open, she hadn't closed it, which told him she wasn't afraid of being with him, and that pleased him. He wasn't certain why she was able to trust him so quickly, but he was grateful that she was. She would need to. He didn't think Franco Matherson was going to give up so easily, not with what Drake and Jake had to say about him. Sevastyan couldn't just go kill the bastard and be done with it, not without a certain risk. He didn't want to bring that risk to Mitya's door. Or Flambé's for that matter. Franco had brothers. In Sevastyan's world, that meant those brothers would come looking for him.

He stalked silently into the room, seeing immediately that Flambé wasn't in the large bed. He used his leopard senses to find her, inhaling sharply. She had a sutble fragrance, one he found particularly pleasing. The combination was of hints of freesia, Moroccan rose and Egyptian jasmine spiced with coriander, cinnamon, cloves and buchu. The fragrance was so subtle it was barely there, but it was particular to Flambé, not a perfume, but natural to her skin. He smelled it in the silk of her hair and he knew when he tasted her, the flavor of the cinnamon and cloves would be there forever on his tongue. Just the thought brought an ache to his cock.

He found her just inside the open door of the closet. That made him want to smile. He didn't. Had she been awake, he might have reprimanded her. In a fire, he would have needed to know where she was. For now, looking down at her face as she lay curled up like a sleepy little kitten, barely making a shadow beneath the blankets she had covering her, his heart turned over. She was getting to him in a big way.

The dim light that recessed into the eaves of the ceiling when the door was open shone down, providing just enough of a glow to spotlight her. Flambé had taken a shower and her hair was still damp. She had braided the thick mass, so the braid was a dark red, a splash of color against the black pillowcase. In her sleep, and without makeup, she looked younger than she did awake. Her eyebrows were red-gold just the way her lashes were.

She was a true redhead, with a smattering of freckles on her face and across her arms. She was obviously careful to cover her skin when she worked in the sun, although he thought that being leopard should provide some protection from the bombardment from the sun's rays. Her hands were small, her wrists narrow. He would have to take that into consideration. He wanted to touch her skin, feel her to see if she felt as soft as she looked, but he had other things to do this night, like make certain she was safe — and send a very strong message to Franco Matherson.

It would do Matherson good to look him up. To see what kind of family he came from. A man like Franco would immediately want to run to Sevastyan's father, try to get the *bratya* to do his dirty work for him, because in spite of the man's arrogance, he would be afraid. Once he learned who he was really dealing with, what kind of shifter Sevastyan was and what kind of leopard he possessed, Matherson wouldn't want to come at him fairly.

In the meantime, Sevastyan would be taking out his pawns one by one.

4

Flambé lay looking up at the ceiling, her heart pounding. She was in the same house with Sevastyan Amurov. What had her female leopard done? She had wanted this, but not permanently. She'd been so out of it. So scared. The attack. The blow to the head. Flamme rising, taking control.

It wasn't like she could blame her leopard. She'd been fantasizing over Sevastyan Amurov for months. Who knew his leopard would be the biggest, baddest brute on the planet, ready to fight for a mate? Of course Flamme would try to find someone to protect them. It wasn't her fault.

On top of everything else, Flambé had been sexually aroused for the last couple of weeks before Flamme's sudden appearance. Her skin had been crawling with need. She should have picked someone up and taken the edge off, but she'd been trying to find a way to meet Sevastyan. She'd had her sights set on him.

She was insane to think she could really be with a man like him — hold his interest for more than five minutes. He was — extraordinary. She had watched him for so long. He hadn't once seen her. Not a single time. Why would he? She'd been a little mouse hiding in the shadows, too timid to ask for what she wanted. What she needed. She always felt she had too much to lose. More, she had too much to protect.

The first time she'd ever laid eyes on Sevastyan she'd known he was the one she needed. He was intimidating in the most delicious way. Totally sexual when she didn't find most men in the least bit hot. Just looking at him from a distance made her go damp. Weak. She knew she shouldn't be all about sex with him, but she was desperate for real relief.

She needed sex nearly all the time but she was never satisfied. Never. Then she saw him and nearly had an orgasm from just looking. She wasn't about to ignore the miracle of feeling true chemistry. Still, nothing was supposed to be permanent. She didn't do permanent. She didn't want it or need it or even trust it, especially with a man like Sevastyan.

She paced for a long time in the room

110

he'd given her to stay in. He was being so nice to her. Sweet, really. He didn't have the reputation for nice — or sweet. He didn't look it either. His eyes were as cold as they could get. When they drifted over her, she found herself shivering in both anticipation and trepidation.

She'd always intended to seduce him. She'd wanted to have sex with him. That had been her intention from the first moment she saw him. But she realized the moment she saw him up close it would be impossible to seduce a man like Sevastyan. He seduced women. It wasn't the other way around. Now, her leopard had taken charge in her weakened state and tied them to him.

She touched the lump on her head. She'd been hit a lot harder than she realized and Flamme had taken advantage. That wouldn't happen again. She couldn't let her leopard out until she figured out what to do. Her heart didn't want to slow down no matter how hard she tried to get her breathing under control.

Her leopard had begun to rise a couple of weeks earlier than she'd admitted to Sevastyan, although she hadn't recognized what was happening, only because she was always desperate for sex. She'd tried to be satisfied with a man she'd known for a short while.

111

He'd asked her out a few times, but she just wasn't interested. She'd faked it and that made her feel terrible, especially since he thought they were really compatible, but the sex left her burning for something more. She had a string of one-night stands with human males she picked up in bars, all totally unsatisfying — and horrible. She detested herself, especially when they wanted her number and she refused to give it to them.

She was lucky enough to get a call from a man named Cain Dufort, who owned a very successful business — a private, exclusive club — and wanted her to come in for a consultation. She would have to sign a nondisclosure agreement, as it was a sex club for clients with unusual tastes. She didn't care. She wasn't someone interested in outing others' personal sexual preferences. She loved her work and if the owner needed work done, she was happy to design whatever it was he needed.

The job wasn't outdoors as she first thought. He wanted a beautiful oasis in the middle of his club. His concept was that he would have drinks served in a garden of paradise. It would be glassed in so those relaxing could enjoy the shows taking place in the various rooms if the curtains were

112

open, or they could just talk with their friends while they relaxed.

Flambé had never been inside a club like the one Cain owned. The moment she was escorted into his office, she knew he was leopard. She recognized the roped muscles and the focused eyes. He carried authority easily, something she reacted to. Even wearing her power clothes, she had to fight against his pull and her natural submission. She knew her reaction to him was caused by the type of leopard she was. She kept her chin up and met his eyes when they talked, not allowing her gaze to stray around to the unusual but beautiful artwork he had in his office. She had glimpsed the pieces as she had entered, and knew they were originals, artwork most likely from Japan, depicting the fascinating practice of Shibari — a rope tying of men and women.

He had taken her around, shown her rooms where there were all kinds of equipment, things that made her ache inside, made her sex flutter and her panties go damp. He showed her racks of instruments as well as benches and wooden crosses, things she had never seen before. There were ropes of various colors and textures. She worked at keeping her breathing even and her heart from pounding. For some reason, she really responded to the rope. This place was exciting and amazing, when she'd been so certain she would never be in the least bit interested in such things.

Cain had looked at her speculatively and asked her if she had ever considered any of the practices. She shook her head and answered honestly that she hadn't. He immediately invited her to come in the evening and watch from his office, where she would be safe and no one would see her or know she was there. At first, she declined, telling him she didn't think that was fair to the others who were in the private rooms, but he assured her that if they opened the curtains, they were fine with anyone who wanted to observe them.

She had gone that first night and stayed alone in his office watching the security screens, a little shocked by some of the things she saw, but mostly excited. Mostly sexually excited. Then Sevastyan Amur had stalked in, looking more confident and arrogant than any man she'd ever seen. He was scarred, rough looking and as dangerous as any man could get. She knew immediately that he was a shifter. He commanded every room he went into. Instantaneous silence fell when he entered a room. It was very clear to her that he could

114

have his choice of any woman — or man for that matter — that he wanted.

She kept her gaze fixed on him as he indicated a woman with a jerk of his head. He wasn't particularly nice as he pointed to a chair when they entered one of the viewing rooms. The woman removed her clothing and folded it neatly as he stalked over to the wall where a row of ropes hung in neat clusters. They were in various colors and made of different types of material. He selected a deep green and an olive color, both ropes looking rough.

Flambé shivered as she watched him return to the woman. Sevastyan looked like a prowling leopard as he circled her, his muscles rippling in his scarred chest. His trousers hung low on his hips. His eyes glowed a vicious, almost dense glacier-turquoise layer over the deep blue ice of the cat's eyes. It was impossible to look away from him. He was magnetic. Spellbinding. So incredibly impressive she forgot to breathe.

He whispered something to the woman, his fingers on her pulse as he moved around her, the rope sliding through his fingers. Flambé was so fascinated her heart began to pound. The woman was nearly swaying as he leaned his head down toward her. Sevastyan was a big man, tall, his shoulders wide, and even though she was tall, he seemed to dwarf her. Flambé knew it was because he dominated the room.

He put his hands on her shoulders and forced her to her knees. The woman knelt obediently. Flambé gasped when Sevastyan grasped her long hair and braided it, weaving it expertly. He shoved the mass over her shoulder and then caught first one arm and then the other, thrusting her forward by putting one hand between her shoulder blades. The woman went down farther, prostrating herself on the floor, so only her bottom was up in the air.

Sevastyan laid the rope against the woman's skin with quick, sure confidence. Every knot was tied with that same sureness from her neck to the curve of her bottom, anchoring around her hips. There was no hesitation. He worked fast, laying his lines and fastening the ropes into a piece of beautiful art, as if she were a canvas. That piece was done in the dark green and he wove it back up her body, laying the knots up her front without seeing what he was doing, laying them almost blindly. She could tell he was laying them perfectly as he built the sleeveless blouse for her.

Standing in front of the woman's bowed

head, Sevastyan suddenly popped the rope, tightening the knots so the entire shirt clamped around her skin. Her body jerked and she cried out, whether in agony or in pleasure it was difficult to tell. The sound was muffled and barely discernable when the audio in the room was only coming over one speaker. It was impossible to hear anything Sevastyan said; he spoke too low as he tied off the rope and picked up the olive-colored one.

Goose bumps broke out all over Flambé's body. Her nipples tightened into hardened peaks. Her breasts ached, straining against the material of her bra. Between her legs, she felt the brush of fire, almost as if that lash had stroked over her clit. She wanted to be that woman. *Desperately.*

Sevastyan pulled the woman's head back by her braid and began to weave the braid into the rope, knotting it every other inch until she was straining, the position awkward, one difficult to maintain. He pulled her arms behind her and wove a harness made of intricate knots from her shoulders, hair and then down her arms to her wrists, so she was completely helpless.

Flambé had never seen anything like it until she'd seen the artwork in Cain's office. She'd looked up the ancient art on the

117

internet and discovered all kinds of information on the practice. It had intrigued and shocked her just a little at all the various ways Shibari was used.

Watching Sevastyan lay those knots, so impersonally, so relentlessly, his face a merciless mask, she felt as if she was being lashed with lightning. She couldn't take her eyes from him as he used his foot to shove the woman's knees wide apart. Heart pounding, she actually watched as he took the woman almost brutally, his body a machine, taking her from behind, not looking at her face, as if she mattered so little he wouldn't look into her eyes. When he was done, he glanced over his shoulder, beckoned, and another man hurried into the room.

Sevastyan tugged on the rope and loosened the knots, first on the olive rope and then on the dark green one. He indicated both loosened ropes to the newcomer and then pointed out shears he'd laid out on a table. The man thanked him and then gently removed the woman's bonds and comforted her, his arms around her, as Sevastyan just turned and strode out without once looking back. It took Flambé a few minutes to realize that the other man was the woman's partner.

She found herself gripping the edge of Cain Dufort's desk, tears swimming in her eyes. Finding out about one's submissive sexual cravings alone in a club when she knew she was leopard and the man she hungered for was also leopard was terrifying. Especially when that man clearly could have cruel tendencies and she was not only attracted to him, she desperately wanted him. She had always been careful to fulfill her sexual needs with human men — except she was never fulfilled.

There was something very, very wrong with her. She had to leave. Get out of that place. That first night, she resolved to *never* meet Sevastyan Amurov. *Never* be in the same room with him. She, more than any other female, knew exactly how dangerous it was to be with a dominating shifter. They could be very cruel, especially to a mate. She was never, *never,* going there.

As days went by, she found herself obsessively thinking of him all the time. It didn't matter how many times she told herself to stop, or how many long hours she put in working; she couldn't control her thoughts. She couldn't sleep. Her body told her he could sate the terrible fire that burned in her night and day. She burned for him, for the things he could do for her. For the world

119

he could open for her. Maybe she could go to Cain. He was interested in her. She could tell. She always could tell when a man was interested. He was also a shifter and she didn't burn for him or obsess over him the way she did over Sevastyan. Would he be able to sate her? She doubted it.

She found herself trying to look Sevastyan up on the internet. She found articles about his cousins, but there was very little on him. That made him all the more mysterious and intriguing to her. In the end, she justified going back to the club because she had to begin work there. She stayed later and later, behind the cordoned-off glass, safe from those playing in the rooms. No one even noticed her there as she diligently planted the trees and bushes, or the delicate little flowers and bulbs that would make up the garden of paradise Cain wanted.

It was a couple of weeks before she saw Sevastyan a second time. Flambé knew he was there before she actually looked up and saw him. Her body reacted. She was on her hands and knees, head down, fingers pushing the dirt gently around plants when chills went down her spine and her sex clenched. Her heart accelerated. Went into overdrive.

She lifted her gaze to look through the glass. He was there, larger than life, crooking an arrogant finger at a woman who preceeded him into a room just across from her. He was so gorgeous. So beyond even what Flambé remembered. Her heart sank. She was never going to be rid of her obsession with him. It was just going to grow and grow. The worst of it was she could tell his leopard was riding him hard. He wore that same expressionless mask, but his eyes were colder, the lines in his face deeper.

A shiver went down her spine, and deep inside, something feral stirred. Sevastyan halted just inside the door to the room and looked around, his eyes glowing, his cat very close to the surface. She froze, not daring to move, staying low, wishing she hadn't stayed so late, but knowing she had just in case this man came in.

Abruptly, Sevastyan turned away, closed the door and pointed to the chair. The woman took off her robe, folded it and placed it on the chair. A man sat in a deep armchair just outside the door. The woman turned her head to look at him. Sevastyan said something, and at once she stiffened and turned back to him. Flambé realized that like the other woman Sevastyan had chosen, this one had a partner. He didn't tolerate any interference. If they were with him, they focused completely on him. Her partner wasn't alone in watching. Many others had drawn up chairs. Flambé counted herself lucky that no one had put theirs in front of her spot.

Sevastyan left the woman standing alone and naked while he inspected a variety of colored ropes hanging on shelves. Eventually he chose several charcoal and brown bundles. He shook the charcoal one out and ran it through his hands as he walked around the woman, talking softly to her. She nodded to him several times. He touched her neck and she leaned into him. Flambé found that small movement very telling. Sevastyan could create intimacy with just his voice and the lightest of touches.

The woman was bound and tied in an elaborate corset and leggings with her breasts and sex framed just like in the pictures in Cain's office. Done in charcoal and brown rope, the knots intricate and beautiful, the work was fascinating. Flambé found it captivating and gorgeous against the skin of the woman Sevastyan worked on. His expression never changed, not when he whispered to her in reassurance and not when he suddenly tightened the ropes. Her expression would change, going from a kind of rapture to shock and pain, settling back to rapture.

In the end, Sevastyan spun her body away from him and once more took her from behind, his body moving hard in hers, lasting a long time, while she seemed to cry out over and over in bliss. Again, it was her partner, after Sevastyan loosened the ropes, who removed them and comforted her, while he simply walked away without a backward glance.

Flambé found herself sitting back on her heels breathing hard, one hand going up to her throat protectively. She didn't know the first thing about that kind of wild sex, and she didn't want to know, did she? But she dreamt of it. No, not of *it*. Not of the sex. Of him. Of Sevastyan. She was more obsessed than ever. There was no getting him out of her head. She needed that kind of sex. Raw. Hot. Rough. Pure fire.

She had gone back to the club repeatedly because she had to work. Cain didn't allow anyone other than her to come there. He said he would prefer the work to take longer rather than risk a violation of his clients' privacy. Cain spent time with her, bringing her coffee, talking with her while she worked, and she liked him. Once or twice she even felt a brief stirring of interest, but it faded quickly. Both times she found him looking at her speculatively, but he never

123

tried to push her into agreeing to any of the sexual offers he made her.

She stayed late most nights and realized Sevastyan only came every couple of weeks and there was no pattern to when he might show up. When he did, he commanded the attention of everyone by his presence alone. She wasn't the only one obsessed with him. He never seemed to notice or care if others were around or watched him. He always chose a woman who had a partner who would care for her. The women he'd tied vied for his attention, but he didn't use them more than the one time. The only person she ever saw him speak to was Cain, and then only briefly in the hall. They seemed to be friendly enough. Flambé wasn't about to ask Cain about him or show interest at all.

In the end she decided one night of crazy sex with Sevastyan would get her over her obsession. He never spent more than one time with a woman. Never. He barely looked at her. So really, it would just be sex, not even a night. She couldn't do it at a club. She was fairly certain of that. She had to figure out a way to casually meet him. She tried to find a nightclub he might frequent, or a bar. Someplace she could go where she might be able to run into him and then be flirtatious enough that he would do his thing and walk away. One time. That should be enough.

She was very committed to saving her species. There were so few of them. They had also been reaching out to the Arabian leopards, slowly bringing one or two into the country as well. It was a very slow process, getting the right elders to help them. She didn't have the time or energy to be in a relationship and she knew a man like Sevastyan Amurov was not the kind of man to be in a loving committed relationship, so the sex was going to be wild and crazy and one time. She didn't trust male shifters at all and she wasn't about to be in a relationship with one.

Now, Flambé rolled over and pushed herself into a sitting position. She'd made a bed for herself in the closet. The main room was just too big for her. A part of her wanted to sneak away and go back to her small studio that felt safe, homey and *hers.* This place was too large and masculine for her and it smelled like Sevastyan. He was everywhere. Stamped into the walls and floor. He might not reside in the rooms, but his presence was everywhere and she found it too overpowering. She hadn't counted on that.

She wasn't a weak person. She could stand up to anyone and often had to when it came to her business and the people she brought into the country to save. Her species of leopard was very submissive to their mate, but they were ferocious fighters and extremely protective of their children. Still, those things Sevastyan had made her feel when she'd been at a distance from him in the club were a thousand times more intense this close to him.

She forced herself to her feet and out into the main bedroom. The privacy screens had been lowered on all the windows, blacking out any light from the moon, but she could see easily in the dark. Pacing, Flambé thought about what to do. She had to be practical. Really assess who she was and what she could do now that she'd met Sevastyan in person. When she'd gotten the request for work, she'd been thrilled. She was going to get the chance she wanted.

The first meeting had to be cancelled because Flamme had made her presence known in a big way. Already, Flambé's body had been crawling with need, her nerve endings alive and raw with a kind of fiery burn that translated to a sexual heat of its own. Her leopard's sudden appearance added even more of an urgency, so much so that she couldn't trust herself to go out of her room. Her body was in a frenzy of need. Hot and aching. She'd called and cancelled, because she couldn't trust herself around him.

At the same time, Franco had contacted her and tried to set up a meeting with her. He let her know he was watching her. That was really frightening and she had been extremely careful, making certain she stuck close to her crew whenever she left her offices or home after that.

The second meeting she was supposed to have with Sevastyan had gone way wrong as well. Her leopard was spinning out of control. Completely. Flambé had found herself on the floor of her room when she'd been so carefully dressing for her meeting with Sevastyan. She'd been thinking of him, fantasizing, and the next thing she knew, she was burning up, her blood so hot, pounding with need so intense she was on the floor on her hands and knees sobbing, hips bucking out of control. Nothing had helped. Toys had made the sensation worse. It had taken what seemed like forever for the terrible sensation to ease enough for her to even text an apology to him. She knew he wasn't a man to be very forgiving.

Now that she'd met him, she realized she

should have taken into consideration what kind of person she was. Who she was. Wild sex was what she totally needed, but not with a man like Sevastyan. Sevastyan was the kind of man who could own a woman with his brand of sex. She should have been paying more attention to how many of those women came back night after night in the hopes of being Sevastyan's choice for the night, even though they had permanent partners.

Sex was a powerful weapon if it was used that way — and it could be wielded as a weapon. Sevastyan clearly was adept at using sex for whatever the reason. She was in so much trouble. "It's not your fault, Flamme," she whispered aloud, and rubbed the swelling on her head for the hundredth time. "You were trying to protect us."

The last thing she expected was for his leopard to claim hers. She paced restlessly again. Her leopard was in her first life cycle. Mistakes were made. She knew that. This had to be a mistake because no way in hell was Flambé going to be claimed by a shifter. She'd be trapped by Sevastyan.

"What do you want, Flambé? What are you doing here? You think things through. Plan things carefully. Since the first time you laid eyes on that man, you've been out of control. You have to pull back and figure this out, because if you don't, it will be too late and you'll never get out of this mess."

She had always talked aloud when she planned anything. She was an only child and most often alone. She lived in the studio because her father took in so many strangers, so her "room" had been the studio to "give her privacy," even as a child. Which really meant give her father many rooms in the house for his women.

She had talked aloud to hear sound. She played music, filling the room with the soothing rhythms so she didn't feel so lonely. Talking to herself in times of stress had become a habit. She was used to small spaces and they comforted her.

"You like him. That was unexpected. You didn't think in terms of liking him. It was supposed to be all about sex." She crossed to the large bed and stared down at it. She hadn't gotten on it so the blankets had remained untouched. There wasn't so much as a wrinkle on the comforter. "He didn't want you upstairs in his personal space and that's good." She looked around the room, a long slow sweep through her leopard's eyes. "This is a nice room that any guest would be happy to be in. He's treating you so politely. Perfect manners."

129

Restlessness had her pacing again. The room was so large and she was able to walk the length, using the sitting room area as well. "You don't matter any more than those women mattered to him. Your leopard matters to his leopard. You know that. You felt it when they connected. If you stay here with him, you'll have that amazing sex you dreamt of, and your leopard will be happy. So will his leopard. This is a great property for the leopards to run free. He wants you for his leopard and to have his children, just the way the other shifters wanted the women for their leopards and to have children. What happened to them? In the end? What happened to your mother? What kind of lives did they have? You know better than to fall for this bullshit."

She paused by the low table and flung herself into the sitting chair so she could drum her fingers on the tabletop, hearing a musical beat in her head. She had to hear something along with the sound of her own voice. "I'm not certain if he's capable of being happy, no matter what he says. He has that place inside him he retreats to where only he can go. I would never really be a part of his life. I'd be . . . lonely. Just the way I've always been. I'm so damn tired of being alone. I hurt all the time now. My body is burning up, even before your rising, Flamme. I'm not complaining about you. I'm not. It was already happening. I wanted him. You know I did. Now, having met him, I know one time would never have been enough."

Her head was pounding again and she wanted to cry. Crying wasn't going to solve anything. They were in a mess. She'd seen too many other shifter women in a mess. Most didn't make it out. She had to find a way.

"Flamme, even for you, I don't know if I can do this. I thought it would be one time with him and then it became something else because we were so scattered and afraid of Franco. I shouldn't have come here, but he was chasing me and he had others close by."

She dropped her forehead into her hand and rubbed at her temples. She couldn't leave now, not with Franco's men watching the place. Not unless . . . Her head went up. She could go out the garage and into the tunnel, the one Sevastyan had driven them through. She would end up at Mitya's. She could text one of her workers to come get her and text Ania that she had an emergency at her home and one of the workers was there to pick her up. The timing would have to be perfect so Ania

131

wouldn't have a chance to call Sevastyan. Once she was back at her house, she could protect herself.

She took a deep breath. "That's plain bullshit and you know it. Franco and Sevastyan are not the kind of men you can fight by locking yourself in your studio and pretending they're just going to go away. If you do this, you'll have to take the first flight out of here. You'll have to set that up as well. Have someone pack a bag and when they pick you up, drive you straight to the airport. You'd have to fly out immediately. That would only be the first step. Sevastyan might let it go, but Franco likes to chase. The hunt is half the fun to him. You might need help in disappearing. Who to go to? And if you go, what about Shanty? The woman coming in from South Africa with her children?"

She was up again, pacing across the room. She had to work her entire escape out step by step and then implement it. She was extremely good at planning. She had planned dozens of flights for men, women and children from other countries, taking them out from under the noses of hunters and bringing them to safety. Surely she could do it for herself.

But if she did, then she'd have to leave a

132

shifter woman with children, one counting on her, out there alone. She'd have to shut down the only underground abused shifter women had available to them because in the end, she'd have to use it for herself. That would be so selfish. She had made such a mess of everything because of her runaway hormones.

She was disciplined. She could surely figure out a way to fix this without ruining everything she'd put in place. When a shifter male abused his mate, he was more brutal and crueler than could be conceived. She'd seen that over and over. She wasn't about to let it happen to her, nor was she going to let others down because she had been so careless in a moment of weakness. She'd find a way out.

Sevastyan signaled to Kirill and Matvei to separate. The two leopards went up and over the roof of the house in order to come down on the back side of it to get to the heavier brush where they could more easily conceal themselves. Sevastyan's leopard, a big brute of a male, a vicious fighter, was scarred and deadly. He had thick white fur scattered with large, widely spaced black rosettes over his head, back, legs and tail.

In the advance sketches Flambé had sent

to him for consideration, she had included plants that would help his leopard blend in with more natural cover. Kirill and Matvei both had larger Amur leopards with the same wider spaced black rosettes, but their background fur was creamier colored rather than a stark white. Sevastyan hadn't thought in terms of needing cover for the leopards other than the trees and heavier brush. Flambé had included color to match their actual breed of leopards. She had also tried to give them as many varied shades as possible, knowing the leopards, although shifters, preferred the cooler weather.

He spotted the first of Franco's spies. The leopard had eyes on the windows of the master bedroom where Flambé was staying. A prickle of uneasiness went down his spine. He turned his head slowly, very carefully, just enough to bring her bank of windows into his sight. No light leaked out from under the privacy screens. What had attracted the spy's attention? He waited a heartbeat. Two. It wasn't that he saw movement behind those screens. He sensed it. Flambé wasn't fast asleep in the closet. She was up and moving in that room.

Cursing under his breath to himself, Sevastyan took advantage of the spy's inattention to his surroundings and began a freeze-frame stalking. It was a slow process, but he was moving out into the open behind the leopard. At any moment the other cat might turn its head and see him, but the closer Sevastyan got, the more of an advantage he would have. He wanted to get this kill over fast so he had more time for the next. The longer it took before the others knew they were being hunted, the easier it would be for him and his men.

The leopard lifted its head, stretching its neck high toward the house, testing the air. Sevastyan rushed the last few feet and was on the other cat, slamming his weight down hard on the spine while he sank his teeth into the throat, driving deep for the killing bite. The spy desperately tried to throw him off, bucking and throwing himself to the ground, trying to roll, but Shturm was an extremely heavy leopard, all roped muscle, an experienced killing machine, and he never once let up with the suffocating bite.

The leopard was gone fast, faster than Shturm was happy with, so it took a few minutes before Sevastyan could regain control of him. They had to drag the body into the brush so none of the enemies could spot the carcass. He didn't want any of the men on his land to escape or communicate with Franco in any way. He wanted them just to disappear. Franco would wonder if Sevastyan had found them and killed them, but his ego wouldn't allow him to believe that he could do so. Then his conspiracy-theory mind would kick in and he'd begin to think his men had deserted him. Their disappearance would drive him crazy, even when his brothers pointed out the obvious to him, that Sevastyan was from a criminal family and of course he'd killed all of Franco's men.

They were leopard and the carcasses had to be burned so there was no chance of their bodies being discovered. All shifters were careful about that law. It mattered little if they were rogue or decent, they protected what was left of their species, although Sevastyan did wonder about men like Franco.

Shturm dragged the dead leopard into the heavier brush and kicked leaves and dirt around it in disgust before he crouched low, waiting for Kirill and Matvei. The two leopards joined him and then all three moved into the thicker grove of trees where three of Franco's men were secreted high in the branches watching the house a good distance away.

Sevastyan had spotted one of the leopards from his second-story window a few hours earlier. The animal had paced on the tree limb several times, unused to staying in one position for very long. By the time he'd been in his early teens, Sevastyan and his leopard had learned the importance of being absolutely still for hours. The consequences to both animal and human if either made the mistake by so much as shrugging a shoulder or easing a cramping muscle had been a severe beating. Consequently, both were adept at disappearing into the shadows, or in many cases, right out in the open without being spotted.

It had taken longer to find the other two animals hidden in the branches of the trees. Sevastyan had slipped out onto his roof and, stretching out in a prone position in one of the indentations beneath the newly built shelters he had constructed for just such a purpose, he patiently watched for his prey.

Eventually another leopard gave himself away by swishing his tail. It was the only movement, but it was enough to disturb the leaves, drawing Sevastyan's attention. He marked the position of the tree and the branch and then began to calculate the position another leopard might be in based on where the first two in the trees were.

Sevastyan had remodeled a good deal of the Dover home for security purposes, paying close attention to the roof and the surroundings. The roof had been problematic when they had been protecting Ania. He didn't want the same difficulties if he was attacked in his home. He had changed the angles on the roofline as well as added places where he — or a sentry — could get into position without being seen and study their enemy.

He backed down the pitched side of the roof where the leopards in the trees couldn't see him from their angle and then made his way back up to the western surveillance indentations. That's when he'd spotted the third cat. This one spent time raking the tree, standing as high up in the top of the tree as possible, making certain to leave his mark, as if Sevastyan's cat wouldn't notice with him being in the branches.

Now, the three Amur leopards made their way silently through the woods, fur not so much as whispering along the leaves as they passed through the brush. Their large paws didn't snap twigs or downed branches as they walked through the vegetation toward the three separate trees, each a distance from one another. They were independent predators, yet used to coordinating their hunts.

It was no surprise to Sevastyan that Shturm made it clear to Kirill's and

138

Matvei's leopards that he was stalking his enemy, the "raker." He considered the leopard disrespectful. This property was Shturm's territory, clearly marked. The female was his, clearly claimed. Any male marking on his trees was challenging him, even if they were coward enough to hide their challenge in the trees where they hoped he wouldn't see. He had seen and he was coming for the leopard. Matvei and Kirill could take the other two leopards.

Franco had originally left six watchers behind, but while Sevastyan was out with Flambé, Matherson had pulled two of his men back. The cameras had caught two of them leaving after a brief exchange on their cell phones. Jeremiah Wheating, one of the youngest of the bodyguards in the Amurovs' employment, had tracked them back to where Franco Matherson was staying in his rented mansion.

Wheating originally worked for Drake Donovan and then was employed by Fyodor. They moved him around quite often because they all liked him a little too much and he was a pain. He was too intelligent and wanted everything too fast. He was particularly close to Ashe, Timur's wife, treating her more like a sister than anything else. In fact, most of the women treated him like a younger brother, which made it difficult for the men to reprimand him. Right now, he was Sevastyan's problem, and one he didn't like having. He didn't coddle people. He never had. He had a little glitch in him the others didn't, no matter how often they told themselves they were the screwed-up ones.

Shturm turned his head once to glance over his shoulder toward the house, to those blacked-out windows, a strange, uneasy feeling snaking through his mind. He had to keep his focus on his enemy, but something wasn't right with his counterpart's woman. His mate wasn't ready, but she was reaching out to him, letting him know something was wrong with Flambé. He would have to turn the form back to Sevastyan as soon as he was done teaching this leopard a lesson. Sevastyan had a way of figuring things out about women very quickly. He always had.

Shturm padded within a hundred feet of the tree the upstart leopard was in. The idiot had once again risen and this time had paced around the branch to try to reach another branch in order to put his mark on that side of the tree as well. He was a good thirty feet up and the foliage was much barer on that side, so the leopard could easily be seen. He stretched and lifted his lips and wrinkled his nose, showing his teeth before spraying the trunk of the tree.

A leopard roared a challenge in the distance and, above him, the spraying shifter nearly fell from the branch. He clawed at the limb and then hastily turned toward the sound to try to get a view. When he couldn't see anything, he began to climb down fast.

Shturm remained very still, his body secreted in the thick bushes. He recognized the powerful voice of Matvei's leopard issuing a triumphant challenge as it attacked again and again, probably already having ripped his adversary to shreds. Most leopards went back again and again to show dominance when the adrenaline was flowing.

The shifter leaping from the tree landed only a few feet from Shturm, but was so focused on the sounds of the intruder and his sawing roars that he didn't even smell the large cat until it was too late. He'd taken several steps and then whirled around just as Shturm burst out of the brush and hit him in the side so hard and fast, several ribs cracked with an audible sound.

The leopard screamed. Far off, there was an answering echo of a scream, as if another leopard had also been hit hard. That would be Kirill and his opponent, but their fight didn't matter. Shturm blocked off all other sounds and focused completely on his rival. This leopard had come to his territory and acted as if he would claim it.

The big cat backed up, allowing the intruder to roll over and stagger to its feet. The moment the golden leopard was up, Shturm rushed him again, hitting him from the other side, breaking ribs and sending him flying. The cat screamed in fear and defiance. Shturm felt no pity. Leopards knew better than to come into a male's territory and issue a challenge unless they were prepared to fight. Shturm was ready to fight for his female anytime.

He caught the rear leg of the cat as it tried to roll over to get to its feet. Laboring to breathe with broken ribs, it was much slower and he bit down hard, snapping the bone and dragging the leopard backward several feet as it shrieked in pain.

Shturm circled the leopard. So far, the other cat hadn't managed to bite or claw him. He let him see that the blood dripping from his jaws was all his enemy's. He kept his gaze on his despised challenger, showing him the venomous hatred. He had no mercy in him. He didn't want the leopard to expect any leniency from him.

He roared his challenge, all but telling the

other animal to get up. He slammed his paw into the ground, shooting dirt into the face of his adversary. He paced back and forth, roaring and slapping contemptuously with his paw to kick dirt over and over toward the fallen leopard. He feinted several rushes, but the leopard refused to try to rise. He circled him twice more before catching his front leg and biting down, breaking through the bone and dragging him back another four feet.

The leopard opened his mouth, but no sound emerged. He appeared almost catatonic. Sevastyan rarely intervened with Shturm in a leopard fight. As far as he was concerned, it was his animal's right to meet any challenger, but this one wasn't exactly a real match. Where Franco had found him was anyone's guess, but the leopard wasn't experienced at all.

Deliver the kill bite.

It is too soon. He was not respectful.

I doubt he knows the laws of any lair. He doesn't know how to fight. It's beneath you to fight him, Shturm. Far beneath you. A kitten could take this one down. Get it over with. We still have to burn the carcasses and remove all evidence that they were ever here.

Shturm didn't like the fact that Sevastyan was right. The leopard lay on the ground

143

panting, eyes half closed and glazed over, blood pouring from his leg wounds, not even attempting to fight back. It was rather silly to continue to "fight" when the other animal refused to engage. It was just that he'd worked himself up to a killing fury and he needed the adrenaline to go somewhere. He wouldn't be alone with it; Sevastyan would feel it as well.

I know, but this isn't right. I thought it would help letting you loose, going hunting, but it hasn't helped either of us. I think our women are too close to the emergence and we're going to have to suffer.

Both knew that wasn't safe either. They could be dangerous under those circumstances. Not just Shturm, but Sevastyan as well. Shturm gave up worrying about it. That was Sevastyan's department. He rushed his enemy and delivered the killing bite.

144

5

Sevastyan stood outside the open door to the master bedroom. He could easily see Flambé's shadow as she paced back and forth across the room. She'd switched on the dim nightlight beside the bed. It threw just enough of a light to give him a good view of her as she went in and out of his vision. He'd paused outside the door because he heard her voice and assumed she was talking on her cell phone to someone. He realized after listening for a few moments that she was talking to herself.

"You're panicking, Flambé, that's what you're doing, and if you panic, your brain doesn't work. You know that. You've been in a panic since Franco ran you off the road. You have to get yourself under control if you're going to carry this through."

Sevastyan had almost stepped into the room to make his presence known, but he halted at the way she worded her own

145

reprimand. Carry what through? He was responsible for his cousin's security. No matter what, he had to know everything that was going on around Mitya and that included his woman, whether she had one foot out the door or not. He stayed very still, getting comfortable, leaning one hip casually against the wall while he listened, a little amused that she talked to herself while she paced.

"You can't have him. It doesn't matter how much you wanted him. All those times at the club watching him. All the nights you couldn't sleep just thinking about him, wishing you could have one night with him. You're not built that way. This is a huge mess and you made it. He didn't. You let his leopard claim yours because you were so scared of Franco. Now Franco is targeting him. That's not fair, Flambé, and you know it. So, make the call, stop putting it off. Find a flight, it doesn't matter where it's going, take the tunnel to Ania's place and have someone meet you with a car and drive you to the airport. Just do it. Who though? Who would do it and be discreet? Who can I count on who Franco won't have a chance of hurting for information?"

The pent-up aggression in Shturm that ran in Sevastyan's veins as well sent a

146

familiar rush of heat burning through him, settling deep in his groin. There was nothing familiar about the raw hunger that slammed into his cock, stretching him beyond what his monster had ever been, to the point of hurting, not just aching. His body reacted to everything she said. Everything she did. He'd known savage, brutal sexual hunger many times, but not like this.

He stepped into the room, every bit as silent as his leopard had been stalking his challenger. Flambé was a few feet from him, facing away so he could see her beautifully shaped ass, but she spun around, her eyes going wide with shock. She was still in the clothes she'd gone to bed in — a lacy thong and a thin clingy stretch lace top that barely covered her full breasts.

Sevastyan caught her hand and turned without saying a word, striding from the room, down the hall, to the staircase.

"Wait." Flambé tried to halt, but he kept walking, taking her with him. He didn't tighten his grip. He didn't walk faster or slower. He didn't look back. He just continued as if he hadn't heard her. He felt the fine tremor that went through her body and when he inhaled, he scented her hot call. He knew when a woman wanted him and

147

Flambé reacted to his sudden show of dominance.

Sevastyan continued walking up the stairs until he came to the door of his private suite. It was locked, and he bent to use a retinal scan to get in so he wouldn't have to let go of his woman. She was still straining back from him, not exactly struggling, but acting reluctant. She hadn't protested other than that first little "Wait."

He took her inside, closed the door deliberately and turned to click all the locks in place — all three of them — forcing her to stand beside him while he did. She glanced up at him, her lashes fluttering, those long red-gold-tipped lashes that made her look so vulnerable. She had a sprinkle of freckles across her nose. He wanted to kiss every one of them, but he resisted.

He indicated the center of the room. "Stand there." He dropped her wrist and waited to see if she would obey him.

Flambé stood looking up at him for a moment and then around his room. He watched her swallow several times. It was a purely masculine room. All his. Large furniture. Thick, carved wood with big posts and heavy spindles, good places for bondage. There were hooks on his ceiling and a pulley system. Mirrors on the wall and ceil-

148

ing. On one side, hanging from the high ceiling, he had constructed a large tree out of knots and wood with a very small hammock made of knots hanging high from one of the limbs. There were shelves with ropes of different colors and textures in bundles.

Sevastyan let her look her fill. He didn't tell her a second time, but he did stare at her with piercing eyes, daring her to disobey him. She pressed her lips together and for one moment she squirmed, her body restless, her skin flushing with heat before she moved to the exact center of the room right under the hook placed there.

"I will be asking you questions, Flambé, and I expect prompt, truthful answers. Do you understand me?"

"Yes."

"You saw me at the club?"

"Yes."

"How did I not see you?" Deliberately he walked behind her, taking care to place his feet, walking so softly it would be impossible for her to know where he was, even with her superior leopard hearing.

"I was working there, planting the garden of paradise for Cain."

He remained silent for a brief moment, drawing out the tension. "Why didn't you tell me immediately that you had seen me at the club?"

She hesitated. Usually a prelude to a lie. Her shoulders straightened. Usually a determination to tell the truth. He needed her to give him the truth always. That was the only way they could build a partnership.

"I was afraid to. I hadn't made up my mind what I was going to do. I thought if I could have you for one night like those other women, I would be satisfied, but then Franco scared me and I ran here and you were very different than I thought. Everything happened too fast. My leopard began acting up and your leopard claimed mine before I really had time to think things through." She hung her head. "I'm not trying to make excuses. This is my fault. I should have been up front with you from the start."

"Yes, you should have." He poured harshness into his voice. Cold. Clipped. He wasn't going to let her think that he excused her, although he thought she had every reason to be confused when Franco and his leopard had run her off the road and then chased her like she was their prey. She had a nasty bump on the head and her leopard had made the decision for her.

She shivered but she stayed straight. Unbending. That made him inexpicably

150

proud of her. "You saw me at the club and didn't tell me. You cancelled meetings with me on two occasions. And tonight, you were planning to leave after my leopard claimed your leopard. I even very carefully went over the rules of our world with you before I allowed Shturm to claim Flamme. Are those things all true, Flambé?"

She nodded. He remained silent. Waiting. He could wait for a lifetime. Eventually she figured out what he was waiting for.

"Yes. All of those things are the truth."

"Your female is my male's mate. He cannot do without her. You belong to me. Do you understand me, Flambé? You aren't going to sneak off in the middle of the night and make me track you down. You will marry me and settle down right here on this piece of property and make it a home with me just like we discussed. We're shifters, not humans, and we don't have the luxury of changing our minds because we get nervous. Do you understand me?"

Flambé wanted more than anything else to turn her head and look at him. Her room had seemed so warm. Hot even. She couldn't stand clothes, let alone blankets. His room was very cold, yet the longer she stood there with him looking at her, not knowing exactly where he was or how far

151

away he was from her, the hotter the fire between her legs seemed to grow.

"Yes, I understand," she said in low tone, knowing he was expecting an answer.

"Take off your shirt, fold it and hand it to me."

His voice was low and totally mesmerizing. The sound played along every nerve ending, sparking little electrical currents that played over her skin and through her body. She obeyed him almost automatically, her nipples so sensitive that when the material slid over them, she nearly cried out. Very carefully, she folded the top, feeling a little helpless, not knowing where he was. She wanted this. She had waited for this. For him. Her body was on fire already, shaking with need, burning for him, and he hadn't done one single thing.

Then his breath was on the nape of her neck, causing a shiver of awareness to run down her spine. His arm stretched out past her ribcage, his hand palm up so she could place the top in it before he withdrew once more. She took a deep breath and let it out, bringing up her arms to wrap them around her body in a comforting hug.

"Keep your arms down."

His tone was low. Velvet soft. Moving over her skin. She actually felt those notes caressing her body. Goose bumps rose. She dropped her arms to her sides immediately.

"Are your panties damp? Or are they soaked, Flambé? You watched me tie those women and you wanted to be one of them. Now that you're here with me, is it better than you hoped?" He was suddenly right behind her again, his warm breath in her ear this time. "Which is it? Damp? Or soaked?"

She swallowed. There was no point in lying to him. He was leopard. He could smell her arousal. Worse, he was going to make her take her panties off and then he'd catch her in a humiliating lie. Better to just own up to it. She wasn't embarrassed about who she was or what she was. Just that she might need more of him than he was willing to or capable of giving her. "Soaked."

"Take them off and give them to me."

Flambé hooked her thumbs in the little thong and slid it down her legs, thankful she kept herself in reasonably fit shape. Although she was very curvy, as were most shifters, she was extremely toned from her work outdoors and moving heavy plants around all day. It was much more difficult to hand him her panties. The little strip of lace was definitely more than just damp and her hand trembled. She found herself wrap-

153

ping her arms around her waist in a hug for comfort again.

"Didn't I tell you to keep your hands at your sides? Now you can lock your fingers behind your head."

She hated that she had forgotten what he'd told her to do. She wasn't that person. She remembered details. She was meticulous over details and she wanted to be very good at this. She had allowed her leopard to rise and be claimed by his, although truthfully, she was a little out of it at the time. Committing to a future meant she would have this. In fact, this might be the only real joy she would have — the only part of Sevastyan he would give to her.

She laced her fingers behind her head obediently. She didn't apologize on purpose. She wasn't going to be that person. She was new at this and a little afraid. If he didn't treat her right, there was no way she was staying. But then, she didn't want to be lulled into a false sense of security. Wasn't that what all of them did? Pretend to be wonderful and then cheat with other women? Beat you? Hurt you? Treat you as if you were so much less than they were?

She didn't want Sevastyan to treat her differently than he had those other women at the club. She knew what to expect from him and she could live with that. If it was just sex and they both went their own way, maybe she could give her leopard a decent life. The second Sevastyan hit her, or wanted anything she wasn't willing to give, she would use her way out.

Flambé waited again as he walked over to the ropes on the other side of the room. He took off his shirt as he studied the ropes and then glanced at her over his shoulder. He selected two bundles of rope, both black, but different textures. She could see one looked smoother than the other. Ignoring her entirely, he walked up three long curving stairs that separated the huge space designated for his sitting-playroom from where his bed was. Sitting on the edge of the bed, he removed his shoes and then slid his jeans down, only to pull on a pair of soft drawstring pants.

Flambé's arms were beginning to tire. She was strong and she was used to being uncomfortable, but the position wasn't one she had ever been in. She had the feeling he was deliberately seeing how long she was capable of holding her arms up before they became wet noodles, which she feared might happen in another few minutes. She called Flamme to aid her. The leopard ignored her, or had completely retreated.

155

Her body began to tremble with the effort. She refused to give in. Tiny beads of sweat broke out, but she wouldn't break. Sevastyan stood up and came to her with that slow, silent stalk he had that set her heart pounding. He ran his finger possessively down the side of her neck, right over her pulse.

"Put your arms down, *plamya*. That was impressive. For a beginner, you did much better than I expected. You have to tell me when you are uncomfortable or if something hurts you, unless the discomfort is deliberate; but that would be discussed ahead of time. I have to know if your circulation is cut off and you have to tell me if your legs or arms or hands start to tingle. The point isn't to injure you. We both should find this practice pleasurable."

Flambé allowed her arms to fall to her sides. The relief was overwhelming as he massaged her arms with firm strokes. "Go sit in the chair near the fireplace." He indicated the high-backed chair that was covered in a dove-gray butter-soft leather.

She pressed her lips together, hesitating. He simply waited, the rope sliding through his fingers over and over, almost hypnotizing her, although he didn't seem to be aware of the effect the sight had on her. She felt awkward being entirely naked, her body damp with arousal. She had nothing between her and the leather of the chair. Straightening her aching shoulders, she stepped past him, feeling the heat pouring off his body and wishing she could snuggle into it. He looked cold and aloof, but he felt hot as hell.

The leather of the chair was as cold as the room was. She sat properly, folding her hands in her lap.

"You don't like to sit like that, baby," he said softly. "We're just talking right now. Get comfortable. Pull your legs up the way you like."

How could he know she did that whenever she sat in a chair and no one was around? She drew her knees up, sliding her heels close to her bottom and wrapping her arms around her legs in a hug. She didn't feel quite so vulnerable, or as on display. Part of her liked being on display for him. She had a good body; not like some of the women at the club he attended, but he never seemed to choose women for their body types. She wasn't altogether certain he paid attention to what the women looked like.

"Pay attention, Flambé. You allow yourself to drift away and you need to learn to focus at all times. Shibari can be a harmful practice if you don't know what you're doing. You're just as responsible as I am for what we do together. It may not seem like it to you as an observer, but your participation is every bit as important as mine to make what we do enjoyable for both parties. Not only are you cheating yourself if you don't come to me with the right attitude, wholly focused and prepared to enjoy the pleasure and magic of our exchange, but it's disrespectful to me and that's something I will not tolerate. When I call you to me for this kind of play, you are not only to shed your clothes, but our bedroom should be the one place you can let every trouble go. I can take those burdens from you and I will. I insist on it."

Flambé kept her eyes on the rope as it moved so smoothly through his hands. He was so confident. So completely assured. She had confidence in her work. When she interviewed. When she confronted danger moving a victim out of a dangerous zone into a holding area until she could get them out of the country and into safety. But here, with him, she felt a thrill of trepidation and for some perverse reason, she craved that feeling. She needed it to feel alive.

"You will eventually develop your own ritual, which will help to center yourself.

You have to let go of all defenses. I want you to allow yourself the freedom of coming to me as emotionally naked as you are physically naked. Trust me to protect you when you're in that vulnerable state."

Her gaze jumped to his face. He hadn't protected those other women. Their partners had done so, removing the ropes from their bodies and comforting them. Would he do that for her? She had no idea what he would or wouldn't do. Did she even want him to? That would give him more of an advantage over her, yet she longed to be in the ropes. She knew that would be the ultimate erotic practice for her.

"You're doing it again, Flambé. When we're talking together, especially about a subject as important as this one, you stay focused. You can't let your mind wander."

She nodded her head. He was right. He spoke in that soft, almost predatory way he had, not threatening exactly, not at all. It was just that his eyes held this piercing, fierce gaze. She knew a leopard's focused stare was disconcerting and Sevastyan had that same stare even in human form. Some shifters had much more animalistic qualities than others, and Sevastyan definitely had the predatory instincts of his fierce counterpart.

"Can you do splits?"

She frowned. No one had ever asked her that before. "I stretch every day and I get close."

"I want you to work at it until you are able to. You also need stamina. We'll go running and work out together. This isn't a practice for the weak. If you enjoy it, Flambé, you have to be in shape and I mean that. It isn't about size or what women perceive as looking good. I've tied all sorts of body sizes and found them beautiful. If you aren't fit, you can be injured or worse."

"I understand." She did. That made sense to her.

"You need to stretch every day. You have to be limber. Do you get motion sickness? Are you afraid of heights?"

She shook her head. "Why would that matter?"

"I find suspension bondage sexy. With you, several very erotic images come to mind. I wouldn't be able to use those scenarios if you had a problem with either, no matter how sensual I found the ideas."

Another wave of heat rushed over her. She hugged herself tighter. It took a great deal of discipline to keep from looking at the tree he had constructed out of knots with the very small hammock hanging from a branch high up.

"Have there been a lot of women here in your bedroom?" She didn't know why she asked, she didn't really want to know the answer. She had watched Sevastyan. He didn't get caught up with the women. It was about the art, the scene, and then the power of the sex. The woman belonged to someone else, who got off on watching her get off on doing something she enjoyed that her partner couldn't provide.

"You are the only woman to come in here. You are the only woman to ever be welcome in this room."

Her heart stuttered. There was an underlying ferocious note to his tone, although he hadn't raised his voice at all.

"Do you share women?" That mattered. She couldn't live with that. She just couldn't.

He studied her face for so long she found herself beginning to tremble. He hadn't changed expression. He still wore that same impossible-to-read mask, but now something flickered in the depths of his eyes, something terrifying. Something that wasn't cat, yet was just as bad as cat. That predatory trait ran deep in him.

Sevastyan suddenly moved then, with the shocking speed of a leopard, covering the

161

distance between them in seconds so that he was towering over her. He caught her chin and tipped her face up, forcing her to look into the flickering flames that were his eyes. "Flambé, if you hear nothing else tonight, you hear this. You are going to be my wife. I will not share you — not ever. No man will put his hands on you and live. That is as plain as I can make it. What we do together is between us and stays that way. Do you understand me? You need to acknowledge to me that you do, because make no mistake, *plamya,* I would kill a man over you just as fast as Shturm would kill a rival over Flamme."

There was no looking away from the fierce fire blazing in his eyes. He meant exactly what he said. There was relief in knowing he didn't intend to suddenly start bringing her to Cain's club and deciding to share her with other men. That would be a deal breaker.

As if he could read her mind, the pad of his thumb swept gently over her lower lip and then he released her chin and stepped away. "The club was an outlet for me when I needed release. I'm a dominant, pure and simple. You recognized that in me the first time you saw me and you reacted to that."

She had. A part of her knew it was more

162

than that. Cain was a dominant, but she hadn't been drawn to him. There had been that one brief second and now she knew it was because her female had been on the verge of the rising. She'd stretched. Sent out a brief preview of what was to come, and then like all females in the beginnings of their coming emergence, settled and vanished as if she didn't exist.

Flambé nodded. "Yes. I did."

"We get married and we stay exclusive. When we have a problem, we talk it out. I know your landscaping business is important to you so it's important to me. You need to keep me in the loop at all times. You'll have to get used to having one of my men with you. Sometimes it might be necessary to curtail your activities and stay closer to home, but only in an emergency. I also know you're passionate about saving other shifters. I have resources that can help you with that. My cousins and friends do as well."

She rubbed her chin on top of her knees and searched for the right words that she hoped didn't sound judgmental when she really was grateful that he understood she wouldn't give up her business or her work helping other shifters. "I try to keep everything legal. I want them to start their lives

163

here in the States right, as citizens with an education and an opportunity to own their own businesses and employ others who need assistance. I want anyone we bring in to be productive citizens."

"I'm very aware you keep everything legal, Flambé. I do my research when anything gets anywhere near my cousin."

His tone sent another shiver traveling down her spine, reminding her she was stark naked and the room was chilly. Once again, she became wholly aware of him as a man. Shifters had the roped muscles of their animal counterparts and Sevastyan's chest had muscles merging with his impressive abdominal muscles that just seemed to continue until they disappeared into his low-slung pants.

"Shall we continue with our previous conversation on rope bondage? I think it's important that you understand what I expect of you and what will keep you safe."

He paced away from her, and she took a deep breath, feeling like she'd been breathing shallowly and needed the air. "Yes." She wanted to learn as much from him as she could, but watching him move was so mesmerizing she feared she might miss what he was saying.

He indicated several very thick rounded

poles that looked as if they were made of bamboo. If they were, she'd never seen bamboo that thick. "I want to work with those, stretching your leg or both legs on them and suspending you in the air, so the splits are important. You have to be comfortable in that stretch for long periods of time. It's important to hydrate. I can't express that enough. You have to take care of your body, Flambé. And you have to talk to me. I know what I'm doing but if one day you're feeling fatigued or you've injured yourself while working, you have to let me know. I can't put you in a position that might make that injury worse. In other words, you don't stay silent just to please me. That won't please me, *plamya,* it will piss me off."

She nodded. "I understand."

"I put a bottle of water on the nightstand for you. Use the bathroom and then drink water. You need to always be hydrated. That's your job when I call you to me. Prepare yourself. Once you're trained, I might want to suspend you from the ceiling. I might choose to put you in any number of poses using any type of rope or a combination of ropes. You will be expected to remain in the position until I choose to allow you out of it."

Her sex clenched wildly in response to his

165

demands. She nodded to show him she was listening because she was afraid she might not be able to speak.

"You saw me at the club. That was entirely different. There I needed to get in and get out. Here, with you, I intend to indulge myself. My cravings. My desires. Fulfill every one of my fantasies as well as work out the various positions I've always wanted to try when I had my own woman. Look at me, Flambé."

She forced herself to meet his eyes. The things he said made her entire body flush with heat and he could see it. He could also smell her arousal.

"I will make certain you will know pleasure beyond anything you've ever experienced. I sound selfish, but if this wasn't something you wanted or needed, we would not be doing it."

She knew if they weren't compatible, she would be one of those women in the club he walked away from and never looked back at, leopard or not. She still wasn't certain what he intended to do after they had sex — if he intended to have sex with her after tying her. She nodded her head to show she understood, but she couldn't have said a word if she tried.

"Tonight, I'm going to show you two different rope textures and what it feels like to be tied. I want to see how well you cope. Some people think they will like it and then reality hits when they realize they're entirely at the mercy of the one tying them and they panic."

She immediately got to her feet, her heart beating fast. She had wanted this for so long but now that the moment was getting close, she suddenly was becoming fearful and she wasn't certain why. He had put a subtle emphasis on the word *mercy* and that mask he wore proclaimed he didn't have much mercy in him. He had also said he would put her in a position until he chose to let her out of it. She wanted that, but it was a scary thought. Everything she wanted from him was frightening.

Flambé hurried to the master bath and closed the door behind her, leaning against it on unsteady legs. The room was enormous, with long double sinks and the coolest shower she'd ever seen in her life. It looked like something out of a movie, but she didn't have time to examine it. She just hoped she could sneak in and use it sometime, just to see all the things it actually did behind all that glass.

She made certain she was clean everywhere and then realized she was stalling.

She wasn't going to let herself be so afraid that she missed her opportunity to try something she really wanted to do. As she re-entered the bedroom, she picked up the water bottle and drank from it. The cold water felt good on the back of her parched throat.

"I run the rope through my hands to make certain all the kinks are worked out and there are no splinters or anything that might be uncomfortable against your skin. Unless I want you uncomfortable, and then I use my artwork to make you that way, or the texture of the rope and positioning of the knots. I am extremely careful. I always will tell you ahead of time."

She had been fascinated by the way he ran the rope through his hands and he'd noticed. He pointed to the spot in the middle of the room again and she obediently went without hesitation. There was something comforting in knowing what was expected of her this time. She stood directly beneath the hook where she knew at some point, he might suspend her in the air like some flying object with his rope and knots. Just the idea of it was almost enough to send her soaring, her blood rushing, heated and wanton.

Flambé thought it was truly crazy how

much she craved this. He circled her in complete silence, adding to her anticipation, to the dreadful need building in terrible waves inside her.

"I'm going to tie you with an easy halter first, Flambé. I want you to get used to the feel of the rope on your skin. There are different types of ropes and I use them for different purposes. I'm going to use cotton on you first because it's soft and gentle on your skin. It has a high burn speed which means it has to run along your skin much faster before your skin blisters."

He had once again stepped away from her and his face was back to that expressionless mask he normally wore. The rope slid through his hands, almost a caress, without him even looking at it, until he found the natural center and folded it in half. She found herself mesmerized by the slide of that rope through his fingers. By him. By the real Sevastyan, this man who controlled himself, his feral leopard, women and that rope so easily.

Flames seemed to dance up her thighs, small little tongues of orange and red, teasing at her nerve endings, flicking at her skin until she wanted to cry out with need. The burn between her legs grew hotter. Her nipples felt on fire, as if he'd pressed two

169

burning matchsticks to them. He hadn't touched her. She had no idea how or why she'd gotten so inflamed, so hungry for him so fast, but she couldn't control her breathing.

He moved behind her and a moan broke from her when he touched her neck, his finger sliding over her pulse. "Shh, baby, you're going to be fine. Give yourself to me."

He ran his hand over her shoulders, a slow, very tender touch. His palm curled around the nape of her neck and slipped around to her throat, barely there, just resting, feeling her heart beating into his palm. It was the most intimate experience she'd ever had and yet he hadn't touched any of the supposed parts of her body that were considered the "sex zones."

She leaned into his hands. Into his body. She felt his strength. He was all male and he made her feel exactly how she wanted to feel, totally feminine and powerful in her femininity. There was beauty in her own strength, in the way she chose to submit to him. She wanted this experience with him. This man was so utterly arrogant and had every reason to be when it came to his skills. But . . .

He suddenly caught both hands and

yanked them behind her back, folding one arm on top of the other decisively. The move was so unexpected she almost moved from the spot he'd told her to stay in, but at the last second she remembered to remain still.

She felt the rope slide over her skin almost lovingly, sending shivers through her entire body. His hands moved on either shoulder, running the lines simultaneously as he began to swiftly build a harness. At the same time, he leaned into her again, his warm breath in her ear. His teeth found her earlobe and bit down.

She yelped.

"All of you, Flambé. You're holding back. Give me all of you. You've already got several indiscretions you have to answer for. Don't keep adding to them." He whispered the warning to her, all while his hands worked with absolute sureness.

She moistened her lips, wishing she didn't understand what he was talking about, but in the back of her mind she hadn't forgotten that he had enumerated her supposed sins as he'd taken her into his room. The two times she'd cancelled on him. The fact that she hadn't told him she had seen him at the club. That seemed to be a very big one to him. He really hadn't been happy about that and she couldn't blame him.

The rope began to weave back and forth over her arms and breasts and under them, around her arms and then down the middle in intricate knots, both front and back. He worked fast, pulling the ropes tight and securing her quickly. She felt almost euphoric as he completed the halter. The knots were beautiful, straight down the valley separating her full breasts, the lines beneath them lifting them up while the ones over the tops delineated the curves artfully.

She ached for him. Burned. Her nipples jutted out at him invitingly. She'd never been so aware of her breasts as feminine and sexy. If this was art, it was erotic art. Sevastyan stepped back to survey his handiwork. His expression didn't change as he circled slowly around her. It was a leopard's prowl, one slow, almost freeze-frame stalk after another. She held very still.

When he returned to the front of her again, he used his foot to nudge her feet farther apart before retrieving the skein of rope he'd left on the bed. This was the rougher texture he'd mentioned earlier. He began running the rope through his hands absently while he returned to her in the same silence, with that same arrogant mask, the one that made her even hotter. This was how she had first seen him, so in control, so completely dominant.

He took his time before he moved close to her. He didn't look at her face, but rather at her breasts. "You shouldn't have missed your appointments with me, Flambé. That will not happen again. From now on, no one is more important in your life. No one. Nothing. You make certain you put us first always."

He spoke in that same low tone. No inflection. No harshness. Just a soft decree. He reached out and gently ran his finger over her right breast, down her aching nipple, and then flicked it hard with his thumb and finger. Heat burst through her and she jumped. He bent his head and sucked her breast into his mouth. She cried out, her legs nearly giving out as pleasure washed over her. Just as abruptly he lifted his head.

"The matter of the club is a much graver offense. You didn't know me before cancelling the appointments with me and I believe you thought you had good reason, so that is forgivable. You saw me at the club and you should have confessed to me immediately, especially after Shturm claimed Flamme. You knew you were wrong for that. Don't speak. I don't want to hear excuses."

He stepped away from her and studied her body, the rope still moving through his hands. "This will be a very simple piece as well. Not telling me about the club is another matter altogether."

He moved behind her and made a simple wrap around her hips twice. At once she could feel the difference in the texture of the rope. The halter was smooth and, although tight, felt nice against her skin. She needed tight. She liked firm pressure. This rope was prickly. Again, Sevastyan worked fast, the knots forming a thong, sliding between her cheeks, positioning perfectly, pulling tight and coming right over the hood of her clit to attach to the two ropes that circled her hips. He pulled the lines even tauter and she gasped as with every movement the knots rubbed and inflamed her body.

He pulled on the ropes as if testing them and each time he did, flames shot through her. She cried out, need burning through her, hips jerking uncontrollably.

"Stay still, I need to make certain these knots are correct." His tone was low, the same, as if she was an inanimate object and his art was all that mattered.

He knew the knots were perfect. He was being a devil. She didn't know if she wanted him to be the devil. That only added to the fiery need building and coiling tighter and tighter until she thought she might go insane.

Sevastyan slid his fingers under the knotted rope and gently ran his knuckles up her belly to her breasts. The knots tugged and rolled over her clit and rubbed and burned deliciously between her cheeks, inflaming every sensitive bundle of nerves she had. His index finger began to brush back and forth under her breast, tracing the curve very gently.

"When you were spying on me at the club, which pose made you want me the most, Flambé? Which was the one that made you decide you had to be with me?"

He bent forward and took her left breast into the heat of his mouth, sucking hard, his tongue fluttering against her nipple and then pressing it tight against the roof of his mouth while his fingers played the rope like a harp, setting the knots dancing over her sex again, setting her on fire. The combination shook her entire being.

She couldn't find her voice. She was helpless, unable to touch him, when she wanted to cradle his head to her breast and keep him there. She was unable to reach that place that would let her fly, although she needed to get there so badly. She wanted that knot to rub and burn over her clit and

175

at the same time she desperately wanted it to stop. The knots running between her cheeks were producing the most erotic sensations, sending waves of heat crashing through her. He added his teeth to the mix, an unexpected tug and sting on her nipple, making her cry out.

"Answer me, Flambé. Which pose?"

Her mind was in utter chaos. She loved him best this way. So in charge. So distant. So arrogant. So completely Sevastyan Amurov. She tried to force air into her lungs, to find a way to breathe through the raging firestorm so she could get to a place where she could think.

"Sevastyan."

He bit down again and she cried out as the sting sent waves of dizzying fire blasting through her, threatening to send her over the edge, but stopping just short. She tried to find relief against that knot, but it wasn't working. She couldn't get there no matter how hard she tried.

"Flambé. You look so beautiful just like this. Open your eyes and look in the mirrors. Look at yourself. And then tell me."

She couldn't. She knew what she would see. The need. The wanton hunger. The desperation only Sevastyan could produce in her. But he was relentless. Merciless. That was why she was so obsessed with and addicted to him. He could make her feel this way when no one else could.

He bit down again on her nipple but this time his teeth remained, and he tugged, stretching, his fingers on the rope, tugging at the same time, dragging those knots up tighter between her cheeks so they rubbed deliciously and dangerously. Sparks erupted. Flames burst through her. She lifted her lashes and forced herself to look in the mirrors that surrounded her.

Moans escaped. She looked so sexy. So completely erotic. So not Flambé. The artwork was beautiful, framing her breasts with the colors of the ropes. She could see marks from his mouth and teeth and that just added to the eroticism of the image. He towered over her with his wide shoulders and muscular body, looking completely merciless while she looked . . . a willing captive. Desperately adoring. More than willing to do anything for him, and she was. She would.

She'd never come close to wanting a man the way she wanted him. She hadn't known her body could crave the things she wanted from him. She hadn't known this kind of need existed on any level.

Sevastyan curled his palm gently around

her throat and tipped her chin up using his thumb. She felt the tug of the ropes, but almost softly, against her skin — like his voice. "Which pose, *plamya*?"

She was going to die if he didn't relieve the terrible coiling need burning through her body. "You," she whispered. "It was just the way you are."

"The pose." His voice never changed. His expression never changed. He wasn't going to relent.

In desperation she told him. "You did one where you braided her hair and arms down her back and tied both legs onto a pole, stretched out in the splits." Her breath was ragged. She could barely think. Her head fell forward onto his shoulder and rested there. "You bent her head forward toward her legs and tied her in that position and then hoisted her into the air and anchored her there."

"And then what?"

She was floating. She couldn't think anymore, remembering that night. She'd never seen anything like it. That had been the night she knew she was in terrible trouble. She'd wanted him all the other nights, but that night she had been burning up for him. She'd actually gone to Cain's office, determined to ask him to train her.

178

To let her be his, so she could have what those women had, but thankfully Cain wasn't there. He'd gone home.

"You did what?"

His voice changed for a moment and a shiver went down her spine. There was a note of rage hidden in that calm and that was worse than anything she could imagine. She'd confessed to him aloud that she'd gone to Cain? What was wrong with her? She couldn't think clearly. She couldn't move her arms or legs. She was too exhausted, but her body burned and burned. For him. For Sevastyan. Worse than she ever thought possible.

"Tell me what happened next, Flambé," he insisted, as if her confession had never taken place.

"You took her and left."

"I fucked her. Say it. I fucked her. Hard."

"Yes. From behind her. You didn't even touch her. You held on to the pole and you fucked her hard from behind. It was very impersonal."

"Exactly, Flambé. It was *very* impersonal. There is absolutely nothing impersonal about any of the things I'm going to do to you. *Ever.* Each of them is going to be very deliberate. And very personal."

179

6

Sevastyan carried Flambé to the bed and gently laid her right in the middle of it. She was shaking. Exhausted. It was her first time being tied and, although he'd constructed a simple harness and knotted thong, leaving the ropes on for a very short time, to a beginner it must have felt like forever. She had done amazing, far better than he could have hoped for.

Between their craving of Shibari and the insanity of the shockingly raw chemistry between them, his woman needed care desperately. He wrapped his arms around her and pulled her tight into his body for comfort. Her hips moved restlessly against him and he couldn't help but push back into her. Wanting her. He'd never wanted a woman more, but he needed to make certain she felt safe.

"I'm right here, *malen'koye plamya.* You're fine. Just breathe. Put your arms around me and look at me. Open your eyes."

She shook her head, but her arms slid obediently around his neck. It took time before her lashes lifted and he found himself staring into green eyes. He leaned down and brushed kisses over her temple. There was recognition there. Pure hunger. None of it leopard. All woman. He was extraordinarily pleased that they had this time between them, man and woman, not their animals driving them.

"Sevastyan." She whispered his name. A soft little plea.

"I'm right here, baby. We're not finished yet. I just want to make certain you're with me all the way on this."

He slid one hand from her throat to her breast, cupping the soft offering, his thumb and finger rolling her nipple firmly. She seemed to respond to firmer pressure rather than gentle. The moment he touched her she arched into him, offering herself to him. He tugged a little harder, watching her expression closely for any signs of discomfort.

Flambé was an open book, not one to hide behind a mask. Pleasure and need were easy to see. His heart stuttered when something else crept into her gaze as it moved over his face. Something he'd never had. Never seen.

181

She looked at him with an expression far too close to reverence. Bordering on real adoration.

Real. He didn't get real. He didn't even deserve it. He was going to turn her life upside down. He knew he would. He would protect her. See to her happiness as best he could. Respect her. But . . . He shifted his body to blanket hers, kissing his way over her face. He could fall in love with her and that would be a disaster for both of them. He couldn't chance really loving her. And he'd fall fast and hard if the way the unfamiliar emotions crowding in were anything to go by.

He had been born with more traits of his animal than many of the shifters. He could be quick-tempered and when it happened, it was bad. Very bad. He had worked hard to ensure he covered it up, held his rage in, but it was there, smoldering below the surface all the time. He was extremely alpha, very dominant, so much so that he had always feared it would be impossible to find a woman who might be willing to accept him. He was also very sexually dominant and at times that burning rage, the dominant trait and his sexual needs came together in a ferocious combination that might frighten any woman. And then there

182

was his love and need of Shibari, his rope art. He would never give that up.

Already he felt possessive of Flambé. Wanting to hold her too close. Afraid of losing her. If he let himself love her, what kind of monster would he turn into? He kissed his way to the creamy swell of her breasts. He loved her skin. He wasn't just oral, the way most shifters were; he was extremely tactile too. He'd been denied the pleasure of indulging in anything so simple as touching a woman's skin or hair for more than a few seconds because Shturm despised every human he came close to and wanted to kill them all. He didn't dare spend more than a few moments with a woman, especially after he fucked them. That was when he was the most vulnerable and his leopard could surface fast and push his way out if Sevastyan wasn't alert.

No one had skin or hair like Flambé. At least if they did, Sevastyan had never been around them. He took his time, exploring every inch of her, claiming her body for his own. He had to open his drawstring pants with one hand and push them off his hips as he suckled her breasts, using teeth and tongue, totally indulging himself while she writhed under him, her hips trying to move but held down by the weight of his body.

She didn't mind him rough. If anything she seemed to want it — want him the way he needed to be.

He loved to hear her little broken cries. The soft sounds of need. His name that came out like a plea. He'd not had that either — not ever — and it was addicting. He took his time moving down her body, kissing his way down her rib cage. He discovered she was very sensitive under her breasts and around her sweet little belly button. She had a strong core, but was very much a woman with a woman's body, and he liked her figure. He wanted her to keep that little bit of a pooch he was certain she detested. It was barely discernable, but soft enough that he spent time nipping with his teeth and taking the sting away with his tongue.

He caught her thighs in his hands and pulled them slowly apart. Wide. Very wide. Her gaze jumped to his face. His shoulders were wider than she realized, and he was going to spend some time indulging himself even more. His smile was deliberately wicked as he stripped off his pants with one hand and then settled between her legs, stretching them even farther. There it was again. *Sevastyan.* His name. That breathy little moan.

He blew warm air over and into her. She smelled delicious. "I told you, baby, you're going to have to be comfortable doing the splits. I like you in this position. You'll find yourself in it often."

He ran his tongue up the inside of her right thigh, over her lips, and circled her inflamed clit. He had teased her clit into a fiery need with his knots, and that hunger hadn't eased. The moment his tongue touched her she cried out and her body jerked, her sex clenched and that warm mixture of spices spilled out of her. He lapped it up, careful to keep from giving her any release.

He repeated the tongue action up her left thigh to her clit and this time flicked it hard after circling it. His name came out loud. Demanding. He smiled as the spice spilled into his mouth and her hips became nearly as frantic as her voice. He held her down easily with one arm laid across her, giving him the use of both hands.

He lifted his head to look at her. Red hair spilled wildly over his black sheets. Her breasts jutted upward, swaying with every movement. She still had rope marks on her skin and he loved that she had the kind of skin that would hold those marks for a long time. Her nipples were hard little peaks, tight, showing him she liked everything he was doing to her.

Sevastyan pushed, first one leg up and over his shoulder, and then the other, opening her even farther to him. She was beautiful, looking wild and vulnerable. Lust had darkened the amber in her eyes to a decided gold and turned the green to an emerald. He loved that look of desperate hunger on her. It added to the raw fire burning through his veins and coiling deep in his gut. He wanted to hold her on the edge for a very long time so he could see her just like this. Her body covered with his marks. His ropes. His fingerprints. His teeth. The strawberries he'd left behind to mark his trails.

He bent his head to her once more and this time he simply devoured her. Ate her the way he hungered for her. Like she was his last meal and he wouldn't leave one single drop behind. He used his tongue like a weapon, stabbing, stroking, petting, sometimes a counterpoint to his fingers and thumb as he flicked and thumped her clit, brushed and circled and then suddenly suckled like a madman. Flambé answered with a drawn-out wail, a moan, and thrust her hips into his mouth, desperate to bring herself off.

Sevastyan immediately eased back with

186

butterfly flutters of his tongue while his fingers and thumb slid between her cheeks to find the skid marks of his knots, brushing back and forth gently, spreading her spicy, cinnamon-clove and Egyptian jasmine honey all over so he could lick that off as well.

"Sevastyan, *please.*" Her voice came out a breathy little sob. A plea.

He lifted his head and rubbed his face leisurely on her thighs before looking up at her. "Please what, Flambé?"

"I need you to . . ." She broke off.

"To?" he prompted and bent his head and sank his teeth into the tender area of her inner thigh, high, up close to her dripping slit. She jerked, more of that precious liquid spilling. He lapped it up and then flicked her inflamed clit. He could keep it up all night. His cock ached painfully, but he was used to ignoring his needs.

"I need your cock," she finally managed.

He lifted his head again. "Where? Your mouth? I wouldn't mind seeing your lips stretched around my cock. I have to admit, since first seeing you, it's been a fantasy of mine. Or here?" Deliberately, he pushed his thumb into her forbidden little hole, clear up to his knuckle. She was already slick from the juices that he'd spread and then

187

licked from her. "Or your sweet little pussy? Exactly where do you want my cock, baby? Because I'm more than willing to give you whatever you want."

He withdrew his thumb and then began lapping at her clit and pussy again, not waiting for her answer. Her breath was coming in ragged gasps, her breasts swaying invitingly with every desperate intake of air. He played his fingers over the sensitive bundle of nerve endings, waiting for her to find her voice, all the while making it difficult.

"My pussy," she managed.

"Sweet little pussy," he corrected, and bit her other thigh. She jerked and cried out, liquid heat glistening for him. She was totally made for a man like him.

He knelt up, drawing her legs around his hips, forcing her body to stay wide open to his. With one hand he circled the base of his cock. He felt heavier and thicker than he'd ever felt in his life. She'd done that to him and he wasn't even in her.

"Look at me, Flambé. Keep your eyes open and look at me." It was a command, nothing less, and he meant it.

Her golden-emerald gaze clung to his. He didn't wait, couldn't wait one moment longer. Without warning her, he slammed home, driving through her snug folds, that tight, scorching-hot tunnel that robbed him of breath. Flames raced through his body, down his spine, roared in his groin and burned like a firestorm in his cock and balls. Nothing that had come before her had prepared him for what she felt like. Nothing. No one.

He needed to move harder. Deeper. To feel that raging storm over and over. He wanted the flames to consume them both. He wrapped his arm around the small of her back, holding her hips off the mattress as he surged into her, driving so hard he nearly pushed her toward the headboard. He could feel every single fold and muscle in her silken sheath clamped around his cock, gripping him with a fury, holding him as if a million fiery tongues licked and teased, as if a voracious mouth sucked at him and fingers pumped to milk him dry. The sensations were unbelievable. He never wanted to stop.

Sevastyan pistoned into her over and over, watching the expressions chase across her face, watching passion and lust war with adoration and trepidation. Tension coiled in her. He felt her heart beating out of control right through her tight tunnel straight to his cock so that the pounding rhythm of his cock hammering into her seemed to match the wild fury of her heart.

He pressed his finger into the seam between her cheeks, sweeping back and forth at that same pulsing pace. Rubbing, pressing into her, brushing those marks that might have caused her discomfort, as if he would erase them and give her so much pleasure she wouldn't remember anything else. All the while, he thrust into her, deep and hard, working her body. His cock was thick and each time he thrust into her, the friction was unbelievable perfection.

Her orgasm hit them both unexpectedly, sweeping through her without warning, nearly taking years of discipline from him as her body clamped down, biting like a vise on his shaft, exquisitely painful, burning, scorching, somewhere between heaven and hell. He kept surging into her, powering through tight folds as they contracted and released over him ferociously.

Flambé's scream was soundless as she orgasmed but then as the first wave began to ease, she moaned, the pitch so perfect and beautiful, it only spurred him on. His body seemed to swell impossibly, a reaction to the place he never wanted to leave. Pure pleasure. Scorching-hot paradise. He tightened his hold on her and drove into her over and over, knowing he would never be able

190

to stop his own release when her body took over again.

He indulged himself, all the while watching her expression, ensuring she was enjoying the ferocious sex. The flames burned over his skin and roared through his body, bursting through his veins. He could feel an unfamiliar boiling in his balls, as if a thick magma had found its way in and now was so overheated it had to find a way out. The eruption was going to be imminent, violent and nothing short of spectacular.

This time he saw fear building in her eyes. Her head thrashed on the pillow as the tension coiled tighter and tighter in her body. Her gaze clung to his and she dug her nails into his arms to anchor herself as if she feared she might fly away. He didn't slow down. It didn't matter that his lungs burned for air. Nothing mattered but that scorching heat that threatened to consume them both. He needed this every bit as much or more than she did.

Sevastyan slammed into her exquisite, perfect sheath one more time, and then her muscles bit down like a vise, clamped so hard he couldn't breathe or think. Thunder roared in his ears. Silken, fiery tongues, millions of them, all scorching hot, licked and worked at his cock, determined to milk him or suck him dry. He could feel that tight tunnel like a burning fist pumping and squeezing his shaft until rope after rope of hot seed coated the walls of her perfect, beautiful, exquisite little pussy over and over.

He allowed himself to collapse over the top of her, but purposefully dropped a little to one side so he didn't crush her with his weight. He kept her legs wrapped around him, his jerking cock in her while they both fought for air. He felt every aftershock of her body ripple right through his spent cock. It was the first time in his life that his cock had ever been fully sated. *Ever.* He closed his eyes and savored the moment. The feeling.

She had done that. Flambé. He didn't try to think beyond the moment. Not right then. He let himself feel her under him. Her body was all feminine. Her scent filled his lungs. He had never thought to have a woman lie in his bed but she felt as if she belonged there. He had prepared his room with the hope — with the idea — that one day he might find his own woman. His cousins had been successful. He hadn't really believed it possible, but when he bought the property from his cousin's wife and renovated it, he had made the specific changes to the bedroom to give himself the hope or the reminder that there was no hope. He was never certain which it was.

"Sevastyan?"

Flambé sounded so tired he was immediately ashamed of indulging himself even further by just lying half over the top of her.

"What is it, baby?" He kept his voice gentle.

"I need to take a bath, but I'm so tired I don't think I can move enough to get back downstairs."

"I didn't make it clear that you would be sleeping with me here in this room from now on? I'm fairly certain I did, Flambé. Maybe you were too excited to listen to me. It's been a long night. We'll move your things in here and I'll program you into the security code so you can come and go as you please. Let me get the water running for your bath while you rest."

He lifted his head and looked down at her face. She had her eyes closed. She looked as if she was already drifting off. He wasn't sure by the expression on her face if she was happy with the idea of sleeping in the bedroom with him. The thought made him smile. Wasn't the woman supposed to *want* to sleep with her man?

193

He brushed kisses over her eyelids and then her nose. "Thank you, *malen'koye plamya*. You were quite amazing as a beginner at our rope practice. I should have taken your picture, but I didn't want to leave you in the ropes too long."

"I loved the ropes."

He could hear the honesty in her voice, but she didn't open her eyes. Her face was very relaxed. He loved the way she looked. He wanted to roll her into him, curl around her and fall asleep just that way. That was an interesting idea to him when it had never occurred to him to sleep with another human being in the same room, let alone in the same bed or touching his skin. When he'd thought about having a woman of his own he hadn't considered exactly where he'd have her sleep. He wanted access to her all night, but he didn't think he would just curl around her and go to sleep. That was what restraints were for — to keep everyone safe.

"I thought the patterns were so beautiful, Sevastyan. You can make anyone look beautiful and sensual in your creations."

That sleepy note in her voice stirred his cock. He forced himself to move, reluctantly withdrawing from the haven of her body. He had already grown semi-hard again just

194

listening to that drowsy, very sensual bedroom voice she had. As he shifted his weight off of her, she curled onto her side away from him. Her hair spilled across the black of his sheets in a bright splash of brilliant crimson silk.

Immediately, because his mind worked that way, images began to form in his head of her tied, the black background under her, red hair spilling around her; his captive, the shifter, strawberry leopard that she was, feminine, soft, bending, yielding, submissive even, until one looked closer and saw her immense power. The ties would have to be just right.

"Or you made my creation look beautiful and sensual," he corrected, and kissed the swelling at her hairline before sliding off the bed to go to the master bath to run the water for her.

While the tub was filling, he cleaned himself and returned to her to find her half asleep. Her lashes fluttered, acknowledging his presence, but she didn't lift her head. He began to pace, trying to decide what to do about the sleeping arrangements.

Flambé sighed and rolled over onto her back to look up at the very high ceiling. "What is it, Sevastyan? I thought we were going to talk things out."

She was going to talk things out with him, he wasn't. But she was right. He was all for honesty. "I want you in this room with me at night, every night. We're getting married as soon as possible and we share sleeping quarters." He made that a firm statement. Her gaze shifted from his and she visibly winced but she didn't argue.

"But?"

There could have been a note of amusement in her voice. He stopped pacing abruptly and swung around to face her again. She was back staring up at the ceiling. Now her hands were linked behind her head. She looked absolutely relaxed. Small. Her hair was still everywhere, as if it was untamable. The sight of it stirred the dominant in him. Or the leopard in him. It didn't matter which. There was more to Flambé than was on the surface and he needed to be aware of that. He couldn't take her for granted. Not for one moment. She was hiding herself from him.

This was a woman who frequently went overseas to find other strawberry leopards or leopards of other subspecies that were slowly becoming extinct. She exhibited no fear when she went into those lairs and explained her plans to the elders. She faced down poachers. Sevastyan had asked that she be investigated and she had been — thoroughly. In Africa and the Middle East, two different poaching factions who trafficked in animal parts and pelts had put out a reward for her death. Drake had known of her and her father long before Sevastyan had asked for a report.

"Before I actually found a woman and claimed her, I made certain there were features built into this room so that I could have my woman close and ensure that she was safe at all times as well. Not only that she was safe, but that I was and our leopards were."

Flambé sat up slowly, pushing her hair back from her face with one hand and looking warily at him with large cat's eyes.

"That you were safe? Why wouldn't you be safe from your woman?"

"I'm an Amurov. My family would always be willing to pay someone to assassinate me."

"I see." She said it slowly, frowning, as though she didn't really see. "So, a woman might go so far as to seduce you and then kill you in your sleep. You wouldn't hear her lies, and neither would your leopard because you'd be so enamored with her that you just would fall all over her, like you did me."

That was a trap if he ever heard one. He

197

set traps, he didn't fall into them. He stared at her without replying.

"What are these sleeping arrangements?" Suspicion colored her voice. She moved to the edge of the bed.

He turned away from her on the pretense of checking the water filling the bathtub. She looked too tempting with her breasts jutting toward him covered in his marks of possession and her hips, mound and thighs marked with the same. Satisfaction coursed through him. He was far more primitive than he ever thought he was. He'd tied so many women, but never once had he wanted to see those rope patterns on their skin. Never had he thought to sink his teeth into them in a claiming bite even though shifters were extremely oral. Now, just the sight of his marks on Flambé had his cock stirring all over again.

It was a large bathtub, but the taps were high pressure and would fill it rather quickly. Steam rose, curling into the air. He liked hot water and he intended to bathe with her. He wanted to start their life together as it would continue. She joined him, surprising him by walking in completely nude, her hands in her hair, winding it into some messy knot that she clearly was well versed in making when she took baths. It didn't

198

seem to matter that her hair spilled out of the knot in disarray; she looked more tempting to him than ever.

"It looks hot." Flambé bent down to test the water with her fingers.

"Very much so." He made it a statement as he put both hands around her waist and lifted her right into the middle of the tub.

She hissed her displeasure, but she didn't try to claw at him to get out as he half expected. The water wasn't so hot it would burn her skin, but it was hot enough to maybe be a little uncomfortable. He'd poured healing salts into it in order to help ease any soreness their wild fucking had created.

Flambé stood for a few minutes as the tub continued to fill with the hot, steamy water. "You were telling me about the sleeping arrangements. Just what are the options? I assume there are options."

His gaze swept over her body deliberately. "I could tie you to our bed in a different position every night. I'm very imaginative. It would take quite a while before we would have to start repeating positions."

"Seems like a fire hazard to me. I think sleeping downstairs appeals to me more." She gave a little sniff of disdain.

He turned off the taps and stepped into

the tub, towering over her. Crowding her, when there was enough room that he didn't have to.

Flambé stepped back and then had to catch at his hips to stop herself from slipping. He continued to stand, trapping her between his larger body and the high side of the tub. Very gently, but with firm command, he put one hand on her shoulder and applied pressure. The order was clear. He wanted her to sit down in the water and he wanted her to do it right there where there was little room between their bodies.

She tilted her head to look up at him, her cat's eyes meeting his for just one moment. There was a brief hint of defiance that had the dominant in him rising fast, a sharp brutal power unfurling in him that raked and clawed just as violently as his leopard. He stared straight into her eyes, letting her see who he was, what he was and what she would always have to deal with.

A part of him detested that he had been born twisted and fucked-up, created by a strain of vile men who thought only of themselves and wanted nothing but power over others. He had fought the cruel streak in his makeup, the raging temper, and he'd kept others safe from both his leopard and himself. He cupped the side of her face and leaned down to take her mouth.

Her lips were soft. Reluctant or not, she opened for him and his tongue swept inside all that heat and glorious fire. The moment he touched her, Flambé surrendered herself into his keeping. More, she gave him as good as he gave her. She matched him flame for flame. She poured liquid accelerant onto the fire, her tongue stroking along his. Dancing with his. Dueling with his. She kissed like sin. She kissed like a fucking angel.

Flambé wasn't in the least bit passive and he knew she never would be. She had a healthy sex drive and she wasn't ashamed of it. She would need that with him. His body raged at him without his leopard driving him. When their leopards got in on the act, the two of them were going to be in trouble. He was looking forward to it.

Kissing Flambé was dangerous, not at all soothing. It was more like lighting a match to a stick of dynamite. He wasn't used to having reactions to women. He didn't give a damn one way or the other about them as a rule, with the exception of his cousins' wives. And even then, when it came to matters of security, he ruled with an iron fist. But Flambé could change all that and he wasn't certain that was a good thing, not

201

when there was so much ugliness in him he fought to keep suppressed.

Sevastyan lifted his head and kept pressure on her shoulder. Flambé blinked up at him like a sleepy kitten, coming out of a fog, looking adorable and sexy at the same time. The steam had put a light dew on her skin so that every inch of her seemed to glow and the pattern of the ropes gleamed red.

Her long lashes did that little flutter that always drew his attention and then she slowly began to sink down, using him to steady herself, her hands on his hips and then gliding lower as she sank. Her face pressed against his abdomen as she moved down, her breath warm. His cock became a monster, hard and aching. He felt her tongue sliding over the broad, sensitive crown, lapping greedily at the leaking drops there and then curling around his shaft and gliding up his heavy sac. Then the inside of his thighs were treated to the feel of her tongue before she settled in the tub.

Flambé drew up her knees and looked up at him, a wicked expression on her face. She raised one eyebrow before resting her chin on her knees. "I believe we were talking about sleeping arrangements."

She was going to be a handful and he

202

couldn't help but love the challenge. Just because she enjoyed his art and her leopard species preferred submission to her male didn't mean she was a pushover by any means. He was in for a lifetime of surprises. He wasn't a man who would ever enjoy the mundane. Flambé appeared to suit him perfectly, although that meant they were going to butt heads more than he'd like.

He sank into the hot water and took the end position of the tub, waiting for her to scoot around to the opposite end. When she did and stretched out her legs, he took her foot to massage it. "You seem very stuck on the sleeping arrangements. Did you have something in mind?" He turned the tables back on her.

She rested her head on the soft pillow angled for her and closed her eyes. "I'm just tired, Sevastyan, and I guess I want to know where I stand with you. I've never really been in a relationship and you're pushing us very fast. I'm willing to sleep downstairs if it makes you uncomfortable to have me be up here with you."

She wasn't lying. She would definitely go back downstairs to the master bedroom. That was the third time she'd suggested it. She was trying to put distance between them.

"No, baby. I want you up here with me." He kept his voice very gentle. "I had preconceived ideas of what it would be like if I found someone. Now that I have you, those ideas aren't the same. I want you close to me."

Her lashes fluttered again. Lifted. She looked at him, seemingly a little hesitant. "I know you don't want anyone sleeping in your bed with you and I understand that. I do, Sevastyan. It doesn't hurt my feelings. I was looking at the tree in your room, which, by the way, is extremely cool. It has that little hammock hanging from a branch. I could sleep there."

He studied the expression on her face as she made the offer. She was actually quite hopeful he would want her to sleep there, which was actually very comical. The tree and hammock had been designed as an art piece, but also to weave a woman into a tight space, possibly an uncomfortable position that would — eventually — give her a sense of rebirth. The experience could release endorphins that were both sexual in nature and a kind of euphoria for the recipient. Perhaps his little Flambé had inadvertently discovered the process without knowing what she was doing, just as a runner could release certain endorphins.

"Thank you for the offer, Flambé. I appreciate it. I do intend to use the hammock with you once you build your stamina in the ropes, but as far as sleeping arrangements, I prefer to have you as close to me as possible. I want to wake up with you right beside me. I find I have need of you close for many reasons."

He wasn't going to elaborate. Most were of a sexual nature, but he was very concerned with her safety. He didn't want her too far from him, especially knowing she had Franco Matherson as a stalker. Or that she had death threats against her. She also had it in her head that she could escape him if things weren't to her liking, and Shturm had claimed her female leopard. While Flambé's father had brought her up in the rules of lair life, he clearly hadn't explained what occurred after the claiming.

Shturm wouldn't be able to give Flamme up. He would follow her to the ends of the earth. Sevastyan didn't blame Flambé for not understanding the rules when she wasn't fully aware of them, but those were things that could get others killed. Others like Cain. He didn't like the fact that she, even for one moment, had considered going to Cain.

"I have a meeting with a supplier tomor-

205

row," Flambé said. "It's important for me to go. I know that you've got all sorts of things you have to do, so can you have one of your bodyguard friends available to come with me? I can't cancel it. I did grab my schedule and I'll get it typed in so I can send it to you and you won't have to be blindsided."

Sevastyan paused the massage, both hands clasping her foot. "Flambé, don't you think you should have told me immediately you had an important meeting?"

"I didn't remember. I have to put in reminders," she said. "I've got so much to do all the time and my reminders keep me on track. Without my phone, I'm kind of lost."

He couldn't fault her for that. No way was he allowing one of his "bodyguard friends" to go with her to meet with her suppliers. Franco had her schedule. And her leopard was close to the emerging.

"I need to know exactly where you're supposed to be and who you're meeting with in the next month, Flambé. If possible, you're going to change those meeting times and days."

Her eyes flew open and she tried to sit up straight but he refused to relinquish his hold on her foot.

206

She glared at him. "I can't just change everyone's meeting times and their days. In some cases, we booked those times months ago. You know how upset you were when I cancelled on you."

He nodded. "Sevastyan Amurov is leopard and you knew that going into it. The majority of your other clients are not. Who else do you work for that is leopard?"

Sevastyan kept his gaze fixed on her face, watching her expression closely. He saw the instant shutter come down. She was a businesswoman, used to protecting her clients, the shifters in particular. She didn't divulge information.

"I am responsible for your security now, Flambé," he reminded gently instead of demanding as he normally might. "I'm not just prying." This was about her landscaping business, not a personal matter between them. He was always going to have to be careful about separating the two if it was possible.

"Jake Bannaconni. Mitya and Fyodor Amurov, your cousins. My father had them as customers, not me. I've never been on their properties, but recently Eli Perez called me. He's a shifter my father worked for. Elijah Lospostos is also a shifter my father worked for and I have an appointment with

207

him later in the month. And Cain Dufort. Those are all the local customers that I have at the moment who are shifters."

His gut tensed. His leopard leapt for the surface, raking and clawing for supremacy. He wanted to do a little clawing of his own but he kept his hands very relaxed as he continued pressing the knots out of her foot. Very gently he put that foot down and picked up the other. That gave him time to breathe away the worst of his rage — the raw edges of it where it was crimson and brutal and desperate for blood.

"Dufort's business? His club?"

"Both. His private residence and his club. I also work at Bannaconni's office buildings and his private residence as well. Bannaconni owns several buildings, as do you and your cousins. My company recently signed a contract to work up designs for them too."

"Is it possible that Franco has infiltrated your company? You have to employ quite a lot of people to cover that many projects as well as non-shifters."

He had to find an easy way to circle back to Cain. He wanted to know if she worked alone at his residence. He knew she worked alone at the club. Cain would never stand for others to be there. He would know she was a shifter. She would have to sign a nondisclosure and if he could, Cain would try to get her in a compromising position in order to ensure she would never blackmail one of his customers. Cain took his word to his clients very seriously.

She sighed. "Anything is possible, Sevastyan. You know that. Most of my employees, at this point, are people I trust. They are those I've helped, provided an education, a place to live, and will eventually help to set them up in business with the hope that they will help others, shifters or non-shifters. The point being to help whatever community they land in. My father made it very clear that if they wanted to return to their original countries after they received an education and could take back something to their lair that would aid their people, all to the good. He wanted to save lairs, not tear them apart. Ours was too far gone to save."

"Strawberry leopards, who knew?" He let himself look at the messy knot on her head. Like her red-gold-tipped lashes, it made her look vulnerable and very sexy.

She sent him a smile. "I really am sorry about the appointment tomorrow, Sevastyan. I would cancel it if I could. This particular supplier is very important to my business and I need him. I had to special order plants that Cain wanted for his club, the garden of paradise. He really likes that garden and constantly wants to add to it. It's proved very profitable for the business and I'd hate to lose him as a client."

She made a little moue with her lips that put steel in his cock. "At first his vision was quite simple, but his clients love it and so does he. It's *really* good for me monetarily, but a pain because he goes online and looks at plants not knowing anything about them before he tells me what he wants. In any case, this particular supplier is my go-to when I have exotics to order fast. Honestly, I'll be all right with just one bodyguard. Franco caught me off guard. I'll be watching for him this time."

Sevastyan tightened his hold on her foot and then began his slow massage again. He didn't have to find a way to circle back to Cain, she'd just given him that. "No worries. I can rearrange my schedule. When you work at Cain's residence, do you have to go out there alone?"

She shook her head. "I don't have that kind of time. I oversee the work. I lay it out, leave, come back at the end of the day to make certain it's what I wanted to have happen and then I check it off as a good day's work. I only work at the club by myself."

He was surprised at the relief he felt. He didn't want to address Cain further with her, not unless it became necessary. She was already falling back asleep, giving in to the earlier exhaustion. He continued the slow massage of her foot and calf until she was nearly out and then he simply stood, lifted her out of the water, dried her off and carried her to their bed.

7

Flambé's meeting with her supplier, a man by the name of Brent Shriver, was actually in San Antonio itself. Ania asked if she could accompany them into town as she wanted to drop by the bakery to see Evangeline and Ashe. Mostly, she said, she wanted to see the twins. Evangeline had the little nursey finished and while she worked in the bakery, the twins were in the playroom. Ania wanted to go sit with them for a little while and get out from under her husband's "bossy" company.

Flambé had looked up at Sevastyan several times for guidance, no doubt hearing the blatant lies in Ania's voice when she gave her excuses for coming, both to Flambé and to her husband. Both knew she lied, but both thought she was teasing Mitya. Truthfully, Sevastyan wanted her driving the car. Ania could handle just about any car on the road and when it was one her father and

212

she had worked on to make into a little road rocket, there were few cars that could overtake it.

Kirill and Matvei were in a car somewhere ahead of them and trailing behind were two others. Leonid Chernov was Kirill's younger brother who had come over with Kirill but had gone his own way for a short while. He'd joined them some time ago but hadn't been put in a trusted position until recently. Sevastyan, being Sevastyan, still wasn't entirely certain of him. Partnering with him was Zakhar Kotov, a man few wanted to cross. He was quiet, watchful, and loyal to Sevastyan and no one else. Not even to Mitya.

Zakhar's father owed money the family couldn't pay. Rolan's lieutenants set their leopards on the family, hunting them down and ripping them to pieces. Sevastyan had saved his life when he was a young man, concealing him from the brutal *vor* and the lieutenants hunting him.

Zakhar had seen the savage beating the *vor,* Sevastyan's own father, had cruelly subjected him to and then his leopard had visited on Shturm. Neither had given away Zakhar's hiding spot. In the end Rolan concluded that Sevastyan couldn't know where Zakhar was hiding. Sevastyan had smuggled Zakhar money and a passport to get out of the country so Rolan couldn't kill him. Eventually, when Sevastyan had left Russia, Zakhar had joined him.

Sevastyan made certain Mitya was well guarded at his home and had promised to remain there before he took off with Flambé. The two cars with the other bodyguards left well ahead of Sevastyan's leaving the Dover estate. He didn't want anyone to think he had bodyguards traveling with them or that he might think they needed them. He wanted Franco to make his move. The sooner he could make certain Flambé was safe to carry on with her landscaping business, the better he'd feel.

He felt a little guilty telling Mitya there might be a five percent chance there could be a problem when he thought it might be higher, but Mitya was every bit as protective of Ania as Sevastyan was of Flambé, so there would have been zero chance of Mitya allowing Ania to go. Ania was becoming restless. Sevastyan could see all the signs in her, where Mitya chose to ignore them. Sevastyan didn't want to be that kind of partner. He knew he was worse than Mitya in lot of ways, but he wanted to see his failings and hopefully correct them so he had a good chance of keeping Flambé happy.

He laid out everything to Ania. He didn't want her going into trouble blindly. Being Ania, she was more than happy to come with him. Not only more than happy to come, she was eager to come. She told Mitya she was driving and danced around the room joyfully, kissing him good-bye before catching up the car keys and proclaiming they were taking her car and did Sevastyan mind?

Flambé was quiet a good portion of the way into San Antonio, looking out the window. She seemed distant from him and Sevastyan found he didn't like it. She moved in the seat as if she couldn't quite be still, her hand rubbing along her arm or her thigh. She sat away from him, clearly trying to avoid touching him.

Shturm? Has Flamme indicated that Flambé is upset? She has been very quiet all morning.

Now that he thought about it, she'd been quiet since they'd had breakfast and he'd taken her with him to Mitya's. He'd left her with Ania while he'd been with Mitya attending endless boring meetings.

Flamme seems — moody. She is resting before rising. She is not talking.

How close is she to rising?

I cannot tell.

215

Still, his leopard was content. Shturm had gone from raging to calm as long as Flambé was close. Sevastyan found he felt the same way. He thought that the female leopard being moody could be affecting Flambé, just as his leopard's moods often affected him.

He reached for her hand, threaded their fingers together and pressed her palm to his thigh. Even though she stiffened slightly, she didn't pull away, and she kept her face turned toward the highway. That wasn't a good sign.

"Look at me, *plamya.*" His voice might have been low, but the order was clear.

She glanced toward the front seat and their driver, but obediently turned her head toward him, her eyes reluctantly meeting his. His belly knotted. Was there hurt there? She wasn't good at subterfuge, but her expression was clouded by the ever-changing color of her eyes.

"We promised each other that we would talk things out. I can't make it right if I don't know what I did. Clearly I did something."

Color swept up her neck into her face. She frowned and shook her head. He liked that she blushed. She was too fair to control that telltale sweep of color.

"Flambé. You know these things add up

fast with me when you don't do me the courtesy of replying. I am asking you a very simple question that requires a very simple answer."

She shook her head a second time and then capitulated, but he could see she was very reluctant and was going to be just as upset with him for forcing her to divulge why she was upset. "You made a big deal about me sleeping in the room with you and then this morning you were gone. You had nothing to say or do with me. I felt . . . abandoned."

She'd felt more than that, he could see. She had been just as sexually frustrated as he had. So much for being noble. His body had awakened him as it did nearly every morning, roaring to life with insane demands, and with Flambé beside him, that voracious hunger had been worse than ever. Even asleep, she had looked exhausted, and some of his marks looked like faint smudges, almost bruises on her skin. Where the night before they'd been erotic, in the morning light he didn't approve of that look. He wasn't going to take any chances with hurting her.

Sevastyan had gotten up quickly and left the room, showering and dressing in the master bedroom downstairs. Flambé's scent

217

still lingered there, surrounding him, entering his lungs every time he took a breath, driving him nearly insane, yet he'd managed to control himself and kept his hands off of her by staying a distance from her.

He rubbed his thumb along the back of her hand. "You should have felt cared for. I don't make a habit of depriving myself."

She stared down at his thumb for such a long time he didn't think she was going to answer him. Then her head tilted back again until her eyes met his. "I was being cared for?"

"Yes, you were. I am never gentle, Flambé, no matter how much I might want to be. Your body needs time to recover."

Her gaze once more jumped to the front seat as if afraid their conversation might be overheard. No doubt it could be, given that leopards had excellent hearing.

He caught her chin and firmly held it. "The only one who matters to you is the man sitting right here. No one else." He wasn't going to tell her about the crazy sex he'd tried not to hear when Mitya and Ania had been so out of control numerous times thanks to their leopards. He was certain it wasn't going to be much better for Flambé with Sevastyan.

"We're talking about something very

important. Sex is extremely important between us. We have privacy screens in our cars for a reason. Right now, if you need sex, or want it, we just raise the screen and we do what we want."

"With other people in the car?" Her eyes went wide.

"What happens when your leopard rises? We need them because there's no other choice when a female leopard goes into heat. And sometimes, Flambé, I'll just want to fuck you because I can't wait five more minutes. That's going to happen." He leaned down to whisper in her ear. "Is that exciting to you? Or upsetting? Tell me the truth."

Her long lashes fluttered, veiled her golden-green eyes, and then she looked directly at him. "It's exciting," she conceded in a low tone. "Scary, but exciting."

She was courageous enough to be honest, which was why she was the perfect partner for him.

"The scary part is why it's important that you trust me to take care of you."

She nodded, but stayed silent. He kept his hand cupping the side of her face, refusing to allow her to turn away from him. Sex was a good subject to keep him distracted, but it wasn't the real problem. There was something more. He pressed the pad of his thumb over her lips and brushed back and forth, staring into her eyes, completely focused. Not blinking. He had that stare down. He was a shifter. An alpha. He was completely dominant. He didn't ever need to raise his voice to bring anyone in line.

"It's never good to attempt to hide anything from me, Flambé. You may as well tell me the rest. What is it that has upset you?"

He kept his thumb brushing across her lips gently, watching her eyes change color. She was upset. Her little leopard was worried. Flambé shifted restlessly in the seat beside him. Again, her hands rubbed along her arms and thighs as though putting out a fire. For a long moment she looked as if she might defy him. She tried to look away, but she couldn't manage, shaking her head twice before closing one hand into a fist.

"I overheard something this morning that bothered me," she admitted. Reluctance edged her voice. She tried to look away from him again, but couldn't.

He knew from experience that he was capable of keeping other alphas held captive with his stare. She didn't have that kind of experience and her leopard was too submissive to break free. He tried to encourage her by gently using his other hand to press her

220

palm deeper into the heat of his thigh. Her heart was beating rapidly, almost as if she was prey and he was the predator. He could hear the sound and it bothered him, but he couldn't let this go. It was too important.

"Anything that bothers you should be given to me immediately, Flambé. I thought we'd established that." Her eyes had gone to that gold with emerald flecks. "Whatever you heard didn't just bother you. You're extremely upset. You're doubting me. Us. My motives for being with you, aren't you?"

He didn't raise his voice or betray the fact that the ever-present rage that sent crimson sheets banding across his vision and had Shturm rearing up, raking and clawing at him, just as enraged at the thought that they might lose the only thing keeping them both sane, was surfacing.

She didn't respond, but her eyes searched his as if she could read his mask. Read what everyone else had failed to in years of trying.

"What did you hear?" he prompted gently.

She glanced toward the front seat again, toward Ania. "I know you said it was just the two of us, but I can't talk about this right here . . ."

"We've got company," Ania announced. "Two car lengths back, one lane over. Com-

221

ing up on us fast, Sevastyan. A Porsche Macan Turbo, fast, and in the right hands, great cars. Make sure you have your seat belts on."

Sevastyan didn't like the conversation interrupted. At some point they were going to be picking it up again, but Ania needed to concentrate on driving and he had to make certain Flambé was protected. On the floor was a bulletproof blanket. The windows of the vehicle were bulletproof and supposedly the car was made encased in a newer bulletproof armor that protected them, but he wasn't taking chances with her safety.

"I'm sorry, Ania, I didn't think he'd really be this stupid." Sevastyan was going to have to answer to his cousin. Already he was texting Mitya, making certain to let him know they were possibly going into a gun battle.

Sevastyan doubted if Franco Matherson was personally in the Porsche chasing them. That wasn't his style. He wouldn't want to put himself in any real danger. Sevastyan had prepared three different places they could ambush anyone coming after them. They'd already passed the first two roads. He'd been fairly certain Matherson would want to keep his kidnaping of Flambé as

222

low-key as possible. The first two roads had been long before they'd gotten onto the freeway. Now, there was only the one exit that would take them toward Evangeline's first home before she married Fyodor.

Sevastyan liked to change up Mitya's routes often. He never wanted to establish a pattern and this was a longer distance, but had far less traffic. The exit looped around in a wide circle that came out on a frontage road. That continued for a mile or two before they would turn off to take a short little connecting road, almost a one-lane that led toward the residential area where Evangeline had bought her home. Sevastyan was certain that short lane was where they would be ambushed if they weren't before then.

"Did the Porsche exit with us?"

"Yes. It's trying to keep a couple of cars between us, but only one other car exited onto this loop. I have a feeling that car might be with them as well, Sevastyan."

There were no nerves in Ania's voice, but then he didn't expect there to be any. Ania had always proved to be a driver beyond compare. She had no doubt in her mind that she could outdrive anyone pursuing them.

"Matvei and Kirill have already back-

223

tracked and set up on the hill just above the turnoff to Evangeline's street. They can cut off anyone you don't shake."

"That's just insulting," Ania said.

Sevastyan laughed. "You love this shit. Poor Mitya. He has no idea."

"He knows. He just doesn't like it."

Sevastyan found himself running Flambé's palm up and down his thigh, pressing it deep. His body felt hot. His cock ached. He couldn't help the way his body reacted when there was danger. Adrenaline translated to sexual hunger every time for him. "We're going to be fine," he assured her.

She nodded, not pulling her hand away. "I'm sure we will."

He glanced down at her face. Flambé wasn't the hysterical type. She was used to danger. She had no problem walking right into the throat of her enemy, but she was the one doing the planning, being in control. It was an altogether different situation relying on someone else when the stakes could be life or death. He understood that. She gave herself to him in the bedroom, but this was a different matter.

He brought her hand up to his mouth. "I really didn't expect him to hit us this soon, Flambé, or I wouldn't have brought Ania with us. Mitya's going to have my hide for this."

"You deserve it too," she said, looking up at him.

There it was again, that brief look, a shadow in her eyes that hadn't been there before. It had slipped in sometime while she was at his cousin's home and there was a distinct wariness in her that hadn't been there before. It was so slight, almost hidden. She was used to hiding her nature from others so whatever she was suddenly leery of was going to be difficult to ferret out if she didn't want to disclose it.

The car braked suddenly, the back end sliding around in a perfect U. They ended up going the opposite way they'd been driving. Sevastyan glanced out his window to see Ania threading a narrow proverbial needle between the Porsche and an SUV as those two vehicles tried to brake. She sped up and headed toward a cross street that would bring her to another road back to their original destination where Sevastyan's men had set up an ambush.

"Nice move, Ania." Sevastyan would never get over her driving abilities.

Mitya was insane not to use her capabilities. She loved driving and she had mad skills. Most of the time she traveled with her husband. He wanted her in the back seat so he could have sex with her. Not that Sevastyan blamed him now that he had Flambé and knew what it was to have his own woman close.

The way his rage had manifested itself into sexual needs had always been a problem and he knew it always would be. The older he had gotten, the harder his body drove him. He practiced disciplined arts to help, but eventually, he was driven to go to the club in spite of the dangers of his leopard. He was always very, very careful. There were many couples there, men who enjoyed watching their woman tied and taken — their women willing to be tied and taken. That was always his number one rule. She had to be willing. He always made certain. He asked her himself away from her partner. Checked her pulse to make certain there was no coercion.

His ropes were easy to remove, and the partner knew how and there were always scissors to cut the woman loose right there. Cain was in his office or on the premises watching if there was a problem once Sevastyan walked away. That way, Shturm had no chance of escaping, no chance of harming the woman, not even at Sevastyan's most vulnerable moment. He was always very, very careful. He never faced the woman. Never kissed her. Never did anything that would set the leopard off. It was never the most satisfying sexual experience, but it got the job done.

Until Flambé. Sevastyan stroked a caress through her hair, wishing they were home and he could talk to her. He wasn't used to doing anything but giving orders. He had the feeling that wasn't going to work in this case.

Ania, in the driver's seat, let out a string of unladylike words. "Clever bastards. They considered we might use this road. Apparently, you have before."

Sevastyan could see that two cars were blocking the street just ahead. Ania only had seconds to make a decision on what to do. Already the Porsche and SUV were coming in behind her. Flambé's breath exploded out of her lungs, but other than that, she made no sound. He wrapped his arm around her shoulder.

Ania spun the car and raced back straight at the Porsche as if playing chicken. Flambé put her hands over her eyes. Sevastyan stared calmly out the front windshield. There was no way whoever was driving that vehicle would be willing to go back to Franco and tell him that they had killed

227

Flambé. Matherson made it clear he wanted her alive.

"I'm so sorry I brought him into your lives," Flambé whispered. "He isn't going to stop."

"No, he won't. Even if he managed to get his hands on you, baby, he'd still go hunting other leopards. He likes it or he wouldn't be doing it. There's no reason to kill other leopards. None at all. There's something very wrong with him. His lair should have taken care of it a long time ago."

Sevastyan tried to comfort her even as he watched the driver of the Porsche desperately pull his vehicle hard to the right while his passenger threw his arm up as if that would save him if the two cars collided at the high rate of speed Ania was traveling. Ania's car sped on past and raced around the bend, back up the slight hill toward the freeway.

"What do you want to do, Sevastyan? Call it off or go to the cul-de-sac by Evangeline's home one more time?"

"Try the lane. Prune Lane. That's where the boys have set up. If our company doesn't follow, we'll head into the city. Mitya's pretty pissed, but apparently he was following us anyway."

Ania laughed. "I'm not surprised."

Nothing seemed to faze his cousin's wife. His own wife was going to think twice before she crossed him, especially in matters of her safety. He glanced down at the top of her silky head. She wasn't saying much, but she kept looking behind them, watching to see if they were being followed.

"We want them to come after us," he said gently.

"We do?" There was trepidation in her voice. "Sevastyan, there were two men in the Porsche. I saw three in the SUV. I couldn't see into the other two cars, but you have to figure at least two men in each. So, at least nine men, maybe more. Even with Kirill, Matvei and the two others I don't know, we're outnumbered. And what are we going to do with them anyway? Ania's a good driver. A great driver. She can get us out of here. We'll lose them and go back to the house. I can call Brent and tell him I have to reschedule. He'll understand. It will be Cain who might be a problem, but I can handle him."

Sevastyan's eyes met Ania's in the rearview mirror just for a moment. He flicked his gaze toward the right, away from the freeway and back toward Prune Lane.

"Cain? Why would he be a problem?" His hand settled around Flambé's nape to begin a slow massage, attempting to ease the tension out of her.

"The plants are for his club, his garden of paradise. They're exotics and we've been waiting for some time for them to come in. It hasn't been easy to get them. I have to have an open time to go to the club when no one is there. He doesn't shut down that often. Coordinating our schedules isn't that easy, but this situation is ridiculous."

"Tell me about his garden. The garden started fairly small although the room itself is huge." He kept her talking to distract her, although he genuinely wanted to know.

"He wanted the garden to be really large but still allow everyone to see into the rooms on either side of it. I had to design the plants and trees to grow so that could be done. In keeping with his themes, I incorporate his apparatuses as much as possible for the plants to grow on. That lets me prune them back and tie them so they grow the way I need them to. I just had a smaller version of a wooden X brought in to plant some of the exotics to grow up and over. It should be quite lovely."

Her voice held both intimate and enthusiastic notes when she spoke of her plants and the garden. It was a huge undertaking and very private between her and Cain, the

230

owner of the club. For the first time in his life, Sevastyan felt the stirrings of jealousy and it was an ugly, demeaning emotion. He didn't like to picture her in Cain's office, close to him, leaning over the man's desk, both poring over the papers she had drawn out, that sensual, intimate note in her voice as she talked about her plants and ideas and how to incorporate his various sexual apparatuses. He didn't want Flambé talking to Cain about anything sexual, let alone an apparatus.

"Did Cain ever offer to show you how those apparatuses work?"

"Yes, but I declined. I wasn't interested in anything but rope. That was beautiful and sensual."

"Did he offer to tie you? He is a rigger. A very good one and a master in suspension." They were coming up on Prune Lane. Ania had slowed the car as if she suspected another ambush.

Just the thought of Cain tying Flambé and suspending her in an erotic pose made him want to rip out Cain's heart. He had never been that kind of man. He wasn't jealous. He wasn't possessive. He certainly didn't care what other man a woman wanted after he tied her in a pose. If she wanted fifty other men, she was welcome to them. Not

Flambé. She was his alone and hopefully he had made that very, very clear to her.

She nodded. "He did. By that time, I think I already was obsessed with you. I didn't tell him because I didn't want to hurt his feelings."

"Cain has many women to choose from, *malen'koye plamya.* You have no need to feel guilty or that you may have hurt his feelings. He owns a club and he's very good at what he does. Women flock to him."

He risked a quick glance at the setup. Everyone was in place. Once again, his eyes met Ania's in the mirror and the car began to move forward with more confidence. Behind them the SUV pulled close, the Porsche behind it. The other two vehicles were nowhere in sight, which meant they'd taken the bait and rushed around to cut them off using the alleyway. His body stirred the way it always did in times of danger. He craved the rush. He needed it.

He caught Flambé's chin and tipped her face up to his to take possession of her mouth. He loved her mouth. It was a hot haven of promised sin. She looked like an angel and kissed like she was Satan's accomplice. Whiskey couldn't burn that hot down his throat. Nothing could. She poured herself into him without reservation, without hesitation. He knew if he unbuttoned that prim little blouse she wore and put his mouth to her breast she would cradle his head to her and offer more.

Flambé tasted like hot cinnamon spiced with just the lightest hint of Moroccan rose and Egyptian jasmine. The moment he tasted that on his tongue, he wanted to rip off her panties, press his mouth between her legs and devour her to get at her unique flavor. He had to stop. He'd gone too long without her and he couldn't start anything, not until this was over.

He had to send Franco Matherson a message. One very loud and clear. One that said not to fuck with him because the man would die if he did. Flambé was off-limits. She was safe and secure and never to be touched, frightened or intimidated again. It didn't matter how much money the shifter had, he wasn't going to win and he would never be safe. Sevastyan could get to him.

He lifted his head to push his forehead against hers, looking into her eyes. "I want you to stay in this car with Ania. Keep your head down and the doors locked. Don't you dare defy me on this, Flambé. This is *my* business." He kissed her forehead and then pushed her down on the seat. "Lock the doors after me, Ania."

233

"You got it." He waited until she allowed the SUV to trap her between the other two cars suddenly rushing at them from out of the alley and she brought their car to a complete stop. He opened the door and was out, rolling away from the car to draw fire away from the women and signal to his men they had open season on Franco's men.

He came to his feet as his men opened covering fire and strode purposefully right up to the passenger side of the Porsche while they were still staring in triumph at the trapped car with Flambé in it. He yanked open the door, put a gun to the passenger's head and pulled the trigger. He shot the driver twice between the eyes as the man turned toward him in a kind of dazed shock. Then he sprinted toward the SUV.

Two more vehicles tore onto the lane, trapping the SUV. Sevastyan barely glanced at the cars, not in the least surprised that Mitya would follow his wife. His own men had already sprung the trap and enclosed the other vehicles Franco had sent, exchanging gunfire but killing the occupants fairly quickly.

Sevastyan came up to the side of the SUV, but Zakhar was there first, giving him a look that said to back off. He smashed the rear window with a tool several times, ducking low as a barrage of bullets met the glass shattering inward. Tossing the tool to Sevastyan, Zakhar waited for Sevastyan to hit the back-passenger window and then duck before he threw the homemade bomb into the vehicle. Tackling Sevastyan, they both hit the ground hard as the SUV was lifted high, rocked and then set back onto the ground, flames coming out from under the doors and through blown-out windows.

"You fucking asshole," Mitya greeted as Sevastyan climbed to his feet. He looked his cousin over carefully. "Are you all right?"

"Yeah, no worries. Thanks, Zakhar. We've got to get these bodies out of here."

"Cleaners are already here. Drivers will move the cars. We have an enclosed one for the SUV. Get out of here." Zakhar's voice was clipped.

Kirill and Matvei escorted Sevastyan back to the car with Mitya and his bodyguards striding right along with him.

Mitya knocked loudly on the driver's door and all but yanked his wife from the car. He continued glaring at Sevastyan.

"Did you think I wouldn't know you were up to something?"

"*I* wasn't up to anything," Sevastyan denied. "I was taking Flambé to see her sup-

235

plier. Ania said she'd drive me. There was a five percent chance that something might go wrong. I told you that ahead of time."

"*When* did you tell me that?"

"The other night. Do you ever listen to one damn thing I say to you? Maybe because Franco Matherson isn't after your woman you don't have to worry about him, but I did make it very clear that asshole was after mine. I also mentioned he was pissed as hell at me."

"Because you challenged him deliberately, Sevastyan," Mitya pointed out. "You thrive on confrontation."

"That's most likely true. Right now, I promised my woman that I would get her to her meeting on time." He also had the hard-on from hell. "You can give your woman a lecture, one of your two billion that will never do any good, and I'll take mine and go."

Sevastyan was already signaling to Kirill to take the driver's seat. He wanted only one other in the car, someone he trusted. He slid into the back seat, keeping his hand on Flambé's shoulder, keeping her down, trying to prevent her from looking too closely at what was happening around them. It resembled a war zone and the mop-up was going too smoothly, too efficiently.

"Are you going to tell me what just happened?" she asked.

"No. Right at the moment, I have other much more urgent things on my mind." He pushed the button for the privacy screen the moment the car started up.

"Strip, Flambé. Everything. Hurry, baby, we don't have much time." His hands dropped to his trousers, easing them open and pushing them off his hips while he watched her take her blouse and bra off. She had generous breasts. Her nipples were strawberry red. They stood out against her pale skin. She kicked off her sandals and hooked her thumbs in her thong and the soft feminine pants she wore, sliding them down her legs to pull them off.

Sevastyan caught her hair in one fist, tilted her head back and took possession of her mouth. The moment he did the fire flared hot and wild between them. He ran one hand from her throat, down the valley between her breasts to the tight red curls, finding liquid heat at her entrance. He pushed two fingers into her and used his thumb to circle and tease her clit while he kissed her over and over until neither could breathe adequately.

"Ride my fingers, baby," he said. "That's right. Just like that." He used his free hand

237

to tug her left nipple. She was very responsive. He dragged his fingers free before she could get off and brought them to her mouth. "Open." When she did, he pushed his fingers in and watched her suck them clean. The sight sent his cock into a frenzy of need.

He caught her breasts in his hands and guided them between his legs. "I need that mouth of yours busy, Flambé. Woke up this morning and had a vision of the way I wanted to tie you and then take your mouth. Hard to get that image out of my head."

His large hand slid into the silk of her hair and closed around it, making a tight fist at the back of her head. He brought her face right to his lap. "We don't have a lot of time before we get to your meeting and we're not getting out of this car until you swallow down every drop I've been storing up all day for you, so I suggest you get busy."

Her hands immediately began stroking his sac, followed by her tongue lapping and caressing. She traced her way up to the base of his cock while her fingers jiggled and teased his balls. Her tongue glided up his shaft and curled around it, getting him wetter and wetter, but she didn't touch the sensitive crown, prolonging his agony. He crushed the bright red hair in his hands, pulling at her scalp. She teased under the broad head with her tongue, sending fire racing down his spine.

Sevastyan shifted on the seat so that he was above her and could angle her head over his cock, forcing her mouth exactly where he needed it to be. He caught one quick glimpse of her eyes and everything in him went still. Just froze.

His body burned like hell. That terrible, savage rage that manifested itself in sexual urgency had him in its grip, and normally, he would have done whatever he needed to do to rid himself of the buildup that never seemed to go away. His cat's edgy needs seemed to feed his own and it took a great deal of discipline to pull back, to loosen his grip in her hair and breathe through the voracious hunger eating him alive. More than anything he wanted her mouth on his cock, but he couldn't get past that one little shadow he caught. One small shadow.

"Fuck." He spat the word, closed his eyes and breathed some more. What was it about this one woman that made him so crazy? She was more than willing to take care of his needs.

Her body was flushed a soft pink, almost red. Her nipples were standing out, totally erect, twin temptations, staring at him. He

239

could scent her particular fragrance calling to him, the one he craved, the one that made him want to throw her onto the back seat and devour her. That had been his intention all along, to make her think he was going to selfishly have her take care of his needs, but then, at the last minute, ensure she got off as well. He wanted to see what she would do. He should have known.

Sevastyan was going to have to be very, very careful in his handling of his strawberry leopard or she wouldn't be happy for long. She might be naturally submissive in the bedroom and he might be naturally dominant. She liked Shibari and to be tied. She liked to be told what to do and pushed to do things she wouldn't think of doing on her own, but he had to always take care of her. He had to always see to her pleasure, make certain that if she gave him anything special, he reciprocated tenfold.

He was never going to be easy to live with. He knew that. He had to make it worth staying with him. She wasn't a woman who would care about money. He had to take care of her. Sexually, they were a good match. Right now, to keep him from confronting her, she was willing to use sex and he wanted to oblige her. His cock raged at him. *Raged.*

240

Her body wanted him, but her mind didn't. He wasn't her choice anymore. At least, there was doubt again. He wanted her to know — absolutely know — that he was the one she chose to spend her life with.

Sevastyan took another deep, controlling breath and exerted more pressure on her scalp to pull her head away from his cock. "Listen to me, Flambé. You don't want this."

Startled, she looked up at him, her eyes going almost pure green. "That's not true, Sevastyan. I do. I don't know why you would think I don't."

He was feeling a little desperate with her mouth so close, the heat on his cock with every word she said. He caught at his trousers and yanked them up, trying not to see the misery in her eyes or feel the very real pain in his cock. He burned like hell. "Just get dressed, *malen'koye plamya,* so we can talk in peace."

She lifted her chin at him, and with the graceful movement of a female leopard was on the other side of the car, pulling on her clothes in silence, dressing with sure efficiency. There had been defiance in her chin lift and he felt that challenge in every cell of his body. He snapped his teeth together, keeping his gaze wholly focused on her. She sat in her seat and buckled her

241

seat belt.

"Start talking."

"I have absolutely no idea what you want to talk about, unless you want to explain your sudden lack of interest in me sexually."

"You're not going to turn this around, Flambé, you know exactly what I'm talking about. Sooner or later we'll be completely alone and you'll run out of excuses. You'll have to have the conversation whether you want to or not."

She sent him another frustrated and very defiant look, which made him want to grab her by the nape of the neck and have her finish the job she'd just started when he'd tried to be a gentleman. The only problem was he was certain that was what she wanted and that he'd be playing right into her hands. He was not willing for her to distract him.

8

Flambé worked for an hour, her gloved hands packing dirt around the fragile roots of the lacy plants she inserted along the little stream Cain insisted she incorporate into his garden of paradise. She had to admit, as the plants had begun to mature, that the garden really was quite beautiful. The greenhouse was cleverly disguised as a huge bar for Cain's patrons to quietly sit at tables and enjoy the various shows going on while they sipped at drinks or just visited with one another. The tables were high enough to see over some of the plants and low enough to accommodate couples who became aroused at what they were watching.

Flambé had planted in stages, allowing the first of the plants to take root before adding the next. She knew Cain wanted to see if he liked what she'd done. She knew he would. She'd been careful to incorporate the various sexual equipment into the garden, although, at first, she thought it was a horrible idea. Now that she understood about his club and the clients, she knew he was right. She was careful to use each piece sparingly and only if it fit in with her theme.

There were groupings of tables and chairs, the tables at different heights, and the chairs were BDSM chairs so they could enjoy one another as they relaxed in the garden. A small path led to a black label bondage couch near the window, where the occupants could view the various shows taking place, but could also take advantage of the various positions they could enjoy while watching. She was careful to keep her precious plants out of harm's way so any enthusiastic couple couldn't hurt an exotic.

There was a spanking bench used as an ottoman and a low cage as an end table, both grouped in a seating area with several comfortable chairs. The garden area ran down the center of the building and Cain liked it so much he was already building an addition to it, enlarging it. His clients loved it. The bar at the front of the building had screens where they could see the various rooms, but the screens didn't provide the intimacy of viewing the way the garden did.

To be honest, Flambé was really very

proud of the design. She'd worked hard to bring it to life. It hadn't been easy to work with Cain at first. His idea of the Garden of Eden clashing with the Garden of Sin had been a little extreme for her. She'd had to envision the concept as another landscaping job, with intriguing puzzles that would have to be solved. She liked puzzles. She liked to find ways to make really bare spaces beautiful. Sometimes clutter needed to be bare. It could be that simple. She needed to spend time in the space and understand it.

She needed a trellis of some kind for the exotics he wanted to grow up and over, to wind around. Cain wanted to incorporate a piece of equipment called St. Andrew's Cross. It was far too big and bulky. She couldn't find a place for it in her space, although she told him in the newer section she would try. Then he came up with a different one. This was a sleeker design, more of an hourglass shape and one she thought she could work with if anchored properly. It was called a BDSM Triangle Cross. She didn't care what it was called as long as it didn't move. Cain's men had installed it a couple of weeks earlier, in the hopes that the plants would arrive.

Flambé hadn't yet decided how best to use the cross. It was situated in a corner

245

where the very expensive plants wouldn't be trampled on by accident. She worked around the space, occasionally stopping to study it. One flowering tree was close to it, but if it became a problem, she would prune it or teach Cain how to.

Usually she could envision exactly how she wanted the flowers and vines to drape over the existing wood to show them off at the height of their beauty, but for some reason, every time she looked at the cross, she thought of Sevastyan and her body reacted. He had been very upset with her when he dropped her off. He'd left two bodyguards, one at the front door and one at the back, basically threatening them within an inch of their lives if anything happened to her.

They had gone back to the house and both had showered and eaten and she'd informed him that the plants had to go into the ground immediately or they would be lost. They were that sensitive. She was fine going to the club alone or with bodyguards. He had said little, but then, he didn't have to. Those focused eyes of his had sent a chill down her spine. She was playing with fire. With the devil.

She just needed time to think. She wasn't someone who usually made snap decisions.

He probably thought she was because she'd accepted his claim on her leopard. She couldn't blame him for his assessment of her. She cursed the fact that she needed sex so much. She didn't want to explain why, and being around Sevastyan had turned that terrible raw need into a craving that was so strong it bordered on obsession of him. She couldn't think straight when he was around.

The worst part was, she'd thought sex would satisfy her and she could walk away, as he did so easily from all those other women — as clearly he could from her. She found, with him, she wasn't built that way. Something about him got to her and not just in a sexual way. He got to her deeper. That was where she was going to get into trouble. She had to figure out very fast what she was going to do. What the truth about Sevastyan Amurov really was.

Normally, she was good at reading people. That was a major part of her gifts. She could size up a person the moment she saw them, spoke to them or just watched or listened to them for a few moments. She could read their character, but even after spending time with Sevastyan and being in his head, he was still an enigma to her. That was frightening in the face of all the rumors about his family and his admissions about

247

them. More, after the things she'd overheard at his cousin's home . . .

There wasn't a single sound. Not one, but Flambé knew he was there. Her body reacted first, goose bumps rising all over her skin. Her nipples hardened. Her sex clenched. She just knew.

She glanced up as Sevastyan entered the long, wide, glassed-in garden of paradise. Her breath caught in her throat. He was wearing only his soft drawstring pants, his chest bare, and there were several bundles of ropes in his hands. He looked remote. Merciless. So completely the man she'd first seen in the club who had robbed her of her ability to think or sleep for weeks on end. She sat back on her heels, blinking up at him as he dimmed the lights in the garden even lower than she already had them.

"Go. Prepare yourself for a very long session. Hurry. I don't want to be waiting long. When you return, come back to this exact spot. Hydrate, Flambé." He indicated the water bottle she'd brought with her and set on the table near the door but hadn't yet touched.

Heart beating fast, Flambé got up and walked to the nearest restroom, ducked inside and took care of business, washing her hands thoroughly and staring at herself in the mirror. She looked terrified and excited beyond belief. He did that to her. A part of her was so afraid he might leave that she hurried back out, catching up the water bottle and drinking from it as she returned to where she'd been working.

He indicated the ground and she knelt back amongst the vines in the exact spot where she'd been planting new flowers.

"Strip. Everything. Fold your clothes neatly and put them on the bench, but do it right from there. Don't get up."

That voice. He issued the command in a low, compelling tone, velvet over steel. The tone seemed to brush along her nerve endings, sending sparks igniting fires in her veins, her sex, her deepest core. She didn't think to object. She didn't want to. She needed to give him everything he demanded or could ever desire. She had needed him from the moment she had first opened her eyes that morning. She didn't care that she still was unsure if she wanted to be in a relationship with him, she wanted sex with him — like this. Just like this.

She unbuttoned her blouse with trembling fingers and folded it just as he ordered, placing it on the bench, which was just barely in reach. Her bra followed, allowing her generous breasts to spill out into the open. At once her nipples tightened in spite of the heat inside the glassed-in garden. She glanced at him from under her lashes, feeling very feminine, but he looked aloof, as if he didn't notice her body at all. For some strange reason, that sent liquid heat dampening her panties. She quickly worked at pulling her jeans and the thong over her hips and down her legs to slide them off along with her sandals.

Once she had her clothes and shoes on the bench, he indicated the ground with the ropes. "Get back on your hands and knees and come to the center just under this tree, close to the cross."

Her heart went crazy as she crawled, using the fluid, sexy movements of her leopard's sleek form, hips undulating temptingly, breasts swaying, as she put each hand and knee carefully down until she got to the exact center under the blossoming tree. She didn't look at him. She stared straight ahead at the thick flowering bushes she'd planted in all directions, the lacy leaves climbing up trellises she'd cleverly provided so anyone sitting at the high tables could see through the glass into the viewing rooms.

Flambé couldn't hear him. Not a whisper of sound. Even his clothing didn't dare slide against a limb or leaf. His fingertips touched her left buttock, nearly making her jump. A whisper of a touch, but it felt like a brand against her skin — searing her straight to the bone. She did her best not to move, but she trembled in anticipation. His fingertips trailed up her spine, feeling like tongues of fire licking along her back.

His legs came into view. His thighs. He seemed so big towering over her. Invincible. She touched her tongue to her lips. He could make her so crazy for him so fast, it was insane. Now he only had one bundle of rope in his hands. Where had he gotten the rope? Had he brought them with him? She knew he had a storage locker at the club. He had a membership there. In fact, Cain considered him a VIP. Just the idea that other club members might catch a glimpse of him or his work brought many members in night after night. Cain had told her that.

It was shocking to her that she had him all to herself. He stood there in silence, looking down at her while her body coiled tighter and tighter, heat gathering along with the need to feel the ropes wrapping her in their embrace. The ropes were so much a part of him. Just keeping her like this, on the edge of anticipation, made that place inside of her all the more open to him.

The rope was a bright red. Crimson. It

slid through his hands, a part of him. She knew he was checking for slivers as it passed through his fingers. He moved over to the cross anchored in the corner and her heart stuttered and then accelerated as he tested the sturdiness of it, pushing against it with the strength of a leopard. It barely moved.

He indicated for her to stand. He didn't help her. He just waited for her to rise and then he walked around her, this time his fingers trailing on her pulse, a whisper of a touch, hand checking to see how cold or warm her skin was. He slipped the rope over her shoulders and began to build a harness in the fast, sure way he had, this one quite different than the one he had used before. The knots were thick, hard, the harness more of a yoke, coming under her breasts and between them, the knots going down to form a diamond around her belly button and then wrap around her waist, thick strands coming from several angles off the diamond for support. He caught her arms behind her and pulled them tight, binding them into the weave of knots going up her back and into the yoke. He added rope positioned directly over her nipples, pulling tight enough that she felt the burn if she moved.

He tied more rope to the diamond and

252

quickly added thick knots down the front of her to her crotch and back between her cheeks as if it were a thong, but the knots were very large, rubbing against her pussy lips and the hood of her clit, spreading her cheeks with any movement. She stayed very still, her lungs filled with the scent of him. Her mind filled with the need of him.

He walked around her, carefully inspecting his ties, checking her pulse as he did. Making certain her skin was warm and her circulation hadn't been cut off. More rope wrapped up very high around her thigh and then around her ankle. He positioned her very close to the cross. The small movement sent the ropes sliding over her body and sent every nerve ending screaming with need.

Her wild gaze jumped to the cross to see his ropes had already been threaded through the various rings at the top of the two wooden beams. He pulled her easily into the air, a slow rise, her weight evenly distributed. Nevertheless, it was shocking and frightening when she was no longer on the ground.

He tightly pulled up the leg tied at the ankle and thigh so her knee was drawn up and out. He secured her knee to her waist, exposing her damp crotch to him. Her sex pulsed. Her heartbeat pounded right through her sheath as he tied her other leg and pulled her knee into position.

Again, he was careful, checking her pulse, touching her body to ensure her circulation wasn't cut off. He stood in front of her, looking down at her in silence for what seemed like forever before he retrieved a small camera from somewhere behind her. He walked around her taking several pictures.

"I hope you're ready to talk to me, Flambé." His tone was casual. Low. Velvet over steel. "You do look really beautiful and so much a part of this garden. I think you outdid yourself. I'm a little jealous. Perhaps you'll have to make us something similar, although for us, I would like you to think in terms of suspension throughout our garden since it is something I like to tie and you like to be in."

He moved very close to her belly and took a closeup of the knots and then backed off to get a closeup of her face. "You have a look of almost ecstasy on your face." He reached out with that same casual way he had and gently moved the rope controlling the knots.

Her breath hissed out; she couldn't help it. The brush over her nipples set them on fire. The knots between her breasts leading down to her sex and back up between her cheeks moved and twisted in such a way that she wanted to ride the knots to see if she could relieve the terrible coiling tension that burned inside of her, but she knew it was impossible. Relief was just out of reach and any movement would only make her need worse.

"We were fine last night, but then after being at Mitya's everything changed." He walked to the side of her and snapped more photographs of the knots. Of her breasts. Returned to the front and moved close to capture the way the knot was positioned right over the hood of her clit. "Tell me what changed."

His voice was exactly the same, as if she were an art object and they were having a casual conversation. She was desperate for sex, her body flushed and so aroused her brain could barely function. He trailed his fingers over her thigh, inside, close to her sex, just stroked for a moment, but that one small touch nearly brought her to orgasm.

"We have all night, Flambé. You look quite beautiful. If you want to be stubborn and not tell me, that won't be a problem. I can lower the suspension to the perfect height to give your body rest while you take care of me. That gives me some respite and we'll start over again. I'll lift you back up and then we'll see how long you want to hold out before you talk to me."

She instantly wanted to hold out just for that alone. She tried desperately not to look at him, not to meet his eyes because he would see, but she couldn't stop her lashes from lifting. Naturally, his eyes were blazing right into hers. Focused. Hypnotic. Knowing. He was already lowering her body to the floor. Slowly, so not one part of her jarred when her bottom touched down other than the insanity of the sexual hunger coursing through her like a firestorm.

The knot positioned directly over her little star was soaked with liquid heat and the moment her weight settled it pushed deep, straight into the bundle of sensitive nerve endings, adding desperation to the flames the knot over her clit and the two pushing into her entrance caused.

He slid the drawstring on his trousers open and withdrew his cock, one hand circling the base of the shaft while the other fisted in her hair, tilting her head back. He rubbed the broad crown back and forth over her mouth, smearing his addicting taste along her lips before suddenly abandoning her hair to press his fingers into her jaw, opening her mouth wide. He pushed his cock deep, stretching her lips all in one swift motion.

"Look at me. Keep your eyes on me. I want to see you like this. Suck hard. That's it, baby. Harder. Swallow me down."

He felt heavy and delicious on her tongue. He took up her mouth. He was big, a monster, but she wanted him. She wanted to do exactly what he asked of her. Everything he asked, but she wasn't certain she could. She concentrated on his cock, using her tongue, her mouth, listening to his instructions as he thrust into her. She knew he was gentle for her. Sevastyan wasn't a gentle lover. He never would be and that was more than half his appeal for her. But this could be a scary situation and he took more care than usual although he thrust deep, his cock pulsing, a dark, erotic, powerful seduction that sent her own body into a frenzy of need.

She found herself sucking even harder just as he demanded, tilting her head back farther to give him a better angle. His cock swelled even more, jerked, felt so hot it was a burning brand as ropes of his seed jetted down her throat. He held himself there, one hand to the back of her head.

"That's it, baby. All of it." He eased back enough for her to breathe. "Clean me up.

All of me. Every drop. Every inch of me."

She wasn't certain he was breathing hard. He looked as aloof as ever. Why was that hot to her? Why was her body so responsive to that? She took her time, her tongue finding every last sticky spot on him. He stepped away from her, casually retied his trousers and retrieved her water bottle. He held it to her mouth so she could drink and then he checked her arms.

"Is your circulation all right?"

"Yes."

"Good." He unwrapped the rope that covered her nipples.

Flambé wasn't happy about that, but she didn't protest. She kept her lashes down, desperate to keep from squirming on the knots. Three of them were in her body now, or at least they felt like it. Sevastyan began to pull her back into a suspended position. He stopped when her breasts were jutting toward him. He leaned forward and took her left one into the heat of his mouth and her entire body jolted. Flames ran up her spine. He sucked hard on her nipple, elongating it as he reached into his pocket and pulled out a small case.

"You'll look particularly lovely in these rubies with this decorative tie." He leaned close and began to attach something that

258

bit into her nipple. "This is a rubber-tipped alligator clamp. Ruby, of course, and weighted with rubies. You'll want to be still so they don't swing while you talk and I take your photograph."

He screwed the clamp tighter, watching her face the entire time. When she took a deep breath and her gaze jumped to his, his finger slid to her slick entrance and pressed deep. "You like this, don't you, baby?"

She swallowed and nodded. She did. It was scary, but she felt like she floating close to euphoria. She couldn't say why, only that she was so very close.

He switched his attention to the other breast and mimicked the same action. When he was satisfied, he lifted her a few more inches into the air. Once again, he tested her pulse and checked to make certain her skin was warm.

To her consternation, he lifted the knot at her clit idly and began to rub back and forth with his finger and then the knot, alternating between them. "What happened at Mitya's house, Flambé?" His thumb hooked in the rope and played for a moment, sending streaks of fire darting to her sex and bottom simultaneously while his fingers and the knot burned over her inflamed clit until she wanted to scream.

She jerked and the rubies dangling from the nipple clamps danced as though possessed, sending flames roaring through her veins straight to her sheath.

"I heard some men talking about me. About a conversation you had with your cousin." She could barely find her voice. Her mind was in chaos. It was difficult to think straight but she was so desperate to have him she thought she might go insane.

Sevastyan stepped back. "Open your eyes, baby, and look at me. You're flying too high to talk and we're not stopping until we have this conversation."

His voice was commanding. There was no disobeying it and she needed the sound of it as an anchor. Flambé forced air into her lungs and opened her eyes, holding her body very still. He was about a foot away from her, maybe less, sucking on one finger, his camera cradled in his hands. He looked so unaffected by everything, so sexy she wanted to hold out even longer but she knew she couldn't.

"Who did you hear talking?"

"I don't know. They were in the next room, but the door was open. I was waiting for you. Ania had gone upstairs to get her things. She said to go ahead and wait in the sitting room and I took a wrong turn. I heard voices and was going to ask where I went wrong, but I heard my name so I just stopped and listened."

Her voice was ragged. Lungs labored. She tried not to hear the sob in her voice. The betrayal. But it was there and if she could hear it, so could he. His expression didn't change.

"Keep going, *malen'koye plamya*. I need to know everything that was said."

She hated this. Hated to tell him. She already felt so vulnerable. Not because she was wrapped naked in the ropes — the ropes comforted her. She had no idea why they did. There was every possibility that Sevastyan knew being in the ropes comforted her. She felt vulnerable because she already wanted to be his. She felt too much for him. Too many weeks had gone by while she fantasized about him and now that she'd been with him, she wanted to belong to him. This wasn't all about sex. The things that were said had crushed her.

"They said you told Mitya that you needed a submissive, any submissive would do and you just had to find a female on her first life cycle."

She kept her gaze fixed on his face, but it was impossible to tell from his expressionless mask what he was thinking. Flamme

261

had chosen Shturm because he could protect them. The little female leopard was on her first life cycle and had been so afraid of Franco Matherson that she was desperate to find a male leopard who would stop him. Flambé had fantasized about Sevastyan for months. When the two had come together, Flamme had risen, taking charge, choosing her mate because it made sense to her.

"They said Mitya pointed out that you'd found exactly what you were looking for in me, a woman you could do anything you wanted to because I was so hot for sex with you I'd do anything for you. I was just the right kind of woman because all I wanted was to be fucked any way you wanted to fuck me. I was a toy for you and I'd let you manipulate me, and they're right, aren't they? Aren't they, Sevastyan?"

She struggled not to cry. She wasn't going to give him that satisfaction. She was tougher than that. They were so right about her. She was hanging in his ropes, desperate for him to fuck her. Nearly begging him to. Humiliating herself by telling him what those men had said — what they all thought of her in his cousin's home.

"I want to know every single thing they said, Flambé, and then I'll address it point by point. I can see overhearing this conver-

262

sation really hurt you and I wish that you had come to me immediately, although I can understand why you didn't. Please continue."

She was grateful that he didn't portray any emotion. His expression didn't change. His voice didn't change and that gave her the courage to keep going.

"They said you don't give a damn about women. About anyone other than your cousins and maybe their wives, but they doubted that. In your families, most of the women are killed after they provide their husbands with sons."

His expression remained the same, that mask was in place. He didn't flinch or look as if anyone was saying anything that was crazy.

"They said that you killed the men watching us at your house. You went out and hunted them down and you killed them, just like you had to have killed the ones following us when we were on our way to see Brent Shriver."

"That's it? That's everything?"

"Only that you told Mitya it was difficult to find a true submissive, especially one your leopard didn't want to rip to shreds, and I was a true submissive and Shturm was enamoured with Flamme."

263

He nodded. "First, Mitya and I did have a discussion some time ago, before I ever met you, that I couldn't hope to find a woman who would suit my particular needs. My cousin is considered rather dark and very sexually demanding. I am much darker and more demanding. Both of us know this and he was worried about me. It was unfortunate that we had the discussion within the hearing of men we trusted."

He reached for the bottle of water again and held it to her lips. "Drink. Do you need to come out of the ropes? Or do you want to continue with the discussion in them?"

She wanted to stay bound. She felt safer. Comforted. "I'm good."

"He knows Shturm is a killer and that it was dangerous for me to go to the club, but it was my only outlet. I was careful, but that solution wasn't going to last forever. As for manipulating you, I suppose I can and will sexually, just like tonight, but you could have said no at any point. Those men are selling you short. When it comes to our sexual relationship, we both, fortunately, enjoy the same thing. Outside of that, we are going to have to work things out. Manipulation is not going to work on you in our day-to-day life."

Flambé knew that much was true. He

couldn't manipulate her outside of the bedroom.

"As for doing whatever I want with someone like you, you love the ropes the way I do, so yes, I can do whatever I want and I don't have to worry that you'll find the things I want or need repulsive. You made that very clear to me, although whoever was gossiping has no idea what they were talking about because they were making shit up. As for being my toy, you aren't anyone's toy. You're my woman and we're partners sexually. You have the right to say what you want or don't want and I'll respect that."

He stepped close to her and cupped her face gently in his hands. "Do I give a damn about most women? No. I love my cousins' wives. I am already falling for you and know that it isn't going to take much to just keep going in all the way. Do I think that's a good thing? No. I don't. Like I said, I'm much darker than Mitya, and I've got things inside me that sometimes escape. They aren't always good. You're capable of unleashing those things."

He stepped away from her again and went back to wherever it was he put the water and camera. He moved around her, taking several closeups of the ruby clamps. "Your life with me isn't going to be easy, Flambé,

265

and I'm not going to pretend it will be, although I will always try to give you everything you want when I can. I'll care for you with everything in me. You'll have that. So that bullshit about not caring for you is just that — bullshit. I know you and your leopard can hear the truth."

She could. The relief was so tremendous she wanted to cry. At the same time, she had been around so many male shifters who were so good at deceiving their mates that a part of her, that hurt part, filed the things those men said away in her head.

"I told you about the lair we came from. The women were murdered after they gave birth to sons. My own mother was murdered. Most times, the sons were expected to participate. I refused. Mitya refused. Gorya, Fyodor and Timur refused. We were forced to leave and all of us have a price on our heads. Again, I shared this with you. Maybe not the details because I don't want you to have nightmares, but we got out."

He suddenly looked directly at her again. "As for hunting the men Matherson had on my property, men he was using to try to kidnap you, damn straight I hunted them and I killed them. I sent him a message loud and clear that he wasn't going to hurt you in any way. He went after you again and I sent him the same message. Mitya added an exclamation point by joining me. I don't think he got exactly who he was messing with at first."

He took several more photographs, put down the camera and then lowered her until her breasts were level with his mouth. "You have to be getting tired." Very quickly he unscrewed the clamp on her right breast and as it dropped into his hand and the blood rushed painfully back, his mouth covered her nipple with soothing heat. He did the same to the left. All the while he tugged and played the rope like the artist he was so that it sang along her nerve endings, bringing them to vivid life.

"Sevastyan." His name came out a plea. Almost a sob.

He quickly shoved the knots aside as he lowered his trousers and, digging his hands into her hips, slammed his cock into her inflamed, slick sheath. The aggressive thrust drove her bottom against the cross so that the thick knot tangled deep in the bundle of sensitive nerve endings. She cried out as flames seemed to lick at her body from the inside out.

He moved in her over and over, relentlessly, feeding the fire until it engulfed her, rushing over her so strongly there wasn't

267

one cell in her body that didn't feel compromised, that didn't feel the contractions in some powerful way.

He continued surging into her harder and deeper, rocking her body, when the solid boards behind her refused to allow any give to them. The position he had her tied had her wide open to him, completely allowing him to drive into her, angling his body to keep his cock positioned perfectly to cause the most friction over her inflamed clit, over her most sensitive spot where her sheath clamped so tightly down on him and grasped and milked at him greedily. Then she felt him erupting like pure fire, coating the walls of her sheath with molten seed, rope after rope triggering more violent shocks until she was hanging in the ropes, unable to keep her head up. Unable to think or breathe properly.

Sevastyan's arms went around her and he lowered her right into his lap as he took her to the floor, loosening the ropes to allow her legs to straighten, rubbing the blood-flow back into them as he did. He quickly unknotted the chain of large knots from the diamond that looped from her front to her back, freeing that thong, and then the binding on her arms. He spent a great deal of time massaging her arms while she sat on his lap.

"I've got you, baby," he murmured softly. "Just rest. You're not hurt anywhere, are you? No place the rope was too tight?" He ran his hand expertly under the remaining halter to check that the bindings weren't digging into her skin.

She shook her head and nuzzled her face into his chest. She was exhausted. She was in excellent physical condition and even though it seemed as if she had been in the ropes a long time, she actually hadn't been. He had even lowered her to give her a break. She knew what he had been doing.

"Good. Even if you're loving what we're doing, Flambé, you have to tell me if something isn't right. We'll correct it and go on. We can't take a chance on you getting hurt." He slipped more rope off her body.

Strangely, the more the rope came off, the more she felt naked and vulnerable without it. She burrowed deeper into him. "I really like being in the ropes."

"That's a good thing since I like tying you. You look beautiful in rope. Some people don't get it, and that's all right. It's not their thing. I needed an outlet for the artist in me as well as that darker side of me. It was also something that helped me stay at a distance

269

and protected the women from my leopard." He brushed a kiss against her neck as he continued to massage her arms and shoulders gently.

She opened her eyes enough to look up at him. "That was so incredibly erotic. A million times better than what I saw you do in that room."

He rubbed his face against hers. "It wouldn't be safe to take you into one of those rooms. There are cameras everywhere. I made certain before I came in here that Cain didn't have any hidden ones. I also made it clear what would happen to him if he ever photographed you. He knows better than to cross me."

She frowned. "I don't understand. Photograph me? What does that mean?"

He scraped his teeth on her bare shoulder and a fission of desire slid down her spine. "You think you're alone when you come here to plant, Flambé. Cain has tried to set you up more than once. He left you alone in his office to watch the screens so you could see what went on in the rooms. He asked if you wanted him to show you the various apparatuses to see how they worked. He's a leopard, a dominant. He recognizes a submissive. He compromises clients to protect his other clients. He never uses footage unless he has to, but he's ruthless enough."

She blinked up at him, trying to understand. She hadn't done anything with Cain. She'd gone to his office that one time, but he hadn't been there.

"Had you gotten yourself off while you were here watching and he caught you on camera, he would have held that over your head," he said bluntly.

Shifters weren't particularly shy about sex and she might not have been as a rule, but she had a very prosperous business and she needed it to help others survive. She wasn't about to throw their lives away because she was so anxious to have sex she wasn't thinking, which was why she was very worried about the emergence of her female leopard.

"I should have thought of that. Not that I was getting myself off in the club."

"Good, although the idea does have its merits."

She laughed softly. "I should have known you'd say that."

"Thank you for trusting me enough to tell me the truth tonight, Flambé. We both know you didn't have to. I was afraid you'd tell me to go to hell, and I wasn't certain how else to get you to feel safe enough to tell me."

271

"I wanted to tell you, I was just so hurt and I was afraid it was true. In a sense, because part of it was true, it was easy to believe the rest. You're so extraordinary, and I feel so ordinary that it's easy enough to believe."

"Flambé." There was warning in his voice.

"You would never have looked at me if I wasn't a submissive and my leopard didn't appeal to Shturm."

His laughter made her toes want to curl. "You would never have looked at me if I wasn't a dominant, a rigger, and Shturm didn't appeal to your little female."

He totally had her there.

"I'm getting a little worried that she isn't making an appearance," he added.

Flambé took a deep breath. Now they were getting into muddy waters. "She was very upset when those men said all those things about me — and about her." She rubbed her palm up and down his thigh. The soft material of his trousers felt sexy over the muscle of his thigh. "Matherson really frightened her as well."

Sevastyan rubbed his chin on top of her head. "She'll probably feel more secure once she sees everything is all right at the house. You can work on the designs and bring your crew out. I really would like you

272

to start an indoor garden like this one that we can build onto the house. I have the perfect spot in mind for it. I've already got the beams in place that would hold the necessary rigging for suspension. I was going to use the garages for something else and changed my mind. I have lofts and pulley systems in place and the high ceilings are there. We'd have to convert the outside walls to glass but that's easy enough. The two garages connect and both are enormous. We could start with one."

Flambé heard the enthusiasm in his voice, but she had to be so careful not to be entirely sucked in. Just the fact that he'd said those things to his cousin about finding a submissive, one on their first life cycle, was another strike against him. It didn't matter how much she loved sex with him or how compatible they were when it came to sex. Eventually, she knew how things ended up with shifters.

She wanted the enthusiasm for the project to be as real later as it was right then. A garden for them was a project they could do together. She wanted something that was theirs. Something they could start their life going forward with. In a perfect world, he would support her business and her need to continue rescuing shifter species as their numbers in the world diminished. She would do her best to understand what he did and try to be supportive. Sadly, she'd seen too much of shifter life. The real world didn't work that way.

"I've got the schedule worked out, Sevastyan." She tried to suppress a yawn. All she really wanted to do was sleep. "My crew will be working on the property in three weeks. That will give me enough time to figure out all the trees, plants and design work, order them, the dirt we'll need and . . ." She trailed off, waving her hand. "I'll take care of the details."

"You do that. I'll take care of the other details." He stood up easily, with her still in his arms.

"What would those be?"

"The marriage license. Where. When. Those kinds of things."

Her heart stuttered. That couldn't happen, no matter what kind of fairy tale she wanted to be living in.

274

9

Sevastyan stared out the window of his cousin's large pool room. He'd known all along the day of reckoning would be coming. No one ever escaped it forever. He had hoped for a little more time. Mitya had already gone through so much and he and Ania had barely started their lives together. They were still dancing around each other, madly in love, but not quite in sync yet.

He sighed and glanced at the door leading to the hallway. Flambé was in a small office most likely hunched over her desk, drawing various sketches for her clients — and for him — to look over. She amazed him with her endless ideas. They were brilliant. She was brilliant. He'd had no time with her. None.

They knew very little about each other and hadn't managed to establish much in the way of trust. He hoped the things he'd told her, what little of himself he'd given

275

her, was enough to get them through the hell that was coming.

Their relationship hadn't progressed no matter how hard he'd tried to move it forward. There were reasons she couldn't get married. She rarely told him anything personal about herself. She responded eagerly to sex wherever and whenever he initiated it, but rarely wanted to be touched outside otherwise. She didn't pull away from him, but she never held his hand or reached out to him, touching his body, especially if anyone else was around. He found their relationship frustrating at times because he didn't understand it — and her leopard had been stubbornly silent, adding to the frustration. Sevastyan knew he wasn't the best at relationships. He had no idea how to be a good partner to a woman, but he tried.

Now, it seemed, time for them had run out. Flambé had courage, but she wasn't a violent person. He was extremely violent. She might fight beside him if she absolutely had to, and he doubted if she would hesitate to kill, but she wasn't the type of person to walk up, stick a gun to someone's head and pull the trigger. She would definitely not be okay with the kinds of things he did in his job. The premise of their work might appeal to her, but not the actual day-to-day process.

He closed his eyes and shook his head. Mitya knew she wasn't like the other women. He'd told Sevastyan. Warned him. Lectured him. Sevastyan didn't need the warnings or the lectures. It was far too late for all of them — especially Flambé. She had to find a way to live with him. He swore to himself he would make things as easy on her as possible, but now, with this new development, life was going to be hell for all of them.

There was no putting off the inevitable and he strode out of the room and down the hall to his cousin's study. Mitya was at his desk reading the reports Drake Donovan sent him on the latest crimes and who they needed to hit and when. Sevastyan didn't bother to knock. He just walked in and shut the door, indicating to Mitya he didn't want anyone, even their most trusted men, to overhear the conversation.

Mitya looked up alertly and turned off his tablet, giving Sevastyan his complete attention.

"Rolan is in the United States. He came in through Miami. Sasha Bogomolov sent word he came in under diplomatic protection." Sasha Bogomolov was one of their

277

shifter allies out of Miami. "Rolan has his own men with him, his security detail. He stayed one night at a hotel and there was a private plane waiting for him and his men. He flew to New Orleans. I find it very telling that New Orleans seems to keep being a repeating factor whenever we have trouble. He was in New Orleans for three days. I've got our people looking into what he did there. Where he went, who he spoke with."

Sevastyan kept his voice completely expressionless. Rolan Amurov was his father, the man who beat his mother to death with his bare fists in front of Sevastyan. Before the life had drained from her, Rolan set his leopard loose on her so the savage animal could tear her apart. Sevastyan would never forget that sight as long as he lived. The rage in him would never be satisfied. The hatred in him was as alive in that moment as it had been when he was a young teen, beaten and bloody, helpless to stop his father from killing his mother.

Still, his heartbeat didn't change. His expression didn't change. His tone didn't either. He met Mitya's eyes without blinking. Without emotion. He was disciplined. He was prepared. He was merciless. "Rolan has sworn to kill you, Fyodor, Timur, Gorya and, of course, me. You first. You bested your father and in order for him to prove to the other lairs that he is the strongest and the most dangerous *vor* of all time, he has to kill you."

Sevastyan knew the real reason Rolan wanted to kill Mitya and Sevastyan both. He despised them. He had despised his older brother Lazar, Mitya's father. Lazar was cruel, crueler even than Rolan.

"Let him come, Sevastyan. He's coming into our territory and he won't be as prepared as he thinks he is," Mitya said.

"From New Orleans he went to Houston. He's gathering men-shifters and he's gathering information. He isn't coming in blind. He isn't as arrogant as Lazar was. Or Patva, for that matter." He named his uncles, both now dead. "Mitya, I'm responsible for Ania's safety and yours. I don't want you to make this harder for me. You gave me your word that you'd abide by my rules. I don't tell you to do things because I want power. I tell you to keep you and Ania safe."

Mitya drummed his fingers on the desk top, betraying his agitation. "Who keeps you safe?"

"I know what I'm doing. You have to have faith in me. I plan for everything. I always have backup plans. You two are the main priority at all times."

Mitya jerked his head toward the hallway. "What about Flambé?"

"She'll be close. I have a safe room. You do as well. Both houses are nearly impossible to gain entrance into. We've locked them down tight."

He wasn't going to be drawn into an idiotic discussion on who he would protect first — his woman or his cousin. That was pointless. He'd been guarding Mitya for as long as he could remember, even back in the old days, back when they were in the lairs. He'd done his best to watch his cousin's back just as Mitya has watched his. Flambé would be safe because few people knew about her. Sevastyan hadn't yet married her. That was a plus. He would insist she was either at Mitya's estate or his. She would do as she was told. She might not like it, but she would do it.

"I gave you my word, Sevastyan," Mitya conceded. "What do you want to do?"

"I've already made the move to get eyes on Rolan. In the meantime, I'm sending for shifters we can trust. We'll build up our own army here. Rolan will probably send in a couple of mercenary shifter teams to test us, someone we won't connect with him. I'm going to suggest to Timur that Fyodor take Evangeline and the twins and go on an extended vacation until I send word that we're clear. Timur and Ashe will go with them. Timur would never allow Fyodor to go anywhere without guarding him. I'm asking Gorya to stay with us. I trust him implicitly."

"It won't be easy getting Fyodor to go."

"He has children," Sevastyan pointed out. "Timur can be very persuasive especially when it comes to Evangeline and the twins' safety. Fyodor has had enough time to learn to trust his judgment."

Mitya tried to give him a hard stare. "Is that some kind of a crack at me?"

Sevastyan shrugged. "Only if you aren't listening." He glanced at his watch. "I've got to get ahold of Drake. I need to pull in some of the others I trust."

"I trust Miron and Rodion Galerkin, but you beat the shit out of them and put them out of commission," Mitya groused. "Was that really necessary?"

Mitya was fishing. He had no idea why Sevastyan had come to the house in the middle of the night a couple of weeks earlier, yanked Miron out of his bed and beat him to a bloody pulp. He'd calmly walked past three guards to find Rodion and done the same to him, almost without breaking a sweat. He'd left both men on the

281

ground and just walked off into the night without a word.

Sevastyan stared at him with cool eyes, never blinking, not bothering to answer. He wouldn't have done it had he not considered it necessary. Mitya could order the men to tell him why, if he wanted to know that bad, but neither man would be able to talk for a while. Sevastyan had made certain of that. The doctor had wired their jaws shut, which meant they couldn't shift for a short period of time. Shifters were fast healers, but their leopards would be furious, and they wouldn't be so happy drinking their food. He figured it might give them some time to think before they gossiped — especially about him.

Mitya sighed. "You're a mean son of a bitch, Sevastyan."

"That's what makes me good at what I do." He planted both hands on the desk and leaned over to look at his cousin. "Mitya, I'm not willing to lose you or Ania. I'll be talking to her, but you do it first. You curb that streak in her so I don't have to. She won't like me much if I have to lock her up."

"She thinks you're going to let her drive."

"Neither of you are going anywhere. The safest place for both of you is right here. I

282

want her out of that garage once I tell you he's actually out of Houston. At the moment, you're safe enough, so if you want to take her to dinner, or do something special, get it done now. You've probably got another week at the most."

Mitya nodded. "Thanks, Sevastyan. I'll let you know my plans well in advance." He cleared his throat. "I know you don't like to talk about this, but I think it's necessary to point out that sometimes leopards can make mistakes on their first life cycles."

"Don't start, Mitya." Sevastyan glared at him. "We've had this conversation three times."

"She doesn't look at you the way a woman should look at her man. You said yourself her leopard hasn't made her presence known for a long time. There could be a mistake."

"You don't know the first thing about her."

"Do you?" Mitya challenged.

Pushing down the inevitable rage, Sevastyan left the room, glanced at his watch again and headed for the small office at the very end of the hall. Just thinking about his woman sent little flames licking over his skin and down his spine. Deliberately he slowed his steps so he could savor the way his body responded to the thought of her. It didn't

283

matter that he'd just been thinking some of the very things Mitya had been saying. He knew Flambé was the right woman for him. He just had to figure out why she wasn't so certain.

His blood turned into a raging inferno while a fireball rolled and twisted in his gut. He'd needed sex all the time before he found Flambé, but he could force himself to go without. Now, she was his addiction. His obsession. He craved the sight of her. The touch of her skin. Her hair. The scent of her. The taste of her.

He dreamt of her. Woke up in the middle of the night reaching for her. Opened his eyes in the morning, his body hard and painful, erotic images pouring into his mind, all of her. Now, the whips of lightning flashing through his body to strike at his cock and balls aroused him with every step he took.

The room given to Flambé to work in was the last of the offices down the long hallway. He yanked open the door and closed it, locking it as he did so. Sometimes, when he came into the room, all he could think of was eating her alive. He would strip her, plant her on the desk and put his mouth between her legs. Now, his cock was a monster, driving him into a frenzy of urgent, almost desperate hunger.

Flambé stood bent over the desk. The light was on under the drawing she was examining and she had a pencil in her mouth, her teeth biting down on it. Her hair spilled down, unusual for her. As a rule she wore it up, but clearly she'd pulled out the tie keeping it drawn away from her face, so the silky mass cascaded down her back. She half turned to look at him over her shoulder.

He was on her in seconds, his leopard fast, the room so small he covered the distance in a one leap. He put a hand between her shoulder blades to press her down until her breasts lay on the surface of the desk.

"Stay still." He reached with both hands to open her jeans, yanking them down along with her panties. "Kick off your shoes and step out of your clothes."

She obeyed him while he pulled her T-shirt up and over her head, ridding her of her bra at the same time. She lifted her body just enough that he could slide the material out from under her before he pressed her down again. He liked her body bare, all that smooth skin for him to see and feel. She didn't seem to like light touches. She winced when he touched her that way, so he always used a firm, hard grip. Possessive strokes.

"The next time I tie you." He used the top of his boot to nudge her legs wide. Then wider still. "I'm going to leave rope marks on your skin so I can see them for a day or two." He opened his jeans and released his burning cock. He bent forward so she could feel the friction of his clothing rubbing along her body just before his teeth nipped her earlobe. His fingers slid into her entrance to find her slick with heat. "I see you like the idea."

"Yes." She whispered her response.

He didn't wait. There was no waiting. He gripped her hips and slammed into her, watching in awe as her body swallowed his cock. She looked so small, stretching to accommodate his size. He felt her sheath, that scorching hot tunnel fighting his invasion, but giving way as he drove through those tight muscles gripping him, the friction unreal. He wanted to roar with ecstasy. She surrounded him like a fiery, silken fist as he surged into her again and again, using his strength, burying himself in that perfect haven he never wanted to leave.

He might want to stay there forever, but he had a job and he needed to ensure he set everything in place for all of his cousins to be safe. He moved faster and deeper in her, watching her body slide into her desk, each

286

jolt causing her breasts to skid and bounce over the glass overlay, adding to the visual appeal as he fucked her hard.

Flambé's bright hair went wild, the silken mass spilling everywhere. Her naked body, nearly buried beneath his fully clothed, much larger one, was a sight, her curves all feminine. Her breath went ragged, labored, hips pushing back into his, desperate for him, as her body coiled tighter and tighter. White-hot lightning lashed at him, struck hard, surrounded and clamped down, strangling his cock. A wicked, silken fist squeezed while a thousand scorching-hot tongues stroked and licked along his shaft and over his crown. Twin out-of-control firestorms settled in his balls, raged there and sent a volcano erupting in hot jetting pulses, coating the walls of her sheath with his semen over and over. Thunder roared while her body rippled powerfully around his.

He lay over the top of her, finding his breath while aftershocks triggered Flambé's body to clamp down over and over around his cock. He savored the feeling, just holding her, wishing for more time with her. When things settled down, he wanted to turn his cousin's security over to Gorya for a couple of weeks and just spend time with Flambé at their home. Just the two of them.

Or take her off where no one would interrupt them.

Reluctantly, he straightened and gently helped her to stand as well, turning her to face him. "Clean me up, baby," he ordered. "I'm short on time or I'd spend a little time with you."

"Because you spend so much time with me when we're here," she said, flicking him a quick glance from under her long red-gold-tipped lashes.

He put his hand on her shoulder. "I visit you at least four times a day before we head home." He put pressure on her until she knelt down. She was gorgeous naked. He loved to look at her body. He couldn't help running his hands from her shoulders over the curves of her breasts to her nipples.

"I don't actually see you those four times, Sevastyan," Flambé pointed out. "You strip me, pick me up, put me on the desk, devour me and leave. Or have me strip, and you bend me over the desk and fuck my brains out, or take me against the wall or on the floor, but then you leave immediately."

He refrained from smiling. She didn't have the least bit of complaint in her voice, although if one took her words, they might think she was complaining. Once, when he called her into his office, which was three

288

times larger than hers, to ask her to go over her schedule with him, he'd gotten a phone call. She had crawled under his desk, unzipped his jeans and sucked him dry. His little Flambé loved sex. He had considered keeping her under that desk with a variety of different ties. He didn't want anyone to come in and find her that way. Their rope work was between them, an intimacy created between the two of them.

She ducked her head and he felt her tongue on the inside of his thighs. It took every bit of discipline he had not to jerk his body. As it was, his muscles reacted, fingers of desire snaking up toward his groin in spite of the explosive release he'd just had. She wrapped her arms around his legs and began to use her tongue in the way of the shifters. They were an oral species, and Flambé was extremely sensual in everything she did with him. She took her time, paying close attention to his body, to every part of him, making certain there wasn't a spot on him she missed.

It was both heaven and hell to feel the rasp of her velvet tongue sliding over his balls and cock, that glide and then the way she took him in her mouth and sucked to make certain he was clean. He wanted to start all over again, but damn it, he was out of time.

He caught her hair in his fist and pulled her head off of him, wanting to roar with rage that his time wasn't his own.

"Get dressed before someone comes in, Flambé."

Her gaze darted to the door. "Didn't you lock it?" Anxiety crept into her eyes.

He pulled her to her feet. "I'm teasing you, *malen'koye plamya.* I'm slipping out. Lock the door behind me and clean up. I'm not certain what time I'll be able to make it home tonight."

"Do you want me to take the car and you catch a ride with someone? Or do you want me to find a ride?" She followed him to the door.

He didn't want her going home without him. It wasn't that he thought there was any immediate danger. He had eyes on Rolan and the man was at present in Houston. As for Matherson, Sevastyan planned on paying him a visit. The shifter didn't want to lose any more of his leopards. He wasn't about to make a move against the Amurovs, especially on their property. He hadn't been able to draw him back to the property or convince him to come after Sevastyan either, no matter how much he'd taunted the coward.

He didn't believe that Matherson would

290

find another woman he thought was easier prey either, as Mitya had suggested several times. There was something very special about Flambé and once you were close to her — and Matherson had been on many occasions — it was difficult not to fall under her spell. That brought him up short. She liked sex. Was it possible she'd had sex with him, a one-night stand before she realized what kind of man he was? He doubted too many men or any shifters would be satisfied with only one night of sex with Flambé. How the hell was he going to ask her a question like that without getting her riled up? She seemed a little moody lately, especially when she was at his cousin's home. Still, he felt he had to know.

"Babe, did you ever hook up with Matherson? Even for a couple of hours?" He just came out with it.

She went very still, the smile fading from her face. Hell. He knew that was going to happen. He didn't change expressions.

"You know what, Sevastyan? I don't want to have this conversation with you. I watched you hook up with several women in that club. I know there had to be so many more. There were, weren't there?" Her eyes glittered like twin emeralds, no amber in them whatsoever.

291

"Yes. That's beside the point. I need to know about you and Matherson."

"You don't need to know about me and anyone else. I didn't ask you about your life before me and I don't expect you to ask about my life before you."

She turned away from him, tossing her wild head of red hair, so much of it, like a crimson mane of fireworks. His leopard roared, raking at him. That volcano inside of him threatened to erupt. He wanted to leap after her, take her to the floor and pound into her with his suddenly engorged cock, but there was a whisper of unease in his mind.

A pattern was developing here, one he so easily could get into. They both were extremely sexual. He was very dominant and she played into that so easily. Was she deliberately provoking him? Provoking his leopard? He was always honest with himself. It would be easy enough to do. She was everything he could possibly want and sex with her was explosive. Unbelievable.

He asked questions of her and the next thing they were having sex — wild, uninhibited sex — not having a conversation. He took a deep breath for control. He had years of discipline. Years of experience. He had to stop reacting with his body and his dominant personality and start figuring out his woman and what exactly she was hiding. If they continued making their relationship all about sex and not about the two of them, they weren't going to get anywhere.

"Flambé, you misunderstood me. I should have explained what I meant." He turned, closed and locked the door. She stood by her desk, turning back to him, her expression wary.

"I would never question you about past lovers out of jealousy, not that I'm not capable of that very unattractive emotion. I'm a possessive man and not into sharing."

"Those women at the club had other men."

He shrugged. "Those men were their partners. In their relationships, they wanted or needed things someone outside their relationship could provide. The male liked to watch and his female liked to be tied and fucked by someone else. I needed release and to be able to practice my art. My leopard wanted to kill anyone I touched. It was the best solution in order to get what I needed and keep everyone safe. I don't want any other man touching you. I thought I made that clear to you. I don't want you touching any other man. I have no intention of being with another woman. My

293

leopard wants only your leopard. We're exclusive in this relationship. I would hope that you feel the same way."

He watched her face, her eyes, the entire time, needing to see, to read her expression. He wanted Shturm to be alert. Did she love and need sex so much that he wasn't enough for her? Was that what was putting that niggling doubt that had been so slowly growing in his mind? Was that what was making his leopard restless? He couldn't believe that he was even entertaining the idea.

Relief crept into her eyes. Relaxed the tension in her face. She didn't want another partner. That helped with the knots in his gut, but there was something elusive about her, something he wasn't quite getting.

"Matherson seems to have a pattern, *malen'koye plamya*. He left his lair when the elders ran him off because, even though with his money he could have hired an army of mercenary shifters to take one of the women and run with her, it was too dangerous. Too much trouble. He goes hunting for easier prey."

She frowned and shook her head, resting one hand on her desk, leaning her weight on her palm and one hip. That small shift in her stance gave him an intriguing view of her body, pushing her bare breasts and one rounded hip forward so that he could just glimpse the fiery curls covering her mound. His body tightened the way it always did when he looked at her. Hot blood roiled in his balls and pounded through his cock. He forced himself to stay in complete control, refusing to react, even though her nipples stood out in stark relief, tempting, enticing him to stop all conversation and just go to her.

"It isn't exactly easy to find women shifters, Sevastyan, as you well know. Most of those people in that club aren't shifters. Cain may own it and he may be a shifter, but the vast majority of his clients are just regular humans. Even going to the rain forests or Africa won't guarantee Franco finding a female shifter."

"That's true, but he found a few. Unfortunately, while he was looking, he got a taste for hunting. We're all leopard, Flambé, never forget that. We aren't human. We may look civilized, but we aren't. Some may be more than others, but the bottom line is, we're leopard and we're predators."

He could see the goose bumps rise on her skin. The heat in her eyes. Her body responded in spite of her determination not to at his declaration. She was a female leopard and there was no doubt that she was wired to find the male who could see to the survival of her children. She might not want to have that trait, but she did. Like him, she was very strong in many of her leopard's attributes.

"Matherson should have moved on. He shouldn't have sent his men against me once he had me investigated, and when his men disappeared, believe me, he had me investigated. The name Amurov, as you know, is very suspect. He had to think in terms of a crime family, yet he still attacked us and tried to get you away from me. I had to wonder why he would do that."

Her gaze dropped to the floor. She moistened her lips with the tip of her tongue. Leopards were oral and their shifter counterparts were equally so. He refused to let his gaze linger on that perfect sinful temptation. The image of her lips stretched around his cock might be in his mind, but he wouldn't let it show on his face. She had to believe he was in control at all times. They seemed to be in some kind of battle and he'd missed the reason why altogether.

"Why would that be, Sevastyan?"

Her voice had gone very soft, but he heard her and was very tuned to her. She didn't seem to realize that the more he tied her, the more he had to learn to read her body, her face, all the little nuances that made up Flambé Carver. He had memorized her body, every damn inch of her. That beautiful face, the bone structure that lay beneath it. He heard the small note of fear and his leopard heard it as well. Shturm clawed and raked, furious. They both knew what that note meant.

"No man would just walk away after fucking you, Flambé. You set up a craving in a man. He gets addicted."

He stalked her with slow, measured steps, purposefully giving her the impression of danger. Letting her see the inherent cruelty in his leopard, in him. He could be without mercy. It made him very good at his job. It also made his leopard a very good mate. He knew it was the very trait that both attracted and repelled her.

She was addicted to him. To their wild, passionate, *feral* relationship. She was addicted to the ropes. She never knew what he was going to do or ask of her and she was addicted to that as well. He kept her off balance and craving him. Flambé might be a submissive woman in the bedroom, but she was a woman with such a demanding sexual nature that unless a man could satisfy her needs, she would move on fast.

He knew he was right about Franco

Matherson. At some time, they must have met casually in a bar. In a nightclub. He'd probably had no idea she was leopard. They'd talked, they'd danced and she'd spent a couple of hours with him and left. A couple of hours hadn't been enough and somewhere along the line he'd realized she was a shifter. Matherson wasn't going to let her go.

Sevastyan stepped right into her. Close. The height difference between them was over a foot. His shoulders were wide. He caught her chin in his hand and forced her to look at him. "Where did you meet him?"

"A club. In South Africa. I was staying at a hotel near the airport."

Her gaze tried to shift away from his, but he refused to allow it, his eyes wholly focused, boring into hers, forcing her to face him. He didn't blink, giving her the stare of his cat. The hunter. She was damn well going to answer him this time. He was standing so close to her he felt her body hitch as she tried to pull in air.

"I was at the bar and he came in. He looked like he could handle himself and I was . . ." She broke off, her voice low.

"Keep going. You were looking for someone to fuck, I get it." He was deliberately crude. He wanted to shake her. He didn't give a damn that she'd been with men before him, only that she hadn't been safe.

"I'm not ashamed, Sevastyan, if you're thinking I am." Her eyes went golden on him. "I do feel guilty because I was so needy that I just wasn't paying attention to the warning signs that were there. I should have been. I let him spot me and it wasn't that hard to get him to take me to his room."

Sevastyan was certain that was the truth. She was beautiful. Small and curvaceous. To a man like Matherson, she would look like someone he could have his way with. Little did he know she was a tigress in the bedroom.

"I knew he was leopard. I could see it in his eyes. He had no idea I was. She wasn't close to rising. I wasn't even sure she would ever rise at that point. He wasn't that great in bed and I just wanted out of there as fast as possible afterward. I had to initiate everything and it isn't my thing, as you well know."

Sevastyan knew that was most of Flambé's problem and why she went out so often seeking partners. She was never satisfied. The men might look like they could satisfy her, but they had no idea how. Thankfully, he did.

"He wanted my phone number. I gave

some lame excuse and that's when I realized I could be in trouble." She shrugged. "I soothed him, made noises like we'd meet up again and then got the hell out of there. I was coming back to the States. I'd never told him where I was from so I didn't think he could find me."

Sevastyan ran his hand down the back of her head, down all that soft silk. He bent and brushed a kiss over her upturned mouth. "Thank you, Flambé. I needed to know or I wouldn't have asked." His thumb slid over her lower lip. "If you need me, baby, text me."

He brushed his mouth very gently over hers a second time and then dropped his hands, although it was difficult not to touch her body when he could feel her hunger for him all over again and his blood pounded through his cock so hard, he thought it might burst.

He strode back across the room, pausing at the door. "Wait for me to bring you home. If you get hungry, text me and I'll get you something to eat, or we'll have dinner with Mitya and Ania."

She shook her head, her hands gripping the edges of the desk until her knuckles turned white. "I'm not that comfortable with them yet."

He dropped his hand on the doorknob, hating to leave her. Not because she was naked and he wanted her all over again, but because she suddenly looked vulnerable and a little unhappy.

Flambé was very self-sufficient. She didn't require entertaining. She didn't ask for much. She hadn't balked when he told her he wanted her to work from his cousin's home rather than theirs even though he knew she would be less comfortable. She didn't object to the bodyguards he sent with her when she went to work on other projects and he couldn't go.

"You mean Mitya. You and Ania are thick as thieves." He couldn't exactly blame her. Mitya hadn't been that welcoming, although that was because he was worried for Sevastyan.

She shrugged. "Go to work, Sevastyan. I'm perfectly fine. I'm trying to design the indoor garden and it's a massive project."

"I thought we were designing that together."

"We are, but I have to put together the skeleton for it. We need a foundation."

Sevastyan nodded his head, not entirely certain what she meant. His mind was already on what he needed to do about Franco Matherson. Closing the door behind him softly, he stalked down the wide hall, wondering what the hell he was going to do about her. She was getting to him. He wasn't so certain he was getting to her. That was the thing about Flambé. She was as elusive as hell.

He set up a security detail to watch over his cousin and those in the residence while he was absent, and he indicated to Kirill and Matvei to accompany him. He wanted to slip away from the Amurov estate without his woman's knowledge. Her office was at the back of the very large house and unless Ania noticed and mentioned his absence to her, she wouldn't be the wiser. In any case, he came and went often. She rarely asked, but if she did, he didn't want to try to lie to her. He would have to tell her the truth and that might not go over very well.

The sun had already set some time ago as they made their way silently through the streets toward the large estate Franco Matherson had leased on the outskirts of San Antonio. They took a roundabout route so if their vehicle was caught on camera, their destination could easily be Evangeline's bakery or one of the many businesses the Amurov family owned. Sevastyan would make certain to stop somewhere along the way long enough to make it appear as if he had a destination that would hold up in court if necessary.

He had reports on Matherson, none of them good. It seemed to him that the man's mental condition was deteriorating slowly over time. He had become somewhat of a megalomaniac, much like Sevastyan's uncle Lazar, who had ruled the lair with such cruelty. He had gotten away with murder so often that he sunk lower and lower over the years, thinking he was entitled to kill anyone who crossed him. That meant that Matherson was doubly dangerous to Flambé, because it made him unpredictable.

"The estate is a few blocks over, Sevastyan. Your club is up two blocks on the left. We could leave the car there, walk to the park and shift and make our way to his home. It's a little risky because it's still a bit of a distance and there's bound to be dogs out, but it's a cover," Kirill ventured.

It was a solid plan. He could go in after he took care of business, talk to Cain for a few minutes and then get back to Flambé. "Sounds good. Let's go for it. But keep your leopards under control. We can't start killing any animals in the neighborhood no matter how obnoxious they are." Dogs were always barky around cats. It was more than annoying.

303

"If you have to spend any time at the club," Matvei added, "you have your locker there. You can get dressed, wander around and let the cameras pick you up. The fucking cops aren't going to know what you do or don't do there."

That wasn't a bad idea either. He'd have that for an alibi when Matherson and his bodyguards disappeared and people started asking questions. The cops always came to the Amurovs. Knowing Matherson had been stalking Flambé, they would question Sevastyan straightaway.

The club parking lot was full, not a bad thing at all. That meant more witnesses to him being there. The three quickly made their way through the dark streets, avoiding any street lights. They jogged through the empty park and cut through a lot that took them to the upscale neighborhood where Matherson leased his estate. It was a two-story contemporary home on one acre behind a tall wrought-tron fence. With a custom pool and multitevel decks, it was a dream home for people and would have been nice for leopards with the landscaping, but Sevastyan doubted if Matherson allowed his men the use of the amenities the place provided — the game room and spa.

He had the blueprints of the house and

had memorized the layout of the yard. As they approached the fence, they stripped, rolled their clothes and placed them in the small bags they could sling around their leopards' necks when traveling. In this case, they stashed them. Shifting, they easily leapt over the fence and landed in the yard. All three let the leopards take a few minutes to inhale, to prowl around in silence to get a feel for the shifters guarding Matherson.

Scents were everywhere, heavy on the ground, in the trees and shrubs. Male leopards had sprayed and raked, claiming territory. Tracks were in the dirt, but there was no sign of anyone, human or leopard. The three split up, Matvei jumping up on the deck to walk around the outside of the house and then up on the roof to look for sentries while Kirill and Sevastyan made their way around to look for a way inside.

Doors were locked, but one window was open about half an inch. It appeared to be stuck and Matherson's men were too lazy to bother with it, or it was a trap. Kirill carefully worked at it until he got it to move. Cautiously his leopard stuck his head in and looked around. He sniffed the air and jerked his head out again, shifting head and shoulders. Sevastyan did the same.

"Something's dead inside," Kirill warned.

"Someone," he corrected. "You're going to need that alibi."

"Let's see what we're facing." Sevastyan hoped whoever they found was Matherson, but he knew it wasn't going to be that easy. Men like Matherson seemed to have the devil guarding them.

Kirill pushed his way inside, Sevastyan right behind him. The house had been abandoned hastily. There were three bodies, two women and one man, all human. All three had been killed by a bullet to the head. None wore clothing. It looked as if there had been a huge party thrown, with wine, champagne and various sorts of liquor bottles strewn everywhere along with glasses and broken bowls of chips. To Sevastyan, the room looked staged.

"We can't stay here, Sevastyan. You have to get to that club fast and make an appearance. The timing has to be right," Kirill said. "Matherson is missing and could be presumed dead if they don't suspect him for this. For some reason, he always seems to get a pass."

"I wonder why that is," Sevastyan said, and shifted back fully to his leopard.

306

10

There was pure satisfaction in watching a barren landscape transform into something lush and beautiful. Flambé loved putting her hands in soil. She found the soil grounded her. She also found that watching the people who worked with her moving the trees into position with confidence and sometimes outright joy made her happy.

She loved what she did at every stage. One of her gifts was talking with the client and catching images of what they really wanted when most of the time they were unable to describe with actual words what they envisioned or needed. Often, the client had no idea what they really wanted and she would look at a space and know, after spending time with them, what would best suit them. She loved providing something special and unique for them.

She enjoyed picking out plants that would suit the various landscapes. She worked in all sorts of areas, the urban and rural. She worked in malls and business buildings as well as clubs and private estates and modest homes. She had very wealthy clients who owned acres of land planted with grapes. Others had ranches. The fact that her clients were so different provided the artist in her with continual varied canvases to work on.

Knowing that Sevastyan had bought the Dover estate and her father had done the original layout and planting of the trees, shaping them into an arboreal highway for the leopards, gave her an extra joy in working the property. She felt as if she needed to make certain every single tree she planted added to the beauty of the original vision. Sevastyan wanted the woods continued all the way to the very edge of the property lines between the Dover and Amurov borders. Her father had planted the trees on the Amurov property as well.

Her goal was to eventually grow the trees to connect the branches, make it easy for leopards to run along the limbs and leap from one tree to the next without hindrance. The trees had to be sturdy, with broad trunks and thick, strong branches that she could twist and shape with wire to get them to grow into the positions she needed. The first step was the planting, and that meant primary spots with plenty of room. The roots had to take hold and grow deep. Other taller trees couldn't block the younger ones from the sun. She took great care to give each tree the best start possible while filling in the woods as best she could.

Flambé had two newer leopards, Rory and Etienne, both strawberry, working near the house planting low shrubbery, plants that flowered at various times of the year but wouldn't ever grow high enough to cause Sevastyan concern when it came to security. No leopard could use the flowers or shrubs to hide in if they tried to sneak up on the house or the residents. She had chosen those plants carefully. Both strawberry leopards were men and they'd been with her working in the field about four months. Both had completed two years of college and done very well prior to coming back to work with her in the business.

Rory had lost his mother to a poacher and had taken a bullet in his left side. He limped when he was tired and probably always would. Flambé had been with him when he'd been shot and she'd pulled him into the cave they often used to shift, held off the poachers until her team showed up and gotten Rory out of there. There had been nothing she could do for his mother but stay with her until the life left her and then burn her body and bury the ashes. There had been too many shifters she'd done that for — sat watching helplessly as the life flowed out of them. It was always quick. Some strawberry leopards bled profusely. It was just the reality.

Blaise Brodeur had worked with her father for years before she had taken over the business. She had come home from college and he was well established, a valued member of the team. She relied heavily on him to help teach the newer shifters after they had completed their educations. He was crouched down beside Etienne, pointing to the roots of a plant as the other shifter gently placed it in the hole dug out for it.

She liked Blaise. He was older than her by several years, but sometimes seemed younger. She liked quiet and he was boisterous. It was just his personality, but she knew, when he persisted in asking her out, that they weren't in the least compatible. She needed sex, and had been tempted a few times to give in to his advances, but she hadn't, mostly because he worked for the company. She had a strict policy about mixing business with pleasure. She was very glad now that she had been careful.

They worked well together and had she

been silly and let her need for sex get in the way, she knew it would have become a huge problem between them. Blaise still hadn't found anyone. It was difficult as a shifter. It wasn't like he didn't pick up women, but like most shifters, they looked for another shifter so their leopards had a mate. Mostly, they wanted to find the right leopard for their cat.

"How's it going?" she asked, putting a hand on Rory's shoulder and leaning over him to inspect his work. She was very particular about her flowers and how close they were planted. How deep they were put into the earth. It mattered to her to give them the best opportunity to grow.

He tipped his head back to look up at her. "We've almost got this section finished. Once we started, they went in fast. I like these little flowers. Why did you alternate the varieties?"

"They bloom at different times. It gives us color all year round. I like to provide that for customers if possible."

Blaise sank back on his heels and sent her a quick grin. "They're both doing great. These two really don't need anyone watching over them. Although this isn't Etienne's dream job, he does excellent work."

Rory was very interested in the landscap-

311

ing business. Like Flambé, he liked the plants and the soil. He enjoyed figuring out designs and what looked good where. He was genuinely trying to learn from her. Etienne did the work, but he wanted to build things. The minute she needed something that required construction, he was the first to volunteer. He never shirked work, but it was clear his love was in wood. Flambé hoped Sevastyan would find him a job with whoever was going to transform the massive garages into their indoor gardens.

Both men flashed Blaise a quick smile. Etienne shrugged, not bothering to deny Blaise's assessment of him. After all, it was the truth.

"I've been studying all the different plants, trying to learn about them," Rory confessed. "There are so many. You're like a walking computer program."

She laughed. "I have to look them up all the time. I might have an idea of what I want but can't remember the name. It's easier when you're working with local plants rather than exotics. You get so you know all the locals not only by sight, but by name."

Rory sat back on his heels and wiped his gloved hand across his forehead, smearing dirt, making Blaise, Etienne and Flambé laugh even more. He just grinned and shrugged, in no way perturbed. They were used to having dirt all over them by the end of the day.

"When is the newcomer being brought in?" Blaise asked.

"She's supposed to get in next week," Flambé said. "Her name's Shanty. She has three young ones. The team managed to get them out as well. That was a miracle because the cameras picked them up and they were seen on the national news. Poachers went after them immediately. I couldn't go, although at first, she wouldn't leave South Africa because I wasn't there. She said she didn't trust anyone but me."

"Had she ever met you?" Rory asked.

"No, I saw those pictures of her for the first time the same as everyone else, when the news reported her. Clearly, she came from a different region. No one recognized her or knew her." Flambé pulled her gloves off. Her hands were beginning to itch. She rubbed at her skin, finding the sensation disturbing. "That was the first time I realized there might be strawberry leopards anywhere besides where our lair was. I wanted to get to her first if for no other reason than to get a few answers — like where did she come from? Is her lair large?

That sort of thing."

She sank down between Rory and Etienne, pulling her legs up tailor fashion. Blaise frowned and moved close in front of her to form a tight circle, his gaze moving over her, inspecting her carefully. "Are you all right? You look very flushed. You did wear sun protection, didn't you?"

She was hot. "Yes. I always do." Her skin burned easily. And marked easily. She wiped at the sweat forming on her forehead.

She'd been a little out of sorts since yesterday evening when Sevastyan had come to take her home. No, it was even before that. She felt moody and on edge. She really wanted to jump all over him, thinking that might help her strange mood, but when they got in the close confines of the car, his scent was very off-putting. She couldn't get that out of her mind, no matter how much she tried.

They hadn't been together but a few weeks and already Sevastyan was back at the club. Cheating. Lying. Showing that he was just exactly like every other shifter male. She knew he was going to be like that, but it still hurt. Did he think she wouldn't smell it all over him? She'd know the smell of sex and sin anywhere. She worked at the club all the time. He was such a lying bastard, just like all of them. Exactly like them. Following the pattern of every shifter male she had ever known. Her skin burned and something moved through her, hot like a furnace, something she couldn't control. She tried to sit very still, breathing, hoping she wouldn't cry. Hoping it would go away and she could just talk normally.

"Why would this Shanty insist on only meeting with you, Flambé?" Etienne persisted suspiciously. "That makes no sense when she'd never met you. I don't like the sound of that."

"You sound like Sevastyan," Flambé accused. "She's scared and alone. I have a certain reputation. My name is fairly well known in that region, you have to admit that. Unfortunately, I had to send word that it was impossible for me to make it. If she wanted to be rescued with her children, she needed to allow my team to extract her. I had to call in a lot of favors for this one."

Etienne and Rory exchanged a look over her head and then looked to Blaise. "What does your man think?" Rory asked.

"He's been in security a long time," Blaise pointed out. "He's got to have gut reactions."

She scowled at the three of them since they seemed to be in agreement. "Since when do you care what Sevastyan Amurov thinks? This is *my* business, what *I* do. He's got his hands full dealing with his cousin. Believe me, Mitya Amurov is difficult to say the least."

She was very uncomfortable in Mitya's presence. She had the feeling Mitya didn't like her very much — not that she liked him. Sevastyan preferred her to work there when she was drawing up her designs. She was very aware that it was for two reasons. He didn't want her out of his sight because he worried Franco might try to have her kidnapped. That was probably the number one reason. Or it was just because he really liked sex. He wanted sex several times a day. She didn't mind that reason at all or she would have objected strenuously. Now, with his latest cheating development, she didn't quite know what she was going to do. She couldn't leave until Shanty was safe. Flambé had to personally interview her and make certain she was set before Flambé could disappear.

Flambé did like Ania and would regret not really getting to know her. She'd never really had the chance to form any friendships, and Ania was the same. Working at the Amurov estate had allowed Flambé to see Ania often and she was beginning to think of her as a

316

genuine friend. Ania popped in with tea or she would call her on the intercom, asking her to come out to the garage where she was working. Ania was designing a car, working on an engine and building it herself. They would sit together, Ania talking excitedly about some new breakthrough while Flambé listened, happy for her.

Flambé was grateful Ania didn't ask her questions about Sevastyan. She didn't know how she felt about him and their relationship. It was complicated. Sevastyan was in charge inside the bedroom or outside of it, no matter what he had said. He was the one in charge and that was very clear. She was used to being her own boss, used to a tremendous amount of alone time. Now she had very little, and truthfully, she found that difficult. She had thought to consult Ania, who seemed happy with Mitya, but now it wouldn't matter.

"Is Mitya Amurov more difficult than Sevastyan?" Rory asked, his eyebrows going up.

"I never said Sevastyan was difficult," Flambé denied. "I said this is my business and he works for Mitya. Don't try to put words in my mouth."

Etienne gave an undignified snort. "Sevastyan Amurov has a reputation, honey. Even you can't pretend he doesn't. I can't imagine that if he thought Little Miss Strawberry and her children were some kind of setup to harm you he wouldn't be cutting them off and putting them in some interrogation room none of us know about."

A chill went down her spine because she had a feeling that might be just a little too close to the truth. "Fortunately, she isn't a plant and there wouldn't be a reason for her to set me up. He has no interrogation room. I know because I've thoroughly searched the house for hidden passageways, and in any case, she isn't his business."

She had searched the house for hidden passageways. There were many. She hadn't found an interrogation room but that didn't mean there wasn't one. That was one of the things about Sevastyan that worried her. He could be very cold. She had seen him that way at the Amurov estate more than once. She'd seen him that way at the club. That was scary to her. She was an emotional person. People mattered to her. They mattered a lot. She risked her life helping them. On the other hand, she knew that side of him appealed to her leopard. It was such a two-edged sword being a shifter.

Her arms itched and she rubbed her skin, glancing up at the sun. Sometimes if she was in the sun too long, she could burn fast and the itch was horrendous. Her legs itched as well and she rubbed her thighs, trying not to squirm. Blaise watched her closely. Not only Blaise, but his leopard, as if both were worried.

"You should probably go up to the house," he suggested.

That suggestion set her teeth on edge. She was getting very tired of men ordering her around. She was getting tired of men in general. All of them. Even the three she was sitting with. And if the itching and sudden burning sensation along her nerve endings didn't stop, she was going to scream.

"Do you have the photograph of Shanty on you?" Etienne asked.

Flambé nodded, refusing to clench her teeth. She didn't look at Blaise. Instead, she unzipped the pouch on her belt and pulled out a picture of a strawberry leopard and three younger leopards trailing after it. Then a second photograph showing a woman with short red hair and two little girls and a boy, all holding hands and staring into the camera. All three men leaned into her to study the photos.

Rory's shoulder brushed her arm, sending small electrical charges zinging through her bloodstream. Etienne leaned across her body and his shoulder touched her breast, the merest brush, but her nipples felt as if they'd burst into twin flames, so hot they'd melt through the material of her work shirt. Her breath caught in her throat and she had to bite down hard on her lower lip as Blaise put his hand on her leg, higher, toward her thigh for balance as he leaned in to look at the photos. His palm felt hotter than hell, an inferno traveling up her thigh to center between her legs in a burst of fire so hot she thought she might go insane. She could only breathe through it and hope no one noticed.

Blaise pulled his hand back and once again his gaze moved over her. This time speculation was there and she feared he had much more knowledge than she did — or the other two men.

"Really, Flambé, you need to get out of the sun," he advised again.

She wanted to claw at him. She actually dug her fingernails into her palm, needing the bite to ground her. Her mind felt chaotic, her body heavy and inflamed.

"This woman isn't from our lair," Rory confirmed. "Clearly she has a mate. Where is he? Did she say?"

It took Flambé several moments to get her breathing under control. Fortunately, all three men had straightened up again and the fierce burning sensation was receding.

"We don't know much at all," she said, ignoring Blaise. "She was pretty hysterical when the team got to her. She said the poachers came and wiped out everyone. That was what she repeated over and over. She didn't make much sense other than that."

The three men exchanged another long look. She wanted to rake her claws right down their faces. What was wrong with them? Didn't they have any compassion in them?

Flambé sighed. The burning sensation receded further, giving her some respite. "What is it? Just straight up tell me. I've been doing this a long time and I've never had so many men all of a sudden act like I can't possibly figure things out without their help."

"It isn't that, Flambé. You're trusting when it comes to our people. You think because there are so few of us and we're hunted by almost everyone that we're all going to help one another. That isn't the case. It should be, but it isn't," Etienne said.

Rory nodded. "You have a soft heart. I was glad when I heard you were with Sevastyan Amurov. I know some of the others were against him, but you need someone

321

strong to tell you no when you go too far. You don't look before you leap."

She was honestly shocked. She *always* planned everything so carefully. She did look before she leaped. What in the world was he talking about? "That's not true. You've only known me a short while. I plan every rescue operation very carefully. Do you have any idea how many shifters we've successfully managed to save?"

"That's not what I'm saying," Rory corrected gently. "You believe anyone contacting you and asking for help. If they're a shifter and they come from a lair that is losing ground fast, that's all you need to know and you're in all the way. You have a price on your head. A very big price. Some shifters are unscrupulous. They wouldn't mind selling you out for the money, and yes, that includes women."

That sounded like something Sevastyan might say if she gave him the chance — which she didn't intend to do. She wasn't going to introduce Rory and Etienne to Sevastyan.

"I've known you a lot longer than a short while, Flambé," Blaise said. "And his assessment is spot on. You do have a soft heart. You believe anyone. You're just too damned trusting. Your father told me he

322

wanted you out of the business of rescuing but you refused."

That was true. She didn't think anyone knew that. Her father had trusted Blaise or he never would have disclosed that information. It was the one topic they'd argued over repeatedly. The disagreement had continued right up until her father was unable to talk. He was adamant that she not continue with his legacy, other than the landscaping business, stating it was too dangerous to rescue shifters anymore. The odds were she would be killed.

She took a breath and met Blaise's eyes, acknowledging he was right. "He was worried," she admitted. "The world is smaller with the internet and it's much more difficult to slip into a country. They see me coming."

"Exactly," Blaise said.

"I'll give what all of you are saying some thought, I promise." She would. She hadn't considered that she wasn't investigating as thoroughly as she should be. Her name and reputation were getting out there. She did have a price on her head. Now Franco Matherson had his sights set on her. "I'll be more careful."

She had an investigator and he was good. She just didn't utilize him to his full potential. She had to do better. She always wanted to extract the shifters as fast as possible so she immediately got down to the planning part. She was excellent at planning the escape routes.

Etienne nodded. "What are they doing on the other side of the house? All those hammers going? I kept thinking I'd have a chance to get over there to look when we took a lunch break, but we were all the way to the back of the property planting trees at the time."

Excitement burst through her. "I forgot to tell you about that project. Sevastyan has two massive garages, both sitting side by side, two stories high, that weren't in use. He wants to convert them to greenhouses, or more like one big tropical paradise. I love the idea of lush plants and trees inside a long glass building."

"That sounds like an enormous undertaking," Rory said.

"Yes, I can't wait to get started. I've already begun sketches, sectioning smaller areas off around where I'll put the larger trees. He's already got massive support beams in, so the outside structure is already there and the builders are framing for the glass now."

"Amurov wants to put in an indoor garden

that large? A tropical garden? It was his idea?" Blaise asked. "What's he specifically looking to do?" There was speculation in his voice.

Like her father, Blaise was interested in environmental landscaping and he would be shocked at the idea of a tropical garden. One the size Sevastyan was asking for might be interesting for leopards, and Blaise might understand that, but the outdoors appealed to him far more. Flambé wouldn't have talked to him about Cain's club garden of paradise even if there hadn't been a nondisclosure in place, so she wasn't about to tell him why Sevastyan wanted a very large indoor tropical garden.

"For something that massive he must plan on utilizing the highest technology available," Rory said. "Temperature control for every section of plants."

"I can't imagine otherwise." Cain had done the same, although he was continually adding to his garden, calling Flambé back to the club to plant new exotics. With the additional space he was adding on, Cain liked to try to find plants no one else had. He pored over catalogs, searching for blossoms and vines to add to the latest section, sending Flambé his ideas, hoping she could get them for him. Often, she had to tell him

325

the plants he'd chosen weren't allowed into the United States, but she always suggested something close to what he wanted.

"Seriously, Flambé," Rory said, "I'd love to be part of that when you start working on it, or even before when you're in the designing phase. I'd like to see how you start to put something that big together."

"Sevastyan has his own ideas, but if I can't get you in on it, if he wants it completely private, I'll have discussions about similar projects."

She didn't have a clue how long it would take to plant the massive indoor garden Sevastyan wanted without a crew. She would have to talk him into at least allowing a crew to plant the bigger bones — the large trees and any boulders or waterfalls she would have to build. He could put in his suspension pulleys and cables after as well as any other apparatuses he chose to incorporate just as she had done in the garden of paradise at Cain's club. She had the feeling that even after she was gone, he would want his garden finished. That bothered her, that he would use it with some other women, but that was the way shifters were, particularly men like Sevastyan, and she had to accept that.

Flambé shifted her weight slightly to ease

the sudden burning down her legs as it returned with a fiery scorching heat. It felt as if a white-hot flame traveled over her skin, licking slowly along her nerve endings. Flamme turned in a languid coquettish roll, stretching in a deliberate flirtatious manner. Rory and Etienne scrambled to their feet, moving uneasily away from her. Blaise rose more slowly just as a dark shadow fell over the top of her.

All three men headed to the work truck without a word to their boss and climbed into it, starting the engine and heading away from the estate at a rather fast pace, following the vehicles already departing. Flambé frowned after them, squirming as the burn between her legs flared and then receded as her cat slowly retreated. She rubbed at her arms and thighs, trying to combat the waves of itching and burning that made her feel so edgy and moody.

Sevastyan stood behind Flambé, breathing deep, taking in the heady scent she was throwing off between her little leopard and her as their cycles merged. Flambé might not have heard him, but it was impossible not to feel the menace of his leopard. Shturm was deadly. Snarling. Clawing for freedom. Raking and fighting his human counterpart for supremacy to get to his rivals. Sevastyan's eyes had gone all cat, glowing a red-hot gold, banding with heat. He fought him back, knowing the leopard was fast enough to go after the trucks and drag the men from inside out onto the ground where he could rip them to pieces.

The female cat had decided to make an appearance, even if it was a small one. It was a risky moment, sandwiched between three males with her mate coming up silently behind her, but at least she had risen. Shturm wasn't the most forgiving of males. He was rough and jealous and moody as hell, but he was very glad that his mate had shown herself.

Already, as if that brief little flare of energy was enough, the female had subsided, leaving Shturm more on edge than ever. Grateful for the years of experience and discipline, Sevastyan controlled his leopard and forced air through his lungs. Very, very gently, he rested one hand on Flambé's shoulder, holding her in place, while he circled the nape of her neck with his palm.

"It looks beautiful out here already, *malen'koye plamya.* It's amazing to me how quickly you've managed to transform the place." He kept his voice very low. Velvet soft. No inflection that might warn her there might be trouble coming.

"I have a good crew." She rubbed her itchy arm across her forehead and tilted her head to look up at him. "They really work hard. I haven't had a chance to look at the greenhouse. Are the builders moving that along fast?"

He nodded, his gaze on the trucks driving away from the property, back to the main road. "It's a huge priority for me, so yes, it's coming along fast. You seemed to be having a very in-depth conversation with three of your workers." He dropped his gaze to her face. "Is everything all right?"

"Yes. I wanted you to meet them. That was Blaise, Rory and Etienne. Blaise is my foreman. Rory is really interested in landscaping but Etienne is definitely more of a builder, not that he shirks work. I thought you could interview him, see what you thought, and if you liked him, find a job for him with a construction crew. If not, no worries."

She started to unfold her legs and stand but he didn't move his hand, holding her in place. She went still, frowning, looking up at him over her shoulder with her large eyes. "Sevastyan?"

"I don't think that really explains your in-depth conversation. It wasn't about plants or building, Flambé. They were extremely concerned about something. All four of you were. Anyone could see that. I thought we agreed not to keep things from each other."

Flambé frowned at him. "Sevastyan, sometimes you can be extremely irritating. *Extremely.* Right now, you're annoying me beyond even your comprehension. I'm tired and hot and thirsty and I want to stand up, so move back and let me."

Sevastyan felt the pool of red inside him expand, roar through his veins, hot and explosive, but he flashed her a smile and extended his hand to her. "I see she really is close, making my woman moody. You don't have a temper, in or out of the bedroom."

Her hand felt small in his palm when he closed his fingers around it. He pulled her to her feet easily and then against him. She was small but solid, soft. He felt her muscles running through her body beneath her astonishing curves. Very gently, he ran his hand up and down her back as if soothing her when he knew that kind of soft touch did anything but. He kept her close against him, not allowing her to step away from his body when he knew she wanted to. She had been very standoffish since they'd returned from Mitya's the night before. In fact, she had withdrawn from him so much that he wanted to shake her.

330

"Only one of us can have a temper, baby, and I'm afraid it's already been established that it's me. Shturm is a real bastard. That makes me one." His hand continued to stroke down her back but now traveled farther to the curve of her spine. His fingers bit deep. Possessively.

"I didn't mean to snap at you, Sevastyan. I really am hot and thirsty. It's been a long day and Flamme chose the worst possible moment to make her first appearance in forever. I wasn't expecting it. I didn't even know what was happening at first. I was all itchy and uncomfortable."

She pressed her forehead to his chest, her first genuine gesture toward him in weeks.

"It was awful. Truly awful. I wish there was a book on this. Maybe I should have asked Ania what to expect. I didn't even recognize it was Flamme making me uncomfortable. At first it felt like I'd been out in the sun too long."

There was a curious reaction in the vicinity of Sevastyan's heart at the lost note in Flambé's voice. She was a woman of confidence and yet this small rising of Flamme had clearly thrown her. She really didn't know what it felt like to have a female make an appearance.

"Let's get you into the house, baby. You

can soak in the tub and tell me all about the conversation with your foreman and the other two workers." There had been affection in her voice for the three men. He would have to go out of his way to get to know them. Make certain they were good men and would always have her best interests at heart.

Thankfully it was a short distance to the front door. The three employees had been working on the plants closest to the front of the house. He could see at a glance the flowers and shrubs were all low to the ground just as they'd discussed. Even without the embellishments of stone or growth and blooms, it was easy to see improvements to the yard already. Flambé had paid attention to everything he'd said about security and there was nothing that would hinder his ability to see danger coming at them. Even so, she had created what would become an amazing landscaping piece for their front yard.

Sevastyan kept his arm around her shoulders as they walked to the front porch. His gaze had been riveted on his woman and the three men deep in conversation from the moment he had rounded the corner of the house and seen them together. The men were too close to her. Flambé's potent scent, so heady to him, had drifted on the wind, inciting his leopard and stirring his own proprietary need of her. He was aware of everything around them in the sense of looking out for danger, but he hadn't taken the time to see what progress had been made on the overall landscaping of his property.

He paused on the large verandah, taking that moment to really absorb what Flambé and her crew had done in the eight hours they'd been working. More trees had been added to the grove already in place, extending it toward Mitya's property as well as toward the house. Quite a bit of progress had been made in that area. Some of the trees appeared quite tall, quite mature, and he could see they had to use a small crane to put them in place. Already, the branches were thick and looped down or upward, but extended outward toward the next tree so a leopard could easily run along the limbs and leap from tree to tree.

"The place looks amazing, Flambé," he reiterated. "You increased the size of our woods by at least another fourth."

"By the time I'm finished with it, we'll have doubled it," she said, suppressing another yawn. "I think I'm getting old. I'm feeling every ache from shoveling dirt."

His gut knotted as he used the eye scan for quick entry. "Babe, why in the world, when you have such a big crew, would you be shoveling dirt? You oversee things, give orders, you don't do manual labor." He took her inside, closed and locked the door behind them.

"When we're putting in those bigger trees, everyone has to help, Sevastyan. You get them in as fast as possible. It's just safer that way." She sounded offhand, a little distracted.

"Go on upstairs and start your bath, Flambé. The chef left our dinner in the kitchen. I just have to turn on the heat. I'll be right up. Make the water hot. You know how I like it." He brushed a kiss on top of her head. He'd already programmed the locks on the doors to open with her retinal scan.

"I'm going to wash my hair," she advised him. "I'll start filling the tub after I rinse off."

He nodded and watched her go up the stairs. She was definitely exhausted, not just from her working day. That had started early, before light even, but most likely from the short, unexpected appearance from her female leopard. Her muscles had to feel abused by the contracting and expanding as

334

the cat pushed against her frame, testing her strength. Shifting could be brutal when one wasn't used to it. He'd forgotten that.

The house was large, and there were two smaller houses on the property for his men and other possible staff, but Sevastyan didn't particularly want anyone around once the day was over. He liked his time alone and since he'd found Flambé, he wanted his time with her uninterrupted. More often than not, he knew he would keep their play in the master bedroom, where he'd set up his domain. With no one in the house and no way to be surprised, he wanted to be able to utilize any room in the house when the mood struck him.

He was pushing fairly hard to get the construction done on transforming the two garages into one massive greenhouse so they could have a tropical garden. He had been thinking about what types of equipment he would want hidden amongst the plants. He liked the idea of waterfalls and streams. He wanted to have very comfortable chairs to relax in and many places to inspire his imagination for tying on the ground as well as in the air. Flambé looked beautiful in ropes and, although new at erotic bondage, she was more than willing to try anything with him. He also wanted a place for the leopards to relax.

She was soaking in the steaming bathwater when he walked in, barefoot and naked himself. He simply stepped into the tub and joined her, sinking into the water opposite her so he could watch her face as they talked. The hot water was working its magic. Her hair was wet and piled on her head. Her face was clean and free of all lines of worry. She looked hopelessly young, as she did sometimes, and very relaxed. Her eyes were closed and she smiled faintly when he joined her, but she didn't open her eyes.

He circled her ankle and picked up her foot to stroke her calf with strong fingers. "You were going to tell me about the conversation that had your crew so concerned, Flambé." He kept his voice low, that velvet-soft, mesmerizing voice that played over her senses, the one she responded to the most.

"They were mostly giving me a hard time about the rescue operations. My team is bringing in a woman and her three children. She was caught on camera recently in her leopard form. Strawberry leopards are so unusual that they make huge headlines if they're seen. She was seen in a big way because she had three kittens with her. Scientists are trying to prove why their spots are red, not black, and where the strawberry leopards come from. But there are so few because poachers want their furs . . ." She broke off, sighing. "It's a big mess."

He waited, not hurrying her. He pushed his thumb into her tense, tight muscle and rubbed until he felt it slowly give way and then massaged gently. There it was again. The truth. Misleading him. What was she hiding?

"They think I trust too much. Maybe I do, Sevastyan. The internet has made it so much more difficult for me to go anywhere without being seen. My father could slip in and out of a country and no one was the wiser, but now, if I take two steps somewhere, Franco knows or those people who put a price on my head are watching the airports and they know."

That was all true. "Is that what these men were worried about?"

Her lashes fluttered and she frowned as she opened her eyes to look at him. "Sort of. It all kind of fits together. Are you sure you want to hear this? I haven't really figured out if they're right or wrong. They gave me a lot to think about."

He didn't want to tell her that he was the only one she needed to figure it out with, but it was the truth. If he didn't get a satisfactory answer from her, he would be talking to all three of the men, one at a time, until he was satisfied. Something in the way they were acting really bothered him. He kept his fingers relaxed as he switched to massaging her other calf.

"Bounce it off me."

"The woman, Shanty is her name, insisted on meeting only with me when she'd never met me. My team was going to extract her, but she wanted me to go to South Africa myself to escort her and the children to the United States. I have a perfectly good team and they explained to her that it was impossible for me to come. When she balked, I had to tell her that if she didn't go with them, we couldn't pull her out. For some reason, all three of the men didn't like that she was insistent I go to her. They thought it was strange."

He kept his gaze on her face. He didn't allow his heart to accelerate or any change to his breathing. If these three men thought there was a problem, there most likely was a problem.

Her teeth sank briefly into her lower lip and then she sighed again. "My father didn't want me to continue with rescuing. He said it was becoming too dangerous." She made the confession in a little rush. "I disagreed with him. It was the only thing we argued about right up until he passed away. I have a team of investigators and they're very good, but maybe the men are right and I hurry them because I'm so afraid of losing someone. I need to be more careful."

Or not do any more rescuing. Sevastyan didn't say it aloud. He was going to consider how to keep her safe and not sound like a dictator. Clearly, she felt passionate about what she did. To just tell her she had to stop when she wouldn't do it for her father wasn't going to work. He needed a better solution.

"It's nice to know the men who work for you also look out for you," Sevastyan said, his voice mild. He was going to make certain he knew everything there was to know about them. He hoped to enlist their aid. He also wanted to talk to her investigation team and find out about this woman, Shanty.

"Don't fall asleep yet, baby. You need to eat. You haven't been eating much at all lately."

11

Sevastyan lay awake for a long time, his body burning hot. Flames licked over his skin and ignited like gunpowder in his veins. It seemed that every time he woke now, Flambé beside him, his body woke first, already in a state of need. He always savored the buildup of heat and fire. He let it happen rather than trying to suppress it the way he had for years. Now, there was his woman.

She lay curled up in a ball the way she did, making herself so small in the middle of their bed, that red hair of hers already spilling out of its braid, proclaiming to him that she couldn't be tamed. She always turned on her side, away from him, as if she could get away in her sleep, but he slept with his body around hers, his arm anchoring her to him, one leg thrown over her so there was no way she could possibly escape.

He enjoyed lying awake while she slept, imagining her tied in various ways. Seeing erotic images of her with the different ropes against her skin. She had such perfect skin for ropes, for the various colors and textures of ropes. She was extremely limber and she had done what he'd asked and stretched every day, several times a day, taking care to get her body into the best shape possible for the rigorous demands needed to be a rope model.

With Sevastyan, she wasn't just his rope model. She was his partner in bondage and sex. He would demand all kinds of difficult erotic things from her that meant she needed to be in top physical condition. He took her training seriously and he was very grateful that she did as well. He studied her face for a long time while she slept. She'd been very quiet, nearly falling asleep in the bath the night before.

Sevastyan had insisted she eat, and she had, but very little. She had been seductive as she readied herself for bed, but he had been aloof, settling himself in a chair across the room from the bed with a book until she finally gave up. She threw herself on top of the covers and almost immediately fell asleep. Denying himself had taken discipline, but she needed rest and he needed time to figure his woman out. He also knew that he had to be the one controlling the

341

sexual situations between them at all times. He was missing something big and if he didn't figure out what that was soon, he might lose her altogether.

There was a problem with her leopard — or with her. He couldn't decide which one it was. Her female was in her first cycle. Male leopards were known to their male counterparts almost from the moment they were born, but it wasn't the same with most shifters. Often, women had no idea if they even had a leopard until she made herself known when their cycles united and she was ready to emerge. That was an intense time for the human female and extremely disorienting, at least based on everything he had observed from Ania's experience.

Flambé's leopard had retreated so far that Shturm couldn't seem to reach her. His male was furious and getting more and more difficult to handle. That meant he was having difficulty controlling the building rage inside of him. Something was very wrong and he had to figure out what it was as quickly as possible.

It was very possible, even probable, that the female leopard was terrified of Shturm. Quite frankly, he was a brute. He would terrify any female leopard, let alone one as small as a strawberry leopard. She had no

342

idea what to do or what to expect, and her human counterpart didn't either. Flambé's body was hypersensitive, so her reaction to the feeling of the female leopard coming close to the surface was distressing. That could suppress her rising.

Or . . . he didn't want to think about the other possibility . . . that Flambé was the one terrified and was somehow stopping her female from rising. Was that even possible? He didn't know. He'd never heard of such a thing, but if he didn't find out soon, Shturm was going to tear him apart to get to the female. The fact that Flamme had come close to the surface around three other males and then retreated when Shturm came close had turned the big male wild.

Sevastyan resisted touching Flambé's face, tracing her high cheekbones with the pads of his fingers. There was a strange melting sensation in the region of his heart from just looking at her that was beginning to alarm him. She was becoming necessary in his life. He liked having her around. He liked hearing her laugh. He wanted to get to know her — the real her — the things about her no one else knew. He wanted her to let him into her life. For the moment, the best he could do was keep her safe, and work on their relationship.

Drake Donovan had his best people along with the Amurov people tracking Matherson. His private jet had filed a flight plan to Miami with nine people aboard. Supposedly Matherson was one of them. From there, the jet had taken those nine people to a small island owned by one of Matherson's friends. He stayed there overnight and left in the afternoon for France. He was expecting confirmation that Matherson was on the plane at any time. He knew the man would come back, but for now, he could concentrate on one enemy at a time.

And he had today with his woman. He needed it to figure out what was going on with her leopard — or her. He caught Flambé's messy topknot and tugged gently. "Time for you to wake up, baby."

As he tugged, he sat up and turned to put his feet on the floor. His heavy sac slid over the side of the bed and his cock strained toward his abdomen. He avoided touching himself when he needed to give in and give himself relief. He kept tugging her head with little gentle movements toward the edge of the bed until she made her usual drowsy murmurs of protest.

Those sounds always put more steel in his cock. He loved her little morning protests before she really woke. Flambé stirred, started to roll over and found his fist in her hair. Her gaze instantly jumped to his face and then swept down his body. Her tongue slid out and moistened her lips. His cock jerked in anticipation.

"Good morning." He kept his tone strictly neutral. "I want you to get ready. Hydrate. Stretch. Don't take long. Come back when you're ready."

She nodded, her long lashes sweeping down, but not before he caught the excitement flaring in her eyes. She was up immediately, gliding to the bathroom in her fluid cat's walk. Her bottom was enticing, hips swaying as she faced away from him.

He stood and stretched, feeling every muscle expand and contract before he began to prepare his scene. He tied the ropes he needed to the suspension cables. Hemp. Plain this time. Not particularly comfortable but not the harshest in his collection by any means. He had plenty of time to think about what he wanted to use that morning and just how he would tie her.

He waited until she returned and stood in the center of the room under the suspension hook before he sauntered into the bathroom. He took his time, knowing she would stand still waiting for him. He knew from experience that waiting built her excitement. The endorphins released in her body would add to the sexual excitement, the hunger building in her as well as the feeling of well-being and comfort in the ropes.

Flambé stood very still, her back straight, head up, but eyes down as he approached her. He circled her, the way he always did, touching her gently, trailing the pads of his fingers along her skin, testing for temperature. Testing her pulse. Murmuring to her, questions about her health, how she was feeling, if she was up for a prolonged scene with him, if her body could take what he planned to do to her. The more he talked, the more he touched her, the more she shivered, her nipples peaking and her hips shifting restlessly.

Sevastyan stopped in front of her, yanked her hands with unusual aggression toward him and immediately bound them together in a fast cuff tie. From there he wove straps that looped around her neck and knotted into her cuffs. He locked her arms down tight, quickly weaving double strands of rope to match the straps and then moving around to her back to knot a harness around her waist to anchor everything to.

Using her cuffed hands to guide her down, her urged her to settle her bottom into the

346

depression in the long egg-shaped crimson chair he'd placed close to her. It was soft and instantly molded to her.

"Lie back, Flambé." He deliberately didn't help her.

She complied, lowering her spine until her neck sunk onto the very edge of the chair so that the back of her skull rested along the edge of it. Grasping her bound hands, he attached them to the ropes he had already affixed to the pulley system overhead. Immediately he caught her right thigh and looped rope around it in two places, working quickly, drawing her leg up toward her belly. Adding in knots, he then attached those to the bindings going down to her ankle so her leg was tied close to her body in a frog-like manner. He attached that leg to the same pulley as her cuffed hands. Grasping her left ankle, he tied it and attached it to a second pulley so that leg was stretched out and straight in the air.

He walked around her, inspecting his work, adjusting the knots, making certain no rope was cutting off her circulation.

"Are you comfortable? Or at least reasonably so?" He stopped at the bottom of the chair, just between her legs. The fiery curls glistened with her damp liquid. Casually he reached down and swept his finger across

347

her slick opening, collecting what he considered his own personal treat. Her sex clenched. It had been a very good decision to let her sleep the night before. She was more than ready to play.

He sucked on his fingers as he walked away from her to stand across the room to study her from different angles. "I have the day off today. You didn't. I know everyone was coming out today to work, but I gave them the day off with pay. They were very happy to hear that."

He watched her carefully. Color flooded her face. Her eyes went fighting mad. He drifted back to her as if he hadn't noticed, trailing his fingers over her body, from her dripping sex to her breasts. Tugging at her nipples, he bent and took her mouth before she could voice a protest. She had opened her mouth and he slid his tongue in and they both caught fire. He rolled her nipple, slid his hand along her soft body until he found her curls and dipped his fingers into that sweet, hot slit. Immediately her sheath bit down hard on his two fingers. He fucked her and then pulled his fingers away before she could get off, pressing them to her mouth, silently instructing her to clean them off. Flambé sucked them clean, her gaze back to need. To desire. To lust. Still, he

348

could see she wanted to protest his heavy-handedness with her business.

Once again, he preempted. He stood just over her head, his hand circling his pulsing cock. "I woke up this morning thinking about your mouth, Flambé. Those lips of yours and how sweet they look when you try so hard to stretch them around me. I love looking at that. You're going to want to get me really wet because you're going to be swallowing me down farther than you ever have. It's not like you can do much else, can you?"

He rubbed the head of his cock over her lips, smearing the droplets of his seed over her mouth back and forth. When he pulled away she licked at her lips, and just that sight sent another heat wave rushing through him. To him, no one was more sensuous than Flambé.

"I think I spent most of the night lying awake next to you, thinking about how I wanted to tie you today. We both are always so busy and we never seem to have time for us."

Deliberately, before she could protest, he bent over her body in the sixty-nine position, laying his cock right over her mouth as he ran his hand over her body, stroking his tongue this time over her clit. The way he had her tied left her sex completely open to him. He pulled back just enough that he could pat her pussy with his hand. Gently. He flicked her clit. Patted harder. Flicked harder. He straightened up and rubbed his cock all over her lips, smearing his semen again. She opened her mouth and he moved back.

"Stay still. I'm taking my time. I was the one awake all night with my body hard as a fucking rock while you got to sleep." He made it an accusation.

Once more, he bent over her, this time much more slowly so that his heavy balls slapped her hair as his cock covered her face and mouth and his chin settled in her mound while he smacked her pussy gently. She was so wet. He licked at the coating on his palm and then repeated the action. His cock hurt, jerking in time to the blood hammering like mad in his veins and the sound of his hand as it played a gentle beat over her pulsing pussy. Her tongue took long swipes at his shaft, adding to the heat running up his spine.

He forced himself to straighten again. To keep his mask in place. To look indifferent, as if nothing affected him when his body was burning and blood pounded through his cock. "Open your mouth."

She complied readily.

"Get me wet, Flambé, or you're going to have a difficult time." He stroked her throat. "You're going to take me deep. You love this. You love my cock, don't you?"

"So much, Sevastyan."

"You concentrate on swallowing me, taking me all the way down. I'm going to try some new things that might scare you, but you'll love them. They'll feel so good, baby. You'll come so hard for me. I promise you will. Get my cock deep. Really deep." He massaged her breasts with his hands roughly. She tried to arch into his hands, silently begging him to continue. "You just have to trust me to take you there."

He saw it in her eyes. That adoration she gave him when they were connected this way, through the ropes. She liked rough play. She even needed it and he gave it to her, pushing his cock into her mouth, letting her tongue lube his shaft first and then pushing deeper, repeating and going a little deeper. The sight of her lips stretching around his girth was so fucking beautiful he knew he'd never get over it. Adding to that was the beauty of her in the ropes and the look in her eyes as she gazed up at him.

Flames rushed down his spine, tore through his body like a fireball straight to

351

his groin. He spent a few minutes letting her get used to his cock, the size of it in her mouth. The angle that helped to open her throat. He bent over her slowly and then pulled back, allowing her to get used to losing the security of his gaze, which kept her feeling safe and focused. When he'd established a rhythm, he cupped the side of her face.

"I'm going to give you something new, baby. Keep taking me deeper. Work at taking me deeper after each breath. You ready for this?"

He kept his gaze fixed on hers. She didn't stop sucking hard, her tongue lashing at him. He pulled back to give her air. She nodded. Her eyes said yes, even with liquid swimming in them. He touched her face to give her courage and show his approval. Very slowly he bent over her, his cock sliding deeper, taking care not to allow his body to shake. He had to appear to be in control.

He had to be careful. He couldn't see her expression. He didn't want her to panic. She couldn't talk nor could she fight him. He had to be aware of the subtlest body movement. He already had gotten her rhythm, when she needed air, but she no longer had the reassurance of his eyes. He timed the first withdrawal of his cock so she could see that she could rely on him to give her the air she would need. When he pushed deep, he smacked her pussy a little harder than he had before and then flicked her clit before sucking it. Her entire body quivered.

Shturm, do you feel her cat close? It makes no sense that she rose when the others were near but disappeared when you came close to her. Flambé is extremely strong, but right now she is vulnerable and in a weakened state. Reach out to Flamme. Draw her to you. Now, Shturm. God, you'd better do your part because I can't hold out.

His leopard rose while his hips thrust over and over, sending his cock into her mouth, matching the rhythm of his hand smacking her. He sucked her clit, using his tongue to fuck her the way his cock was using her mouth. He felt his leopard close to the surface, the male nearly as ferocious in that moment as he was, demanding his mate.

His head was already nearly exploding with the way her mouth felt so tight around his cock. It was difficult to force himself to pull back. His cock was at her throat. She was good at controlling her gag reflex and this time he smacked harder, flicked and sucked. Then it was several smacks. He was adding fucking her with his fingers, flicking and sucking as he was gently pushing his hips deeper each time he let her have air.

It was difficult to think, almost impossible. He knew he had to stay in control. This was dangerous all the way around, but she was pulling hard at his cock with her fierce suction, surrounding him with a scorching, moist fire so tight she was squeezing and then lashing him with her velvet tongue as he pulled back. The feeling was unlike anything he'd experienced.

He felt his leopard close to the surface, moving in him, a fierce beast, demanding the female come close. At once her presence was there, her heat adding to the fire in Flambé's body. Sevastyan felt the change, the added sensitivity. Already Flambé's nerve endings were extremely responsive to the merest touch. A brush of his finger, no matter how light, could set a flame going off in her bloodstream. He was tuned to the slightest change in his partner when he worked with someone. He had to be. He'd never known any woman's body to be as sensitive as Flambé's body was.

As the female leopard came closer to the surface and her hormones merged with Flambé's, the sensations he created when he smacked and flicked her heightened the coiling tension in her belly, in her sex. He'd deliberately chosen a new sexual technique to incite the leopard as well as Flambé.

She was rocking her hips, pushing herself into his mouth, raising her pussy to his hand, desperate for him to put out the flames he'd created, and the coiling tension that just wound tighter and tighter in her body. By now the fur would be moving under her skin, creating an itch, only now it would feel different, more like the brush of fire, strokes of flames over and over as if he was licking her with a fiery brand. Her moans vibrated through his cock, adding to the ecstasy so that he wanted to prolong the session, not end it, although he didn't see how it was possible.

Her body was so close. His was too. He wanted to feel the tight clasp of her throat and this time he pushed deep, all the way, letting his cock feel that squeeze while he spanked her soaked pussy hard enough to bring her to a violent orgasm. Between his mouth, fingers and smacking palm he prolonged the orgasm while he rocketed long jets of hot semen over and over into her. It was all he could do to keep his feet and pull back so she could breathe.

Sevastyan, in all his years of dark sexual practices, had never experienced such a violent or long, intense release like that one. His body felt like he had been thrown into

355

another world, a fiery ascension that took him to a place of pure feeling. He looked down at her face. Pure beauty. She coughed once but managed to keep breathing, not choke.

He waited, catching his breath, his gaze fixed on her face assessing her the entire time. He needed to make certain she was all right, that he hadn't hurt or damaged her. Above all else, her safety came first. After that, he wanted her addiction to him to grow. That was very, very important. Something was terribly wrong between them and he absolutely knew that the only real possibility he had to keep Flambé tied to him was the sex that no one else could give her. He was going to give her things that would blow her mind. Things she'd never thought of. Things she knew she'd never get anywhere else or from anyone else.

Her lashes fluttered but she didn't quite open her eyes. When he was certain he was able, he walked across the room to the small bar and retrieved a bottle of cold water for her. He took his time, looking casual as he returned to gently lift her head and hold the bottle to her lips.

"What did you think, *malen'koye plamya*? Is that something you like? Would you want to do it again in a different way? I wanted to distract you the first time to see if you would enjoy it. Your body seemed to, but sometimes the head doesn't always agree with the body." He brushed a kiss over her temple. Kept it tender. Loving even. He felt tender and loving toward her, but he knew he had to be careful of giving her too many of those gestures when she didn't want them from him.

She drank slowly, letting the cool water trickle over her throat. He was a big man and her throat had to be sore. The water had to feel good. When she turned her face away from the bottle, he lowered her head back down over the chair. She wasn't finished and she would expect him to insist they finish their ritual. He stepped close to give her access, drinking from the same bottle, resting one hand on the ropes as he leaned toward her mouth.

Her tongue felt exquisite as she lapped at him. There was nothing so decadent as his woman taking care of him in the early-morning hours after the blow job of the century. Her face was smeared with his seed when she finished, and she looked disheveled and well used.

Again, he needed a minute to get himself under control and he spent it looking at her, assessing her. Thanking the universe that she was in it with him. Her tight red curls were wet and gleaming with their combined sex and when he opened the privacy screen they glistened along with her thighs. He picked up the camera and slowly walked around her, taking shots from every angle.

"You do look beautiful, Flambé. I want to have a book of my ties with you as my model. The ropes always look so good against your skin." Deliberately he moved close to take a picture of her spread legs. "And you react so beautifully to erotic bondage."

"I know you're not going to show those to anyone." She said it, but there was the smallest hint of doubt in her voice. Her voice was husky.

He turned away from her, putting the camera down so he could pull the knots loose. He was always careful not to leave her tied too long. She was building up her stamina, but she wasn't ready to stay for any prolonged period of time. He checked her pulse and her hands, legs, arms and feet for warmth and then pulled her onto his lap to rock her gently.

"Woman, I've told you a million times, I don't share." He nuzzled the top of her head. "We both need a shower and then you can show me what you've been working on for our garden. I've got a few ideas I want to talk to you about so you can keep them in mind when you're designing."

She cuddled into him the way she did after he tied her. It was the only time he got that from her and he savored every second he had with her. She felt small and fragile to him, when now that he knew her, he was well aware that wasn't the truth at all.

"There's going to be so much room, Sevastyan. Almost too much. I think we're going to have to do this in sections, otherwise it will be too overwhelming." Her voice was very low, husky, and she sounded distracted. Still very much on edge.

"That's what you said when I wanted to build up the little wooded area to a much larger forest." He rubbed his chin again over the top of her hair.

Sevastyan massaged Flambé's arms and breasts, a firm rub that was very sensual, circling her nipples and then moving his fingers down to her belly to massage there as well. She was still experiencing little ripples, aftershocks that shook her. He could feel them moving through her body and his massage added to the sensations. He wanted to keep those sensations going, just for a little while longer.

She moaned and turned her head into his

359

chest, spreading her legs for him as he pushed his fist against her wet, inflamed pussy, his knuckles rubbing. She pressed down tight, riding his knuckles as he continued the massage, his teeth biting her shoulder, tongue soothing, then teeth stinging again.

Shturm, keep talking to your female. I want you to coax her to the surface. You are going to reclaim her, just in case, for some reason, she didn't understand the first time what that meant. She's young and it's her first cycle. We need to know if she realizes you are her mate.

Sevastyan very gently pulled his fist out from between Flambé's legs. She made a low sound of protest and tried to catch at his wrist to hold his knuckles in place there. He nuzzled her bare neck again, and then wrapped his arms around her tight, his hands cupping her breasts, thumbs sliding over her nipples. He bit down on her shoulder, his teeth sinking into her delicate skin. She cried out and rocked her hips, sliding one leg over his thigh, trying to find a way to ease the terrible building pressure between her legs.

The male leopard pushed at him, rubbing close to the surface. The female was close, unable to resist with Flambé in such a highly sexual state. She stretched and rolled, flirting outrageously with Shturm. She pressed against Flambé and made it known that she wanted out soon. That she wanted her mate.

Be gentle, Shturm. Make it count. Don't make a mistake. Clearly, she's in her first life cycle and doesn't know what she's doing. If you want her and you're absolutely certain she's your mate, you claim her and let her know no other male is going to take what's ours. That we'll fight to the death for them. She didn't get that the first time around.

Holding Flambé tight, Sevastyan shifted just his head and allowed the male leopard to take that form.

Hurry, Sevastyan hissed to the cat, knowing Flambé was too weak to stop the female from responding if she had been doing so, but he didn't like her in need without meeting that need. Not when it was so acute.

Shturm didn't waste time. He sank his teeth into the back of Flambé's shoulder, calling to the female, sending her reassurance that he was strong and fierce and that no other male could defeat him. That he would fight for her and defend her. That his claim on her would always stand. No other male would ever harm her or Flambé. His human was as fierce and protective as he was and would take equal care of Flambé.

The female rose to him, touching the edges of his teeth, accepting the claim for the second time. She stayed close this time, pressing toward the male, assuring him with images that he was her choice.

Ask her why she is taking so long to emerge. Sevastyan kept his arms tight around Flambé, locking her to him, his large hands completely covering her breasts, her nipples pressing deep into his palms. He rolled his wrists so that the massage was subtle, but kept pressure on those twin points of flame. Her hips rocked and bucked against his thigh.

Flambé fears you. Shturm shifted, giving back the form, retreating to allow Sevastyan to process the answer the female leopard had given the male in stark images. *She holds Flamme back.*

Sevastyan dipped his head low to kiss the wounds on Flambé's shoulder, wondering why Flambé would be afraid of him. What she would fear. She didn't fear being tied in the rope when she was the most vulnerable. That was when she was the most honest of all.

"I love that you're so sensitive," he whispered, his thumb sliding over her nipple.

"When I clamp you, you shudder with pleasure. Your entire body responds."

"I don't, not all the time. Sometimes the smallest sensation and I burn. I know that's why I need sex all the time. Even fabric against my skin can make me start to burn. It's the worst. Or my hair falling down my back, which is why I try to wear it up all the time."

She was giving him all kinds of ammunition, things he could use to help her, but things, when they were playing erotic Kinbaku together, he could use to add to her sexual needs. He slid one hand lower, to her belly, massaged there while his other played with her breast. He understood now why she liked rough. Why she responded to a rougher touch and not a gentle one.

"Sometimes if I wear a thong, the types of lace between my cheeks will start to rub and then this fire starts building until I need something or someone to put it out. I don't understand why I'm like this. I tried to talk to other strawberry leopards, the females, but they didn't want to talk about it. They would burst into tears and turn away, so my guess is we're all the same. It has to be our skin, our nerve endings too close to the surface or something."

She pressed her hand over her other breast

and rocked her hips harder. When that didn't help, she tried to close her legs as if she could rub her thighs together, but he had her on his lap and he kept his legs wide, preventing her from getting relief that way. His hand slid lower, massaging her mound, his knuckles dipping low to rub her wet lips and then back up to trail through her tight curls.

"I need sex all the time." There was a small sob in her voice and she pressed her face tight against his chest.

"You've got me now, Flambé. You don't have to go to bars every night, or try to find someone to help you out during the day. I just happen to have a voracious sex drive, as you well know. We were meant to be." He let a ghost of a smile creep into his tone.

Her hand slid down his arm to grasp his wrist. Once again, she tried to push his fist between her legs. He didn't let her. Instead, he put his mouth against her ear. "Tell me what you want, *malen'koye plamya.*"

Her entire body trembled. "You know that's so hard for me. To ask for anything sexual."

"You weren't listening properly, baby, and if you were in the ropes, you would be waiting a long time before you'd get relief, but you're in a terrible state so I'll let you figure it out. Think about what I said to you." He had made it a command. In the bedroom, he commanded.

She hesitated. "I still need your cock, Sevastyan."

It was a whisper, in that husky voice that reminded him of his cock down her throat. Every time he heard her speak in that tone, images and feelings immediately rose of the spectacular fireworks she'd produced in his body. There was no one like Flambé. No other match for him.

Her head tilted back and her eyes filled with dark lust, somewhere between gold and green. His cock was already aware with the cats so close and both females throwing off enough hormones to bring every leopard snarling and fighting for a mate within a hundred miles running to them. Still, he waited.

Her tongue moistened her dry lips. His seed was all over her face, shiny, beginning to dry. She was a mess but sexy as hell to a shifter who needed a woman willing to have the kind of dirty sex he needed. He was voracious in his appetites and kinks. He wanted one woman but he wanted her devoted to him. Willing to indulge him.

"Please."

His heart felt as if a vise squeezed it hard.

"You need me, baby, you know I'm yours." Very gently, his hands went to her waist and he lifted and turned her so her body faced his. "Straddle me."

Blood from Shturm's puncture wounds still trickled down her shoulders, but she hadn't even seemed to notice that he'd reclaimed the female, or that part of her extreme sensitivity was due to her cat being close. She wrapped her fingers around the base of his cock and held him steady as she slowly sank down, sheathing him in her tight folds. She threw her head back as her burning folds engulfed him.

He wanted to do a little head throwing of his own. She was pure scorching fire. The look on her face, a kind of ecstasy, only added to the beauty as she rode him, sliding over his cock, her muscles squeezing tight. He caught her hips and slowed her down, not allowing the frantic pace she tried to set.

"Shh, baby, relax, take it slow and easy," he coaxed, setting the rhythm. Her body was a silken sheath, so scorching hot, grabbing at him with greedy fingers and squeezing down over and over as she pumped her sexy pussy over his cock.

Her breasts jolted and swayed invitingly with every movement of her body, dancing for him as she ground down, her breath coming in panting sobs. Deliberately, he slid one hand up from her hip to her breast and flicked her taut nipple. She gasped as if he'd held a flame to it. He pinched and tugged and then ran his finger from her breast slowly down her belly straight to where their bodies came together.

"Look at us, baby. Look at the way you take me inside you."

He circled her clit and then flicked it just as he had her nipple. She cried out and clamped down hard with her muscles around his cock — rode him harder, breaking the slow rhythm. He pinched, using his finger and thumb, holding her little inflamed clit hostage while he pumped into her, surging with his hips and then suddenly letting her go so the blood flowed back. She cried out again as he gently flicked and teased the inflamed bud, while she pressed down harder into him, her muscles like a vise.

"One day I'm going to do a tie with clamps on your nipples and clit, *malen'koye plamya.* I'll have you dripping with jewels and rope both. You always look so damn sexy." Sevastyan slid his hands up her hips to her waist, holding her, needing to hold her. Wishing he could find a way to reach her other than through sex. He was willing

367

to take what he could get, but she was perfect. So damn perfect.

The roaring started. Thunder in his ears. He felt the volcano in him, that deep dark well of savage, red-molten rage that only Flambé seemed to be able to tame. Even if it was for a short while, a small respite, she still managed. The sounds she made told him she was close. He recognized every little sign of Flambé's needs, every tiny nuance, expression, moan of pleasure, sob of desire or lust, her body language, he knew all of that and yet nothing of her. Nothing of his woman.

He caught her close and held her heart to heart as her body clamped down hard on his and the tidal wave took her, took them together. She dropped her head on his chest, her arms sliding around his neck in absolute exhaustion. He could feel her heart beating, surrounding his cock, the same rhythm against his chest. If the emotion welling up in him was actually love, he wouldn't have been surprised. It was stark, raw, overwhelming. And all for her.

He buried his face in the silky mess of her hair, taking advantage while he could. It wouldn't last. She didn't want him. He got that. Even Mitya got that. He was so angry with Mitya taking it out on him, but the truth was still the same. She didn't want him. He would have to face that soon.

She had completely collapsed into him, breathing raggedly, her face pressed against his chest, eyes closed tightly. He kept his arms around her, holding her close to him, their hearts beating hard. He was leopard and he could hear them both hammering out of control. His began to settle first. He opened his eyes to look down at her, just to drink her in while she wasn't paying attention.

Flambé was at her most vulnerable in the ropes, during sex and right after. Those were the only times he felt he had the real woman. The rest of the time she was so elusive he was certain she was moving just out of his reach, always one step ahead of him. He was very intelligent and used to being the smartest man in the room, even if few others were aware of it. To have Flambé always eluding him was both intriguing and disconcerting.

A flash of red caught his eye and he tightened his hold on her and sat straighter to look over her shoulder. She was bleeding from the puncture wounds. His heart jumped.

Shturm. How deep did you bite?

Not too deep. You said to make certain my

369

claim was established and I did.

Sevastyan cursed silently. He had said that. *Did you close the wounds with your saliva?* He couldn't remember if the male cat had licked the bites or not. He had the first time, but they'd been shallow punctures. These, clearly, were deeper.

No, she was distressed and I shifted.

What had he read about her mother dying in childbirth? She'd hemorrhaged. He'd had Ania do some investigating for him and several of the strawberry leopards had died from hemorrhaging. This was a careless mistake. He took a deep breath, refusing to panic. He stood up, lifting her off of him and into his arms, taking her to the bed and laying her facedown. She barely moved she was so exhausted.

Shturm, you're going to clean those wounds. Shift now. Sevastyan was in no mood to take any bullshit from his leopard. *Be gentle with her.*

For once the cat obeyed without giving him any lip. Shturm lapped at the puncture wounds, and then shifted again. Sevastyan hurriedly yanked the first-aid kit from behind the bar where he'd stashed it. He cleaned the bite marks thoroughly, noting that even with the cat cleaning them they were still bleeding. It wasn't a lot of blood, but enough that it told him she would have trouble if she really got a deep cut — or she had a baby. He wasn't like so many others of his species — he wasn't all about having children to save the shifters.

He tried butterfly bandages and waited to see if they would stop the flow of blood. If that didn't work, he would put a stitch in each of the bites. He was also contacting the doctor immediately. He wasn't taking chances with her.

"Sevastyan?" Flambé's voice was husky. Drowsy.

"Shh baby, just lie still."

"I need to clean up."

"I'll get you cleaned up in a few minutes. I'm admiring my handiwork. The ropes looked good on your skin." He smoothed his hand over her thigh where the marks from the ropes were still faint.

She didn't respond. The butterfly bandages were holding. Relief spread through him. He contemplated the perils of landscaping and how many ways she could cut herself while working as he ran a hot bath for the two of them. He'd given the cook and housecleaners the day off as well so after he bathed her, he'd put her back to bed and he'd fix brunch while she slept. That would give him time to try to figure out why she was afraid of him.

She never acted afraid of him. It would stand to reason that if she was, she wouldn't let him tie her. She would never trust him the way she had that morning. Nothing about the situation made any sense.

Sevastyan scooped her off the bed and carried her into the bathroom once the tub was filled. He'd added bath salts to the water to help heal any soreness. She curled into his chest, feeling lightweight, almost insubstantial to him. There were rope marks on her body as well as marks from his mouth and hands. She had skin that displayed his artwork beautifully. Someday, he'd take pictures of her body after he removed the ropes as well as with the various ties on.

"Sevastyan." His name came out a husky protest as he sat down in the tub, her body between his legs, the hot water nearly to her neck. "It's too hot."

"It's good for you." He caught her chin and pulled her head back against his shoulder so he could wash her face. "Keep your eyes closed. I like your face all shiny with my seed, baby, but you might not like it as much as I do."

Flambé reached back over her shoulder and wrapped her arm around his neck. It was the first real spontaneous gesture of affection she'd ever made toward him that wasn't sexual since his leopard had claimed hers. He knew she'd done it because she was half asleep, but he'd take what he could get. He was very gentle as he washed her face. She fell asleep as he held her, just soaking her body, letting the salts have time to do their work.

The moment he began to soap her body, it didn't matter how gentle he was, he could see how sensitive her skin was, particularly now that hormones were raging. If she always had trouble with her nerve endings so close, the merging of the leopard and human cycles had worsened the effects. Her body shuddered with every touch no matter how careful or impersonal he was. He forced himself to use stronger, harder strokes, even though it went against everything he wanted to do, and she quieted.

When he washed between her legs she cried out and turned her face into his shoulder, biting down hard with her teeth, not realizing she was biting him. He murmured to her soothingly and finished, wrapping her once in a towel rather than trying to dry her off, and then putting her in bed and letting her air-dry.

He checked the butterfly bandages and

then pressed a kiss into the middle of her back before heading downstairs to the kitchen.

12

Sevastyan poured Flambé a cup of coffee. "Tell me about your father. You don't really talk about him that much."

He kept his gaze fixed on her face. She was dressed in loose-fitting casual clothes. Nothing sexy about a pair of soft cotton, dark navy pants and a thin cotton ombré top, but for some reason he found her sexier than ever. Her face was devoid of all makeup and her hair was shiny clean, piled high on her head in that messy knot she favored. He knew it was to keep it off her skin, where before he thought it was to prevent the mass from bothering her while she worked or from getting it wet when she was in the tub.

"I don't?" Her long lashes lifted and then she stared down into her coffee cup as if it would somehow help her to remember if she talked about her father or not. Her lashes were naked of all mascara, strawberry blond with those red-gold tips that got to him every time.

He had studied the photographs of the leopards in South Africa, interested to see what her species looked like. They were very small. The heaviest female strawberry leopard known so far was only sixty pounds. That was extremely small for a shifter. He was Amurov and his male was a big brute, coming in close to two hundred pounds of pure muscle.

"No, baby, you don't. I never met him. What was he like?"

She moved her shoulders as if she was stiff. "Why did your leopard bite me again?"

"Flambé." He pushed warning into his voice. Mild. But still a warning. "Things got heated in the bedroom. Is there a reason you don't want to talk about your father?"

She shrugged. "It's just difficult to know what to say about him." She pushed the coffee away after taking a sip. "He was great with plants. Really great." Enthusiasm slipped into her voice.

She hadn't eaten much. She'd pushed the food around on her plate more than she'd actually put it in her mouth. He got her a bottle of cold water from the refrigerator and set it close to her hand, removing the coffee cup. "Honey, if you don't like what I make for you, you need to tell me. I can cook other things. I just don't admit it to the family. The chef can make anything for us and I can reheat it."

Flambé sat up straight and shook her head, her eyes meeting his. "No. This is good, Sevastyan. I'm not a big eater as a rule."

Her voice was very low. Husky. It played along his nerve endings. He watched her take a long drink of water and work her throat. A drop of water from the condensation on the bottle splashed on her top and stained the color a darker hue.

"I know Leland was amazing with his business, Flambé, but that doesn't tell me anything about what he was like as a father. Or as a husband. I know he took a mate very late in his life. Your mother was a good twenty years younger than he was. She was a chef, wasn't she?"

He was a rigger, a rope artist, and he paid close attention to everything to do with his partners, but now, especially to his mate. The slightest change in her breathing, the sweep of her lashes, the press of her lips. She was very uncomfortable discussing anything to do with her parents on a personal level.

"You know my mother died in childbirth, right?"

His heart stuttered. Clenched hard enough that it gave him pause. The moment he saw those steady trickles of blood running down her shoulder from Shturm's claiming bite he knew something was wrong. He felt protective of Flambé. Not just protective. His sentiment went far beyond that. They'd spent time together, but mostly he expressed his passions in his art. He allowed his emotions for her to be wrapped up in his rope. He felt his connection growing with every knot, every tie. The touches on her skin. The sex was inflammatory, wild, the best, but it wasn't nearly as intimate as the laying of the ropes. Wrapping her up — in him.

"Yes, *malen'koye plamya,* I'm well aware your mother died in childbirth. That's one of the reasons I'm against you having children. I don't want to risk you. I know it's practically impossible for birth control to work for shifters, so I'd like to talk to a doctor about how to keep that from happening or how to best take care of it before you're at risk."

She tilted her chin at him. "Has it occurred to you that I might want children?"

The moment she gave him that defiant little chin lift of hers, Shturm roared and his body stirred, his dominant side rising fast. "Naturally. Which is why I said I was against *you* having children. I don't want you carrying our children. We can use a surrogate. There has to be a safer way. When we find it, we'll have children if you want them."

He kept his tone mild, as if he wasn't laying down the law when he was, because he damn well wasn't going to lose her. He doubted if the strawberry leopards had been wiped out just from poachers. He thought it more likely was from whatever caused them to hemorrhage when they had even a slight cut.

The moment he realized she could be like her mother — a hemophiliac — that it could be genetic, he had set in motion everything he could to aid her. His people were researching. Evangeline, Ashe, Ania. Drake's people. Jake Bannaconni's people. Sevastyan had already texted Jake Bannaconni's doctor, a renowned shifter, asking his advice. He knew there were ways to help treat bleeding disorders. That fast he had an incredible team to make certain Flambé lived a long life — with him. It did make him grateful for the life he led. There were some positive things to it. The thought of losing her was already beyond his comprehension.

"How did your parents meet? Did your

father ever tell you?"

Flambé pulled her legs up under her, curling into herself there on the window seat in the kitchen. She looked away from him, her fingers circling the water bottle. "Yes. I was curious of course. She was one of the females he rescued. He put her through culinary school. According to him, she loved to cook and was very good at it."

"She had a reputation," Sevastyan encouraged when she fell silent. "Evangeline told me she was a chef at Baume, the renowned French restaurant in downtown San Antonio. She would have had to be amazing to work there."

Flambé sent him a brief smile and then turned back to look out the window. She looked so alone he wanted to gather her up in his arms. It took effort to stay in his chair and just observe her.

Shturm, pay close attention. She is guarding herself. Holding herself so close. He wanted the impression of his leopard as well. More than once he had been forced to interrogate prisoners and Shturm's observations had been helpful. This was more important to his life — and his leopard's — than anything else.

"Keep going, baby. Tell me about them."

"He wanted children and he never found

his mate. The species was nearly extinct. He said it stood to reason that his mate had already been killed. She was in her first cycle."

She turned and looked at him again. Straight. Her eyes meeting his. Her eyes were nearly emerald. Was there hostility there? Some kind of accusation? Her lashes lowered and she turned her head before he could read her.

Shturm?

She doesn't trust us. Either one of us.

He waited a heartbeat, turning his leopard's assessment over and over in his mind, letting it process. "Your father told you that your mother was in her first life cycle but that he had another mate?"

"Yes."

Short. Clipped. By all accounts, Flambé and her father had gotten along very well. They didn't argue. They were good friends. The only thing she'd gone against her father on had been continuing with her rescuing of the leopard species going extinct. Other than that one thing, everyone, including Flambé, said she didn't fight with her father. But then, Flambé didn't argue with Sevastyan either.

"Did he talk to you about their life together?" He pushed her just a little bit when

381

he knew she was reluctant to talk to him about her parents.

She took another drink of water and then swung her legs off the little bench seat to stand up, stretching. "He didn't. I asked a couple of other people I knew, friends of hers, and they told me things. They weren't exactly nice things. I want to go for a run."

"That's a good idea." He stood up as well. "I think after this morning, we both need a little action." He gathered the plates from the table.

Flambé instantly cleared the silverware and mugs. She began washing the dishes as he scraped the food she didn't eat into the compost she'd set up for the plants.

"What did her friends tell you?"

She shrugged. "Nothing good. They're both gone so I guess it doesn't matter."

He went hot inside. Red hot. Raging. It mattered. "He didn't hit her — or you, did he?"

"No. Nothing like that."

He could barely hear her and she was standing right beside him. Close. She smelled like cinnamon and Egyptian jasmine. At once he got that taste for her in his mouth. On his tongue. She set up a craving there was no denying. Franco Matherson was going to be a big problem sometime

382

in the future as much as they both might want to think he was gone. There was no getting a woman like Flambé out of one's mind.

Her parents. He needed to do some digging into what life had been like for her mother with her father. "When did you move out to that little studio? How old were you?"

The Carver property was fairly extensive, landscaped beautifully, so much so that it was a showpiece. The house was a long, U-shaped, single-story dwelling with many bedrooms and a wide covered verandah. There were two other houses, both of which had been built as dwellings for the male shifters who worked for them or the rescues who were training under her father. The studio was off by itself a distance from the main house.

She finished washing the dishes and wandered back to the window, avoiding his gaze. "I was seven. He needed the bedroom."

Sevastyan felt like Shturm did most of the time, wanting to claw and rake, to break free and murder something or someone. She was very subdued, no expression in her voice, but he had been to her property with her to get her things.

The studio was situated right next to a koi

383

pond where lavender and lacy ferns sprang around the wide bluish-black rock and tree limbs wept long green fringe into the water. The walkway leading to the studio was paved in the same bluish-black stones and the building fit perfectly with the setting, a small artsy one-bedroom cottage with a kitchenette and bathroom. The porch overlooked the pond, as did the front windows, giving Flambé a wonderful view, but that view would be far different as an adult than it would be as a child, not to mention it wouldn't have been all that safe for a child alone.

"Get your shoes, baby," he said softly.

He was the one who needed to run now. His body raged at him. Normally he would have turned to sex, going to Cain's club, losing himself in the sheer beauty of tying the ropes, laying down a masterpiece on a blank canvas, and after, giving his body the release it needed, a totally unsatisfying mindless fuck that never did anything but let some of the volcanic rage go long enough to get by for a few days or, if he was lucky, weeks.

Now that he had Flambé, everything was different. His art was personal. Her body was the perfect canvas and each time he tied her, no matter how he decided to lay the ropes on her body, the color or texture, the pattern, it had to be on her because she was the one who made his art a masterpiece. She made it come alive. She took his cock and actually, in spite of his addiction to her, sated him enough that he could sleep. She managed to quiet the ferocious rage in him that he had thought was impossible to ever tame. Sadly, whatever she needed from him he wasn't giving her — yet. He was determined to figure it out. His little strawberry leopard mattered to him, whether she thought so or not.

He waited for her at the bottom of the stairs. She hadn't tried to change one thing in the house. She hadn't asked for her own office. She'd barely moved her clothes into their bedroom. Each time he'd named a day to get married, she'd come up with an excuse why she couldn't make that work. He was so busy with Mitya's business, so used to being at his cousin's beck and call, that he'd let that all slide. The only thing he'd really demanded of Flambé was for her to work at Mitya's estate when she was drawing up plans and to sleep in their bedroom. She'd given him both.

He gave a low growl as he paced back and forth. How was he different than anyone else in her life? He was truly neglectful of

385

her. He needed to find a way to spend more time with her, to make her know she was his priority. They had sex. Crazy, kinky, hot, wild, insane, insatiable sex. She distracted him with sex and he let her. He distracted her with sex and she let him. Their relationship was founded on sex and seemed to be about sex. She was comfortable with that and wanted to keep it that way. She hid herself from him unless . . .

Sevastyan abruptly stopped pacing. Flambé couldn't hide from him when she was in the ropes. She was too vulnerable and open to him. Too connected to him. That was the one place she was honest with him whether she wanted to be or not. He had to be careful though. He couldn't use that too much or too often. In any case, he would prefer to have her trust him. He wanted her to *want* to get to know him. To want to share his home.

Shturm leapt just as he scented her. It was more than scenting her. He felt her in his skin, that was how connected to her he was. He looked up, watching her come to him. She looked confident, very much Flambé, but he knew her every subtlety now, every little sign, and she was nervous. It was there in the tension of her fingers as she twisted them together to keep them still as she descended the staircase. It was the way she held her head, her shoulders very straight, not nearly as relaxed as normal. She definitely had a problem relating to him when they were alone and they weren't having sex.

Deliberately, he allowed his gaze to sweep over her, and then he held out his hand. She had no choice but to take it or to be rude. There was just the briefest of hesitations before she put her hand in his. He doubted if too many others would have even noticed the slip. He closed his fingers around hers firmly and drew her in close to his body, walking her to the front door.

"I thought we could walk around to the back of the house to warm up and then jog to the woods and run once we get in them. You had to have created pathways between the trees and I'd like to see the new ones that were planted. It looks so beautiful from a distance and I haven't had time to get up close to appreciate it. You do amazing work, Flambé. I don't tell you enough."

She glanced up at him, looking surprised. "You tell me."

"No, I don't. I have to drive around the city quite a bit with Mitya and I make it a practice to find all the places you've worked. I like to see what you've done. I know it has nothing at all to do with me, but it gives me a sense of pride that I even know you when I look at the various places you've transformed. The downtown park in particular was the biggest shock to me. I saw all the before and after pictures. That was your project alone, wasn't it? Your vision?"

He felt the tension slowly leaving her body. She did love her work, another connection he could make with her if she just would let him. He hadn't realized until he was around her how much he liked plants and trees. It was the leopard in him, needing to climb, needing the camouflage around him.

"I underbid that project for the city, but I really wanted to do it," Flambé admitted. "I wanted a place for everyone of all ages to be able to go. Somewhere peaceful."

"I think you managed it beautifully and it seems easy to maintain."

"I tried. The other project I really enjoyed was the Golden Dragon Restaurant. They have such a beautiful piece of property to work with and the owner just let me do what I felt was best. Most owners have a million ideas and they don't have a clue what types of plants work with their soil or terrain. I was able to give him a small fall tumbling over rocks into a small stream that feeds a koi pond. The gardens are gorgeous and grew up fast. I wanted the trees to be colorful, and Japanese maples fill that bill, especially dwarf maples, but the sun is too hot here for them."

Her voice was still low and husky, but her joy created an intimacy between them that hadn't been there before. He had slowed his steps to match her shorter ones. He wanted to watch her face, but he'd been too long in security, always looking out for danger, and she was too precious to him to take chances with. His gaze swept the roof of every building, rocks, bushes, trees, anything that might hide an enemy, but his attention was riveted on her. He counted on his leopard to be a sentry, to warn him if there was trouble close by.

"Was there a way to solve the problem?"

"There's always a way, Sevastyan. I just had to give it some thought. I wanted those crimson reds and gorgeous yellows and bright greens. Even some of the branches and trunks can be red when the leaves fall. I planted taller shade trees first and then the dwarf trees once the shade trees took root and were a certainty to make it. The Golden Dragon is known for its garden almost as much as it is for its food now, and the garden is still quite young."

He slung his arm around her neck and

pulled her in close to drop a kiss on top of her head. "You're so damn smart and talented, woman. I've developed a real love of plants just looking at all the various gardens you've worked on around the city."

He let her go. They were at the back of the house, where they could easily begin to jog. He set an easy pace. He had much longer legs, so it was a matter of making certain she wasn't running to keep up. When he was certain she was comfortable with their pace, he continued the conversation.

"I bought a bunch of catalogues when you were talking to Brent Shriver, your supplier."

"Sevastyan." She almost wailed his name. "Why would you do that? I have tons of catalogues. And I mostly use him for exotic plants. His prices are higher than the norm."

"You don't seem to like talking about your work with me. I thought if I educated myself on the plants it would help. I like having them in the house as well as outside. I'm really anxious to start planning the indoor garden with you. I thought about what you said, that it might be too big and we might have to do it in sections. I hadn't thought that it could be overwhelming. You're just one person and it is very personal since we're incorporating bondage equipment as part of the basic décor."

He caught her green gaze going amber, flashing at him before she turned her face forward, toward the trees. She jogged almost a yard before she replied. "I'm sorry if I gave you the impression that I didn't want to discuss my work with you. I guess I thought you'd find it boring. You work late and whatever you do is . . . complicated. I don't even know exactly what it is you do."

There was always going to be that lying between them. His work. There was no getting around that and no getting out of it. He was what he was. What he'd been born into. She already suspected. She heard the rumors. Hell, he'd told her. She saw him get out of a car and she might not have witnessed him shooting someone, but she certainly suspected that he had. He'd admitted to her that he'd hunted and killed the men who were waiting to kidnap her on his property. Once her leopard emerged, she would know what he was.

Sevastyan stayed quiet. There wasn't much to say. He looked down at the top of her head, at the messy topknot of impossibly bright red hair. It was definitely red. And very thick and wild. Untamed. That should have given him a clue right there. He'd been so damned complacent, so ar-

391

rogant just because she liked the ropes. Because she craved sex the way he did. Not exactly the same way. Her body was very sensitive, her nerve endings burning close to the surface, causing the sensations to be almost painful.

They were coming up on the trees and he indicated for her to go ahead of him and set the pace. She had a shorter stride and she could run full out and still not be anywhere near as fast as he was. He didn't want her to know how fast he could run. Sevastyan kept himself in top fighting shape at all times. Amur leopards were fast and could leap amazing distances, both horizontally and vertically. Shturm had set records at both running and leaping. He could turn in midair and switch directions. He was also in top fighting form and far more experienced than most males. There was no doubt that he could keep his mate safe.

Sevastyan followed her through the path in the woods. It was narrow and wound in and out of the trees. She was faster than he thought she would be and she clearly was used to running. He should have known. He had used extreme exercise to stave off the terrible craving for sexual needs as long as he possibly could before he had Flambé in his life. She ran like a machine, her body flexible, muscles rippling beneath her thin tank and bunching in her thighs.

The rope marks were visible on her legs and arms. Her running top was short, ending just below her bra and exposing the line of rope knots down her back that still showed so beautifully on her skin. They fell into a rhythm easily, moving through the trees and bushes, and even with the fast pace, he found himself liking the way his marks of possession looked on her. He felt primitive toward her. Even predatory, much like his male leopard; primal, not wanting any other male close to her. He'd never experienced any emotion even close to what he was feeling.

Running gave him time to assess his unusual and unhealthy sentiments. He knew part of it was the fact that her leopard hadn't emerged yet and his leopard was raging, prowling closer and closer to the surface every hour. Shturm was growing impatient just when Sevastyan was certain that he needed patience now more than ever.

"Head back to the house, baby," he called out. "To the twin garages. I've had something I wanted to talk to you about."

For a minute he wasn't certain she would respond, but then she chose a path that would loop them back toward their home. He hadn't been paying close attention to their route until that moment. She had run in the opposite direction of his cousin's property, staying clear of any chance meeting with any of the shifters who might be working near the property lines. They weren't that close, but they could have been.

Once out of the trees and into the clearing, Sevastyan lengthened his stride and paced himself beside her. "Are you ashamed for anyone to see my rope marks on you?" That would hurt. He knew it shouldn't. Most women wouldn't want others to see that they enjoyed being tied, but somehow he equated her being ashamed of the rope patterns with a rejection of him.

He caught just a brief glimpse of her eyes glittering green and gold, and then she was looking straight ahead again as she ran. "They belong to me and no one else. You gave them to me, like a gift. It felt intimate between us."

He heard the truth in the husky vibration of her voice. She sounded close to tears and that was the last thing he wanted. Her answer was unexpected and pleasing.

He took his time before responding. "That's why no one has ever been in our room. After it was renovated, I did all the other work myself so that when I found you, no one else had ever touched the equipment or seen it. It was just for you. For us. That's the way I want our garden ultimately to be. Visitors can look from the outside, but I don't want them in it. That will be ours and our leopards'."

They got back to the house and he retrieved water and towels for them. She splashed water on her face and then drank thirstily, her gaze on the rope marks on her wrists and forearms. "I suppose I have to be careful when I'm going to meet with clients."

Was there regret in her voice? He nodded solemnly. "I'll pay attention to your work schedule and be mindful of how I tie you. I don't have to leave marks that will stay. Most will fade in a few hours. These won't last."

Both carrying waters, they walked around the large house, down to the area where Dover had originally built the massive garages where he kept and worked on his cars. Ania's family had been obsessed with cars and they could take them apart and put them back together, making them ten times better when they did so. The garages were used for making their cars fast enough to outrun anything on the road.

The garages were easily two stories high. The second stories consisted of long wooden lofts made up of very thick beams. The pulley systems the Dovers used to haul engines out of the cars hung from the beams. Crude staircases gave access to the lofts that ran the long length of the buildings. The two garages had been empty since Ania had moved out and sold the property to Sevastyan.

At first, she hadn't wanted to sell. The property had been in her family for a long time and it was difficult for her to think of letting it go, but her life was committed to Mitya and she eventually decided she wanted Sevastyan to have the Dover estate. He had been there so many times and had unconsciously been making plans for it. Once living there, he'd discovered, the house and grounds had plenty of secrets, such as the tunnel leading between the properties. There was a second tunnel that led out to the highway. The Dovers believed in being careful. They weren't quite as paranoid as he was, but he appreciated their efforts and was taking advantage of some of them.

Sevastyan led Flambé into the first garage, through the cavernous interior over to the far wall that separated the two garages. That wall was shared by the second garage. He stared up at the high ceilings and then the loft made up of the thick beams.

"I've spent a lot of time in here thinking about our leopards. Right here" — he put his hand on the wall — "this will come down when we open it up. If we planted a really big tree here, one with a thick trunk and large branches that grow out in both directions, as well as up toward the loft, we could create a really amazing space for our leopards."

"Our leopards?" Flambé echoed, spinning around to look up at him, shock on her face. She had been wandering around, not really paying him much attention, but now she was wholly focused on him.

He nodded, ignoring her look of total surprise. "When we tear the wall down, and utilize both garages, the space will be large enough for the leopards to really roam around, especially if we keep the loft. They'd have a climbing area, a place to rest, and several ways to escape from either side of the garden. If we got in trouble, they would be safe and so would we."

Flambé stared up at the planks of wood overhead that still made up the loft where the pulley system that had dragged engines out of cars had been. She walked away from him and then out farther, where she continued to study the loft from different angles.

"We could make stairs to the roof in various directions from the loft. Long ones so they weren't noticeable and the leopards could use them as perches or places to rest if they wanted," she added. "I like the idea of a large tree here. I'd have to bring in a big crane and we'd need to put the roots down deep. That would require a very large hole."

Sevastyan couldn't help but drink in her expression. When she started talking about her work, the love of her plants and the designs she created, she practically glowed. She forgot all about being guarded and became totally enthusiastic. Clearly, she could envision the garden even better than he could.

"If we make the tree the focal point, the branches extending not only up toward the loft and roof but down toward the ground and whatever we choose to plant there, as well as outward to both sides of the garden, it could be extraordinary," she continued. "I was thinking more along the lines of a water feature as a focal point, but this is brilliant when you not only consider the leopards and their needs, but any number of ways to escape danger." She tapped her thigh with the water bottle. "Really, Sevastyan, this is good."

"If you use a mature tree, how can you train the branches in the directions you want them to go?" He'd been curious about that. Most of the trees she planted were young enough that she could work with the immature limbs, twisting them and encouraging them gently, using materials to sculpt them in the forms and ways she wanted them to go. She could make a living tree a piece of art, and often did.

"It is more difficult with a mature tree," Flambé conceded, "but we've got many already planted on our property that my father began years ago with the idea in mind that we might need to use them for special clients. There weren't that many shifters in this area, but he planned ahead. I'm doing the same thing. When I take an older tree, I plant several more and work on them in order to shape them accordingly. Still . . ." She broke off, looking up at the loft, shaking her head with a small smile. "I don't think we have anything close to the size we'd need. I'll have to find one of our fastest-growing, tallest trees and try to accelerate it a bit."

"It would be great if the branches could extend out in both directions, encompass-

399

ing both garages fairly equally to bring the two buildings together so they look as if they were always supposed to be one building." He flashed a small smile. "Not to mention, a strong tree branch would be an anchor for good suspension."

She laughed. "Naturally you'd think like that."

"And you weren't?" he challenged.

She blushed. "I suppose I was." Flambé rubbed her arm and then rolled the water bottle over her skin.

Sevastyan dropped his gaze to her arm. Her skin had turned a rosy strawberry and something seemed to run under it for just a moment. Shturm roared. The wave receded.

She frowned and indicated they start back to the house, turning away from him, quickening her steps in an effort to put distance between them. His longer strides made that impossible.

"What's wrong, Flambé?" He poured concern into his voice. "Did you hurt yourself?"

She shook her head. "It's nothing. I should have put on more sunscreen. I'm so fair I burn easily."

She stepped back when he reached around her to open the door, avoiding his body brushing hers. He didn't let that happen, crowding her just a little. A little shiver went through her. Definitely sensitive. He followed her up the stairs, watching the sway of her ass. She had a way of moving that could make any man notice.

Sevastyan waited until they were in the bedroom and he'd closed the door and leaned against it. "Go in and shower. When you come out, I'll put lotion on you."

Her tongue touched her lips and her eyes went green and gold, flicking to his face, barely meeting his gaze then shying away. Already, the haze was starting. She was equating their bedroom with his place of domination. He also wanted it be her safe place. Her haven. She was still very torn. In the ropes she felt safe. But outside of them, she was emotionally terrified. That dichotomy just didn't make sense.

He stepped close to her and cupped her chin, sliding his thumb over her lower lip. "Baby, take your shower."

"You rubbing lotion on my skin will make me burn so hot I'll go insane, Sevastyan," she confessed in a low voice, as if she felt guilty.

His thumb strummed her lower lip like an instrument, knowing her sex was keeping that same pulse. "That's not a bad thing, Flambé. We're in our room. Even if we were

401

downstairs and you were burning hot, I'd take care of you. This is our home. If we were having a dinner party and you needed me, you just crook your little finger and I'll figure it out. It's my job to put the fire out." He bent his head and brushed a kiss across her eyes. "I like my job."

"Why did your cat bite me again? This morning, when you were holding me, he bit me. I was so far gone, I barely knew it, but he did. Flamme rose again. I felt her for a moment. She went wild. Why did he do that?"

He slid his hands down her body to find the hem of her tank. "Shturm has been worried about your little female." He pulled the shirt over her head and removed her sports bra, spilling her breasts into the cooler air. Gently he cupped the full mounds, thumbs sliding over her nipples. "I love how responsive you are. One small touch and you're ready for anything." He tugged and rolled with equal gentleness. When she shivered, he pinched with much more firmness.

"Why has he been worried?"

"She should have been making more appearances, even if they were brief. He wanted to ensure she knew he would take care of her and you. That he'd protect both of you."

402

"But he didn't have to claim her again, did he?" she protested.

He clamped down on her nipples, pinching between his thumb and finger, leaning forward to kiss her neck. "Take off your shorts, Flambé. When you move your hips like that, is the material rubbing? When you rub does it burn?" He increased the pressure on her nipples, distracting her. "I thought about that when you were running ahead of me, the friction between your legs. What kind of panties I wanted to buy for you so you could run and I could torment you and know you were thinking about me while you ran. Were you, baby? Were you thinking about my cock and what it could do to you? How it can make you scream?"

She gasped and came up on her toes. "Yes." The confession came out in a rush. "You're all I thought about. You're mostly what I think about when I'm not working."

He bent his head to her left breast and sucked, pressing her nipple to the roof of his mouth and then teasing it with a lash of his tongue. She had rope marks around both breasts. Those marks were the deepest. He traced the circles while he gave her right breast equal attention. When he lifted his head, he spun her around abruptly and gave her a little push toward the bathroom, swatting her ass. "Shower."

By the time Flambé returned, he had everything he wanted set out beside his favorite chair. He showered, taking his time, knowing she was waiting for him naked, walking around the room because he hadn't told her to stand, hadn't indicated that he was going to tie her. The anticipation was building in her.

In spite of her desire to deny that her hormones were getting out of control, her female leopard rising to add to the fire already continually spreading through her nerve endings, Flambé couldn't stay still. Restless, she rubbed her thighs together and paced the floor, casting glances toward the glass door and then toward his chair and the things he had set out.

Sevastyan came into the bedroom completely naked. He knew he looked intimidating. He was big, a brutal-looking man with a thick, wide chest covered in defined muscles and various scars. His cock could be intimidating as well, but Flambé never found it that way. She always seemed fascinated, always prepared to be adoring. What man didn't want his woman to have adoration for his cock?

He sank into his chair and beckoned her to stand in front of him, facing him. Immediately he pushed her thighs apart. "Are you burning up now?" He kept his voice soft. That same tone that told her he was in charge and expected answers. His fingers moved up her inner thigh slowly, brushing flames deliberately.

"Yes."

"Here?" He flicked her already exposed clit and she moaned. She was totally inflamed. He flicked a second time a little harder and she had to steady herself, a cry breaking free. "Yes, right there. Everywhere."

"I can see that. Kneel down, legs apart, and let me get this lotion on your arms and shoulders and then I'll see what I can do to help. Keep your knees wide, and face me so I can rub this on your breasts as well."

Obediently, Flambé sank down, not paying much attention until her sex hit the knots in the rough rug made of sisal rope. He had painstakingly made the rug himself, tying the knots and then weaving the rounds until he had a good-sized piece he could use. He'd stashed it just in case it could be useful someday. He was very glad he'd done so when she gave another little cry and rocked her hips.

"Baby, you need to try to stay still for me." The rough rope would play over her burning sex and the knots would slide on her tender inflamed parts, adding to the coiling tension so that she would strain for release.

He took the lotion and began a slow massage into her neck and shoulders. At first, the lotion had a soothing effect on her skin. He knew it would. It had natural aloe vera in it, but his touch on her body was sensual, whispering over her pressure points, the ones that triggered her needs, that ones that heightened her awareness of him. His hands slid from her arms to her breasts, massaging the lotion into the full mounds, cupping the soft weight and massaging lotion into the undersides, not wanting to be neglectful.

"Turn around for me. No, don't get up, just spin around, keep your knees wide."

She closed her eyes and obeyed him, grinding down on the knots as she did, rocking her hips forward, a kind of long groaning sound of need escaping. He simply continued with the slow massage, starting with her neck, digging his fingers deep into her tense muscles, finding every trigger point. Occasionally, he bent forward and nipped at her earlobe or whispered a kiss along her ear, watching the goose bumps rise on her skin.

When her skin was glowing and she felt

406

hot, when she couldn't stop moving, he put the lotion down and reached around to her front, very gently covering her breasts with his palms. "Baby, if you prefer, you can go lie on the bed and I'll make love to you slow and easy and take away that burn right now. I've never tied you twice in one day and you're already climbing out of your skull. That can either be a good thing or a bad thing. I don't want you burning to the point of hurting. I want you burning to the point of anticipating. If you want to stop, we'll stop, and I'll give you my cock, let you sleep while I make us dinner and then you can rest again."

He fell silent and waited. Flambé didn't disappoint him. She tilted her back until it was nearly in his lap, her nipples hard little points of flame in his palms.

"Or what?"

"I've wanted to build a pattern called the necklace on you. I think it will look beautiful. It really depends on how tired you are." One finger slid back and forth along the side of her breast, adding to the flickering flames of electricity snapping over her skin.

Her hips rocked. She kept her head in his lap, her back stretched, her breasts thrust into his palms. "I'm never too tired for you to tie me, Sevastyan."

407

His heart stuttered. He heard the note of truth leopards couldn't hide from one another. She had seen the bundle of green rope, silk, a stark contrast to the sisal rope rubbing on her bare pussy. He reached one hand for it, keeping the other on her, rubbing gently, reassuringly, soothing her.

The necklace was a beautiful pattern. He wanted to add a couple of variations to it, but essentially, he would tie it the way it had been done for many years. There was no screwing with perfection. He pulled her hands behind her back and looped her wrists and then wove a quick cuff and open lace glove over them. Pulling her head back farther and down toward her hands, and hands up toward her head, he quickly braided her hair into the rope and the rope and hair into the line with her cuffed hands. Now her head was anchored and she was unable to move it.

He checked her pulse, whispered encouragement and kissed her as he looked down at her body. The light had changed in the room. Evening had shifted the sun so that the ball had dropped from the sky, creating orange-red streaks that were already fading to bluish grays.

Shadows fell across Flambé's face. Already she looked as if she was slipping into subspace, and he wanted her focused completely on him. He caught the rope and tugged hard, snapping it against her scalp, causing it to sting, bringing her eyes flying open. He waited until she was looking at him and nowhere else. He snaked the green rope around her neck and began to weave it in the intricate pattern that was high up on her neck and made its way down to her breasts until the ropes were draped and pulled over them in loops, covering the mounds and nipples at an angle, two strands at a time. Each weave ran around to the back and was threaded into the bindings of her hands and back up to the necklace ties at her neck.

When Sevastyan was finished, Flambé was kneeling on his rug made of sisal rope, her naked inflamed thighs and clit pressed tight into the knots there. Her hips bucked continually, riding the knots, her body bent almost backwards. At the same time, the necklace around her throat and breasts seemed almost demure in contrast to the sordid display of her open legs.

He moved out from behind her, camera in hand, and took several shots of his work, then several shots of her face before seating himself once again. He tugged on her braided hair, letting the knots unravel,

409

watching them slide away quickly. He'd deliberately used ones that could easily be removed fast. His woman was just about done.

When he had the ropes off of her, he lifted her, carried her to the bed and took her down to the mattress, his body blanketing hers. Murmuring soothingly to her, he kissed her over and over, stealing her breath, wanting to steal her heart. Her soul. God, she was the most amazing woman he'd ever found.

He had no idea he could be tender. He was a rough man, especially when it came to sex, but for her, there was tenderness. She was slick and hot, and so tight that when he pushed into her folds slowly, filling her, he didn't think he could make his way into that snug tunnel. She gasped, her lashes suddenly lifting in alarm, eyes staring straight into his, her fingernails biting deep into his shoulders. She shook her head at him, fear creeping into the gold of her gaze.

"What is it, baby?" he murmured, one hand stroking her mound, her inner thighs, circling her clit, feeling her body shudder as her pussy swallowed another inch of him. "Look at you taking me." It was an erotic sight, seeing himself disappear into her body. "Look at us, Flambé."

Her gaze slid from his face to their joined bodies. Her feminine form was flushed, covered in his rope marks, in strawberries where he'd left his personal marks behind, on her breasts, her thighs, one on her neck, but low so it wouldn't show when she wore a shirt. She had a business and she was the boss.

He dipped his head and kissed her throat. The action sent his cock sliding another inch into her. She shuddered. Her sheath, scorching hot, tightened like a vise around him. His breath hissed out. He stopped moving and watched her face. That beautiful face while she squirmed and did her best to try to impale herself on him.

"We're doing slow and easy, Flambé."

She shook her head, looking as if she might fling herself off the bed and run.

He began to move again, because it was impossible not to. He needed to bury himself all the way, to feel her body surrounding his. It was easy to drown in her eyes. She didn't want to look at him like this; he could see her trying to escape their connection. It was too deep. Too visceral. She shook her head again. "Faster. Harder. Not like this."

"Just like this, Flambé. It's good, baby. You know it is." He whispered the truth to her, and it came out like a sin between them instead of the growing love he was trying to convey.

He detested that he wasn't good at romance, at telling his woman what he wanted her to know. He could do it with his ropes, but she didn't hear him. He was trying with his body, but she didn't want it. Verbally, he couldn't get the words out that would reassure her, because in the world he grew up in, those words were a death sentence. He had to try to reach her someway and she only let him close through sex or ropes.

He did a slow surge forward with his hips, forcing her tight petals to give way and open for him. This time he didn't stop but, all while holding her gaze to his, buried his cock deep in her. The burn turned to flames licking hot and wild over and around him, feeling as if the fire was consuming him in a new and different way. That shocked him. Judging by her expression, the feeling shocked her as well.

They were both used to hot and wild. Fast and furious. Slow and easy was so different, but equally as good, very moving. So much so that terror had crept into her eyes. He tried to reassure her, but a part of him was feeling that same fear. She had taken him over when he wasn't looking. When he'd

412

been so busy binding her to him. Wanting his own woman for all the wrong reasons and realizing, when he had her, what the right reasons were.

He moved in her, sharing her body, her haven, in intimacy unlike he'd ever experienced in his life with another being. The fire built and built like a slow-moving storm, flames licking all over his skin, all over hers, touching and receding and then coming back again, leaving them both breathless.

"Sevastyan." She whispered his name.

He heard a note in her voice that had never been there before. She didn't want to admit true feelings to him. To herself. But they were there.

He kept moving, building the heat between them, that slow, easy build that was anything but easy. The fire began to roar. Became a storm of emotion. Her body clamped down on his without warning, a scorching-hot grip, a blaze of fire so hot his cock jerked and pulsed, erupting in a wild storm of white-hot ropes of semen, a volcano there was no stopping.

Flambé's body seemed to have one continuous orgasm in response, so that even when he collapsed over the top of her, careful to keep his weight to one side to keep from crushing her, every movement sent powerful ripples through her. Her arms crept around his neck and she buried her face against his chest, hiding her expression.

"I want us to try together, Flambé," he whispered in her ear. "I know it's scary to you. Neither of us has ever done this, but let's try." He waited, closing his eyes. Hoping. Hearing his own heartbeat. Feeling her body rippling with such magic around his. "We're good together. I know we are. Let's try, baby."

She was very quiet for a long time. Her head nod was barely there. He felt it and his heart turned inside out. It wasn't much, but he'd take it. She always felt so elusive to him, like she had one foot out the door. At least it was somewhere to start.

13

Sevastyan didn't think his mood could get much fouler. If Mitya didn't fucking start cooperating with him, he was going to take out a gun and shoot him himself. How could the entire world spin out of control overnight? He'd been gone one damn day. You'd think he'd taken a month off, not one single day, but Mitya was acting as if he'd deserted him.

"Get your head out of your ass, Mitya. How can I be responsible for what Ania decided to do while I was gone? She's your wife. You're the one who is supposed to handle her, not me. As for Rolan disappearing, he had to have help. He had to have known we had eyes on him. Someone ratted us out. Unless you think that's me, stop yelling at me and let me think."

"Maybe if you'd been here instead of fucking that woman every five seconds, none of this would have happened. We wouldn't have been short of bodyguards if she hadn't run sniveling to you that someone hurt her feelings, and Ania wouldn't have gotten hurt . . ."

"Damn it, Mitya, that's bullshit and you know it. Ania takes chances. That isn't my fault or Flambé's fault. Miron and Rodion overheard our conversation and had no fucking right to repeat anything we said. None. They know better."

Sevastyan pressed his hand to his pounding head. Mitya was insane over Ania. He knew that. Ania had gotten it into her head to climb to the top of the loft when no one was around. She'd been in the garage working on her engine and just got frustrated. Instead of utilizing the skills of her leopard, she tried climbing the human way, missed a step and fell. She broke her wrist. Of course Mitya was going to lose his mind, but blaming Sevastyan — or worse, blaming Flambé — was ridiculous. To make matters worse, they'd lost eyes on Rolan. That meant Sevastyan was going to have to lock everyone down tight. He'd be everyone's enemy.

"Whoa. Miron and Rodion overheard what conversation? What did they repeat?" Mitya's voice was suddenly low. Menacing. "Something that had to do with Flambé?"

Sevastyan turned to face him. To glare at

416

him. "Suffice it to say it wasn't very nice. I can't go into this with you right now. I have things to straighten out."

He paced across the room again, Shturm raking at him cruelly. His leopard had never been so on edge. He couldn't calm the cat. He was meaner, more ferocious and tenser than he'd ever been, ready to rip anyone apart at the least provocation. This wasn't the time for Mitya — or anyone else — to defy or cross him.

Mitya seemed to be having equally as hard a time. Ordinarily, Sevastyan would be feeling just as upset over Ania's broken wrist. Maybe that was partially the reason for his own furious temper. Why hadn't anyone taken more care with her?

"No one should be repeating our personal conversations about our women, Sevastyan," Mitya said, his tone indicating that he might just add his own retribution to Sevastyan's.

"Hence the beating," Sevastyan pointed out.

He forced air through his lungs, letting the positive sift through his brain rapidly. He had two teams of shifters already available to him. Drake Donovan had been very fast to answer his call for help. Gorya and Timur had listened to him. Without hesitation, they had managed to get Fyodor,

Evangeline, the twins and Ashe out of harm's way. They were supposedly vacationing in an undisclosed area. Knowing Timur, wherever they were, no matter how fun, they were locked down tight and very safe. Gorya had elected to stay and help protect Mitya, Ania and Sevastyan.

Sevastyan forced himself to stop pacing, ignored Mitya and faced his cousin Gorya. "I appreciate that you stayed behind, Gorya. Rolan's hired quite the force to send against us. Most are mercenaries, not shifters. I'm fairly positive he'll send in those men first to test our defenses. Or while we're fighting them off, his shifters will try to come in quietly under cover of their fire. Mitya and Ania have a safe room that's hidden and well supplied. They could live there for well over a month if necessary and they have three escape routes for both leopard and human from that room."

"What will you do with your woman?" Gorya asked. He was draped on the wall, tall, lithe, even a little lean, all muscle, looking deceptively lazy. He was all muscle and flexible spine, a fighting machine, but he appeared to be easygoing, until one looked into his eyes — eyes that right now showed his concern for Sevastyan. He was always

418

the peacemaker for his more volatile cousins.

Sevastyan sent Mitya a glaring challenge, one that betrayed the fact that Shturm was extremely close and furious. His eyes were all cat, pure amber, gleaming with malice at his cousin, daring Mitya to allow his leopard out.

"I had planned to have her go into the safe room with Mitya and Ania, but that's impossible." Even as he threw the accusation out there, he knew it wasn't really Mitya's fault. Part of his anger was the fact that he was beginning to think Mitya was right in that Flambé was never going to feel anything for him but her need for sex.

He turned to stalk out before Gorya could try to appease him. He didn't want to be appeased. He wanted to let Shturm loose to fight the way he needed to fight. He could taste the rage in his gut now, a dark red that spread through his body, flowed in his veins, consuming both of them.

"Sevastyan." Mitya stopped him at the door. "Wait. I know I'm acting crazy. I can't seem to calm my leopard. He's furious no matter what I do." He sat at his desk, his head in his hand. "There're things that have been going on that we need to talk about . . ." He broke off as someone

419

knocked on the door.

Sevastyan was standing beside it and recognized Ania's scent immediately. He opened the door and caught the unmistakable fragrance of his woman too. She was farther down the hall, standing several feet away, not even looking their way. She looked small, alone, too alone. The hallway was wide, the walls tall to accommodate the high ceilings, emphasizing her small frame. She kept her head turned away from Mitya's office even when Ania spoke.

"I'm taking Flambé out to my garage to see my project, Mitya. Is it really necessary for us to have to wade through, like, seventy-five shifter guards to just get from here to my workspace?" There was a hint of amusement in Ania's voice.

Sevastyan wasn't amused. "Ania, Mitya doesn't have a say in who is guarding you right now, only I do. We're under lockdown. Just accept that anywhere you go on the property there are going to be guards. Lots of them. At some point, you might be told not to leave the house. If you can't accept that, you might be forced to stay in a room. You know me. You know I don't fuck around with your safety." He liked Ania a lot — okay, if he ever used the word *love,* he could admit he had that emotion for Ania. He didn't like to be harsh with her, but he'd rather be harsh than have her end up dead.

He knew Flambé liked Ania. If Flambé had allowed herself any friend from inside his circle, it was Ania. Now that he actually thought about it, he'd never seen her with any other friend. She didn't talk on the phone to other women. She didn't tell him she was going to go meet someone for drinks. When she did get calls, and those calls were numerous and could last for long periods of time, she was all business. He didn't want to alienate Ania, not against him and certainly not against Flambé. Still, her safety and Flambé's had to come first. In the end, if either woman died, so did their man. That was the bottom line.

Ania looked from her husband to him, going from challenging to vulnerable in one short moment. That look cut deep. He'd caught brief flashes of something very close to that in Flambé's eyes. Ania moved past him, quicksilver like Ania was, and he didn't have time to move out of her way. She brushed up against him and he scented blood. Ania? Bleeding? That time of the month maybe, but it didn't seem quite right. It wasn't his business, but still, it was worrisome.

Frowning, he pushed back against the

wall, folding his arms across his chest, leaving the door open. He wanted to be able to keep an eye on Flambé while Ania talked to Mitya.

The moment Ania moved into the room, Mitya's hard features softened. He spun his chair around immediately, his blue eyes sweeping over her from head to toe as if checking her for damage.

"I'm sorry I interrupted you, Mitya. I wanted to take Flambé to see my latest work out in the garage, but I should have just texted you or Sevastyan. I had no idea Rolan was anywhere near."

That told Sevastyan that Mitya shared their history with his wife. He and Gorya exchanged a long look. Ania had gone through one war already with their family when Lazar, Mitya's father, had come to kill him. It couldn't be easy to ask her to go through another.

Sevastyan studied Ania. She hadn't hesitated as she crossed the room to go straight to her husband. She leaned into him. Everything about her body language screamed that she adored him. When she tilted her face up to his, the love on her face was almost so blinding, so intimate, it seemed wrong to witness it. Mitya bent toward her, his hands gentle as he cupped her face.

"We aren't certain where he is, *kotyonok,*" he replied, calling his wife *kitten,* his nickname for her. "We just have to make certain you're safe."

Sevastyan glanced down the hall to Flambé. She never touched him outside of sex. She didn't move her body close to his even when they were alone. She didn't lean into him. There was no look of adoration unless he had her in the ropes, one of the reasons he wanted to tie her more and more. He loved that look on her face and in her eyes when he took her. She kept herself emotionally — and to an extent, physically — away from him.

He went very still inside. All along, his cousin had tried to tell him that he had made a mistake with his choice. He thought it was more about him being fucked up. He'd known all along he was, but then all of them, every Amurov, had thought they were — until they found their mate. Sevastyan had been different. The others had been able to stop having sex when their leopards had gone so crazy and wanted to tear apart any partners. Sevastyan had been unable to do so.

The craving for sex had grown stronger in him. The worse the rage, the more the need for sex built until he had no choice but to go to the club. Not that the differences ended there. Mitya might be extremely dominant, but his sex didn't border on brutal. He didn't want or need the kind of kink Sevastyan did.

Ania loved Mitya. She really loved him. He knew Evangeline loved Fyodor. Ashe loved Timur. Flambé didn't want to even connect with him no matter what he tried to do. He reached out over and over to her. Every time he thought he was close, she retreated. Granted, he didn't know the first damn thing about a relationship, but he was trying. He was going to have to face the fact that there was something wrong with him.

Abruptly, he turned and stalked out of the office, straight down the hall to Flambé. They'd had a good day the day before; at least, he thought they'd made progress. Today, she'd come with him to work and she'd been quiet, thoughtful, but she hadn't completely retreated from him as she normally would have. He knew she didn't like his cousin and avoided him as much as she could. Mitya was often rude to her. He was going to talk to his cousin and ask him to try with her, even though Mitya didn't understand her.

He walked right up to Flambé where she stood, back pressed against the wall. There

424

was nowhere for her to retreat. She straightened to her full height, which compared to his was ridiculous, so she tilted her head up as he caged her in, his hands on either side of her, his chest a barrier as his eyes blazed down into hers.

"Is there something wrong with me?"

Her long lashes fluttered. She looked genuinely puzzled. "What are you talking about?" She blinked again and her eye color changed. She gleamed with golden fury. She turned her head toward the office and he heard the hiss of rage. Behind her, where she'd braced herself against the wall with one hand, claws dug into perfect wood. "That bastard. Does he do that to make himself feel better? No, Sevastyan. There's nothing wrong with you."

"He isn't really a bastard."

"You know he is."

"Ania loves him."

"I know she does."

"But you can't love me. What's wrong with me?"

Her breath caught in her throat. Her lashes went down and then swept back up. The fury faded and for a moment he caught fear mixed with something so close to what he was certain was love his heart clutched tight in his chest. So tight it hurt. Burned.

She did feel something for him and it terrified her. Still, he didn't trust himself. He wanted to believe it so much he might have made up that very brief look. She *had* become protective of him for just a few moments, even if now she was stiff and prickly.

Shturm? He turned to the one companion he could count on. Through every nightmare, his leopard had been there for him, trying to protect him, trying to give him truth and stand for him, guard him when there was no one else. *Does she feel anything at all for me besides fear? Anything like Ania feels for Mitya?*

He tried to convey tender feelings much like he felt for his leopard, but it was hard when one had to use images. Shturm had been in the world a long time now, hearing and learning, and he was intelligent. He picked up words, but Sevastyan wasn't certain if he grasped the concept of love.

She does.

Shturm felt aggressive. Every bit as moody and ready to fight as he did. He needed to be cool and in control when he planned his strategy against a master strategist like Rolan. At least his leopard had given him some much needed reassurance. Flambé was still running scared, but she had developed some feelings for him in spite of herself.

"There've been some complications, baby. Maybe danger. Remember I told you about my father, Rolan, and how much he despises us? He slipped into the States and was in Houston. I had eyes on him but he got past them and now he's in the wind. I've got to lock everyone down."

She nodded. "I understand. Do you want me to go home?"

He shook his head. "I'd prefer you work here where I know you're safe. Our house is safe, but when I have my eyes on you, I just feel better. Ania said she wanted to take you out to her garage and show you something. The two of you can carry on as normal, just with a team watching over you. They'll stay out of your way as much as possible. Ania is used to it and hopefully you'll get used to it as well."

He saw the beginnings of a protest, but she locked it down immediately. He detested that. She didn't argue. He wished she would. Before, he took her compliance as part of her submissive nature, but now he doubted her silence had anything at all to do with compliance or even submission. Outside of sex, and from the little he'd managed to get out of her, Flambé didn't show her submissive side to many. She most likely simply didn't argue and went her own way

427

when she chose. That was not a good thing for him.

Ania came up to them. "I'd like to show Flambé some of the things I've been working on, Sevastyan." Her tone was placating. She put her hand on his arm and looked up at him. He could see the affection in her eyes.

Flambé made a single sound, a low vibrating noise in her throat that was a growl, cut off by a choking cough. Sevastyan immediately caught her arms and pulled her to him, worried her throat might still be sore. He'd given her honey in tea before she went to bed and again that morning before they'd come to his work. The moment he gathered her against him, he felt his male leopard's smug satisfaction.

They did not like another female touching us.

Sevastyan felt a little smug himself even though Flambé all but pushed off his chest to get away. She might not ever be one of those women who was overly demonstrative toward him in public. He resisted catching her red topknot and tugging her head back so he could take command of her mouth and light a match to her dynamite. Instead he brushed a kiss on top of her head.

428

"Have fun with Ania, baby," he murmured.

Flambé followed Ania down the hall, past her office to the very end where the back door leading to the garage and gardens were. She found it really quite lovely, but wished she could implement a few changes. The pavers were perfect, the darker colors showing off the flowers and bushes with their variegated leaves, but the path wasn't quite wide enough and needed more of a definition. She would plant some more lacy vines going up trellises and the low fencing around the walkways leading to the garage.

"Are you all right, Flambé?" Ania asked as she stepped back to allow Zinoviy and Vikenti, the two bodyguards, to enter the garage while she stayed waiting for them to ensure no one was lying in wait to harm her in any way. Two other bodyguards, Trey Sinclair and Kyanite Boston, remained with them. They kept their distance, facing away from the two women, scanning the grounds around them, all senses enhanced by their leopards. Ania ignored all of the them as if she wasn't aware they were hovering close.

Flambé refused to allow Flamme even close to the surface, although she would have felt safer. The bodyguards were too close and the female was getting far too near her heat. Flambé's body already was so sensitive to touch without the added hormones of her female, she didn't dare allow her to rise even for a moment with the men in close proximity. It would be a disaster for everyone. She had no doubt in her mind that Sevastyan would murder any male that challenged him for her — and they would if Flamme or she became seductive.

"Yes, I'm just uncomfortable." She kept her voice as low as possible. Leopards could hear about five times better than humans and sometimes, depending upon the shifter, even better. She was careful, but she knew the guards probably heard her — and scented her. It was impossible to cover the scent of a female in heat, no matter how she tried.

"We'll be inside in a minute and the guards will stay outside," Ania assured.

They waited in silence, Flambé studying the way Ania cradled her wrist. The cast was slim and one that could be removed when necessary. It seemed very unlikely that a leopard could break her wrist. She tried to imagine various ways it could happen and none seemed too likely.

Eventually, Zinoviy and Vikenti returned and gave Ania the go-ahead. She flashed

430

them a smile and hurried inside but didn't close the door. "I love my space. No one comes uninvited, without my permission, unless Sevastyan says we're on lockdown for a reason," Ania informed her. "I told Mitya I wanted a place to design my own cars, work on engines and just disappear for a few hours without feeling like I was getting swallowed up in his world."

"This is your dream? What you want above all other things?" Flambé asked. She'd been out to the garage with Ania several times before and had seen the drawings and custom works, but often wondered if Mitya had given her the job to push her into staying close to home.

Ania nodded and indicated the room built mostly of glass off to one side where several comfortable chairs formed a cozy circle. "Let's go in there. I like that room. I chose everything in it. The carpet, the chairs, the privacy drapes, all of it."

"Why do you have privacy drapes if no one comes in here?" Flambé asked curiously, following Ania around car parts and the engine hanging from the complicated pulley system.

Ania, a slight flush on her face, gestured toward the very comfortable chairs as she closed the door. "There are times when I

431

welcome my husband's visits. Sevastyan or one of the other bodyguards is never far away. We can get a little crazy sometimes."

Flambé curled up in the soft blue of the chair. The fabric rubbed over the sensitive skin of her arm, sending a terrible burning wave over her body. She forced herself to stay still, knowing from experience the sensation would go away if she could just ride it out.

"Well, whatever you use this room for, I like how you designed it. It's beautiful and feminine, right in the middle of your garage with car parts, tools and engines everywhere. It's sort of a counterpoint to the tools, like an oasis. When I design my gardens, I sometimes use something similar to make a statement."

"What would be my statement?" Ania stretched out in her chair, her legs in front of her, feet on an ottoman.

"That you're feminine but you have a wealth of knowledge in a field that is predominately male. You're not willing to give up being feminine to prove to anyone that you probably know far more than most others when it comes to taking a car apart and putting it back together. You don't feel you have anything to prove at all and I think that's a powerful statement."

Ania stared at her for a moment. "You get that just from me putting together this little office?"

"And the way you're sitting in the chair. You're relaxed and open. You're not closed off at all. You spent time putting together your office and choosing each piece inside it." Flambé gestured to the glass windows that looked into the garage where the engine hung. "Clearly you enjoy looking at your work, so you're excited about what you do."

Flambé was well aware she would appear closed off if anyone studied the way she was sitting. She had curled up, made herself small, legs tucked under her, the classic way to look non-threatening. "How did you manage to hurt your wrist, Ania?" She was very careful to keep her tone interested. There wasn't a single accusatory note in her voice.

Ania rubbed her forearm. "I feel so silly." She gestured toward the far corner where there was a series of wooden planks going up to the roof. They were vertical, straight up, and each was a good distance apart. "I decided to climb those and I just fell. I wasn't paying attention."

Flambé closed her eyes and shook her head. How often had she heard the same ridiculous excuse from a female shifter? She

433

took a deep breath. "Leopards don't fall, Ania. And if they do, they have flexible spines and they turn in midair and catch themselves. If Mitya hurts you, I can help you." She kept her voice low. "I know it seems like there's no way out, but there is."

Ania sat up slowly, her gaze meeting Flambé's steadily. "Flambé, Mitya didn't hurt me. He would never hurt me. Never. I really did fall. I was crying and I wasn't paying attention to what I was doing. I never should have been climbing when I was so distraught."

Flambé could hear the truth in her voice. She waited a few moments to get her heartbeat under control. She'd almost ruined everything. This woman was Sevastyan's cousin's wife. She most likely told her husband everything. "Why were you crying? You certainly don't have to tell me if it's too personal. Friendships are so rare for me and I . . ." Deliberately she trailed off. She genuinely wanted to know, but it was necessary to divert Ania's attention from her terrible error.

Ania stared down at the cast on her wrist for so long Flambé didn't think she would reply, but then she took a breath and looked up. "I had just miscarried for the second time. I was really upset. I know it wasn't my fault but I felt like somehow I couldn't do what every other woman in the world seemed to do so easily. I want a child. I didn't think I did, but once I knew I was pregnant, I was so happy. Mitya, of course, is only worried about me; at least, that's what he says, but I know he hurts as well. I hate that this happened a second time."

Flambé looked around the office to discover the box of tissues a table away. She retrieved the box and handed it to Ania, who had begun to cry. "I'm so sorry, Ania. How terrible. I had no idea. What did the doctor say?"

"He said these things happen and that it doesn't mean I can't carry, but that he'd run some tests. I know Mitya thinks it's him, and that if for some reason he can't give me children I'd want to leave him, but I wouldn't. It would hurt not to have them, but it would hurt more not to have him."

"If it's you who can't have children, would he leave you?" Flambé asked, her voice very soft. She knew she shouldn't push, but she couldn't help herself. "Is that what you think?"

Ania shook her head. "That's the last thing Mitya would do. He's told me a million times he doesn't care if we have children or not. I can hear truth. He means it. I

435

just wanted the baby . . ." Ania trailed off.

Flambé scraped her teeth back and forth on the pad of her finger, wishing she had words to comfort Ania, but there were no words. No way to comfort, not in this situation.

Ania's gaze was suddenly very focused on her, and Flambé could see her cat watching her as well. "Does Sevastyan hit you, Flambé? I've known him forever and I can't imagine it, but they say you never know. It's okay to tell me. He's very intense, and dominant. Really, if you needed help, I would help you."

The direct question caused a sudden queasiness in the pit of her stomach. She'd done that so many times, lulled a woman into a false sense of security and then asked the important question — was she a victim of domestic violence? It was so much more complicated with shifters. Leopards were involved as well as their human counterparts, and leopards were so much more difficult to get away from.

Flambé shook her head, rubbing her palms up and down her arms, suddenly covered in goose bumps. "When he tries that, it will only be once."

"When?" Ania leaned toward her. "Why would you expect Sevastyan would hit you?

436

Has he done something to indicate that he might hurt you, Flambé? If he has, you need to tell me. Your leopard should indicate to you if there is a problem, but if she hasn't, if she is too afraid and you can't rely on her . . ."

"No, no," Flambé cut her off hastily. The conversation had taken an unexpected turn. She had thought to protect Ania and all of a sudden Ania was trying to protect her. Unfortunately, Ania didn't understand that her husband would always put Sevastyan before anyone else. Ania was so in love with Mitya that she was blind to that. "I don't want you to think Sevastyan has done anything to me. He hasn't. It's just that . . ." She shrugged and sent Ania a smile, breaking off as if that was the end of the conversation.

Ania frowned, clearly not wanting to drop the subject. "Why would you think that Mitya would hit me? Or hurt me in any way?"

Flambé sighed. This was her fault and she had to play it out. She just had to be so careful. Really, really careful. There was so much at stake, too many lives. She'd misread the situation, or at least Ania's commitment to her husband. "Shifters can be very cruel, can't they? In the end, women

437

have very little say and eventually their mates often resort to violence."

Ania sank back into her chair, looking horrified. "Has that been your experience with shifters in your lair? What about your friends, Flambé? What have they said about their lairs? I haven't heard you mention any of your friends. Do I know them? Like yours, my family was in this area for a long time. Maybe we know some of the same people."

Flambé shook her head. "I doubt it. My friends were women like me, strawberry leopards, although those women came in from other countries to try to make a life here. I only got close to a few of them. They didn't make it or they moved away." In spite of every effort to keep herself under control, grief welled up along with guilt, so strong she felt her heart might shatter. She pressed her hand hard over her breast.

Ania, with her sharp eyes, couldn't fail to see that telltale gesture. "Oh, Flambé. What happened?"

Flambé shrugged, tried to look casual. She was talking too much. That was why she didn't get close to anyone. She didn't dare let down her guard. "It doesn't really matter one way or the other. I'm just really sorry about you losing the baby and glad

438

Mitya is good to you."

"Honey, I hate that you have such a bad idea of male shifters. I don't know what it's like where you come from, but not all shifters are cruel to their mates."

Flambé's eyebrow shot up. "Are you going to tell me that your husband didn't tell you that in his lair the men murdered the mothers of their children after they gave them sons? Or that they sold their daughters to other lairs to shifters who would do the same thing to them?"

She couldn't sit still and she jumped up, her leopard close, driving her to a restless pacing, her breath coming far too fast. There was a strange roaring in her ears and heat rushed through her veins. Beneath her skin, something grotesque moved, causing a terrible itch that left a burn in its wake. She could actually see her skin lift. The entity moved like a wave through her body, leaving behind a firestorm that raged through her until she wanted to scream.

"You should text Sevastyan," Ania suggested gently. "Your cat is so close and she's giving you fits. I know what that's like and it's so uncomfortable, Flambé."

Flambé wanted to claw her own skin off. "*Uncomfortable* is a mild word, but I've been told strawberry leopards tend to feel

439

things in a slightly different way. This is torture and it manifests itself in a horrible sensation." She tried to rub her arms, hating to touch her skin. Her clothes hurt, let along touching with her palm. "I'm a mess. I'm sorry, Ania, I came out here hoping to comfort you and you're trying to comfort me."

"Why don't you want to call Sevastyan to help you?" Ania got up to go to the refrigerator she had in the corner of the office. "I know he's working, but you're his first priority."

"I'm not, you know. Mitya is." Flambé gratefully took the water from Ania and drank quite a bit down, hoping to put out some of the fire. It didn't seem to help so she entreated her leopard, trying to soothe her. *Go back to sleep, Flamme. When we're alone, I'll let you out to run. We'll be home and no one will be around and you can run free.* She made it a promise, meaning it, at least hoping to. Maybe she could let her leopard emerge with no one around. Maybe they could do it together and once Shanty got there, they could just disappear.

"Sevastyan might be head of security here, but you're his woman. Your cat is in heat and she's his leopard's mate."

"Is she? She's in her first cycle. So is his

440

leopard. From what I understood from the other strawberry leopard women when I talked to them, it is very easy to get it wrong when you don't know what you're doing and your leopard is in heat."

Flambé didn't want to add that strawberry leopard shifters were notoriously sexual. It was a curse. That made it even easier to accept a male when one was in the throes of a sexual burn they couldn't control. Not to mention, she'd been dazed from a blow to the head and *Flamme* had made the decision for them, half scared out of her mind. Worse, she'd been influenced by Flambé's continual fantasies regarding Sevastyan Amurov.

She turned away from Ania and paced closer to the glass doors that stared out into the cavernous garage. She longed for the freedom of the outdoors and her plants. It was easier there in the open air, hidden in the foliage, to control the terrible cravings that racked her body at times, the ones she knew had aided in destroying the women of her species. So many things had contributed, but this curse was one of the worst.

She didn't cry, because like everything else in her world, she couldn't give anything away. She didn't have friends anymore because she couldn't take the loss. Nor could she trust anyone with the lives she held in her hands. She breathed in and out, giving her leopard air. Giving herself air. Telling herself it would pass, just like everything else horrific in her world.

"Do you feel you've made a mistake? Does your leopard?" Ania asked.

Keeping her back to Ania, Flambé shrugged. "I have no idea because I don't know what to expect. I'm very nervous and so is she. She keeps hiding." She kept her answer simple and what one would anticipate from a woman whose leopard hadn't emerged and who had no one to instruct her in what might happen.

Immediately, Ania was all sympathy. "It's natural for both of you to be nervous, Flambé. It doesn't help that Sevastyan is so dominant and his leopard must be as well. I imagine his male must scare your female every time she starts to rise."

Flamme was settling, and the terrible itching was receding, allowing the chaos in Flambé's head to slowly dissipate. She took several deeper breaths and turned back to Ania. "His male is quite terrifying," she acknowledged. He was. Maybe not so much to Flamme, but he was to Flambé.

That leopard wasn't the kind to ever let his female go once he mated with her. Twice now, he'd claimed her. He'd dripped his chemical into her body via his saliva and there might be traces, even if she used scent-blockers, for him to track her. He would be persistent. He was that kind of cat. Sevastyan was that kind of man. She pushed down panic and made herself smile at Ania.

"I'm taking it one day at a time." She had to be so careful that every word she said was strictly the truth. She drank more water and sat back down, letting Ania talk to her about how good it could be when a male leopard protected his mate and really cared for her. It sounded like a fairy tale to her.

The sun had long since set before Ania and Flambé returned to the house. Sevastyan was aware of every minute ticking by. He'd checked on them dozens of times, ensuring they were looked after. He'd sent food out and it was reported that neither woman ate much. He didn't like that. He had a battle plan to set up. The property was large and he wanted to make certain every point of entry was covered. Every team knew what was expected of them. Mitya and Ania had to be covered at all times. Still, he wanted to make certain the women were cared for.

He was tired and he'd been without his

443

woman far too long. Shturm was in a foul mood, raging at the long separation, especially when he knew his mate was close to rising. It was a dangerous time to be away from Flambé. Sevastyan hadn't gone so long without sex since he'd been with her, his body now used to getting rid of the buildup of aggression just by stalking down the hall, going to her office and finding her there, always willing to be with him. Always ready for him. One lousy day without and he found himself in such a foul mood he wasn't fit to be in anyone's company.

Ania came to Mitya's office with Flambé, but as usual, his woman just stood outside in the hallway, waiting with Kirill and Matvei for him. Ania kissed Mitya as he stood up and went to her, meeting her halfway.

"I'm tired, honey. I'm going to lie down."

"I'll meet you upstairs," Mitya said.

Ania nodded, and patted Sevastyan's arm as she passed him, waving at Flambé as she rounded the corner to go to the staircase leading to the master bedroom.

"Everything's in place, Mitya, stick close to the house," Sevastyan reiterated. "Call me if anything is out of the ordinary."

A dozen strobes flashed and then went off abruptly. Instantly everyone went quiet. He stepped in front of Mitya, and Kirill and Matvei did the same with Flambé and Sevastyan.

"Someone came up the front drive, Zinoviy," Sevastyan said softly into his radio.

"Cops. Two of them."

Sevastyan exchanged a long look with Mitya, who cursed. There was another long silence while they all waited.

Vikenti came down the hall toward them. "The cops are here to talk to Sevastyan," he announced. "Ray Harding and Jeff Myers. I've got them in the front room. Zinoviy is watching them, making certain they don't try to plant any bugs."

Flambé frowned. "Why would the police want to talk to you, Sevastyan?"

"They always want to talk to us about something, *malen'koye plamya.*" Sevastyan gave her his most casual smile and started down the hall.

Mitya went with him, Kirill and Matvei followed along with Vikenti. Flambé trailed after them. Mitya stopped abruptly, which meant all of them did, including Sevastyan. Mitya whirled around and shook his head at her.

"There's no need for you to come, Flambé," Mitya stated. "I'm sure you have plenty of work to do."

445

She went very still and for the first time every man in the room felt her leopard rise. It was fast and the little female was furious. The mood of a female leopard was palpable. Impossible to ignore. Edgy. Dangerous.

Flambé's skin glowed. "You aren't my leopard's mate." Each word was very distinctive. Her gaze swept past Mitya to meet Sevastyan's. She was all cat in that moment. Her eyes pure green. It was a challenge. She was forcing a choice in front of the men.

Sevastyan fucking hated what he knew he had to do. This was going to cost him and he was already on shaky ground with her. He hadn't sealed her to him, but he couldn't afford for Flambé to overhear anything the cops asked him about the night he'd left Mitya's to go hunting Franco Matherson.

"Baby, go to your office." He spoke softly but it was a command, nothing less. "You can wait for me there."

Flambé looked at him for one long moment and then she was gone. Her leopard was gone as well. He felt the retreat. The suppression. They all did. She turned and walked away from him, straight toward the back of the house, which could mean anything. He was fairly certain she wasn't heading to her office, more likely straight to the back door.

He had no idea where Rolan was. He had no idea where Franco Matherson was. He swore under his breath. His sins seemed to be piling up. He stood for a long moment staring down at the floor before turning his icy gaze on his cousin. "You can fucking burn in hell, Mitya. I won't be forgiving that shit anytime soon. When this is over, you can find yourself a new head of security. Kirill, I need you to watch over her for me. If I lose her, I lose everything."

He turned his back on his cousin, not waiting for his response, and stalked down the hall to the cops, knowing they were there to ask him about Franco Matherson and the feud they supposedly had. Matherson could burn in hell as well.

Stalking down the hall straight into the sitting room where the cops waited for him, he entered, letting his rage fill the air, blasting hot, violent red. He knew they felt the feral emotion. The walls could barely contain the predator in him. Shturm raged with him, a cruel, deadly leopard, furious and determined to break free, to kill anyone in his way so he could get to his mate.

"Gentlemen. Make this fast and to the point. I'm busy and you've come at a very bad time for me, so this had better not be a fucking bullshit harassment visit." He didn't

447

bother to take one of the chairs as Mitya did, but remained standing as the other bodyguards had done. "Let's get started."

14

Kirill and Matvei had conveyed to Sevastyan that there had been a very brief argument at the back door with Flambé the night before. Flambé wanted to leave Mitya's house, just as Sevastyan had known she would, and they had refused to allow it. She'd asked if she was a prisoner, and they had tried to be as gentle as possible with her, reminding her there could be danger. He knew they genuinely liked her. Who wouldn't — other than Mitya. Mitya seemed to really dislike her. And she disliked him.

Mitya. Sevastyan knew he wasn't being fair to his cousin. Mitya was trying to protect him, just as he'd tried for years, when he was a child. Looking at it from his perspective, Flambé appeared as cold as ice to Sevastyan. She wouldn't so much as hold his hand. If one compared Ania, with her loving, adoring looks at her husband, touching him every chance she got, to Flambé,

449

who wouldn't go near Sevastyan, who could blame Mitya for thinking Flambé had no feelings for him? Sevastyan didn't really believe she did either. He hoped for it, but he didn't believe it. Still, his leopard was mated to hers.

Sevastyan sighed and paced back and forth across the kitchen floor. He was barefoot, wearing only a pair of soft pants riding low on his hips, wondering if he should try to use a tie to get Flambé to talk to him. She had refused all night. He didn't blame her. She was silent on the ride home in the car, but the bodyguards were with them. He hadn't tried to talk to her either.

The moment they arrived in the house, she'd gone straight upstairs and was in the shower. She'd spent a great deal of time there. He knew she was crying. He fucking hated that with every breath he drew, but he wasn't certain how to handle her tears. She was completely closed off from him. She'd shut him out. He felt the distance between them. He didn't just feel it, Shturm felt it as well. His cat prowled and snarled, pacing back and forth as if afraid she might bolt, taking his mate with her.

No matter how many ways he'd opened the conversation, trying to explain, she had shut it down, turning away from him, acting indifferent, uncaring, curling into the smallest ball he'd ever seen in the middle of their bed while he was so restless, his body raging at him for relief, desperate to rid itself of the buildup of aggression that was worsening by the moment. He didn't want to use the ropes. He wanted to talk to Flambé, to try to sort out what was between them, to come to terms together and commit to each other.

Her leopard had to emerge soon. The few glimpses he'd manage to catch, the female had been potent, bordering on desperate. She was so close. Heaven help him, but she needed to make her appearance before Rolan made his. Somehow, and he wasn't certain how, he had to make this right with Flambé.

The fragrance with little hints of freesia, Moroccan rose and Egyptian jasmine spiced with cinnamon, cloves and coriander drifted to him. He inhaled deeply, taking her into his lungs. She smelled like heaven to him. The moment he scented her, he tasted her on his tongue. That set up a craving. He was addicted to that taste, the combination.

He turned to greet her. She looked pale, dark circles under her eyes. She'd slept restlessly. "Good morning." He didn't have a great opening line and he needed one.

Desperately. They had to talk things out.

She nodded to him. To get to the coffee pot, she'd have to walk past him. She could skirt around the long kitchen aisle, but that would only prove she was avoiding him. She didn't even look at the coffee pot. She went straight to the refrigerator, took out a bottle of water, and went out the door to the verandah.

Sevastyan sighed and followed her. "We're going to have to talk about it, Flambé."

She leaned against the railing, staring out over the expanse of property. She didn't even turn her head. "I don't see any point. You explain. I accept the explanation. Then everything goes to hell all over again. It's kind of a vicious cycle, Sevastyan." She took a sip of water. "Do you know what I like about plants? About trees and shrubs? You can count on them. They're always going to perform the same way." She glanced at him over her shoulder. "I'm beginning to see that in you. I just had different expectations." Her half smile held no humor. "Leopards don't really change their spots."

"What does that mean?"

She turned away from him. It never failed to amaze him how much she appealed to him. Everything about her. He should have been telling her that from the start. Now, if

452

he said it she wouldn't believe him. He tried to think what Mitya did for Ania. Mitya could be tough, even brutal, and Ania and Mitya had a very healthy sex life, but what were the small things that his cousin did that made Ania know he loved her beyond all else?

Actions were always so much better than words. He'd made the mistake of relying on their sex life, their connection through the ropes, and not putting any real thought into the little things that would have reassured Flambé that he meant to put her first in their life together. Had he done that, what had transpired the night before wouldn't have caused such a visceral reaction.

"You have to be who you are, Sevastyan. I have to be who I am. It's that simple when you really come down to it."

"What do you think I'm like?"

"You know what you're like. I don't have to tell you." She pushed her hair back and then pressed the water bottle to her temple. "I've got a bit of a headache. I think I need caffeine. If you'll excuse me." She turned away from him and went back inside.

Cursing under his breath, Sevastyan followed her in. The moment the door swung closed, the strobes went off, indicating someone had driven onto the property.

"We've got company, Flambé," he called out and snagged a gun, going to the front door, eyes on the security screen. "Stay out of sight."

She didn't answer him, but he knew she wouldn't disobey. Flambé might be upset with him, but she would never compromise either one of their safety out of spite. Savastyan recognized Cain Dufort as he strode confidently up the walkway and then up the stairs to ring the doorbell.

Sevastyan opened the door slowly, warily, the gun in his fist, ready to kill Cain if the man made one wrong move. "You didn't call ahead, Cain. I wasn't expecting visitors this morning."

"I'm sorry. I don't want to sound overly dramatic but I need to talk to you and I don't know if someone is listening to either of our phones."

Sevastyan shoved the gun into the waistband of his pants and stepped back, indicating for Cain to enter the house. As he closed the door, turning to keep Cain in sight, he caught sight of Flambé coming from the kitchen. She had a smile on her face, not for him, but for Cain. Even her eyes were lit up. He detested that Cain Dufort could make her smile so spontaneously like that while she was so guarded around him.

454

"Cain, how lovely to see you. There's a fresh pot of coffee. Would you like a cup?" She went right up to him as if she might plant a kiss on his cheek.

Shturm roared with rage and leapt toward Cain, raking at Sevastyan to break free. Sevastyan circled Flambé's upper arm with false gentleness and pulled her away from the other man, around his body and behind him. "I doubt he'll be staying that long. What can I do for you, Cain?" Sevastyan focused completely on the club owner, letting him see how close his leopard was. How close the danger really was.

Cain shook his head. "I'm sorry, Sevastyan, I had to come. I know Flambé's close to the emergence, but the cops came to the club asking questions about you. They claimed they questioned you and you said you were at the club that night. They asked for the proof. I refused to give them tapes, but they're asking for photographic evidence. I won't give it to them without your consent."

Flambé stiffened. He felt her step away from him.

"Flambé, go upstairs and wait for me," Sevastyan said. He spoke very quietly, but it was an order.

He found it difficult to maintain when his

455

leopard was losing control, due to having a large, unclaimed leopard in his prime be so close to his mate when she was near the emergence. That would be bad enough, but Flambé wasn't committed to Sevastyan. She seemed to look on Cain with more favor. That put Sevastyan on edge, coloring the edges of his world a dark red and stirring the terrible well of rage that was always present, no matter how hard he tried to suppress it.

Flambé barely glanced at him as she walked past him. He was surprised that she actually went without a protest. Her shoulders were straight, her head up. She was barely speaking after the fiasco with Mitya and now hearing from Cain that he'd been at the club, he could imagine what she thought. He should have just told her. Truthfully, he hadn't thought about it. He didn't want her knowing he'd been stalking Matherson to kill him.

"Give them the photos, Cain," Sevastyan said once Flambé had disappeared from their sight and he heard the soft closing of the master bedroom door. "I don't have anything to hide. They did question me. Apparently, there was some party at a place Matherson was renting and the cops found dead bodies. How they think I could possibly be involved I have no idea. Matherson apparently disappeared. I had my people check and his private plane is gone. It was my bad luck to drop by the club to see you that night to ask to take a look at the garden Flambé planted for you. I only saw it the one time and I wasn't paying attention to it."

"Yes, you mentioned that you came to get her and took advantage of being alone in my little paradise. I wish I'd been there."

"It was just as well you weren't. I would hate to have to do in one of my good friends." Sevastyan put an edgy humor into his voice. "I'd like her to make us a garden. Something a little different, but I thought your idea was a good one."

Cain grinned at him. "I do like your woman. I wasn't certain she was leopard, although I was beginning to suspect. It was my bad luck that you recognized what she was and claimed her before I ever got a chance. I need to find a mate for mine before it's too late or he's going to rip me or someone else apart." The smile faded. He turned and walked toward the door. "You need something, let me know. There aren't too many of us to count on."

"I was shocked that my leopard was so fiercely certain hers was his mate. He wanted her and he immediately was protective of her. There was zero hesitation on his part. Don't stay in your office all the time, or your club. You might want to talk to Flambé once her leopard's emerged and she's through the heat cycle. It's possible she could introduce you to a few shifter women. But, Cain" — his voice went from friendly to cautionary — "don't claim one unless you're certain you're going to treat her right, with respect. It isn't fair to take one and then toss her aside and continue your lifestyle. Incorporating her into it is one thing, but leaving her behind is another altogether."

Cain nodded. "I'll talk to Flambé when you give me the go-ahead."

Sevastyan saw him out, closed the door and watched him until the car had pulled down the driveway and he was certain the club owner had driven off the property. He stood for a time at the bottom of the stairs, feeling like he was starting all over again with Flambé. She had trust issues, big ones, and he hadn't even scratched the surface with what the problems between them were. Now this happened.

Sighing, he went up to her. It felt like a hell of a long way up those stairs. Their bedroom was empty. He looked around. It was perfectly neat, not so much as a wrinkle in the perfectly made bed. Flambé didn't throw tantrums. She didn't yell. She didn't fight. She retreated. She withdrew. She took herself far, far away. He could tell himself he had her, but he knew he didn't.

He padded silently across the room, stalking her like the predator he was. He was leopard. A shifter. A very dominant alpha. She was a shifter and they lived by shifter law. No one broke those laws. She knew that. He crossed to the slider and stood for a moment regarding his elusive strawberry leopard.

Flambé sat outside on the balcony watching birds hopping from one branch to another in the trees, busy calling to one another as they flitted about. She didn't look up or acknowledge him. She wasn't drinking the fresh coffee he'd brewed. She had the same cold bottle of water. She preferred water to most drinks.

"I owe you an explanation." Sevastyan pulled his chair around to sit facing her rather than beside her. He wanted to see her expression. Her eyes. Right now, she refused to look at him, even when he was right in front of her, larger than life. The night before, she had cried. He'd seen the evidence of her tears on her face, but she hadn't talked to him. Hadn't let him in. Now, she was more closed off than ever.

"I told you, I don't need an explanation."

There was no expression whatsoever in her voice.

He tried not to glance at his watch. He had to get to Mitya's house soon. Time was getting away from them. He knew if he even mentioned his cousin's home or his work, he wouldn't have a chance to make things right with Flambé. "You're going to get one. There was a reason I went to the club."

She sighed. "Of course there was a reason you went to the club, Sevastyan. The first time I ever saw you it was at the club. I know what you do there. I knew you went there. I'm leopard, or did you forget that? I smelled it on you. All those men and women. The sex. It isn't that difficult. I waited for you to give me an explanation and you didn't. If you were going to, you would have at the time. Not now. Not when you humiliated me in front of your cousin and men by pointing out to me that I'm exactly what he said I was, a sex object to you and nothing more. Your toy, I believe I was called. I didn't expect you to be going to the club already, but I knew, sooner or later, you'd go back to it."

She shrugged and continued to stare

straight ahead as if she was talking to the landscape. "Fortunately, I have a very strong sex drive and I'm familiar with the club and what goes on there. Had you just been honest in the first place and told me that was the kind of open relationship we were going to have, I would have understood the rules."

In spite of his determination to work things out, that one little line and the casual way she said it sent crimson fire rushing through his veins. Shturm roared a challenge and leapt at him, clawing and raking wildly.

"What exactly does that mean, Flambé?" He kept his voice low, strictly velvet, back to the dominant in him.

She shrugged again and took a drink of water. "Don't you have to go to work? Naturally, I prefer to work from home. We both know this house is extremely safe. You went out of your way to make certain no one could break into it and there's a tunnel between the two properties no one knows about. I don't want to set foot in your cousin's home. It would be utterly humiliating to me."

He was fucked any way he responded to that. If he forced her, he was the worst partner on the face of the earth, but if he didn't, he would be seriously worried and

461

divided constantly over her protection. And then there was the question of what the hell her statement about the club meant. They had a lot to clear up.

"Flambé, what exactly did you mean about you and the club? I absolutely require an answer."

"I meant, as far as I'm concerned, since I'm considered a sex object anyway and you feel you can go to the club and do whatever you want, there's no reason I shouldn't go. It certainly shouldn't bother you."

Shturm rose so fast that for a moment Sevastyan actually had to struggle with him for supremacy. *What do you think you're doing? If you hurt her, you hurt Flamme. Back off.* Sevastyan stayed very still, breathing down the ever-present rage, reminding himself that Flambé was very hurt. Mitya had dismissed her in a cutting way and Sevastyan had let it stand in front of everyone, leading her to believe that the original things said about her were what they all thought of her — were what *he* thought of her.

She had smelled the club on him when he'd come home to her and she hadn't said a word, waiting for him to give her an explanation. When he hadn't, she'd pulled back. It was no wonder she had suppressed

Flamme. The two had to be confused. Hurt and confused. He couldn't compound errors by scaring them both with his temper and Shturm's.

"There is a complete misunderstanding, Flambé, but I can see how that would happen. I'm going to start with the club. I did go there and I didn't want you to know."

She started to stir, moving as if she might stop him from speaking. He could feel her hurt, although she tried hard to keep it from him, but he was very tuned to her. He was a rigger and he'd had her in the ropes far too many times not to read the slightest nuance. He wanted to pull her into his arms and comfort her, but he knew she wouldn't allow it. Mitya — and he — had stripped her of her pride.

That damned first conversation Miron and Rodion had overheard and repeated where she could hear it, making her feel as if she were nothing but an object for him to have readily available for him to have sex with, that had started it. That was on him, not Mitya. His cousin couldn't be blamed for that. Mitya treating her as if she wasn't important, not his fiancée, not his woman or Shturm's mate. Even that was on him because he never took the time to fully explain to his cousin what was going on

463

between Flambé and him. He should have. He didn't want anyone to know he couldn't handle his relationship — or his fear that he might somehow lose her.

"I would like you to hear me out. Please let Flamme close to the surface so there is no mistaking whether or not I speak the truth. I needed an alibi that night. I planned on killing Matherson and I didn't want you to know. The cops can track cars through traffic cameras and it just so happened that the place he was renting was a short distance from the club. We parked in the lot and made our way on foot to the residence he had leased."

Flambé continued to look out over the property. The one thing he didn't like about the open acreage was the fact that there were several knolls where a good sniper could conceal himself in the branches of a tree or up on a boulder. If Flambé was out on the balcony she could be killed. Inside the room, the bulletproof glass would save her, but if she was outside, that would be a problem. He needed a way to combat that. He forced his mind to stay with his explanation.

"Matherson and his crew were gone, but there were three dead bodies left behind, all human. I knew I could be in trouble if the cops came asking questions — and they might, given the fact that Matherson had been pounding on my door a few weeks earlier. The cops like to harass our family. So, I went into the club, changed and walked around, making certain to be on Cain's security tapes, and then spent some time talking with him in his office about the gardens. At no time did I tie another woman or use one for sex. I didn't provide a demo for anyone. I did what was necessary for an alibi and that was it."

His head was pounding, never a good sign. His body ached, every muscle, an even worse sign. When he got like that, he knew he was getting close to a time when, before he had Flambé, he was going to have to go to the club for a long session. He would have to choose a partner who was no novice with Shibari, who could be in the ropes for long periods of time and could take a little discomfort and fairly savage sex.

Her leopard was throwing off hormones. Flambé was throwing off hormones. His male's testosterone was off the charts; so was his. Flambé declaring she would go to the club and hook up with other dominants was a challenge. Cain coming to the house and Flambé responding to him the way she did set his teeth on edge. Her very silence could be construed as a challenge. The coming war with Rolan put him on edge. It was all brewing together into one perfect storm.

"As for what happened yesterday when the cops came to question me and Mitya acted like an ass . . ."

"I would prefer not to talk about it," she interrupted.

"We have to talk about. I hurt you. I knew it was going to hurt you. I didn't want you in that room with them and neither did Mitya. He sounded like the ass he can be when he stopped you from coming with us."

She shook her head but refused to look at him. It might have been a mistake to make an excuse for Mitya. He should just keep his cousin out of it.

"The cops tried to shut down Evangeline's business when they couldn't get to Fyodor or Timur. They made a show of going into her bakery when customers would be there, during her busiest hours. Your business means the world to you. I know that. I didn't have the time to explain to you that I didn't want them to know we were together. Not yet. Not until I could put a plan together to better protect your landscaping business. We aren't married yet. We aren't partners. I have no real way to help you. The only thing I had was to keep you out of sight. And I knew they were going to question me about the club. I had to figure out a way to tell you I was planning on killing Matherson."

She brought the bottle of water to her lips and drank. He glanced at his watch and inwardly cursed. This wasn't going well. Words didn't mean a whole hell of a lot. Had she humiliated him in front of everyone, he wouldn't have been so easily persuaded by a simple explanation, especially if he'd overheard the things said about him in the beginning of their relationship.

"I know this is bad timing, Flambé," he began. He had to go to Mitya's. Rolan could already be sending a crew to attack. He had to be there.

She shook her head. "I'm not ever going to that house again. Not ever. If you insist, you will have to tie me up and drag me there and I'll fight you every step of the way. There will never be forgiveness. Not ever. The moment I can, I'll run."

He heard truth in every word. This was the worst possible situation. "Flambé, Flamme is close to rising. Rolan is in the wind. He could send an army against us."

She turned her head and looked him straight in the eye. "I will never go to that house again. Never. For any reason. If

Flamme rises, you're close and there's the tunnel. You can get to us. I will never be humiliated like that again or be around those he has purposely made me into nothing more than your toy in front of."

"He hasn't done that."

"You are very quick to defend him and yet he said that to you and you have no idea if he's said it to his men. He certainly has no respect for me. I don't really care, Sevastyan, one way or another what he thinks of me. I will not go to that house. You have pointed out repeatedly that we're safe as long as we're inside, and I'll give you my word I'll stay inside."

There it was. Her word. He heard the ring of truth in everything she said. Shturm heard it as well. He had a choice. He could be an utter bastard and serve himself, keeping her close to him so he could have peace of mind, or he could give her at least one thing, and come home hoping she would feel more at peace in their home and more ready to talk to him. He detested leaving her there.

"I would want to leave Kirill and Matvei with you. They can stay downstairs if you're uncomfortable. You have a mini-kitchen up here. Or I can ask them to stay outside. If

we're attacked, they would have to come inside."

"They can stay downstairs. It's soundproof up here. I can intercom them if I need to. They can intercom me. I'll be fine." For the first time there was expression in her voice. Not much, but at least something indicating she wasn't completely remote from him.

That didn't loosen the knots tied so tight in his belly. "You will send for me the moment you feel her rise." He made it an order.

She nodded.

Sevastyan stood, towering over her, feeling as if they hadn't really sorted anything at all out. There was such a distance between them it may as well have been an entire ocean. He brushed a kiss on top of her head, but she didn't even look up. Cursing, he stalked into the bedroom, changed and stormed out, leaving behind instructions to his bodyguards, and then went to talk to his cousin.

Mitya was waiting in his office. Ania was curled up on the little bench seat by the window. She looked very nervous and she got up as Sevastyan entered, going to him and putting her arms around him. "Mitya told me what happened yesterday. I'm so sorry. Flambé was already so troubled. I

469

should have stayed."

Sevastyan frowned down at her. "What do you mean she was already so troubled?"

Ania gave him another hug and went back to her seat at the window. "She's confused about whether or not her female and your male made the right choice. They're both very scared. I think she's witnessed a tremendous amount of shifter abuse."

Sevastyan lifted his head alertly. That made sense. "She got more of that here." He knew he was being unfair, but rage was too close and fear of losing Flambé too great. He wanted to blame Mitya. He wanted it to be his cousin's fault, but he knew it was really his own. "Exactly why the hell do you dislike her so much, Mitya?" he demanded, whirling around to face his cousin. Even that was a silly question. He knew why.

"She doesn't love you. You deserve to be loved." Mitya shoved his chair back from his desk so hard it fell over backward. "You can be as angry as you want, Sevastyan, but it's the truth. I've watched her from the beginning. I tried to warn you. I know you're tired of being alone. I know you need to go to that club and work your aggression out on whatever the hell you do there, but some little submissive willing to play her

470

part just to get off because you're hot in bed isn't the same as someone who will be devoted to you because she loves you. I want that for you. She doesn't touch you. She won't hold your hand or touch your face, or lean into you. There's nothing at all. *Nothing.* She gives you nothing and I want so much more for you."

That was all true. Sevastyan couldn't say it wasn't. He was suddenly damned tired.

"Mitya." Ania's voice was the calm in the middle of the storm. "I don't know what you've been doing or saying to Flambé, but I can assure you, she does very much care for Sevastyan. She might not want to. She's afraid. I'd go so far as to say she's terrified. Forgive me, Sevastyan, but there was so much fear that I even asked her if you had harmed her in some way, when I can't imagine you harming any woman. She has really been traumatized by shifters, male shifters. I asked her about female friends and her answer was very strange. She said they were gone or dead. I thought that was extremely interesting — and sad."

"You didn't follow up?" Mitya demanded.

Ania didn't so much as flinch at his tone. "I didn't dare. She was on the verge of flight. I wanted to make certain she saw me as a friend. She needs one. I thought if we

471

spent time together, she might relax enough to confide in me. It might not be then, but eventually. At one point, her leopard was close, pushing very near to the surface. I could see it hurt her. Not like it does when one first shifts, but just the closeness of her leopard beneath her skin."

Sevastyan rubbed his arms as if he could soothe Flambé. "For some reason, her nerve endings seem too close or something. I'm going to have the doc look into it. She says they burn all the time. It gets so much worse when her leopard pushes close. Her mother bled to death in childbirth. I suspect that's how their species has mostly died out. The doc wants her to do some testing. He says he can start her on shots to help her blood clot."

"Why wouldn't her father have done that when she was just a child?" Mitya asked.

"That's a very good question," Sevastyan said. "But I'm not certain of any of this."

"When her leopard was close, I had mine talk to hers. It was quick, but Flamme, that's her leopard's name, is very certain of Sevastyan's leopard. She thinks he can protect them. She believes Flambé cares a lot for Sevastyan but is so afraid that she may take them too far away and he will never find them. Never. The leopards never

472

can. That's what she said. The leopards never can. What could that mean?"

There was a long silence. Mitya held out his hand to Ania. She put her smaller hand in his immediately. Mitya shook his head and sighed, shoving at his hair with his free hand. "I'm sorry, Sevastyan. This entire mess is my fault. I should have given her the benefit of the doubt and trusted your judgment. She's so reserved. And small. I think I always pictured you with this lioness of a woman and one who gives you hell, kind of like Ashe does Timur. What a mess." He sank down on the window seat beside his wife and looked at her. "Tell me what you think I should do to fix this."

Sevastyan thought it was significant that Mitya didn't ask him what should be done. He trusted Ania's advice more. Sevastyan should have gone to Ania for advice as well before he had thoroughly fucked up the relationship.

"You're going to have to go to her and apologize and tell her why you were such an ass, Mitya. Tell her you were worried about Sevastyan and why."

Mitya groaned. "He has to take back that he won't work as my head of security."

"No, he doesn't. You were an ass to Flambé and she deserves an apology and

473

you know it," Ania said. "Stop trying to get out of an apology to Sevastyan. You have to do that as well. One has nothing to do with the other."

Mitya looked at him, clearly steeling himself to make the ultimate sacrifice. Sevastyan stopped him, shaking his head and even stepping back. "Don't. Not yet. We've got a couple of things we need to hash out before either of us talks about apologies."

Mitya stood again and this time he tugged Ania to her feet, his gaze steady on Sevastyan's face, knowing the discussion he was going to force between them was going to be an ugly one.

Mitya brought Ania's knuckles to his mouth and kissed them. "If you don't mind, *kotyonok,* I would very much like to speak to my cousin alone."

"Of course, honey, just know that I love him dearly, and I want to be able to have both Sevastyan and Flambé to dinner at our house sometime in the future." She went up on her toes, brushed a kiss on her husband's jaw and left the den.

The office was spacious, but when two large men with big male leopards in their primes faced off in adversarial positions, that space became small immediately. Mitya put the length of the room between them.

"This has to do with Rolan? Your father?"

"You know very well Rolan is not my father," Sevastyan accused. "When I was a teenager, I told myself you didn't know, that I was protecting you from that knowledge. I quickly came to realize after habitually being subjected to beatings by both Rolan and Lazar, and their lieutenants, that there was no way Lazar, in his cruelty, wouldn't have informed you or your mother of what he had done."

Sevastyan's gaze, banded with heat, never left Mitya's. Shturm was close. They trained with the best every day. They never stopped. He loved Mitya, but betrayal was an ugly thing. In their family, fathers turned on mothers and daughters and even sons and nephews, killing them. It was the norm in his world.

"Yes," Mitya admitted softly, "I knew. Lazar rubbed it in my mother's face one night when Rolan's wife came over pregnant. Rolan was out of town and Tatiana, your mother, was staying with us. Lazar kept taunting her, saying he was going to tell Rolan and Rolan would beat her until she lost the baby. His laughter was so ugly. I remember thinking how disgusting he was and how lucky she would be if she lost the baby. He

475

wouldn't have anything to hold over her head."

"But he didn't tell Rolan."

"No, he didn't. So, after she had you, Lazar forced Tatiana to sleep with him. He'd make her come to the house and bring you. I'd have to take care of you while he took Mom and her into the bedroom. Sometimes he wouldn't go into the bedroom so he could show me what two women could do together to pleasure a man. I can't tell you how many times I thought about killing you, killing us both, so those two women would be free of him. So *we* would be free of him."

Mitya turned away from Sevastyan, balling his hands into two tight fists. "When you were not even a year and half, he liked kicking you around in front of the women. Hard. Beating you with his fists. He wanted me to join in. He would let his leopard out to threaten to eat you. When I wouldn't help him, he let his leopard loose on me or the women. He was a fucking dick. A monster." He turned back to Sevastyan. "He didn't get much better as you got older, although he never beat you when Rolan was around. When did you find out?"

"I was a teenager. Lazar told Rolan. He was so smug. Rolan made the mistake of having his lair be too prosperous and other

476

lairs took note of it. We'd swallowed two smaller territories that were right on the harbors and that gave us more control than Lazar. We also had taken a small but very critical piece of land that bordered the main highway controlling the railway."

Mitya studied his face for a long time before speaking. "You were fifteen years old and you were already that fucking smart, Sevastyan. You told Rolan exactly what he needed to do to get the advantage over the other *vors,* didn't you? You were the one running the business. That's why the arms deals were suddenly going so smoothly and no one could figure out where the weapons were being kept. Lazar was going crazy. He tried to bribe so many of Rolan's top men, but by the time he hit the location, the weapons were gone."

Sevastyan couldn't help but hear the pride in his voice, but that didn't matter to him now. He hadn't once taken his eyes from Mitya. His gaze hadn't wavered, the heat still as white-hot as ever. Trapped inside his soul, a crimson rage blazed a molten fire so deep and strong he knew it would never be put out. He waited for the answer. He needed to know the why of it.

He had Lazar's venom running in his veins. He knew that. Mitya knew it. They

477

both shared a legacy of brutality and cruelty. There was no denying Sevastyan had borne the brunt of the hatred and ire of both Rolan and Lazar. He had aided Rolan in outsmarting Lazar only to have Lazar gleefully spew his secret truth — that Sevastyan was Lazar's son, not Rolan's. At the same time, there was no denying that, as Lazar's son, Mitya lived in hell every minute of the day.

"Yes, I took over running the lair, although completely behind the scenes," Sevastyan admitted. "Rolan was a good fighter, but he wasn't good at planning battles and worse at business. I could see the bigger picture. Once Lazar told him the truth, that I was his son, not Rolan's, Rolan despised me. He took every opportunity to find ways to hurt me. He needed me, but he hated me. He threatened to kill you all the time. He hated you almost more than he hated me. He thought you mattered to Lazar. He knew I didn't. Hell, even Rolan used to worry that Lazar was too ugly to you, too hard on you, but it never bothered him when Lazar kicked the crap out of me or my leopard. It wasn't like I mattered to any of them. Not Rolan. Not Lazar. And certainly not to you."

Mitya's eyebrow shot up. "You're changing history, Sevastyan, and I'm not sure why. You might have the right to ask questions, but think back. Who stood in front of you? Who took beatings for you? Later, when you were a teen, you watched my back, that's true, but we did it for each other."

Sevastyan shoved both hands through his hair in agitation. Over the years, he'd come to accept that his role was always to be in the background. He found he preferred it that way, but the rage in him built and built. The more the others heaped their cruel brutal beatings and forced him to fight, the more his leopard learned in the battles to protect his human. Sevastyan learned to fight as well, to become proficient in all weapons until he was a killing machine just as his leopard was. He was exactly what Rolan and Lazar had shaped him into.

"I tried to counter what they did to you, but I was in a different lair, Sevastyan, not around you as much as I would have liked," Mitya pointed out. "You often heard things before I did. More than once you took my back, and I thought it was because of our relationship, that you knew, like I did, that we only had each other."

Sevastyan didn't think that deserved an answer. "You had plenty of opportunities to acknowledge the relationship, but you

479

didn't. Not once. In fact, you avoided me for the most part. You seemed to have an aversion to me unless you needed someone to fight with you or go out on a drug raid."

Mitya shrugged. "You were the best. The fastest. The deadliest. You still are. I don't know another shifter capable of taking you down. In a battle, I'm going to choose to have the best with me every time. That made perfect sense and no one would question my choice or my reason for choosing to have you with me. And I didn't want you left behind alone in either lair."

"What does that mean?"

"What do you think it means?" Mitya sounded annoyed, the way he often did. "No one could be better than Lazar. You were a kid, Sevastyan. A big kid, maybe, all muscle, but you were still a kid. Already you had a reputation, and it was growing too fast. How do you think he was going to react to hearing about some kid being the best? The deadliest? The fastest? You were already getting a reputation as someone the women liked being with. They didn't run screaming from you. They smiled and flirted with you. That was going to get you killed in a very ugly way. And if he ever found out you were the one running Rolan's lair, his business, besting Lazar, he would have emptied a gun

480

in your belly and then let his leopard devour you."

Sevastyan knew that was all the truth. Lazar had an ego that wouldn't stop. Sevastyan hadn't helped Rolan succeed in running the lair so efficiently to please Rolan or make money; it was to best Lazar. To know he was undercutting him at every turn. Taking away his business slowly.

Sevastyan studied Lazar's territory and all of his imports and exports. He knew where he kept his weapons and drugs. He knew the pipelines and the routes he used for trafficking. Systematically he began to interrupt them. He was careful and used only those men he could trust. He stashed any contraband in places no one would think to look and then stayed quiet while Lazar and his men went crazy looking everywhere. Their leopards were let loose to track, but Sevastyan used scent blockers and he mixed up scents to throw the leopards off.

"I protected you the only way I could, making sure to take you on every raid if he wasn't with me," Mitya said, "and leaving you behind if he was."

"You left, Mitya, when Fyodor did, after he killed his father and wiped out his lair, but you never said one word to me. You never sent for me, or asked me to go with

481

you. You left me there to face both of them alone."

Sevastyan's tone was mild. His dominant voice. The one he used that was low, almost soft, that played over nerve endings, but carried his absolute will. He didn't sound as if he might leap across the room in a full-out attack, but Shturm was waiting, prowling, pushing so close when Sevastyan closed his fist his nails dug into his palms like claws.

"I got out with my life and nothing else. There was no time to get word to you or anyone else. Lazar heard Patva was dead and he raced to the lair to see for himself. I got out while I could. The rumors were flying about Fyodor, Gorya and Timur. I hoped you got out and when you finally joined me, I welcomed you."

"But you never once acknowledged me."

"Lazar wasn't dead. Rolan wasn't dead. As long as either was alive, I wasn't going to give them more reason to want you dead. You're a killing machine, Sevastyan. You're intelligent and you can do things I can't. I spent most of my life protecting you whether or not you want to acknowledge or believe that. You're all the family I had until Ania. I wasn't going to allow Lazar to take you away from me. I knew the moment Lazar thought you were important to me he would

482

move heaven and earth to kill you. The same with Rolan. So, I never gave that to them."

"Or to me. You could have acknowledged to me that you knew I was your brother and that it mattered to you. They weren't here and I was. It mattered to me, Mitya."

"True. I could have. Or you could have. But you didn't. Instead, you chose to be head of security. I wasn't about to give you an excuse to leave. And you would have. If I had let Fyodor and the others know you were my brother, you would have left."

"You don't know that."

"You're an arrogant bastard, Sevastyan, mean as a snake, worse even than I am. You know it and so do I. Half the time you're just looking for a fight. You're intelligent and your brain needs to stay active. You have to have sex all the time in order not to rip someone to pieces and it has to be your way. Everything has to be your way. You take control of everything around you. Do you really believe that had I come out and acknowledged you as my brother that you wouldn't have manufactured an excuse and left? You would have. You don't want to be on equal terms with me. You don't want anyone to look at you and see you."

Maybe everything Mitya said was the truth, but that didn't stop Sevastyan from wanting to rip his face off. Or have the satisfaction of punching his fist right through his mouth and feel the familiar crunch of teeth breaking.

"You still should have made that acknowledgment, Mitya," Sevastyan said, not knowing why it was so important Mitya understand that someone had to see him. Just one damn person.

Mitya regarded him for a long time in silence and then he finally shook his head. "You don't get it, Sevastyan. I've acknowledged you from the moment I found out your mother was pregnant with you. I acknowledged you when I took care of you and he hurt our mothers. I have always acknowledged you. I've always known you were my brother. I've always looked out for you, whether you thought so or not. I might not be the best at showing it, or saying it, but you're my brother and no one is going to harm you while I'm around. Why the hell do you think I made such an ass of myself around Flambé?"

The pressure in Sevastyan's chest was like a great stone pressing down on him. Mitya had no more of an idea of how to have a relationship than he did. They were the most dysfunctional family there was.

"Does Ania know?"

"That you're my brother, not my cousin?" Mitya scowled at him. "I don't hide anything from Ania that I don't have to. Especially when it comes to my family. Of course she knows. She loves you, even if you're as fucked-up as hell and you order us all around."

Sevastyan's phone buzzed and he pulled it free of his pocket just as strobes flashed a warning through the office. He glanced down at the warning text on his phone. "Take Ania and get to the safe room. I'll keep you informed. The cameras should be working so you should have live feed, both visual and audio. Don't come out for any reason. I've got this."

He turned away and then stopped, not turning back. "Something happens to me, you take care of her. Flambé. You make certain she's safe and happy, Mitya. Give me your word."

"You have it, Sevastyan."

485

15

Sevastyan texted one-handed to alert Kirill and Matvei that Rolan's first wave of attackers were making their move. He wanted them inside the house and to double-check that the house was locked down with Flambé inside. He texted Flambé next.

Trouble starting here, baby. Rolan is bringing it. Stay inside and be safe.

He waited, his heart beating hard. He shouldn't have left her behind.

Am inside our room. Will be fine. You be safe, Sevastyan.

At least she'd given him that much. He hurried to the control room where two relatively new employees manned the screens. Both were Evangeline's brothers. Ambroise Tregre served in the Navy and was an up-and-coming artist. He seemed a

486

dreamer, a man Sevastyan would have thought useless when it came to security, but Tregre never forgot a single detail once he saw something. He had a photographic memory. More, he was astonishing with computers.

Christophe Tregre, after a stint in the service, had trained with an elite unit of Drake's in the Borneo rain forest but returned to ensure his younger brother and sister were safe from his treacherous father and uncle. He then began training in the security force under Timur. He had excellent fighting skills, but not as much experience as Sevastyan would like. He was Fyodor's brother-in-law, which meant he was sacred. Family. Sevastyan wasn't going to put him at risk if he could help it. Christophe was a strategist, a good one. So, he was in the control room.

Sevastyan leaned over his shoulder. "What are we looking at? Rolan wouldn't throw his best men at us yet. He's testing us."

"He's testing us with some pretty heavy numbers," Christophe replied. "He's got five teams coming in. The way they're moving, they look like shifters to me. Where would he manage to get that many?"

"Mercenaries. Rolan has money. He can pay top dollar." Sevastyan should know, he'd helped to earn it. He kept his eyes glued to the screens. One team was moving in the trees, running along the branches, still in human form, but Christophe was right, they were too sure-footed in the trees carrying their weapons to be anything but shifters. "He must have been in Houston to pick them up off ships coming in. These men aren't from around here. He's recruited them from other places."

Sevastyan studied the shifters moving in the trees. They ran along the branches almost without looking. These men had honed their skills in the rain forests. He texted Kyanite Boston, a man who had spent several years with Drake Donovan in the rain forest rescuing kidnapping victims. Kyanite came immediately, slipping into the control room silently, coming to stand to the side of him to look at the same screen.

"You recognize any of them?"

In the dark, it might be considered impossible, but leopards recognized one another and often shifters did as well, just by movement. By body language. They might be a good distance away, but Sevastyan could see these men were professionals. It wouldn't be long before most of them were dead, but he wanted to know where they came from. Where Rolan was recruiting.

488

Kyanite nodded slowly. "Worked with two of them when I was down in Panama. They kept to themselves. Good trackers, both of them. The other three are from Borneo. They were from a lair several miles from the one Drake grew up in. Sorry to see them here, but not too surprised."

Rolan knew about the shifters training in the rain forests. The internet made advertising so easy these days. Shifters wanted work. Action. They were predators and living in cities didn't appeal to most of them. They were born to hunt so quite a few preferred mercenary work.

Sevastyan turned his attention to the team coming from the main road straight to the front of the house. Team two was coming on foot, spreading out, five men, using the low shrubbery for cover as they approached the house. That looked like the easiest entry point, when it was actually the most dangerous of all.

He'd designed the renovations himself when Mitya had moved in. The roof lines on the house and garages were completely made over, giving him places for his snipers to have higher ground but also cover when they needed it. He'd set his snipers at various locations and they were just waiting for his word to take out the first wave of Ro-

489

lan's men.

Team three came in from Sevastyan's property, using a fast-moving truck without lights and then abandoning that before running to converge with the others, making their way on the ground through the thicker woods Flambé's father had planted years earlier.

Team four came in from the opposite side, running also to cover the distance. They had the battlegrounds to cover, where Sevastyan trained his men daily in simulated wars, in hand-to-hand combat, in taking apart bombs. He left nothing to chance with Mitya's security, and that included keeping the leopards in fighting condition. The open fields were there for a reason. There were gently rolling hills, downed trees and shallow caves dug out so his men could train for every possibility. Sevastyan and his men knew every inch of those acres where they trained.

The last team had the responsibility of covering the others, hanging back to be in position to break into the house and kill Sevastyan and Mitya when the others made their entry. Sevastyan shook his head. Rolan had always insisted he could plan his battles. He'd always sucked at it. Even at fourteen and fifteen, Sevastyan had listened and then

490

changed everything the moment he'd left Rolan with the others to actually go into combat. The men had learned to listen to him instead of Rolan. It was what had kept them alive.

"Do you have sights on team five and team one?" Sevastyan asked. He narrowed his gaze, looking closer at the screen, trying to peer behind those members of team five in the trees. Was something moving?

"That's affirmative," Logan Shields responded. "Give us the go."

"It's a go," Sevastyan confirmed. He didn't look to see if his snipers took out their ten intended victims. He looked beyond the five mercenaries dropping like stones in the trees to the shadows suddenly going still behind them. Something was definitely there, but he couldn't make it out. Suddenly, he was uneasy.

"Christophe, can you bring up the images in the trees team five was in? Right behind them, following them on the branches. Ambroise, you're very quiet over there. Did you see anything?"

"I don't see anything," Christophe said, leaning forward, forcing the screen image larger and larger until it was nothing but gray pixels. He turned in his seat to look at Sevastyan. "All five team members went

491

down hard. Those were kill shots."

Sevastyan ignored that. He knew his snipers had scored kill shots. That wasn't the point. The point was, someone besides Rolan had put together this assault on Mitya's home and team five weren't the only ones in those trees.

"Bring up team one again now. The earlier screens of them." He'd been looking at the men. Seeing what they wanted him to see. Seeing what he expected to see. Thinking he was the smartest damn man in the room. Those men were a sacrifice, pawns to test his defenses. He'd known that, but he hadn't known they would already be utilizing what they learned. They knew the snipers were on the roof of the house, but now they knew they were on the garages.

"Hurry, Christophe. Ambroise, answer me. What the fuck am I missing? What's out there? What's behind these men coming at us?"

"Leopards," Ambroise whispered. "An entire army of leopards and they're coming right at us fast."

Flambé paced back and forth, restless, trying desperately to figure out what to do. She had made up her mind to leave the moment Shanty and her three children arrived. She

492

would ensure the woman was in the program and then she'd make use of her own underground for the domestic violence shifter victims. She'd have to shut it down as soon as she entered it. No one else could ever know about it or use it again.

Sevastyan and Shturm were far too dangerous. Far too intelligent. And she was way too susceptible to the man. Flamme had proved herself to be too susceptible to the leopard. If she actually decided to make a run for it, she couldn't look back because she'd change her mind.

Every muscle in her body hurt. She knew why. She hadn't had sex with Sevastyan. She'd ignored him and in doing so, ignored her own needs. The buildup of hormones between Flamme and her was getting scary. Her skin felt hot to the touch. She felt as if she were burning from the inside out.

Suppressing her leopard was getting much more difficult. When she was alone, she allowed her to come close to the surface, but it hurt, and every single time the pain only got worse. Flambé thought that, with time, she'd get used to the feel of her surfacing, but that hadn't happened. Her nerve endings seemed much more inflamed. The sensations burned through her body like a blowtorch, taking her breath, robbing her of

493

her ability to think. She couldn't bear the feel of fabric against her skin, so she stripped, tearing at her clothes and flinging them aside, grateful that no one could get into the master bedroom.

Naked, she paced faster, desperate to outrun the horrible way her skin burned and itched. Strands of hair fell, snaking down from the messy knot she'd hastily twisted on top of her head, snaking down across her bare back and sliding across her buttocks. She had to bite back a scream as a thousand tongues licked at her skin, points of white-hot flames flicking at her on the end of each of them. Tears tracked down her face as she caught at the ponytail and desperately tried to re-loop, pulling the thick strands back up off her skin.

This was so much worse than it ever had been. "Flamme, he isn't here. Shturm isn't here. You can't rise when he isn't here." She made it a mantra. No leopard could rise without their mate around, right? That had to be right. She was beginning to think she wouldn't be able to control the situation. She didn't know. She just didn't know. She hadn't asked enough questions.

Her breath came in ragged sobs, her lungs heaving. The burning between her legs grew and grew until it felt like a blowtorch. The

494

terrible knots in her stomach, that pressure inside, coiled tighter and tighter until she thought she might die.

Hands shaking, she looked around the room helplessly, desperate enough to call him. Sevastyan. She'd promised herself she wouldn't. She wouldn't be like the others. She wouldn't put herself in the hands of a man. She'd never seen it work out. Not once. She didn't know a single decent man. A shifter. They were all horrible. They all cheated. Were abusive. In the end he would hurt her. But this . . .

She forced herself to the window, looking out over the trees and shrubs, the beauty she'd helped to create. He'd acted as if he'd actually been so proud of her. She'd seen it on his face. It was difficult to hide the truth from a leopard. There was so much about Sevastyan she didn't understand. She wanted him to be real, but if she was wrong, she wouldn't just pay with her life, she would pay with Flamme's life as well. She'd sworn to protect her leopard.

She pressed up against the coolness of the glass, her breasts on fire, her nipples two pinpoints of flames. She thought the cold would help, but it was so much worse, almost as if the cold were really hot wax poured over her breasts instead of cold. She

495

cried out and jerked back, stumbling toward the bed.

She needed relief. She had to have some relief. In her closet, that huge monstrosity of a room that passed for a closet, she had a drawer where she kept a variety of feminine toys. When she had forced herself to stay away from the bars, she had used the toys to try to give herself at least a little respite. Hopefully, they would help.

Her skin lifted, a wave moving so that deep inside molten heat expanded and contracted like the inside of a volcano, as if it was breathing in and out, right before its final explosion. The feeling set every cell in her body, every nerve ending on fire. Between her legs and in her deepest core, she burned so hot she thought she'd go insane.

She could barely keep her feet as she made her way to the closet and yanked open the door. It was absurd to have such a large area to store clothes. It was bigger than her little studio. Sometimes, when she woke in the middle of the night, she thought to sneak into it and sleep, but she knew if she moved, she'd wake Sevastyan.

In any case, when she woke, she was instantly aware of his body curved around hers, large and hot. He was always hot. He took up so much space. He had a way of tucking his cock tight against her. He was mostly hard, even in his sleep, and she wanted to turn and take him in her mouth, feel the weight of him on her tongue. See how long it would take before he took control from her.

She groaned. This wasn't the time to be thinking about his cock, not when her entire body was hurting so bad and poor Flamme was so close and was as desperate for her mate as Flambé was. Yanking several toys from the lower drawer, she stumbled back to the bed, knelt on the floor and turned on the Rabbit. She was already so slick.

She found herself chanting Sevastyan's name and forced herself to stop. This had to work. She bent over the side of the bed and the moment she did, her breasts pushed into the duvet, the material making her cry out, and then sob. She pushed the toy into her and held it tight against her clit, her knuckles against the mattress to help hold it in place.

It was the biggest mistake of her life. A blaze of fiery agony shot through her and then pulsed and pulsed, refusing to relent even when she threw the toy across the room. Her leopard pushed closer to the surface and Flambé's body contorted unexpectedly, her arms and legs joints cracking.

Through it all, terrible sensations of electrical shocks snapped over her skin while lightning seemed to strike deep in her inflamed sex over and over, hitting hard, scoring deeper burns with each strike.

She had to call him. She *had* to. She had no choice. Sevastyan and Shturm had to get to them and hopefully know what to do. She crawled blindly around the room on her hands and knees for a few minutes, tears making it impossible to see, while she searched for her cell phone. Thunder roared in her ears and chaos reigned in her head so it was impossible to think clearly. She couldn't remember where it was. The sexual agony in her body didn't let up for a moment as she hoped it would while she hunted along throughout the room on her hands and knees. Finally, out of sheer blind luck, she put her hand on it.

She texted Sevastyan immediately. Need you now. You have to come.

She waited, sweat pouring off her body. It seemed like hours, when she knew it wasn't, while she waited. She just needed reassurance that he was there and that he'd hurry to her. That he wouldn't waste any time. She'd never asked him for anything. He'd know. He'd come.

What's wrong?

She blinked several times to try to bring the words into focus. It wasn't what she expected, but then she didn't really know what to expect. Two tears splashed onto her screen, turning it watery. She kept breathing, trying not to scream, trying not to rip at her own skin with her fingernails. The pain was excruciating.

Flamme rising. I can't stop her. You have to come. He would come. He would have to. If not for her, he would do it for his leopard. Shturm would never go without his female. She had felt the male's possessive attitude so many times. His impatience. His demands. He had wanted Flamme to emerge, and when she hadn't, he had been upset. Sevastyan would bring the male. They would come. Flambé rested her forehead on the floor, sobbing. Trying to control the terrible pain, trying to get on top of it.

The wait seemed like forever again. Too long. It shouldn't take that long for him to type *On my way.* Right? It shouldn't. On her hands and knees, bottom in the air, she rocked her body back and forth. This was the worst. How did anyone survive? A heat could last seven days. Longer. Was it like this the entire time? She would never last. Never. Could one just take pills and knock

499

themselves out? Why hadn't she thought of that earlier and *why wasn't he answering her?*

Flambé, follow my instructions carefully. Get to the garage, to the Jeep and drive into the tunnel. You know where the entrance is. You have to get to me.

She stared in horror at the instructions, not believing what she was seeing. He wanted her to go to Mitya's home in her present state, desperate for sex, where every leopard on that odious man's estate would know she was there for Sevastyan to *service* her? And if she would actually do that, which she wouldn't, how could she possibly get there? He had no idea the state she was in. It was impossible. She couldn't even see straight, let alone drive a car.

She pressed her forehead harder into the floor. So much for believing that Sevastyan was going to ever choose her over his cousin. Why the hell did she think for one moment to believe any damn thing he said? Her body twisted. Contorted. She fell sideways onto the floor. The burn on her skin was unimaginable, unlike anything she'd ever felt. It had to stop. She had to find a way to make it stop.

The image of two male leopards rose in

her mind. They were downstairs in her house right now with no knowledge of what was happening in the master bedroom. If she went down to them, there would be no way they could resist her. No way their leopards could resist Flamme. Mitya had all but told them she was nothing but a sex object to Sevastyan, a toy. For all she knew, he had told them he shared her. He shared the women in the club.

Flambé. Come to me right now. Use the tunnel. Stay in the tunnel.

For one terrible moment, she was so desperate she actually considered the idea of going down to the leopards. If she was wrong about Sevastyan, he would kill them. If she wasn't, she would never be able to live with herself anyway. She had told him she would *never* go to his cousin's home and she meant it. She wouldn't prove him right about her either.

So your cousin can have his laugh. Fuck you both.

Grinding her teeth together, she crawled to the bed and gripped the post to pull herself back to her feet. It was impossible to think with chaos in her head, the terrible

501

roaring and the blowtorch inside of her burning its way through her skin. She screamed and tore at own skin with her fingernails as the thing inside her lifted her skin over and over. She had to help Flamme get out or they both were going to die. Things crawled on her. Slithered over her. Licked at her. The sensations were so terrible she wanted to vomit.

War going on. I can't leave. Get to entrance of tunnel.
I'll meet you and take care of both of you.

Flambé flung her phone away from her. She didn't want anything more to do with him or his leopard. There was no way to get downstairs, let alone to the garage, or a car. And she'd never go to him now. Never.

She would take Flamme and disappear the moment she knew Shanty and her children were safe. She just had to get through the next few hours. Find a place to ride it out. Find a way. A bath? Hot water? What would work? There had to be something. She just needed to use her brains. Tears blinded her, streamed down her face, and she wanted to claw at her eyes because they burned too. There were no more brains in her head. Her

502

skull was on fire.

She'd interviewed a lot of female shifters, but there had only been a total of thirteen female strawberry leopards who she had ever heard of prior to the recent find. Her mother had been one but she was dead before Flambé was born so that left twelve. Four of those women had died before Flambé was fifteen. Six, Flambé had helped disappear. Two worked for her and she kept a close eye on them. They had separate apartments in a secure building. They had their own money and her private cell number in case of emergencies.

Flambé had smuggled seven other shifter women out from under the noses of their partners when they had called the emergency line for help. She'd been extremely careful. Everyone helping was putting their life on the line. More often than not, male leopards furious at losing their partner were in a killing frenzy when hunting for their "mate."

It didn't seem to matter what species of shifter they were, what lair they came from, the males appeared to be abusive to their mates. She detested them all. Now she just detested everything shifter. She crawled around the floor, blind, sobbing, trying to take her own skin off her body while her leopard thrashed and clawed, desperate to break free.

Cursing, Sevastyan turned and ran toward the front yard, calling into the phone for the snipers to take out teams two, three and four. He reiterated that all leopards with signature blue dots were theirs and not to be shot. Kill anything else. He was grateful that he'd had the foresight to call for help from his cousins, Elijah Lospostos and Drake Donovan, and even Joshua Tregre, all of whom sent teams of leopards to defend his cousin's home.

He glanced down at his cell as he ran and his steps faltered. Flambé. Calling him home. She'd never called him for anything. Not ever. He answered her fast as he stripped. Fuck. Her leopard was rising. He gave her hasty instructions.

"How many coming at us, Ambroise?" he asked.

"Looks like about fifty. They have the house surrounded."

The sniper rifles were sounding off, but leopards were shadows and they had made progress coming in behind the sacrifices, unseen for quite a distance. Sevastyan didn't have time. He waited impatiently for Flambé to tell him she'd come. It wasn't like he

504

could send Kirill and Matvei after her. No male leopard could go near her.

He stared down at her text, not believing his eyes when her answer came, but he should have known. He swore at the top of his lungs in his native language and then shifted on the run, trusting Ambroise to lock up after the leopards exited the house. No one could get inside. Even if they tried burning Mitya and Ania out, they couldn't get to them.

Sevastyan couldn't think about Flambé and what was happening to her, not when vicious leopards invaded the property from every direction. They were coming at the house from the trees, across the rolling hills, the meadow, the paths in the woods, even the road in front of the house.

"Coming up over the back fence to try for the roof," Christophe reported.

The leopards would find that a hard landing. Sevastyan had been prepared for them using the fences as a spring-board to the rooftop of the house. The roof was ringed with hidden spears. As the cats landed on the sharpened points, they shrieked, the sound piercing the night. Their bellies were punctured, their bodies caught and held until one of the men on the rooftop turned and fired, putting them out of their misery, killing them.

"Back patio, going for the fence and patio," Christophe continued.

The back patio seemed another good entry point. That was directly off the kitchen. The herb and vegetable gardens surrounded the patio where tables and chairs had a covered awning. Ania enjoyed sitting outside, especially in the mornings, with her coffee. Two leopards leapt onto the overhead covering and one clawed his way up the side of the column to the thick support beam, attempting to drag himself onto the roof from that angle.

The awning ripped slightly, just a minute tear, but all three leopards dug their claws into the support beam. Their thick stiletto-like claws struck metal in the beam. The three dug deeper for a better purchase and a flash went off, a small explosion knocking them backward, blowing them apart, so that fur, bones, blood and muscle and sinew rained down.

The first wave of leopards hit the front yard of the house, ten of them, coming in fast, males in their prime, scarred from numerous battles, confident in the knowledge that they were experienced. They expected their opponents, although mafia, to be from the city and easily overcome by

506

their sheer numbers, not to mention weak, with few skills.

Sevastyan had already spotted the commander of the team, a big bastard, golden coat with large fancy rosettes. He had allowed his men to sweep into the yard, running at the house to come at the porch as if they could somehow break down the doors or windows just with their sheer numbers. They were big leopards and maybe that tactic had worked for them in the past, but Rolan should have prepared them better for his opponent.

Sevastyan's leopards were either born in the same lair in Russia as he had been, or one of his uncle's lairs. They'd trained as he had. If not in Russia, they'd been born and trained in the rain forests. All of his shifters were experienced fighters, skilled in every kind of battle with leopards or man. He would put his men or leopards up against Rolan's anytime.

Shturm shouldered a big brute of a male out of his way, furious that these leopards were keeping him from his mate, and rushed toward the commander. The golden leopard hadn't yet spotted him. He was too busy stalking Zakhar. Zakhar's leopard was never that far from Shturm. He was a big Amur, very distinctive with his thick white undercoat, and his dark rosettes so close together and so large that he looked as if he had a black top coat over the white undercoat. No one had a pelt like Zakhar. His leopard was simply named Istrebitel, meaning *fighter.*

Had the golden leopard not been so confident, he might have been paying a little more attention to the scars in Istrebitel's strange markings. Instead, he stalked the leopard, weaving in and out of the other combatants. Shturm went low to the ground, allowing two leopards who tried to ram into his sides to slam into each other hard while he slid between two fighting males, bringing him closer to his target.

The golden male bunched his legs under him, readying for the charge, his eyes in a focused stare. Zakhar faced a younger male, one coming into his prime, eager for battle, already charging the larger Amur leopard, attempting to drive him off his feet. Shturm knew it was a ploy to keep Istrebitel's attention on him in order for the golden leopard to leap on his back and break his spine, delivering the killing bite quickly.

At the last possible second, as the younger male came rushing in, Istrebitel leapt into the air, right over the top of him, whirling in midair to face the golden leopard who couldn't stop his charge. Istrebitel landed hard on the younger male's back, snapping the spine, just as the golden leopard's intention toward him had been. The young male screamed, flopping to the ground, unable to rise.

Istrebitel reared up, going onto his hind legs to meet the incoming charge of the golden leopard. Shturm charged from behind him, seizing one of the commander's back legs and snapping it in two with a vicious bite. The golden leopard fell over backward. Istrebitel rushed in and bit down on the throat of the leopard while Shturm eviscerated him with one sharp claw and then left Zakhar to finish both leopards off while he went looking for other prey.

It took time to kill all ten leopards and by that time, the next wave had swept into the side yard from the woods. Drake's team was there to stop them, but security was Sevastyan's job. He didn't just simply hand it over to others. He shifted enough to get information.

"Ambroise. Closest threat."

"Sneaking up on the garage. Two factions, looks close to twenty count. These leopards joined forces, coming in from your property and the meadow. They have someone directing them up on the hill just past the meadow

509

out of my line of sight. He's calling the shots."

Sevastyan snagged his phone as he hurried around the side of the house toward the garage. "Christophe, send me another team. We'll need at least another five leopards, maybe more."

"Roger that," Christophe said.

There were no more messages from Flambé. He read the last one from her again. So your cousin can have his laugh. Fuck you both. Did she really believe that?

Damn it. She'd made it more than clear that she believed Mitya thought her nothing but a sex object. Did she think he'd deliberately leave her if there was any way he could get to her? What if she couldn't get to him?

He texted with one thumb as fast as he could. Baby, please, for God's sake. I'm in the middle of a fucking nightmare here. I need to know you're safe. At least get into the tunnel. I can come to you there.

He didn't know how, but he'd find a way. He could get away. There had to be a way. He couldn't leave her in need. Shturm couldn't leave Flamme. If nothing else, he could see for himself she was alive and well. See how bad it really was for her.

There was no answer by the time he'd rounded the corner of the house, and he'd

510

run out of options. He had to shift. He shoved the phone into the side column of the verandah and shifted while he ran, knowing Zakhar, Zinoviy and Vikenti were right behind him, their leopards coming equally as fast. A shot rang out and he felt a burn along his left shoulder. They had sharpshooters as well. Fuckin' Ambroise had missed that. He'd have a talk with him about that. You couldn't afford to make mistakes in Mitya's security. He didn't accept excuses.

Three shots answered, two from the garage roof and one from on top of the house. He hoped like hell they dropped the sniper. That had come from somewhere along that hill just beyond the meadow. He knew the exact spot a sniper would choose because he'd been there hundreds of times. His men had been there hundreds of times. They'd damn well better not miss, because he'd pointed that place out to them as a weak spot in their defenses.

Sevastyan ran into a solid wall of leopards. It looked like a sea of spots coming at him out of the dark. That didn't slow Shturm down in the least. If anything, he sprinted, choosing his target, malevolent eyes staring at his next victim as he rushed toward the big male. This was a pale black leopard, the

511

darker rosettes spread throughout his coat.

Zakhar came up on his left, Kyanite on his right. Zinoviy and Vikenti had dropped back and spread out farther so that they flanked him. Behind them more leopards borrowed from Mitya's various friends joined him as they tore straight into the sea of leopards coming at them. There were no more shots fired, at least not at the leopards coming together in a fierce clash of claws and teeth. Sevastyan wasn't certain if that was because the other side didn't have another sniper or they had no way to identify their leopards in combat.

His snipers began to systematically shoot one bullet at a time, making each count. He had reiterated over and over that they were not to take a shot in a combat situation with leopards unless they were absolutely certain who they were shooting at. Leopards fighting were ferocious and fluid. They rolled on the ground, raking and clawing at one another, changing position. They leapt into the air, turning with flexible spines, tearing and charging, smashing like freight trains to drive one another off their feet. They rose up on hind legs, biting at genitals and trying to eviscerate their target. There was no telling how suddenly one would switch from one side to the other. Sevastyan had drilled it into his shooters not to make mistakes. He didn't want them to take a shot, even a critical one, if they weren't absolutely sure of it.

His leopards wore small blue dots in their fur to identify them, seen only by his snipers, but that didn't guarantee that in the heat of battle, when the leopards were rolling around, a bullet couldn't hit one accidently. No one ever wanted to answer to Sevastyan if that happened — so they made certain it didn't happen.

Shturm used his claw to rip at an exposed throat, not that it would get him much. Their coats were so thick and loose, it was difficult to actually get down to skin and bone, but he opened the unwary male up as he passed him in his effort to get to the one he sought, the black-coated leopard who he was certain was the commander taking his orders from whoever was out behind the meadow.

The moment you kill this one, head for the meadow. You need to kill the one directing them all, Shturm, Sevastyan instructed his leopard.

He could only hope Rolan was arrogant enough to assume he could actually plan and direct a battle with mercenaries. Rolan would have someone aiding him, a man in charge of the mercenaries, one they all took orders from. Rolan would have a lieutenant. Who would be his second-in-command? That would be the man he would rely heavily on. That man would first recruit someone to find and then hire mercenaries from all over the world. He would want reliable ones, experienced in fighting. Who would be Rolan's lieutenant?

Shturm was on his opponent, the two leopards coming together like two stallions, rearing up on their powerful hind legs, slashing at each other with hooked claws and terrible teeth. Shturm turned slightly to avoid getting his genitals slashed while he delivered a deep rip down the side of his opponent, slicing right through thick fur with practiced care to get to the skin covering muscles. He tore those open long before his front legs came back to the ground.

The leopard howled its hatred and pain, whirling to face Shturm, calling to another leopard for aid. His companions were otherwise occupied and, in any case, Shturm drove into his side, hitting him so hard he knocked him off his feet. There was an audible crack as ribs broke. The cat screamed loudly, turning its head toward the meadow.

Down, roll, Sevastyan commanded, nearly

514

taking over the leopard's form.

Shturm rolled right over the top of the fallen leopard, dropping to the ground on the other side of him, teeth buried in his throat in a suffocating bite just as a bullet skimmed across the leopard's back where Shturm had been. He now had the body of the leopard between him and the meadow.

The moment a shot was fired from the meadow, there was an answer from the garage roof. Sevastyan hoped he'd chosen the right snipers. He needed them to make those kill shots every time. The moment the leopard was dead, Shturm lifted his head cautiously and looked toward the meadow and their enemies. Sevastyan was still racking his brain for who Rolan could have gotten for a decent lieutenant. Whoever had put this attack together was good. Had Sevastyan not brought in so much help, he would have been in trouble.

Shturm, remember the kid — Conrad. His name was Conrad something. He was a couple of years younger than I was and he was always hanging around, staying close, staying real quiet. He was learning. A smart kid. It's got to be him.

You helped him. Stole food for him. For his family. Took the blame for his mistakes. Taught him to use a gun, taught him to fight,

515

Shturm objected.

It's him. Rolan would use him. He thinks when I confront the kid, I'll hesitate. He also thinks because I trained Conrad, he'll be able to best you. He forgets that there are a lot of years between then and now.

The kid trained as well in the intervening years, Shturm reminded with a disdainful huff.

Sevastyan pushed down all emotion. Rolan should have remembered that even at a young age, he'd learned to separate from all feeling and take his punishments, no matter how cruel Rolan, Lazar or their leopards could be.

Shturm broke free of the fighting leopards, but he did so out of sight of anyone in the meadow watching. He had thrown himself back into the middle of the dark fray, all those bodies of leopards, and had made his way to the edge of the landscaping where higher bushes marked the beginning of the routes to the trees or the meadow. Shturm took the trail to the meadow, only as he did so, he crouched low, almost on his belly.

It didn't take long before Istrebitel joined him, silently dragging his body, using his toes to dig into the surfaces so that he made no sound as they crept across the meadow they spent hours training in every day.

Vikenti and Zinoviy, looking almost like twin golden leopards with their dark bursts of rosettes covering their bodies all the way down their long tails and up over their ears and faces, were on either side of Istrebitel and Shturm, approximately six feet apart. Kyanite's powerful male joined them, all muscle, a rare Persian leopard who had migrated to Borneo and found Drake Donovan like so many others. They made up their team, the one Sevastyan had trained for the last year to cover anything that might threaten Mitya and Ania from this open side of the house. A battle might rage near it, but this side was always going to be the one place they were weakest.

Sevastyan directed Shturm toward the one knoll that would provide the lieutenant, those directing the battle from the distance and their sniper a good view of the entire front of Mitya's property as well as the roof of the house and most of the garage. He had always known this was where he would have to end any real concentrated battle to kill his cousin.

Shturm scented the enemy long before he reached them. He heard them talking in low voices, worried that they'd lost sight of the big male. They argued for a few minutes over which other leopard was running

517

second to Sevastyan's mean son-of-a-bitch male. One voice insisted it was the strange dark coat over white. He was never far from Shturm.

"Where is he, Oliver?" The voice was harsh. Guttural. Angry. Recognizable. "You were supposed to have eyes on him at all times."

Rolan. It was the man Sevastyan had thought was his father until he was a teen. He was the man who had murdered his mother and had tormented him, making his life hell in spite of all the things Sevastyan had done to help him against Lazar. His heart accelerated. Shturm pulled his lips back in a grimace, showing his teeth, lifting his face to the air, scenting Rolan along with four other men. The kid, Conrad, was one of them. Shturm never forgot a scent.

Oliver laughed, his amusement genuine. "This Sevastyan is clearly a bogeyman. We should all be so afraid of him. Why is it I've never heard of him? I've been in this business a long time and I know all the names of the ones you want to stay clear of. Sevastyan is not on that list."

Oliver had to be the mercenary, the supplier. He was Conrad's choice to supply the leopard teams.

"You haven't noticed we've lost a lot of

men?" Conrad asked quietly. "And you must know the name Amurov."

"We expected to lose men," Oliver snapped. "And in Russia, yes, Amurov is respected. Rolan is Amurov. These are the men who ran like cowards from them."

Conrad sighed. "You aren't paying attention. We've got one sniper left. They've annihilated more than half our shifters. I'd say even more than that. We can't see around to the back of the house and no one has called in a report. I say we pull back. Call them back, fade away, regroup and come up with a different plan."

"No," Rolan protested, his voice lashing with his hatred. "I want them dead. We're here. I've got the plans to his house. Mitya thinks he's safe because he has Sevastyan guarding him. I want them all dead. Their mates, their children, all of them. Every last one of them. Wipe them out." He spat on the ground to emphasize his declaration.

"Fuck yeah," Oliver agreed.

"Rolan," Conrad reiterated quietly. "I think you should get to the truck and we should leave now. Oliver can run his teams from here. He's quite capable."

Shturm, wait, Sevastyan cautioned when his leopard pressed forward on his belly, fury making the animal shake.

Sevastyan couldn't imagine ever having his primary objective, the one he guarded, sitting on a knoll where he could be attacked by leopards who could sneak into a house and drag out a victim under the noses of those inside without them knowing. What kind of warning system would Conrad have? What kind of defense? He had to have set up something to protect Rolan.

Oliver believed he was attacking shifters who had been out of the field for so long they would be weak. Once he pushed past their outer guards, the man believed he could easily sweep in and kill everyone in the house. Conrad was already seeing the handwriting on the wall.

Sevastyan was aware there was still one more sniper hidden, waiting for his chance at killing Shturm, believing him to be fighting the leopards in the front to keep them from entering the house. That sniper had to be found and disposed of.

Tell the others to find anything Conrad planted to alert him to a leopard's presence. He's hidden something here. There's danger, Shturm. Let them know. Be very cautious.

"I can handle it here by myself," Oliver taunted. "You go ahead and run. I'll catch up with you and bring you your boy's head on a platter." He snickered, a dismissing, arrogant sound that would never have bothered Sevastyan, but was certain to get to Rolan.

"I don't run," Rolan snapped predictably, irritated all over again.

"No," Conrad said. "You never have, Rolan. But you're not needed here. It's foolish to stay and be in the way while Oliver is running his men, carrying out the assault, when you could be arranging transport as well as payment for everyone."

Shturm and Istrebitel used the freeze-frame stalk of their kind to move closer to the knoll, straining to uncover any devices Conrad might have planted to give him advance warning should intruders creep up on them. Various male leopards had scent-marked the entire area around the knoll in an effort to drown out any other smells. As tactics went, it was a good one, one that Sevastyan had used more than once as a teenager to confuse Lazar's leopards when they were hunting for their stolen goods. Conrad had stolen that technique from him.

The leopards stayed very low, lost among the brush, the sea of spots camouflaging them, even Istrebitel with his strange coloring. They blended into the grasses and the dark and light as the clouds moved overhead with the slight wind. They used every sense to unravel the chemical patterns left behind on the ground.

It was Bahadur, Kyanite's male, who first sniffed out the strange odor buried beneath the pungent stench of a virile leopard marking territory. Once found, the leopards could easily identify the bomb buried shallowly just beneath the surface. If one of the heavy males stepped on the plate, activating the bomb, once he stepped off the bomb would go off and the animal would be dead, serving to alert Rolan and his team that they weren't alone.

Sevastyan had no doubt that if those bombs hadn't been found and Conrad and the others retreated, they would have left the bombs behind for members of his security force to step on at a later date. That didn't endear any of them to him. He instructed Shturm to make a wide circle around the knoll in order to find any others hidden from view. They knew there was a sniper. He had to be located and disposed of. There was no way Conrad didn't have someone watching their backtrail. And they had a driver. Maybe more than one.

The sniper was right where Sevastyan expected him to be, lying flat on the highest boulder on the knoll, stretched out, his spotter beside him, looking toward the house with a pair of night-vision goggles.

"You see him, Vagel?" the sniper asked, his eye to the scope. "Conrad's getting antsy."

"I lost him a few minutes ago. I'm with Conrad. We've got too many down and if anyone took that big monster out, I can't find his body."

Vikenti and Zinoviy stepped carefully over the hidden bombs and began to climb up the side of the boulder, using claws to drag their bodies up to the top. Had the two men lying in wait bothered to examine any of the sides of the rock they'd climbed, other than the easy route up, they would have found numerous claw marks scored into the rock where the leopards had practiced.

The two cats lifted their heads above the top to spot their prey, eyes focused, staring as they slowly pulled their bodies fully onto the boulder. There could be no mistake. They had to be on the two men simultaneously and deliver suffocating bites to the throat, killing them before either man could make a sound and alert the three men on the knoll.

It wasn't the first time the two brothers had let their leopards loose on enemies when necessary, and they had perfected the art of their concurrent attack. Once on the rock, they separated, coming at their intended targets from different angles. Vikenti kept his focused gaze on the sniper. He had to wait until the man no longer had his finger on the trigger. There could be no mistake. Once the leopard attacked, even in his death throes, the sniper couldn't accidently pull the trigger and warn the other leopards that they were anywhere close.

Both leopards crept closer until they were in striking range. They waited, crouched. Ready to charge. Never taking their gaze from their victims. The sniper suddenly pulled his head up to wipe his forehead on his arm, his finger coming away from the trigger. Both leopards charged simultaneously, were on the men, delivering the killing bite before either man knew they were even there. The biggest struggle was to force the leopards to back silently away from their victims. That was always the most difficult moment after a kill.

Sevastyan had the utmost faith in both Vikenti and Zinoviy. He knew they would do their jobs. He had only to do his. Holding back Shturm was no easy feat when he smelled the male leopards marking territory, especially with his female in her heat. She was in her first life cycle and any one of the leopards might mate with her, forcing her choice. Shturm was fully aware of that and was not about to allow any other male near her. He wanted to challenge all the males. He wanted them dead.

Shturm remembered Rolan and his cruelty. Rolan's leopard had ripped into Shturm and Sevastyan when they had been very young, long before Shturm, as a kitten, had learned how to fight back or how to protect Sevastyan. He hated Rolan and his leopard. He remembered Conrad and the way Sevastyan had helped him. That Conrad was aiding Rolan in trying to kill Sevastyan was a betrayal, and Shturm believed he deserved death. Shturm was eager to see that both of them died in a very harsh manner.

"Rolan." Conrad used a cautionary voice. "Oliver has this under control. By the time he returns you could have the transport arranged and they could be gone so there are no ties to you. He's been instructed to make it look as if the families from Houston attacked and killed them. You can't be in the country and neither can any of Oliver's men."

"We didn't get Fyodor or Timur," Rolan reminded, his voice almost whiny.

"That doesn't matter. They won't be expecting an attack when we come after them. They'll buy the fact that the Houston families wanted Mitya and Sevastyan dead. There seemed to be bad blood between them. There were implications in the news about it." Conrad was patient. "We'll get them."

"Fine. Let's go." Rolan capitulated all at once, staring at the downed leopards in the front of the house.

"Oliver, get your men back to the cargo ship as soon as you're done. Have them bring any bodies with them," Conrad ordered, proving who was really in charge. "No one can be left behind or they might be traced to you."

"I know what I'm doing." Oliver wasn't paying much attention. His gaze was fixed on the battle. Only minutes had gone by, but things weren't adding up. His men hadn't come around from the other sides to pour into the front as they'd been instructed. No one had called in to say they'd breached the back. He could see bodies lying in the yard. Too many bodies and most looked like his men. He still hadn't spotted the big leopard they were supposed to kill.

Conrad waited for Rolan to strip and roll his clothes, put them in his bag around his neck and shift. Rolan's leopard, Diktator, had a thick, darker Amur gray undercoat

526

with darker rosettes scattered in wide patterns all over his lengthy body. He wasn't short and compact, rather long and lithe. Rolan had given his leopard the name when he was very young because the kitten had been so much bigger. He'd been almost twice Rolan's length when he was a toddler. He'd referred to him as big brother. He'd never made the mistake of calling his leopard big brother in front of Lazar, because Lazar would have had his leopard harass and hurt Diktator.

Conrad's leopard was younger, definitely in his prime, a big male with a long, thick, ivory-and-gray undercoat and distinct black rosettes down his spine and then falling over his body, tail, face and ears in a beautiful pattern. He was a powerful male and knew it. He fell back to protect the older male as Diktator set out for the road on the far side of the meadow.

Once Rolan made up his mind to leave, he set a fast pace, moving around the bombs and heading straight for the trucks and the transports that had carried the men to the property. They'd come in the back way, over the dirt road leading to Mitya's property, not wanting to be seen. The teams had then dispersed to their assigned locations before closing in on the house.

The moment Rolan and Conrad were away from the knoll, Sevastyan and Zakhar fell in behind them. Kyanite watched them go and then he instructed his leopard, Bahadur, whose name meant *warrior,* to step around the bomb and climb up the knoll to stalk Oliver. His leopard, although big and very powerful, was also extremely stealthy, able to be just as silent as any of the other smaller leopards he had trained or worked with.

Bahadur crawled on his belly up the knoll, careful to keep from disturbing any loose dirt that would roll down the hill and be heard by Oliver. He kept downwind. Oliver, a shifter, would be using all senses. At this point, there was no doubt he had to be aware the battle hadn't gone as planned. Kyanite could clearly hear him calling softly into his radio, demanding each of his units call in to him with a report. His voice was tense, no longer confident or arrogant. No one answered him.

Bahadur had him in sight now. Crouched only thirty feet away, in the higher grasses, he watched as Oliver threw the radio down and stripped, turning to face the same way Rolan and Conrad had gone. As he shifted, Bahadur charged, hitting him in the side with such force it drove the contorting half human, half leopard off the knoll onto the ground below. Bahadur leapt after him, landing on the creature as he desperately tried to finish shifting with broken bones.

Oliver's leopard swiped at Bahadur's throat, but Kyanite's leopard was far too experienced and there was no target for the downed creature to get to. He ripped open the belly of the half human, half leopard and then delivered the kill bite to the exposed throat as the creature tried to roll. Bahadur stayed several moments, making certain Oliver was dead, and then, taking direction from his human companion, turned to follow Sevastyan and Zakhar. Vikenti's and Zinoviy's leopards joined him.

Sevastyan and Zakhar split up. They knew the terrain much better than Conrad and Rolan, who had studied it only from a map. They circled around and got ahead of their enemies, placing themselves well between them and the road where their transports were, where drivers might see or hear if they called out for help.

Shturm targeted Conrad's leopard. To him, the animal was the biggest threat. Rolan was past his prime and appeared ill. If Istrebitel didn't get him, then he would follow up. Both leopards knew the others would be coming to help kill the drivers of

529

the transports. If nothing else, they could cut Rolan off from the others and take him down at their leisure. Conrad was the most important.

Shturm watched Rolan go past, the leopard sprinting for the trucks, wasting energy, not even considering that he might be stalked. Conrad's leopard wasn't that far behind. Shturm charged him straight on, full speed, hatred driving him every step of the way. Smerch, Conrad's leopard, had no choice but to meet the charge head-on. He reared up at the last minute in a kind of desperation. The leopards came together, slashing with claws and teeth at faces, bellies and genitals.

Shturm's claw ripped a chunk of fur and flesh from Smerch's face, nearly taking his right eye. The other leopard just managed to turn his head in time. They crashed to the ground together in a tangle of claws and teeth, Shturm, taking full advantage of his powerful jaws, clamping on the other cat's precious jewels and ripping while digging at his belly with claws as they rolled over and over in the grass.

Desperate, Smerch tried to break away, to get any advantage at all, clawing for purchase on the ground so he could get to his feet, but Shturm kept tearing at him, slicing

530

at him relentlessly, mercilessly, clamping down on his back paw and crunching, dragging the leopard back to him when Smerch would have crawled a distance away.

Conrad looked up through Smerch's eyes to see Sevastyan looking down at him through Shturm's eyes. He made one last effort to save his leopard, a sneak attack, coming at the big brute from under his belly to the throat, but Shturm countered the move easily and bit down hard on his throat, holding, suffocating him, waiting until the life was gone out of his rival.

It was much more difficult to get Shturm to back off. He kept leaving the carcass but then returning, slapping leaves and debris at it and roaring a challenge to any other male who dared stay in the territory near his female. Finally Sevastyan was able to get him to run in the direction he needed him to go.

The still night air carried the sound of their growls a great distance, just as the sound of the battle around Mitya's house could be heard. If those men driving the transport trucks heard, they must not have thought much about it because no one came to Conrad's aid, not even Rolan.

Diktator, Rolan's leopard, skidded to a halt and swung around at the sound of the terrible sawing growls and challenging roars, so distinctive of leopards fighting. He paused for a moment and then turned and raced toward the safety of the trucks. He was sprinting hard, his legs shaky, not used to running anymore, when something hit him from the side. A bright hot pain spread through his body and he knew his lung burst.

His legs went out from under him and he tumbled, rolling over and over, coughing as blood filled his throat and nostrils. He tried to stand, but then went down, his sides heaving. He watched as the leopard approached, not even coming at him fast, as if he didn't even count. As if he wasn't a *vor,* a leader of the *bratya,* his lair one of the most feared.

Diktator snarled at him, showed his yellow, stained teeth, but didn't move, sides heaving as he tried to gather his strength. The leopard just watched him with malevolent eyes. The leopard had a strange, distinctive coat. Pure white underneath with a scarred, dark coat on top. Where had he seen him before? He should know him. He *had* seen him, a long time ago in Russia, but Rolan's memory was going.

Without warning the leopard attacked, moved so fast he was a blur, just a streak of spots, and there was a terrible crunch and more flashing pain as the leopard bit through the bone of his right back leg. Diktator howled. The leopard retreated, once more circling, staying just out of reach, looking as if Rolan's leopard was nothing at all and Rolan no more than the lowest creature inhabiting the earth. Rolan wanted to scream at him, to tell him differently, but he didn't dare.

Minutes later, three more leopards joined Diktator. One was a powerful Persian leopard, the other two were Amur leopards. They paced back and forth, circling Diktator. Another two minutes, and there was no mistaking Shturm, Sevastyan's leopard. Rolan's heart sank. He should have known the reason the leopard hadn't come in for the kill.

Conrad had tried to warn him a dozen times against coming to the States. He'd told him to leave it alone, that Mitya and Sevastyan were long gone and weren't coming back. Even after Lazar had been killed by Mitya and Sevastyan, the betrayal had eaten away at Rolan until he couldn't think of anything else. He wanted Lazar's sons dead. He *needed* them dead.

Shturm trotted up to the other leopards and all of them looked in the direction of the trucks. It was clear Oliver was dead. Most likely, everyone was dead. He'd failed all around. Rolan was weary. Diktator was weary. He let Sevastyan come to him. There were ways. There were always ways. He could act conciliatory. Pretend he wanted to talk. He shifted, just partially, his head, luring Sevastyan in. Making him vulnerable. That was all Diktator would need.

Shturm stepped close. Rolan's heart accelerated. He could see Sevastyan's eyes looking back at him. He was going to shift. He told Diktator to be ready, to go for Sevastyan's throat, his most vulnerable place, if he shifted only partially so they could talk.

"Lazar did us all such a disservice, teaching us such hatred," he began, watching. Feeling triumphant. Gleeful.

Shturm leaned in before Rolan could shift back, put his jaws around the man's head and bit down hard, crushing the skull as if it was no more than an eggshell. He pulled back and looked down at the leopard with contempt before delivering a second bite to the throat. He turned and followed the other leopards to the transports and the drivers.

Sevastyan was going to help with dispatching them and then he would leave the mop-up to his security force so he could get

534

to Flambé and make certain she and Flamme were all right. He had no idea what was going on with her, since she wouldn't answer him and he couldn't send Kirill and Matvei up to the master bedroom to check on her. But the sense of urgency was riding him hard.

16

From very far away, Flambé heard voices talking in hushed tones. Strong arms lifted her, turned her. She cried out when pain burst through her. Sevastyan's voice soothed her when nothing else could. His tone was like a velvet cloth stroking a cool liquid over the burning flames consuming her skin.

"It's all right, baby. The doc is here." The words penetrated but they didn't make sense to her. He rocked her. Something sharp stuck her arm. She wanted to tell them she couldn't bleed anymore or she would die. The bleeding would just go on forever but maybe that was the best way to go. She would just quietly slip away.

"No, you're not going to escape me, not by dying, *malen'koye plamya.* Let's see what the doc can do to make this better for you. At least make you comfortable." Cool lips brushed her eyelids.

How could she be comfortable when her

536

leopard could never emerge? It was agony to feel the sexual hunger, the terrible craving and burning through the nerve endings that were too raw and sensitive, so much so that she couldn't handle the change. What shifter failed her leopard like that?

"She will come out, Flambé," that steady voice replied. So certain. Strong. No doubts. So Sevastyan. She could always count on him whether she liked it or not. Right now, she had no choice. She was a mess. She was weak. Blind. Her body shaking uncontrollably.

"We will find a way to keep you from hurting so much." His hand moved in her hair, stroking back the damp mass from her forehead.

"Get her in the shower. Get the blood off her and then get her into the tub." That was another male voice. Very authoritative. "She nearly tore her own skin off trying to get her leopard out."

Two men in the room? That terrified her. She tried to struggle. Sevastyan was far too strong and she was in no shape to do anything but whimper when her raw skin pushed too hard against his.

"The doctor is here, Flambé. You're safe. I'm not going to let anything happen to you."

She shook her head. She couldn't get into the shower, even if the other man was a doctor. Didn't he understand what that would do to her? The moment the water hit her skin, those drops on her already raw nerve endings would be agony. She wouldn't be able to stand it. She'd go completely insane.

"We have to get the blood off you, baby. The moment I do, we'll put you in the bath. There's a compound in the water that will help to ease the sensations you're feeling. He gave you a shot that will help as well. I know this will be bad, but only for a moment, and I'll use the gentle rain setting. Hold on to me. Breathe with me. I'll get you through it."

She shook her head wildly. "Not gentle." She could barely get the words out. Any light sensation was far worse. It caused terrible burning and painful jabbing through her body.

"I understand. Firm hold, hard rain. That's why you like the rope."

Sevastyan wasn't giving her a choice. She was going to have to go under the water. She buried her face against his chest as he carried her, and his arms were tight. Although the idea of a shower was terrifying, and she'd made up her mind that Sevastyan was evil and cruel like all men, she took

538

comfort in his presence. He was strong, solid and completely confident. She could rely on him.

Flambé could barely get her mind to work, but she was shocked that Sevastyan had brought a doctor to the house. She had never imagined that he would care that much. She could hear them still talking to each other as Sevastyan tested the water to make certain it was the proper temperature.

"She has a very rare genetic condition. There isn't a lot of research associated with it because so few have it, and research dollars, as you know, Sevastyan, are a numbers game. I imagine there are others of her species who have the same condition."

"Is it associated with being a hemophiliac?" Sevastyan asked. He put his lips against her ear. "Breathe, baby. I'm right here with you. Count in your head. This will only take two minutes. I'm going to lower your feet to the floor, but I won't let you fall."

She tried not to tense up. She wanted to hear the conversation. They were talking about her. Not just her. Other strawberry leopards. Sevastyan kept one arm around her as he allowed her feet to drop to the floor. She was dizzy, swaying. Her stomach protested. Lurched with the need to vomit.

539

She tried to concentrate on the conversation.

"No, although, in this instance, both are genetic."

The moment the water hit her skin she forgot all about listening and heard herself scream. A thousand knives stabbed point first deep into her body, causing an indescribable agony, but along with that, white-hot flames burned along every nerve ending, sending conflicting messages through her. Her breath slammed out of her lungs as Sevastyan used a handheld sprayer to remove the blood that had seeped from her pores and coated her body. The tears she'd made in her skin where she'd torn strips off with her own fingernails when the pain was too severe and her leopard had been so desperate were on fire all over again.

"Stop, stop, you have to stop." She wasn't above begging. Tears burned in her eyes and she didn't care that he saw.

"Almost over, baby, I'm sorry. I know it hurts." It didn't matter that he sounded soft and soothing, or that he wanted to hold her close and rock her.

She didn't know what to feel. How to feel. Her body was insane. "I can't take this. I really can't. I can't do this anymore, Sevastyan." She couldn't. He didn't understand what it was like to be trapped in such an ugly cycle.

He turned off the water and lifted her again, his arms strong and tight. She hadn't managed to open her eyes and she didn't want to. She was too humiliated, afraid she was everything Mitya had implied. She was in agony and yet her body was desperate for sex. Burning. She couldn't stop sobbing and she didn't care that there were witnesses.

"Statistics show most are lost to suicide," the other voice said. "No one can stay in that state for so long and survive. It's so much worse for a shifter, particularly a female in a heat."

"Well, that's not happening to her," Sevastyan declared, as if by his decree, she would obey. He sounded fierce.

He sank into the bath water, Flambé cradled in his arms as if she meant something to him. She felt as if she did when she was this close to him. It was so strange how he could make her feel that way, especially after being in the ropes. That was when he held her the tightest, the way the ropes did, locked to him, the pressure firm, not at all light, aggravating the sensation in her nerves. She braced herself as the water closed over her body, almost to her neck. Instead of hurting her, there seemed to be a

541

soothing quality to it.

She tipped her face up and did her best to open her eyes, although that hurt even to make that small move.

"Don't, Flambé. You need to rest up. There is no stopping Flamme. You can't trap her in your body. She needs to emerge."

The moment Sevastyan told her the truth she'd known all along, she panicked. She had done her best to help Flamme, but in the end, the pain was too great and her leopard had backed off to spare her.

"It will kill both of us. It would be kinder to just euthanize us like they do animals." She said it to the doctor. "I tried. I couldn't stand the pain. I'm really tough, but I couldn't do it, not even for her."

Her fingernails dug into Sevastyan's arm. She didn't want to start crying again. It seemed as if she'd been crying for hours. Her head hurt, but that was because her skull felt too big, pushing and pushing, just like her jaw. Everything ached. Every joint. Every muscle. How did women do this? How did any shifter do it?

"No one is going to euthanize you, Flambé," Sevastyan said. His soothing voice was gone and his firm, commanding tone was very much in evidence. "Just relax and rest. I'm here, the doctor is going to give us

542

both instructions and we're going to get you through this. He does need you to answer a few questions. They're very important and we might not have a lot of time. Try to concentrate, baby." One hand began to massage her scalp.

"Did you try the shots to help you with clotting?"

Flambé turned her head toward the voice. She managed to pry her eyes open enough to see a man sitting across the room staring at a computer screen, not at her. The lights were off in the room, which helped considerably. "No, my father said they wouldn't work. My mother had tried something like that and they didn't work for her."

The doctor frowned and glanced up, shook his head and then typed more. "That was over twenty years ago. I think your father was wrong. I think you and any other strawberry leopards with this problem need to be tested and put on the shots if they are appropriate as soon as possible. I've given you pills to help with clotting now, and one shot. What are you taking?"

"Iron."

"Have you heard of gene therapy?"

"No."

"Simplified, we introduce a virus into your system, not the kind of virus that makes you

543

sick, but one that introduces a copy of the gene that encodes for the clotting factor you're missing. The hope would be that if it works for you, your body would begin producing your own clotting factor normally. I'd like you to provide me with a list of your clients who are hemophiliacs so we can get them into treatment as soon as possible."

"That can wait until we get Flambé through her heat, Doc. The most important person to me is her. I don't like that she's so fucking miserable and in pain."

Flambé was a little shocked at the intensity in Sevastyan's voice. She flicked her gaze up quickly to look at the strong line of his jaw. That was the best she could do. Even her eyelashes seemed to hurt, although the water was definitely soothing on her skin. The heat helped her sore muscles. Whatever was in the water brought some semblance of peace to her burning sex. She wanted to stay there forever, locked in the safety of Sevastyan's arms surrounded by that hot, soothing water.

"We'll get her through the heat."

"And I don't want her pregnant. She'd not dying in childbirth. Until you get this bleeding thing under control permanently, and you can tell me she's safe, she's not going to have a baby. Hell, I'm wrapping her up in Bubble Wrap."

"Her leopard is in heat. Their cycles are in sync, Sevastyan," the doctor said, his tone mild as he stared straight ahead at the monitor. "That's why her leopard is emerging. Birth control doesn't work on female leopards. She may or may not get pregnant. I've told you that already. There's nothing you can do about that."

"I'd rather give her up than let something happen to her."

Flambé felt Sevastyan's chin drop to the top of her head, nuzzling her there until strands of her hair were tangled in the shadow along his jaw. She closed her eyes against her reaction to the idea of Sevastyan voluntarily giving her up. It was ludicrous and so very silly of her to vacillate back and forth, but she wanted him to want her the way she wanted him.

"Before you ask, condoms don't work with your kind of sex," the doc said. "You'd break them most of the time. We'll just have to work fast to get her blood to clot."

"We won't have sex," Sevastyan declared. "I can live without it until you say it's safe for her. I'm not losing her. I don't have anything without her, doc. Nothing that means a damn thing, so figure this out."

"She's in heat, Sevastyan, you're going to have to have sex." The doctor didn't even look up. "Flambé, had the burning sensations been increasing prior to you noticing your leopard beginning to show herself or were they staying the same?"

She had to pull her mind back to the questions the doctor was asking and off of Sevastyan's declarations. She wanted to hold those to her, listen over and over to his tone, his voice, study the words, the way he said each one of them. She forced herself to think about the doctor's questions. "It was pretty much the same."

"The sensations weren't just in your vaginal region, but all over your body?"

"All over." She curled deeper into Sevastyan's arms.

"Interesting. This is a much rarer form of persistent genital arousal disorder. I've only seen this before in a few other shifters. As I said, it's genetic. The nerves in your body form pathways and send signals to your brain. Harder pressure feels better than soft?"

"Yes. If someone touches me when I'm like that, it burns so bad I can't stand it. The tighter or harder the pressure, the better the feeling."

In spite of being in the soothing water, a

546

wave of itching burned across her skin. Her breath caught in her throat. She recognized immediately what was going to happen. Throughout the night, the pattern had repeated itself until she had clawed at her own skin to try to remove it in an effort to allow her leopard freedom.

"Sevastyan." There was despair. Fear. No hiding it from him.

"Her leopard is rising, Doc," Sevastyan said, surging to his feet, Flambé cradled to his chest as if she weighed nothing at all. Water poured off both of them.

The doctor closed his laptop and pointed toward a large bottle of lotion. "Rub that all over her. Rub it on your penis. That will help her with the burning sensations. You can get her through this, just remember everything I told you. The minute you get her back here, repeat all the same steps I've given to you. The pills, the shower, the bath, the lotion. Every time." He lifted his hand as he started out of the room. "I'll want to see her the minute you get her through this heat cycle so we can start working on the clotting problem."

"Thanks, Doc," Sevastyan said as the doctor left them alone.

Flambé had to hold on to the post of their bed to keep from falling when he set her on her feet. He patted her dry with a towel before he began to rub the lotion into her skin. He used firm, strong strokes, massaging it in. She expected the feel of his fingers on her coupled with the lotion itself to burn, but it actually felt good against the growing heat in her body. Deep inside her, a volcano was forming. Hot magma pooled all over again, welling up and spreading, to burn through her veins in a slow scorching well of fire.

"Sevastyan." His name came out a breathy moan. A plea for understanding. "I can't go through that again. I tried. I did everything I could. I couldn't even get down the stairs."

"I know you did, baby. I came upstairs and saw the smears of blood first thing when I walked through the door. My heart just about stopped. There was blood everywhere. For a minute, I thought you were dead."

His voice had gone strictly neutral. She couldn't help looking up at his face. It didn't do her any good. He was wearing his unreadable mask. In some ways that was a comfort. Sevastyan wore that mask when he became that man — the one she'd first seen at the club — the one who would insist on his way no matter what. She would need that man if she was really going to help

548

Flamme emerge because she didn't think she had the courage to face that kind of agony again.

"According to Ania, the emergence is uncomfortable the first time for both you and your leopard. You're in a highly sexual state. It isn't just part of your condition, it really is a part of the emergence. I'm here with you. I can help you with that and Doc says this lotion will help with your nerve endings so they don't burn quite as much."

"What if I can't do it?" There was apprehension in her voice.

Sevastyan ignored her question. "I've sent everyone home. We're the only ones here. We're going to go downstairs and let Flamme come to the surface. Once she's out, she can run free with Shturm so they can have their time together. When they come back, we'll go through the steps the doctor gave us so when the next wave comes, we'll be ready." He spoke very matter-of-factly. Completely confident, as if there was no question that she could shift.

"Sevastyan." She repeated his name. Needing him to see how afraid she was.

His hands were gentle on her waist and he turned her to face him. "Look at me, Flambé."

He used that voice, the one that brooked

no argument. She wasn't in his ropes but she might as well have been. She lifted her lashes and looked into his glittering, turquoise-over-icy-blue eyes. Once she looked into his eyes, there was no looking away. She was caught there as certainly as if he had tied her.

"You will do this because you have no other choice. Flamme will die if you don't get her out. If she dies, you die, and I'm not willing for that to happen. I will get you through this. Do you understand me?"

She pressed her lips together and nodded.

He leaned down and brushed a kiss over her mouth. A touch, no more, featherlight, but it was enough to remind her of all the times he'd touched her before he tied her, giving her courage. Telling her he was there for her. She was safe with him.

"Get ready. You know what to do. You need to be prepared for a long session, but you only have a few minutes. Can you walk or should I carry you?"

She managed to pull her gaze from his to look back to the bathroom. She doubted if she could manage and he'd drilled it into her that she always had to be honest with him before he tied her. She'd slipped into that space in her head. "I don't think I can walk that far, Sevastyan."

He lifted her immediately and carried her straight to the bathroom, putting her down beside the perfect porcelain toilet. Any other time she might have been embarrassed, but she didn't have that luxury. The heat inside was welling up, the volcano spewing that terrible hot lava into her belly and veins so that it spread fast, a wildfire out of control.

Breathing through it, she did exactly what she had always done when Flambé knew she was going to be tied. She concentrated on how he might tie her. On preparing her mind, shedding herself, giving herself to him, letting go of all fears, giving them to him. He handed her the bottle and she took it, drinking down the cool water, feeling it flow over her throat. His hands were big. Sure. When the rope moved through his hands, it was always such an extension of him. He always wrapped her in him, tight. Secure. She handed him back the water bottle and turned toward the mirror, determined to do something with her hair, ensure it stayed up so not one single strand would touch her skin when the sensations worsened.

A burst of flame between her legs nearly shattered her, and she tried not to cry out, not to make a sound, but suddenly her hunger for him was voracious. Her breasts

551

felt too heavy, aching. Nipples on fire. Her hands involuntarily slid down her body, as the flames licked at her skin everywhere.

Sevastyan caught her hands and brought them to his abdomen, stroking her palms over the heavy muscles there, lower. He curled her fingers around the girth of his cock. Her breath rushed out of her lungs. His cock was thick and long and already she could taste him in her mouth. The moment his shaft was in her palm and her fist had closed around him, he felt hot and heavy and so *hers*. Need and hunger rose so sharp and fast, an urgent demand that had her moving into him, her mouth watering, her gaze dropping to that beautiful crown where he was already leaking delicious pearly drops she needed desperately.

"We're going downstairs, Flambé." Sevastyan's voice was low. Velvet soft, sweeping over her body, fanning the flames. "I'm going to be carrying you and while I do, you think about my cock and nothing else. Not your body and what's happening to it. That's for me to think about. I take care of your body. You take care of mine."

He lifted her in his arms, once again cradling her close to his chest. She wanted to cry when she was forced to let go of his cock. She wrapped her arms around his

552

neck and buried her face against his shoulder as he carried her down the stairs, through the house and straight outside.

She hadn't thought he meant they would actually be going outside, where the cool night air would hit her body, fanning the flames even more. She breathed deep, trying to concentrate on Sevastyan. "I need your voice. Talk to me." His voice steadied her. "Touch me the way you do when I'm in the ropes."

He set her down on the covered front porch, but near the corner where two supporting columns came together in a vee, making a small alcove. There was one on either side of the porch. He set her down, facing the railing so she could hold on to the beams if she felt weak. He stood directly in front of her.

"Spread your legs, baby."

Her heart accelerated. Her body was so hot she thought she might spontaneously combust, but she did realize that the lotion, or maybe the bath, had helped. She wasn't trying to rip her skin off, even though the terrible hunger was building and her skin felt as if one touch might make her go insane if she couldn't have sex immediately. Her hips wouldn't stop moving, no matter how hard she tried to keep them still. The

553

moment she spread her legs, the cool air hit her clit and her sex screamed at her.

He sat up on the railing, casually circling his cock with his fist. "I'm going to touch you, get your body used to the feel of my hands on you. There's no way to fuck you, Flambé, the way you need to be fucked without my hands and mouth all over you." His voice was the one he used when he expected obedience. His dominant voice. The one she always responded to, and now, more than ever, she desperately needed it.

"You are going to think about nothing else but pleasing me. Taking care of me. Not yourself. This isn't about you. I'm the most important thing in your world. You want me to feel the most pleasure you've ever given me. That's all that's going to be in your head. Anything else comes in, you push it out. Do you understand me?"

Her gaze was riveted to his fist, that casual slide as he pumped up and down, and those little white drops that made her mouth water. Her entire body shook with need. The idea of his hands touching her skin was terrifying to her, but at the same time, she needed his cock. In her mouth. Inside her. Everywhere. She was going to die if the fire inside burned any hotter, and it had just started.

554

Sevastyan reached out in his abrupt way, grasped her hair and pulled her close, almost making her lose her balance. It was the same firm, decisive movement he used when tying her hands. It got her attention instantly. He didn't let loose of her hair, but instead, tilted her head back more.

"I asked you a question."

She touched her tongue to her lips. "Yes. I understand. I'll try."

"I don't expect you to try, Flambé. I expect you to do it." There was no give in him. "We are going to succeed."

She nodded and stared into his eyes. He could mesmerize her with his eyes. He had no idea the control he had over her with his eyes and his voice. Or maybe he did. His touch. The confident way the rope slid through his hands. When she watched that, she knew she associated the rope with him. That he wrapped her with himself when he wrapped her with that rope. She wanted him — wanted that same feeling of safety she got in the ropes when she was outside of the knots when she was with him. She needed it now more than ever.

She leaned into him and let her hands shape his thighs, feel his muscles. He sat with his thighs apart. He always was so casual about nudity. Most shifters were. He

555

was particularly beautiful to her and she needed to get her mind right, to put him first so she wouldn't jump back when she accidently brushed her nipple against his leg as she leaned to close.

He covered her breast with his palm and she had to smother a cry as flames shot straight to her sex. Deep inside that volcano grew hotter, sending thick rivers of molten lava running through her veins to every part of her body, igniting bundles of nerve endings. He left his hand over her breast while the other stayed in her hair. Both hands felt aggressive, rough, the touch possessive, not at all light or tentative. Her body reacted with flaring heat, but less pain.

"I want your mouth on me, Flambé."

She licked up his inner thigh and then over and around his velvety balls before complying, getting him wet, running her tongue up and down that thick shaft. Teasing under his crown, running along the thick vein and back down to the base. She licked at the drops that instantly tasted like an aphrodisiac, sucking at them and swallowed them down, eager for more, before she slowly engulfed that broad head.

Sevastyan took a deep controlling breath and removed his hand very carefully from between his leg and her breast, murmuring soothingly to her as he did so. He kept his voice steady, disciplined, the voice he used when tying, knowing she responded to that best. Just that movement would send streaks of fire darting from her nipple to her clit. He felt her body flinch and her mouth clamp down around his cock as she did her best to ignore the sensations building.

Quickly, he tore out the scrunchie she'd haphazardly put her hair up with and gathered the mass tighter, twisting it quickly, braiding it partially so it would stay higher and off her skin, even if they got wild, which there was no question would happen. Once he had it up, he put the scrunchie back in, securing the mass even tighter than she'd had it to make sure it wouldn't fall. It wasn't an easy task when her mouth was surrounding him with such heat.

He stroked her shoulders, using rougher touches. He'd noticed before the kinds of brushes on her skin that heightened her pleasure or could confuse her body, bringing her too close to pain to make the touch truly pleasurable. He might be a dominant, and he preferred erotic bondage and intense play, but not if it hurt her. The moment she said it hurt, he would stop and they would never repeat the act again. She needed firm, not light, and he massaged her arms and shoulders, her neck, digging his fingers into her muscles as if he owned her.

He caressed the sides of her breasts with firm strokes of his knuckles and then his fist. She nearly swallowed him whole. Her gaze jumped to his for reassurance. He let his eyes do the talking, knowing his showed his dark lust for her. He felt her mouth grow hotter, nearly scorching him. Her hips rocked. Beneath her skin something moved aggressively and liquid formed in her eyes.

"I've got you, baby," he reassured. "We're there. She's close."

He continued to move his hands over her body, a slow assault, touching her in all the places he knew she loved the most, every touch a heavy stroke of ownership, concentrating on her, not on the sensations she was creating in him, for him, nearly driving him insane. He traced her ribs and then traced under her breasts before forcing himself to remove his cock from her mouth, although it was one of the most difficult things he had ever done. He felt like he might shatter, he was so hard. He caught up the bottle of lotion he'd had the presence of mind to bring and poured it into his palm to lather over his aching cock.

"Sevastyan." Flambé's body trembled and she reached out to him, the expression of terror and lust on her face breaking his heart.

Slipping from the railing, he crouched down, his hands on her thighs, fingers digging deep, loving her the only way he could tell her. Taking care of her. Showing her she wasn't alone and whatever she needed, no matter what it was, he could find a way to be that for her. He stroked his tongue up her thigh. She felt so delicate. Her entire body shuddered. Her hands clamped down on his shoulders. He was careful to go slow when she tried to force fast.

He knew she felt desperate, but fast wasn't good for her — not yet. She needed a slow assault so her body could accept his. He had to use the utmost care in every touch when her body was this sensitive. The lotion and balm the doc had given them would only go so far to calm her nerves. The shots he gave her for clotting and hopefully, again, to help with her hypersensitive nerves, wouldn't last forever. He was the one who had to learn her body and how to touch her to relieve the burn. He was an expert when it came to reading her and she mattered that much to him. He would take it slow and keep his touch as firm as possible to get her body ready for his.

She didn't have to love him back. He

559

probably wouldn't know what to do with it if she did. No one ever had. He had the feeling she hadn't ever felt loved. That was going to change. He knew he loved her. He didn't know when or how it started, it just crept up on him, but he wasn't going to let her feel alone. She would always know she could count on him.

Tying was a personal art. He had to know every subtle sign his model gave him. He'd always been extremely careful of every person he'd tied, but Flambé was more than just a rope model to him, she had become his world. Her nails bit into his shoulders and she cried out as he nipped at her inner thigh and murmured soothingly, letting her feel the warmth of his breath against the sensitive nerves bursting like fire beneath her delicate lips and inflamed clit.

"I've got you, baby, you have to trust that I'll get you through this."

He repeated the mantra over and over between kisses and licks. Between lapping more aggressively and settling his mouth over her slick heat and finally devouring the addicting spice, that combination of cinnamon, cloves, a hint of coriander and jasmine that was all Flambé. That combination along with the spicy hormones she was throwing off were beginning to make him feel as desperate as she was, but he forced his body under control, ignoring the thunder roaring in his head and the fire pounding through his veins.

Flambé's breath was ragged, hitching, frantic. "Please, please, please. Sevastyan. I need you right now."

Sevastyan stood up slowly, forcing himself to take his time, giving her that steady control, wanting her to see that no matter how far she spun out of control, he was always there for her, calm when he had to be. He could be completely counted on. Disciplined when there could be none. He studied her face for a long minute, tipping her chin up to his while his gaze drifted over her, making certain she was all right and her body could accept his.

His hands went to her waist, testing, lifting her, sitting her on the railing, spreading her thighs apart so he could stand between them. "Clean my face, baby."

Beyond frantic, Flambé leaned forward, her tongue licking at the liquid on his jaws while he cupped the weight of her breasts in his palms, his thumbs sliding over her nipples, carefully watching her face. Before she would have screamed in agony; now, she seemed to move into his hands, finding pleasure, not pain. He tugged on her left

561

nipple hard, pinching down, experimenting. Sex could get wild, savage even, definitely brutal. He wanted to see if she could handle his touch when they would get real with their bonding sex.

She threw her head back, crying out again, but the sound was one of need, not pain. Her little whisper of *Sevastyan* sent hot blood pounding through his cock. All the time taken in preparation seemed to have worked. Her body responded. Instead of wanting to claw her own skin off, she wanted him inside her, wanted his hands and mouth on her.

He kissed his way down the line of her throat, teeth nipping while she wrapped her legs tight around his waist, trying to press her slick sex tight against him. He held her while he kissed her mouth, over and over, letting the flames take them both higher and higher. Kissing her was literally like igniting alcohol, turning them both to living flames. Her name was very apropos. Kissing her was very much like lighting a match to a stick of dynamite. She moved him every time. Intimate. Sensual. Darkly lustful. Damn-right sexy. All Flambé.

He kissed his way down her throat, his teeth nipping, tongue easing the sting. Her hips rocked against his abs. Her sex was hot-

562

ter than hell so that his cock pulsed and jerked, rubbing between their bodies. Locking her to him with one hand to keep her from falling off the railing, he drew her left breast into his mouth and sucked hard, pulling strongly. With his free hand, he tugged and rolled her right nipple. With every tug he felt the answering liquid heat pressing hot against his abs as she ground herself against him.

He used his teeth on her left nipple and then pressed it to the roof of his mouth before marking her breast to his satisfaction and then switching to her right breast. She gasped, her arms cradling his head to her, holding him close, watching him feed, crying out as he went from gentle to rough and back again. All the while her body moved frantically against his in an effort to relieve the desperate burning.

Sevastyan caught at her waist again and she dropped her legs so she could stand, although she was trembling. "Put your hands on the lower rails," he instructed. He was already positioning her hands, turning her away from him, pushing her head down, bending her at the waist.

Flambé was nearly sobbing. "Hurry, Sevastyan. I can barely stand it." She pushed back with her hips.

"Widen your legs." He kept his voice calm, in control, commanding, when all he wanted to do was bury himself deep and lose himself in her. He didn't want her to panic at the last moment.

Shturm was so close, a monstrous presence, waiting to break free at the first opportunity to claim his mate. That meant Flamme was equally as close. Flambé had to be petrified when her first experience of trying to get the leopard out had been pure agony. Sevastyan could only hope that he'd adequately prepared her body.

Flambé followed his instructions immediately, just as she did when she was tied. He stroked his hand down her hair to reassure her. He slid his hand down the nape of her neck and then her spine to steady her before he lodged the broad head of his cock in that hot, slick entrance. She was so hot she felt like she might burn him alive. When he looked down at them, it seemed impossible for her little body to take him inside her. He was never certain she could take him, and he knew she felt the same way, especially when he pushed into her and she gasped, her breath catching in her lungs.

That first slow breach, as her body swallowed the sensitive crown of his cock, devouring him, taking him in, surrounding him with her silken fire, was like nothing he'd ever encountered. That first entry, when she was so tight, was impossible to tell for either one of them whether it was ecstasy or agony. But there was no way he could stop. No way she wanted him to stop.

Little beads of sweat dotted his forehead. He felt almost like a feral animal. A predator, wild and savage, claiming his mate just as his counterpart was desperate to claim Flamme. No matter how often Sevastyan took Flambé, it was as if it was always the first time. He could barely breathe between the sight of his cock disappearing into her body and the feel of her tight walls clasping him, squeezing down and embracing him with a thousand tongues of pure flame.

He caught her hips in his hands and slammed his body home, driving through those tight reluctant petals, feeling the friction rub over his cock like scorching-hot silk. He had always been pure raw sex and Flambé responded to that. Was addicted to that. She craved rough. Needed it. She craved dirty and he gave it to her. He needed it just as much as she did. She screamed and rammed her hips back into his equally as hard, sending sparks racing up his spine to short-circuit his brain.

He tried to be careful of her, to stay in

control, but it was nearly impossible with the drive of his leopard and Flambé completely caught up in the brutal throes of her heat. She was wild, half-mad with need, pleading for more, begging him for more, and he gave it to her, swatting her cheeks to spread the heat to nerve endings, burying his thumb knuckle deep between her cheeks and fucking her as he rode her hard.

Sevastyan lifted her feet off the ground and pounded into her, his cock so scorching hot, so diamond hard and full, he never wanted the insanity to end. He no longer cared that he was acting crazy, a man possessed by a demon. He felt demonic. Flambé had spiraled out of control right along with him, a kind of madness claiming the two of them so that she responded to everything he did to her, begging for more.

It didn't matter how hard he rode her, if he bit, spanked, used his fingers or brutally used his cock, she screamed for more and he gave her more. He just grew hotter and hotter. Thicker and fuller. Plain steel burying himself as deep as possible while her body coiled tighter and tighter as if it was a silken tunnel slowly constricting his cock.

Flambé let out a low cry of agonized ecstasy. The sound started as a moan and just kept coming until it crescendoed into a long wail as her body bit down hard on his, so that he wanted to give that same shout of agonized ecstasy. Unbelievably, as a vise went, it was vicious, clamping down on his cock so tight it drove the breath from his lungs, but at the same time, it felt so fucking good the roaring in his head replaced his ability to think.

A thousand silken fingers, hot as hell, milked his cock as it jerked hard, jetting ropes of semen coating her sheath, triggering a multitude of orgasms so that one ran into another. Her cries were continuous, her body shivering as the powerful ripples claimed her.

How close is her female, Shturm?

She's right there. She's hurting, Sevastyan, she's got to get out this time.

Sevastyan could feel the genuine concern in his leopard. He refused to tense up. He withdrew slowly. Flambé cried out again, this time at the sting of his cock hooking her. He turned her around, forcing air through his lungs, walking to the open porch and setting her down, one hand to her shoulder, not giving her time to think.

"Get on your hands and knees, Flambé." He used his dominant voice. "You aren't finished."

Her hips were moving continuously. A sob

567

of despair escaped. "I'm still burning."

"Yes, I know. That's the heat. It will build again fast. I want your mouth cleaning me." He couldn't let her think while her leopard pushed forward. The moment Flambé obeyed, going to her hands and knees, and her tongue ran up his thigh and licked along his shaft, he signaled to his leopard. *Call her out. Bring her to you.*

Shturm was an extremely powerful male and his will was strong. He exerted pressure on the little female, calling to her, assuring her that Sevastyan would take care of Flambé, not allow anything to happen to her while she shifted, but she had to hurry, not hesitate. Sevastyan saw Flambé's skin begin to ripple as if something was alive beneath it. Her front arms contorted and she gasped and went down to her elbows, an expression of terror coming over her face.

"Look at me," Sevastyan demanded in his low, carrying tone, all velvet and steel. "Flambé. Look at me now."

She was used to obeying him when tied and she did so automatically. She lifted her gaze to him.

"Relax into it, give yourself to it the way you do the ropes. Keep your eyes on me at all times. You are not to look away. Do you understand? No matter how it feels." He

568

reached down and framed her face with both hands. "We're in this together. You trust me to get us through this. Keep your eyes on me."

Flamme was definitely in her first life cycle. The change came in little stops and starts, very awkwardly but steadily, with Shturm coaching her. Her back legs were covered in fur first. Then her spine and tail, belly and front legs. Finally, her head and ears and jaw. Extraordinary. Her jeweled green eyes clung to his the entire time.

Sevastyan had never seen anything like her. She was very small for a leopard. Ginger in color with red rosettes instead of black. Her undercoat beneath the ginger was white, the overall length quite long and thick. She was quite unique and beautiful. He could see why poachers hunted them the moment they were spotted.

"You're still there, Flambé, just in the background. When they've had their time together, Shturm will guide them home. I'll instruct you to shift and bring you upstairs to shower and bathe in the liquid the doc gave us. I'll put the lotion on you to help. He has a balm he wants me to use inside you to help. The heat will last seven days. We're going to get you through this, baby. I promise. I'm so proud of you. Look what

569

you've done. You got her out. She's alive. You did it." He bent his head and pressed a kiss to the top of Flamme's head, right between her ears. "Take good care of them, Shturm."

Shturm pushed at him and Sevastyan stepped back to give his big male his freedom. The leopard certainly deserved happiness after all the cruelty that he'd suffered at the hands of Rolan and Lazar for years. Neither Sevastyan nor Shturm had ever thought this day would come. Sevastyan hoped Shturm's mate would be far more devoted to the leopard than Flambé was to him.

17

"It's a good idea that you take a shower and prepare yourself for a very long and intense tie this afternoon, Flambé," Sevastyan greeted. "Don't forget to use the lotion the doc gave us. Hydrate. After yesterday, it's very important that you stay hydrated. Come downstairs when you're ready."

He'd been up early and was already dressed in his soft drawstring pants. Just the way he was dressed and barefoot would signal to her that he wanted to tie her. "Flamme's heat will last at least seven more days. Mitya knows I won't be coming in and I've informed your foreman you won't. I told him not to call unless there's an emergency."

"I think I can handle my own business." She sat up in the middle of the bed, giving him her little haughty look, chin tilted. There were dark circles under her eyes that got to him, but he refused to see them. They

571

had some things to sort out and with Flambé, there seemed to be only one way she would really talk to him. There was a bite mark on her shoulder. His teeth. Not Shturm's. He felt some satisfaction in that.

He turned his coolest gaze on her and didn't reply to her statement. "I'll be downstairs waiting for you."

"Downstairs?"

"That's what I said. Do you need me to repeat myself again?"

She shivered and wrapped her arms around herself, looking very confused as she shook her head. That was good. He wanted her off balance. He needed her to be that way. He turned and walked out of the room without looking back. That was another thing. He'd studied the tapes of the times she'd observed him at the club. His demeanor. He realized it was the way he took charge that appealed to Flambé. She needed that, yet at the same time, she needed to feel safe. He was good at giving her both.

Sevastyan had helped her shower and bathe, massaged lotion into her skin and put her to bed after the leopards had their time together and had returned in the early morning hours. He'd permitted himself a brief rest and then spent the rest of the time talking to the doctor and doing as much

572

research as possible into the condition she had. There wasn't a lot on it, other than for humans and what little the doctor had given him for shifters. The data had been bleak. The number of suicides for their kind had been high. There was nothing really known about strawberry leopards. He wanted that changed.

He had already set up his rigging, which was suspended above a small couch he brought into his den. The large O-ring was hung from a single chain suspended from the ceiling. He would tie his ropes off that, four of them. One that would go for her arm and breast harness. One her waist. The other two her legs. The ties themselves were classics, the harness and legs ties, but the position itself was known as Patience for a reason. She could stay there for a while and contemplate what he had to say. Think about her reply and then if he didn't like what she had to say, she could think about it some more. They had all day.

If the leopards decided to make an appearance, he could cut her loose fast and when they returned, he would once more follow the doctor's instructions to keep her safe. He would then tie her in the classic Lesson to Be Learned tie. They had seven days. They might be a long seven days for her, but they were going to work their shit out. She didn't like talking to him unless she was in the ropes, so she was going to spend a lot of her time in ropes.

He understood why she liked being in the ropes now. Not only why she liked it, but why she needed it. The ropes were tight enough that they felt good on her raw nerve endings. When she became sexually aroused, the bonds helped to keep the terrible burning from turning to pain. He wished she'd been able to articulate to him that she needed rough for a reason.

He took his coffee outside and leaned on the railing. He was never going to be able to come onto their front porch again and look at those two end alcoves without thinking of the wild sex they'd shared. He was already thinking about their indoor garden and how he wanted her to incorporate places for their leopards, but also various heavy beams for suspension. He pulled inspiration from everywhere for his erotic tying. The more he had been around Flambé, watching her with her love of plants, the more he'd studied plants so he could share that interest with her.

Because he loved the practice of tying, he recognized the rope — hemp — used for tying plants. Already, he bought hemp as a

574

rule, and then prepared his own rope, boiling it and preparing it properly himself. He dyed the rope the colors he wanted and then stored the various ropes for use at the club. Now they were stored at the house for one person only. Immediately he had begun to see so many beautiful visuals in the plants and artistic ties with Flambé. He would be able to incorporate those ties with her in the indoor garden the two of them visualized together.

He wanted a state-of-the-art garden so it would be easy to care for. He didn't want to have to employ gardeners to take care of something that he wanted private for the two of them. He frowned, thinking about that. Perhaps they should consider making their garden smaller. If they did, it would be less space for their leopards, and fewer ways they could escape if trouble came for them. He would have to talk to Flambé about it, get her opinion. He honestly didn't give a damn what others thought about his love for rope art, but he knew she was more reluctant to have it known that she craved to be tied.

Sevastyan was back inside the kitchen pouring himself a second cup of coffee when Flambé came down the stairs. She was naked, as he had requested, her hair damp from the shower and pulled back from her head with a cloth band. She had marks on her body, not rope marks, but his personal marks of possession, ones he'd never put on her before, and he found he liked them there.

He went to her, cupped one side of her face to lean down and take her mouth in a gentle kiss. She looked like she needed it. Immediately, she parted her soft lips for him so he could slide his tongue inside her mouth. She tasted of flame and cinnamon. A little bit like nerves. His woman. Off balance when she should have all the confidence in the world. When he lifted his head she chased after him, needing more.

He took her hand and led her into the den. The room was deliberately cooler by a few degrees than the rest of the house. She glanced at the small couch he'd positioned in the corner of the room, the chain and large ring above it. Her gaze flicked uncertainly to his face. He wore no expression as he walked over to the table where he'd set up his equipment.

Flambé stretched. A good sign. She wanted to be ready for a long session with him. She might be sore from the long night and day of sex, fear and wild leopard shifting, but she was ready to be wrapped in the comforting embrace of the ropes. He loved her more and more for that.

"Are you hungry? You don't seem to eat breakfast, although it's nearly two in the afternoon."

She shook her head. "No, for some reason, when I first get up, I have no appetite. I think, when I was a child, I never ate breakfast, which I know is completely wrong, but that's how I was programmed. Thank you for yesterday, for helping me with Flamme. I was so afraid she'd be trapped in me forever. You . . . surprised me."

"You never expect much from me." He kept his tone strictly neutral. He knew she didn't.

She started to protest. He could see it on her face, but then she stopped because, truthfully, what could she say? She didn't expect much of him. She thought he would cheat on her. She thought he was a liar. That he would eventually beat her. Ania had told him the conversation Flambé had shared with her. She'd been very upset to discover Flambé had such a poor opinion of shifters.

Flambé stared at the floor, looking lost in thought, even when he had selected his natural-colored hemp rope and come up to her using his decisive walk, the one that normally would have brought her full attention to him. The center point of the rope was automatically in his hand. He ran the rope through his fingers, checking over and over to make certain there were no splinters or debris in it, although he had never used it on anyone else and it had been stored properly. Still, just moving the rope could get kinks out of it so it would lie properly against Flambé's skin.

He ran his finger along her cheek and then down her shoulder and back, checking her body temperature before grasping both shoulders and moving her very quickly and decisively into position close to the couch in the shadowy corner of the room. He pulled her arms behind her back and quickly tied them. He used a breast harness going under her breasts and around each beautiful mound, knotting in the middle between them, framing them beautifully, straps coming up and around to the back so there was no weight on her neck. Both arms and her body would help bear the weight of her suspension.

Sevastyan ran his hand down her belly and caressed her bottom every time he moved around her with the ropes as he created his webbing to the O-ring and her right leg, now outstretched, while she balanced on her left. Every touch increased her awareness of him and of her body, of her sexual needs.

Her ankle, thigh — in two places — and waist were all connected to the O-ring for stability. He quickly wrapped his rope around her left thigh and connected it to her left ankle and slowly bent her leg until her heel touched the back of her thigh. He anchored her thigh and ankle to the O-ring so she was suspended just above the couch as if she was lying sideways on it.

Very deliberately, Sevastyan ran his hand over her body once more to check for any problems. "Are you uncomfortable? Any tingling? Blood supply cut off? Nerve endings painful?" Again, he slid his hand into her palm, checking to make certain her hands were warm.

She shook her head.

"Good then." He reached up and gently tugged on the rope until he swung her slowly around, added another smaller rope already knotted and pressed it into her mouth like a bit — a gag, bringing the two ends around to tie them into the harness at her back. "This is a patience tie, at least my version of it, Flambé." He turned her back around very slowly so she was facing toward the center of the room.

Sevastyan backed off until he was a distance from her. He crouched down and looked up at her, studying her carefully, her expression, her body language. He was very skilled at reading people. At reading shifters. At reading women. At interrogation.

"We have quite a bit to work out between us because, contrary to what you believe, you aren't going to run off to wherever you think you can go to get away from me. I know you've got that in mind. It's not that I blame you. I really don't."

He kept his tone mild. He refused to plead with her, nor did he want her to think he was asking for anything from her — he wasn't. Shturm deserved to have his mate. He'd been good to the little leopard. He'd been careful of her. Like Sevastyan, he was rough, but he'd taken as much care as a wild brute of a creature could possibly do. There was affection there and it would only grow with each encounter between the mating pair.

"But I've been in this relationship from the beginning and you haven't. You kept pulling back no matter what I did to reach out to you. You didn't tell me one damn thing that would have helped me understand what you were thinking or feeling. You didn't give me a way to help you physically.

You didn't tell me about your fears of shifting or what could happen."

He could see the protest on her face, in her body language. He'd been right to gag her. She would have interrupted. Protested her innocence. She was already forming her defense instead of listening. He fell silent and rose, walking over to the table. His coffee had grown cold. In any case it was time to switch to water. He had to stay hydrated as well. The leopards would be wanting to come out to run, play and mate later in the evening. He had to be at full strength to see Flambé through it.

She looked so beautiful in the ropes. He liked this particular tie. It was simple. Not at all fancy, no special knots, and whenever he tied her hands behind her back like that, he made certain he could get them out fast in case she began to lose feeling.

Walking back to face her across the room, where she could see him, he leaned against the wall, looking casual, taking a slow drink of water, studying her. Just looking at her could make his heart accelerate, the air move through his lungs faster. All that red hair, bright like the sun, those eyes that were green or gold by turns, depending upon her mood, but it was the little things he'd learned about her that moved him the most.

"You told me you saw me first at the club and you were drawn to me. I saw you when you were talking to one of the workers on the property. A curvy, obviously shifter woman with dark blonde hair. She was hunched over and looked like she was upset. I was a good distance away and I couldn't hear what you said to her, or read your lips because you were turned at an angle, but your body language was very protective."

He didn't take his gaze from her as he talked and he could read the subtle difference in her. She had stiffened slightly, was holding herself very still, waiting.

"You crouched down beside her, put your arm around her and talked to her for a long time. You weren't in the least bit caring of time passing or being on the clock. You made certain that she was taken care of. I know that your business means everything to you. Your customers matter and those plants matter. That woman mattered to you more. I thought you were the most extraordinary woman I'd ever seen in my life."

He kept his gaze on her. That mattered to her. She didn't want his opinion of her to affect her, but it did. She didn't want to believe in him, but she heard truth, as did Flamme. She didn't want to rely on her leopard's senses, but they were there and she couldn't help but draw on them.

"I can't help what I am. My father, Rolan, was a *vor* in the *bratya.* The lair was fucked-up, and he was cruel and enjoyed the power of hurting others every chance he got. His older brother, Lazar, was Mitya's father and controlled a much larger lair. He was also a *vor* with a worse reputation, much deserved. It turns out, Lazar, not Rolan, was actually my father. While my mother, Tatiana, was pregnant with me, Lazar delighted in tormenting and terrifying her, saying that he would tell Rolan so he would beat her to death. He didn't, of course, because that would end his fun."

Unexpected emotion welled up. It came out of nowhere and hit him hard. He turned away from her and took another drink of cool water, let it slide down his throat to soothe him. He'd been alone all of his life. He reminded himself he didn't need anyone and he didn't need what he'd never had. He waited until he was absolutely certain his voice was under complete control before he paced back in front of her with those same deliberate steps he'd used to walk away.

"Lazar tormented both his wife and my mother, and eventually, when he thought Rolan was too close to me and I was getting

583

to the point I might be able to aid his brother, he told Rolan the truth. Rolan murdered my mother and proceeded to make my life and Shturm's life as miserable as he possibly could. I was beaten daily until Shturm couldn't take it and he would emerge and Rolan would let his leopard loose on him. When Rolan wasn't attacking us, Lazar was. They both despised us. Rolan despised Mitya as well and vowed to kill him."

He once more went to her, needing to touch her. She was compassionate. He didn't want her pity. He could see that now in her expressive eyes. That look wouldn't be there in another minute, but right now, while she was still looking at him with something close to caring, he was going to touch her again.

First, he slid his arms around her to fit his hands over hers to ensure she wasn't cold and hadn't lost any feeling. He slipped his fingers through the ropes to check that none of the strands put any pressure on her skin. Very gently he allowed the pads of his fingers to skim down her belly to her mound. Next, he caught the ropes of her harness to tug her close. Her breasts were a temptation impossible to resist. So beautiful. So feminine. That was Flambé. All

584

woman and willing to give herself to him when she was in his ropes.

Sevastyan settled his mouth over her right breast, flicking her nipple with his tongue, his free hand feeding her to him. She was warm and soft and sensual, her body arching into him, even though there was little play in the ropes and nowhere for her to go. She still moved into him, making little delicious moans around the bit in her mouth. Abruptly, he pulled back. As much as he wanted her, he couldn't fall into her trap and make this about sex. If he was going to clear the air between them, he had to get her on board.

He put distance between them because it was impossible not to touch her if he was close. She didn't need to know that. She thought him cold, and maybe it was far better that she always thought that.

"I'm making a point, Flambé. I was raised in a lair, brought up to torture, to interrogate, to be the one to raid other territories Rolan wanted to take over. Eventually, I devised the plans to strike at Lazar's drug and gun pipelines, to disrupt them, hoping to weaken him. When Mitya left Russia, he left without a word to me, but I still followed him, found him and guarded him as his cousin, not his brother. I do his dirty

585

work for him. I always have. I'm always going to be that man, Flambé. I'm not a good man. I do my best to never hurt someone who doesn't deserve it. I investigate carefully, but I'm ruthless and I don't have the mercy and compassion in me that someone like you has in them."

Again, as he paced, he kept his gaze fixed on her face. She hadn't taken her eyes off of him as he made his confession. He shrugged and once again crouched down in front of her.

"The thing is this, baby. The moment I saw you, I wanted you for myself. Then, Shturm claimed Flamme. She was very certain. Then you both backed off. I couldn't tell if it was you or your leopard, and I had to find out. When you're in the ropes or anytime we have sex, you're one hundred percent in, but then you retreat. You don't really want to sleep in bed with me. You want to curl up in a little ball. You'd much rather sleep in the hammock above the bed, not with me. I try to reach out to you and your immediate response is sex."

She squirmed in the ropes, a flush coloring her body a soft rose. She couldn't deny a single word he said. It was all true.

"Shturm deserves Flamme whether or not I deserve you. I can provide you with a good

586

home. I can give you the kind of sex you need whenever you want it and I'll be faithful to you. I don't believe in beating women. You don't have to love me, Flambé, but I do want respect. And I won't tolerate you going to the club or having one-night stands. I wouldn't hurt you, but I would kill your lover."

He told her that truth in the same mild tone he had told her everything else, looking her straight in the eye, needing her to see that he meant it.

"What I'm going to do now is ask you if you're ready to tell me why you feel so strongly about shifter males being such bad mates. And what you're really doing that you're afraid to tell me with your rescue business."

She stiffened again and this time not only looked afraid, but gave a little shake of her head.

He shrugged his shoulders again. "I have no problem if you feel the desire to hang around in the ropes all day. Sooner or later Flamme will rise. I'll cut you free and we'll let the leopards have their fun. We can start again when you're rested. We're going to get past this, because there really isn't a way to begin a life together until you talk to me. I told you the truth about me. None of it was

587

good, but then you made it plain you didn't really want anything to do with me other than a sexual relationship. I've accepted that, although there are a few rules. We can go over those while you're thinking things over."

A strobe went off. He turned, without seeming to hurry, making his way to the table where his tablet was. Matvei and Kirill were patrolling and had deliberately tripped a wire in the denser woods to the back of the property. He sent them a quick text to indicate all was well, in their prearranged code.

"As I said, you will show respect for me at all times, particularly in front of others. I will expect you to sleep in the master bedroom with me in my bed unless we discuss it ahead of time for other reasons. As you're very aware, like you, I enjoy a healthy sex drive and like to have you close to me. You will not sleep with others, male or female, as long as we're mates. I'd prefer to get married, but as you seem violently opposed to the idea, I refuse to make that mandatory and will take that off the table."

He stayed at the table, looking out the window, completely out of her line of sight. His heart felt peculiarly heavy. He refused to acknowledge the feeling.

"We're going to be truthful with each other. If you ask me a question, be certain you really want the answer, because I will be giving you the truth. When I ask you a question, I will expect the truth from you." He pressed his palm on the window, just for a moment, not letting himself breathe. Not letting himself admit that just once he'd wanted something for himself.

There was a long silence. Minutes passed. Sevastyan forced himself to take another long drink of water and then he went to her and removed the rope circling her mouth, gently wiping her lips before holding the bottle up for her to take a drink. Her green eyes had golden flecks in them, and they stayed on his the entire time he took care of her.

"Are you ready to talk to me, Flambé?" He kept his tone the exact same. Mild. Not trying to sway her one way or the other.

"Are you finished with the rules?"

"There are more, far too many to list in one day."

Her lashes fluttered. A faint smile pulled at her full lips. It was all he could do not to stare at her mouth instead of her eyes. She was so beautiful when she smiled.

"I am afraid," she suddenly admitted. "I was so shocked when Flamme enticed

589

Shturm to claim her. She was terrified when Franco ran us off the road and he attacked me. He was so much bigger and even with my training, I barely was able to get away. He followed me off the road and into the woods. Had I not had prior knowledge of the terrain, he might have caught me. Flamme felt she put us in that position with her heat."

"There was Shturm, the biggest badass leopard she'd ever come across," he supplied.

"Exactly. She chose him and enticed him, luring him to her like a little hussy. She was determined that he would keep Franco and his leopard from claiming us or ever hurting us."

Sevastyan narrowed his eyes at her, allowing Shturm close so she could see the merciless gold glaring at her. He reached for the bit again. "Don't fucking talk to me if you're going to mix lies with truth, Flambé." He started to shove the knot in her mouth.

"Wait." It came out muffled. Her eyes went wide. A little wild. A sheen of tears.

Ordinarily, he would have tied off that rope and walked away, allowing the sudden surge of rage-fueled adrenaline pouring through his body to be walked off, but those

590

tears left him stripped of anger and very vulnerable to her. He yanked the knot away from her and just stood waiting.

"She did choose Shturm to protect us. She was so scared. I was too. I was disoriented from the blow to my head and I couldn't stop her. After that, I suppressed her because I was too afraid to rely on her. I didn't think she really knew what she was doing. You're a big man and could easily hurt me, which meant your leopard was big and could really hurt her. She didn't take that into consideration. I was just so shocked and didn't know what to do or how to get out of a claiming. I knew mistakes could be made with a first time so there was a huge chance she was wrong."

"But you didn't think it was a good idea to share your confusion with me?" He kept his tone mild when that ever-present pool of rage threatened to swamp him.

"I wanted you even more than Flamme wanted Shturm," she confessed in a small voice, her gaze sliding away from his.

There was no mistaking the ring of honesty or her embarrassment at the admission. She was giving him something back for all the truth he'd given her. He remained silent, waiting for her to gather her courage to speak again.

"As long as I just could keep what we had between us to great sex, I could handle things, but when we'd stop and I was with you, and you'd do nice things for me, or say things I didn't expect, it was more terrifying than Franco's attack." The admission came in a small voice. "I knew better than to let myself believe in you. Shifter men use women and then throw them away. I see it all the time. Maybe it's just the way shifter men are so primal — I don't know, and I really don't care, but I'm not going to get caught in that horrible emotional mess that keeps women in a place they shouldn't be." Now there was defiance and anger creeping into her tone.

Sevastyan paced across the room while he turned over and over in his mind what she'd revealed to him. It wasn't anything entirely unexpected. Ania had prepared him for Flambé's opinion of shifter males. He'd reinforced that belief when Mitya had told her in front of his men to go back to the office and instead of reprimanding Mitya, Sevastyan had sided with his cousin against her — or at least it had looked that way. He'd explained his reasonings to her, but already he'd had too many sins against him.

He stayed silent, willing her to tell him more. To show her that he expected more,

592

he returned to the spot just a few feet from her and crouched down, looking up at her, his gaze meeting hers. Waiting. She pressed her lips together. He knew it was difficult. He had opened up to her. Told her his truth. The worst of him, knowing he would never have her fully, but accepting it because his leopard deserved to have his mate, and, as humbling as the truth was, he would take Flambé on any terms.

"My father rescued shifters, that much is true," Flambé said, her voice very low and hesitant. "I think, in the beginning, his heart was in the right place. Maybe it always was. So many of the shifter species' numbers are so low it's scary. He thought if he could bring some to the United States and give them a good start here, they could bring others and it would set up a chain to help. The landscaping business thrived and he bought the property so he could build dorms and the big house with multiple bedrooms."

Her voice broke and she coughed as if to keep from crying. It took discipline not to go to her and wrap his arms around her. He consoled himself with the fact that the ropes were the substitute for his arms. She accepted the ropes when she wouldn't — or couldn't — accept his arms.

"He slept with a lot of the female shifters. They were given rooms in his home and sometimes they went into heat, or they were attracted to him. In any case, however it started, for whatever reason, he found himself surrounded with women and he didn't want to give that up. He became addicted to all that ready sex. He told himself they were willing. Whether they were or just thought they had to give him whatever he wanted because they were afraid in a new country, who knows?"

"Did you hear differently?" He couldn't let that go.

She took a breath. A deep one. He moved closer to her, again acting as if he was checking the ropes, her temperature, but more to offer comfort. Running his hand over her hair, down the nape of her neck, along her shoulder. Brief touches, but ones he knew she responded to when she was tied.

"Yes. Later. When I asked about my mother. She was a strawberry leopard and he apparently was quite enamored with her."

Sevastyan could well imagine if she was anything like her daughter. Hot like the sun, all fiery passion in bed. She would have been irresistible to a man like Flambé's father.

"He had several women housed there, but she was his favorite. He put her through culinary school but when she got a job, he wanted her to mate with him, marry him. He talked her into it. She was . . . like me. She needed sex all the time. It was getting worse, according to her friends, so she said yes. He got her pregnant, but he was never faithful. He kept other shifter women in the house and carried on with them while she was pregnant. It was quite horrible for her because her need never let up."

Sevastyan could see the stark fear in her. Not only could he see it on her face, but he felt it pouring off of her in waves. She was terrified of that same fate. It was all making sense to him. It hurt that she would think that of him, but if her own father would do such a thing, why would he think she should trust a complete stranger, one she'd first seen at a sex club?

"He put me out of the house when I was seven because he wanted my room. He had several rooms for his women but it wasn't enough and he wanted me out of the way. What was the difference between taking their passports and forcing them to work for nothing, and making them think they

595

had to have sex and do whatever was asked of them? Because he did that. He never beat them and he always treated them the same, paid for educations, got them started in business, that sort of thing. If anything, he might have been slower to help the ones sleeping with him. But many of the women still felt as if they had no choice."

"Did they tell you that?"

"After his death, not when I was a child."

"Did you ever talk to him about it?"

"I tried once when I was talking about my mother and her medical history. He got very angry with me and denied that he ever forced any woman to sleep with him. He said he and my mother agreed to an open marriage and the arrangement wasn't my business. That's when he told me the clotting shots wouldn't work and I wasn't going to live long. He also told me to stop rescuing, that with the cameras now it was making things impossible to get in and out of countries without the poachers knowing we were coming. It was one long terrible argument. He died a couple of days later."

"But you continue to insist on rescuing as many shifters as possible." Sevastyan kept his voice very mild. He wanted to shift the conversation to what she was really doing, because something was going on that had nothing to do with what her father had been doing. He thought her father's rescue operation had been used as a cover for her real operation.

"I can't bring that many shifters in," she denied. "Not if I want them legal."

She wasn't going to volunteer any information. She was too closed off. He was going to have to nudge her harder. Sevastyan sighed and shook his head. He draped himself casually against the opposite wall and let the silence stretch out between them. He knew each minute that went by, her anxiety rose. He let a good ten minutes pass.

"The problem with being tied to a man like me, baby, is you get it from both parts of me. The man raised in a lair with father who was a *vor*. That interrogator, trained to read everything around him. I had to pay attention to every detail so that nothing ever escaped me in Rolan's territory as well as the territories in the surrounding lairs. You also have the dominant, who enjoys rope art. I have to be able to read every subtle nuance of my partner's body. Every little tell of her body, her expression, her temperature, anything at all that changes. And then there's Shturm. He's Flamme's mate. Animals, unlike humans, don't lie to or deceive

597

their mates. Put that all together and that makes it very difficult for you to hide anything from me for any length of time."

She began to look alarmed. She was getting it. He went to her again and tipped up her face and took her mouth. His kiss was very gentle. Trying to keep it gentle was difficult when she was like kissing a flashfire, but he managed, because his woman deserved gentle. He trailed the pad of his thumb over her lower lip just once.

"Tell me what you're doing, Flambé. I'm in a position to help you. I have resources all over the world. I won't take over, I'll just give you whatever you need. At some point, you're going to have to trust someone. I want that someone to be me."

He saw the very real struggle on her face. She wanted to believe him, but she had so much to lose if he wasn't the man he had tried to show her he was.

She took a deep breath. "Get me out of the ropes, please, Sevastyan. If I'm going to take this chance, I'm going to have the courage myself without a crutch."

He pulled her body against his, more so she couldn't see his face than for any other reason. He wasn't certain he could keep a mask when he'd been doing it his entire life. She had more courage than anyone he knew. The knot on her hands was a simple one. He had to be able to protect her by getting her hands loose if her circulation was cut off at any point or they had unexpected visitors. Once her hands were free, she put her arms around his neck as he worked through the knots.

Sevastyan lifted her into his arms and carried her to the wide armchair he found the most comfortable, settling there with her on his lap. She was trembling, not uncommon after she spent time in the ropes. He held her, rocking her gently, soothing her, letting her come back slowly, not pushing her to talk to him until she was ready.

Flambé snuggled into him and he pulled a blanket around her. Some models were hot when they came out of the ropes but Flambé always seemed cold, even after they had wild, crazy sex, with the exception of her leopard's heat. He was never in a hurry when he had her in his arms. The fact that her body temperature was cool meant her female was resting as well.

Sevastyan couldn't detect her nerve endings flaring up with the terrible burning that plagued Flambé, so he took advantage while he could, massaging her shoulders and arms and down her back, reveling in his ability to touch her freely without worrying that he might hurt her.

Eventually she began to rally, reaching for the water herself and sitting up on her own. She gave him a little half smile before she slipped off his lap and wrapped herself in the blanket, covering her body and taking the chair opposite his.

"This is hard for me to talk about, Sevastyan."

"I know it is. I know it's difficult to give anyone that level of trust, but I swear on my leopard, I won't break faith with you, Flambé. Everything I've promised you, I meant."

She was silent for so long he wasn't positive she would be able to overcome her fears. "I started an underground system for shifter women to get away from abusive mates." Flambé blurted it out all at once, no hedging.

Sevastyan had expected something like that, at least that she was attempting to set something up, but he still found her news shocking. He leaned toward her. "You have it up and running? You actually have a woman you've managed to hide from an abusive shifter?" He couldn't keep the admiration from his voice.

Really? Who could do that? A woman could go to Drake Donovan and ask for his protection, but the leopard had the right to challenge Donovan to fight for her and the fight was to the death. Donovan had family and a lair. She could go to the head of her lair, but chances were good she would be told she had to go back to her mate. No one had ever been able to hide from one's mate. A leopard could track their mate too easily.

"More than one. Several."

His heart thudded. Now things were adding up much faster to him. "Franco Matherson. Tell me about him. Who is he really? Did he have a mate who ran from him?"

"Not him. He has a friend named Basil Andino. I brought Andino's mate, Karisa, out about eighteen months ago, maybe a little longer. She was in bad shape. Basil isn't a really nice man. He'd gone off with his friends thinking she was cowed and would stay put while he partied with other women. Karisa was pregnant, but she lost the babies because he beat her so badly. When he finally came home, he would have come home to lots of blood and clots and a big mess. It would have looked as if she might have died."

"Did he know she was bleeding before he left? Possibly losing his children?" Sevastyan asked. He knew he sounded grim. He felt

601

grim. He had friends he could reach out to. Basil Andino wasn't going to be around much longer.

"He had to have."

"It wasn't an easy rescue by any means and I had to do it without my usual team. I could only use a few trusted women. She's safe enough now, but Basil won't stop looking for her. Franco apparently decided he could figure out how she got away. He started putting it together that I had helped shifters come to the United States and work here, although he had no idea if I was really involved in getting women away from abusive shifters. There just weren't any other leads. I didn't know he had anything to do with Basil."

"You met at the bar."

She nodded. "I was having a difficult time and needed sex. He thought he was so great at sex that if I was involved in Karisa's disappearance, he could easily get me to talk. I don't think he has an idea one way or the other if I'm involved, but he won't let it go. This was months after I'd helped Karisa. He hadn't been near Basil either or I would have smelled him."

"Come on, baby, you need to eat something before the leopards decide to make another appearance. We can talk while I'm warming us dinner."

"It has to be something light, Sevastyan. I don't think I can eat much yet." She stood up, one hand on the arm of the chair.

Sevastyan inspected her carefully in one swift, encompassing glance. She looked tired. He had been careful with the ropes, but the marks were on her body, her thighs and ankles, the marks of the breast harness. His mouth and teeth. Faint bruises from the leopards tussling. But there were no tears in her skin, no signs of bleeding under her skin. She wasn't squirming uncomfortably or looking terrified or as if she might jump off the nearest bridge.

"What sounds good?" He held out his hand to her and was gratified when she didn't hesitate to take it. "I can do a breakfast for you or soup, or just sandwiches."

"Soup sounds good, although that's not going to do much for you." There was a hint of worry in her voice.

That was one of the things he loved about her. She was nurturing by nature. She was always going to look out for him whether she was in love with him or not. She did little things no one else had ever done for him. He didn't take anything for granted.

"I'll have a sandwich with the soup, Flambé," he assured, feeling her hand in

603

his. She had a firm grip despite her hand being small. That was another thing about her he loved. She might look delicate, but she was leopard, her core was strong, her muscles, her backbone both flexible and steel.

"The moment I realized something was off about Franco, I got away from him, covered my tracks and made my way back home. I don't think it was that hard for him to find me. We do bring shifters here legitimately all the time. They work here. Go to school. Become citizens. Set up their own businesses. He was trying to track Karisa. That's what took so much time. I made certain there were multiple places for Basil and his leopard to hunt for her. Franco had to have gone to each of those places first."

She perched on one of the high stools, her blanket slipping open to reveal her breasts with the faint marks of his mouth and teeth over the generous curves and the reddish marks of the rope knots in the valley between her breasts. His cock stirred in sheer male satisfaction. He opened the refrigerator and took out the cannister of homemade soup the chef had already prepared.

"You always prepare for every contingency. I noticed when you do your drawings for clients you make several, no matter how

604

good the first one is. And when you were doing the ones for this property and you were creating escapes for the leopards, you made certain there were dozens of possibilities to choose from."

He'd been proud of her for that way of thinking. She was like him in that regard, a general planning out a battle yet in a completely different way, he'd thought at the time. Now, he realized, she wasn't all that different.

She gave him a small smile. "It's difficult enough for human women to get away from their abusers or stalkers, but shifters? They have leopards who can track them. That can make it nearly impossible. Depending on the country, it can be impossible."

"There is a difference between a mating pair, real mates, and mates who come together like your parents did for the wrong reasons. You know that, don't you?" he said carefully. He didn't look at her, keeping his attention on the soup instead.

There was a small silence. "I'm not certain what you mean."

"Real mates, those belonging together, will find each other over and over. They won't tolerate any other mate during their life cycle. It would be impossible to be abusive. Surely you can see that Shturm wouldn't harm Flamme and would protect her with his life. That means he would do the same for you." He glanced at her in order to read her expression.

She had her chin propped up on the heel of her hand, her gaze on his face as he worked.

"I feel the same way about you. I told you that. I would never hurt you, nor would I allow anyone else to harm you. There was no mistake when Shturm and Flamme found each other. I was drawn to you and I think you were drawn to me, whether you want to insist it was all sex or not. Maybe for you it is, and that's enough." He shrugged his shoulders, trying not to feel the piercing ache in the region of his chest.

Flambé sat up straighter, the blanket slipping off one shoulder just a little more. "It's not just about sex. I think you know that. You scare me. The things you make me feel scare me." She sounded a little reluctant, cautious, almost shy, a characteristic he didn't usually equate with her, but she didn't find it easy to admit her emotions to him.

He poured the soup into two tall, thick mugs and made himself a quick sandwich while he thought over her soft confession. She clearly didn't want to talk about how

606

she felt. He was willing to let that go until he was in bed with her, or at least until they weren't eating.

"Let's take the food outside and you can tell me the rest about your underground railway for shifter women. It had to be very difficult to set up." He poured genuine admiration into his voice.

She looked so relieved as she slid off the stool that he couldn't help smiling. She left the blanket behind as they went out onto the back patio where the large awning shaded their bodies from the sun's rays.

"I was fortunate in that there were several women already in place across the United States who had their own businesses," Flambé said. She sipped at the mug of soup and shaded her eyes as she looked out toward the woods with long branches. "See how the branches reach toward one another and nearly touch? I kept looking at all the various trees that had been planted over the years for the shifters and how they were shaped. My father showed me how to work with them when we were molding and growing them on our property before transferring them to a client's. That stuck in my mind. I flew to a city near each of the women and then rented a car and drove to their business and just talked with them.

607

Visited."

He could imagine his cautious Flambé doing just that. She was personable. Talking about her landscaping business, steering the conversation around to her mother. Listening to them about their past with her. She'd chosen women who hadn't mated and preferred not to. She didn't broach the subject of helping abused shifter women disappear immediately, but she did talk about how more and more she was seeing their women with nowhere to go.

"I could judge the level of sympathy," she said. "And also, whether they were willing to do something about it. Or at least if I thought they could. I went back a second time to the ones I thought might be willing to help."

"You would need a scent blocker so a leopard would never be able to catch your scent or be able to track their female's."

She nodded. "I'd heard rumors about a woman in New Orleans who was amazing with perfumes. Really amazing. I went to see her. I thought it possible she could come up with a product that could drown out our scents. I was very nervous talking to her at first. I told her I needed everything to be strictly confidential and she agreed. She was very sympathetic when I told her what I needed. She said she'd accidently come up with a scent blocker that worked on leopards, although it wasn't perfect. She asked when I needed the product. I told her as soon as possible and she sent me a sample three weeks later. Within a month, I had something that has worked to perfection. So far, as long as I've had the time to use it properly, I've gotten my client and me both away without incident."

"What kind of product?" He was certain he knew the woman she spoke of. If that particular scent blocker was better than the original she'd accidently made as a byproduct, it would be nearly impossible to trace the women.

"Both an oral and a spray used together." Flambé sounded distracted. She put down the mug, rubbing at her skin, a sudden flush coming over body.

Immediately, Sevastyan put down his food as well, recognizing the signs. "Come here, baby. Let's get your hair up fast."

She stood between his legs while he scooped up her hair tighter. She ignored what he was doing, her hungry gaze dropping to his cock, and then she went to her knees, her mouth finding him as if that was her entire world. For a moment he forgot what he was doing as he watched her lips

609

stretching around his thick girth. She looked sexy kneeling between his thighs, lust darkening her eyes.

Her mouth felt hot and tight as she sucked hard, her tongue lapping at him, getting him slick and wet. All the while she moaned, the sound vibrating through his cock while her hand stroked and jiggled his balls. Her hips rocked and bucked while she squirmed with need, feeding off the leaking droplets from the broad crown.

Sevastyan managed to get her hair up and then his hands went to her breasts, kneading, massaging in time to the rhythmic pull of her mouth. She was moaning around his cock, the sound as desperate as he felt. He flicked and tugged her nipples and she cried out and took him deeper into her mouth as if she might swallow him all the way down.

He wanted her to finish him off but he needed to be in her. Her body needed his. The desperate sounds she was making, the way her body was moving, the heat was taking her too fast and he didn't want her nerve endings to take her over before the little leopard had a chance to emerge. He caught her hair and tugged, forcing her head up, to bring her mouth away from his cock.

Flambé cried out and chased after his cock, but he shook his head. "Turn around, baby. Hands and knees." He all but knocked the chair over as he went down to his knees behind her. He wanted her ready for her leopard so the transition would be fast.

Flambé obeyed him, turning, breathing raggedly. Panting. "Hurry. I can't stand it. I'm burning up already."

She was slick and hot. He didn't wait. He caught her hips and slammed into her, throwing his head back as her tight tunnel surrounded him with all that scorching heat, threatening to burn him alive. Paradise or hell. He was back and he wanted to live there.

18

"We've got company, Flambé," Sevastyan warned. He glanced at the screen a second time, cursing under his breath.

Flambé sat up, looking around her, long lashes fluttering like they did when she was barely awake. "What time is it?" She pushed at the stray strands of hair falling around her face and looked up at him with her green eyes.

His stomach tightened. His cock instantly hardened. "Midafternoon, baby. You haven't been asleep that long." She looked almost fragile, dark circles under her eyes.

The doc had been waiting for them when they'd come back that afternoon, sitting in his truck, ignoring Shturm's warning snarls. He'd barely glanced at the two leopards as they padded up onto the porch. Shturm nudged Flamme into the house with his heavier shoulder as she all but stumbled, clearly exhausted. The large male sent the

612

doctor several warning glares over his shoulder but the man had continued to stare at his tablet from inside the safety of his truck.

The doctor had waited patiently while Sevastyan had seen to Flambé, showering, bathing and putting the lotion on her with meticulous care before putting her to bed. The doctor had given Flambé the blood clotting shots and then spent some time with Sevastyan teaching him how to give the shots while they talked gene therapy. The doctor wanted him to have Flambé talk the two other strawberry shifter females into coming to him for help as well.

"Who's here, Sevastyan? You don't look happy to see them." She threw back the sheet and put her feet on the floor, stretching, making an effort to wake up.

"Mitya and Ania. I can send them away. You don't have to see them." Their relationship was fragile. He didn't want to take a chance on anything interfering between them.

He narrowed his eyes, looking more closely at her body as she stood. There were faint bruises on her hips and inner thighs. He'd been rough with her. He'd tried to be careful. He stepped closer to her and bent his mouth to brush a kiss over her lips. Was

613

there a shadow along the corner of her mouth? He swept his thumb over it gently.

"You don't have to send them away, Sevastyan. I'll go take a shower and be right down. It just takes me a minute to wake up, that's all," she protested, frowning at him. "You've still got that look on your face." She reached up and rubbed at his mouth. "What's wrong?"

"Was I too rough with you? It's impossible to be gentle, Flambé." He tried to stay in control, but the leopards were rising, she was so out of control, the sex was so good, everything came together in such a perfect storm. Yet he worried about the rare condition she had and if they could get her leopard out before her nerves began to flare too badly. She had to have rough or touching caused tremendous pain.

Flambé wrapped her arms around his waist and pressed her face against his chest, shocking him. She rarely gave him any kind of sign of affection. "You're never *too* rough with me, Sevastyan. You give me exactly what I need and want. You take unbelievably great care of me." She tipped her face up to his. "I'll be very fast at getting ready, I promise."

To cover the way his heart accelerated, he brought his palm up to cup the back of her scalp but shook his head. "I want you to follow the routine Doc laid out." When she made a face at him, he gave her a stern look. "To the *letter.* It's working so far. We've got a few more days of your female's heat and we don't want to take the chance of anything going wrong. It isn't going to hurt them to wait and they'll understand. I'll make coffee for them, water and food for us and we'll wait on the front porch for you." He made it an order even though he tried not to. "As it is, you'll have to wear clothes and your skin will be sensitive. So, make sure you do everything exactly as the doc laid it out."

"I knew you were going to be bossy." She let go of him, gave him a snippy look and headed for the master bath.

Sevastyan made his way downstairs, put on the coffee and met with Mitya and Ania on the front verandah. The property had been in Ania's family prior to him buying it from her. He'd made quite a few extensive renovations to it and he was a little anxious, afraid she'd be upset. It had been her childhood home and he knew she loved it. Not only had he renovated the house and garages, but a good part of the two hundred acres had been planted in grapes. The Dovers didn't make wine, but they sold the grapes to a winery. He had reduced the vineyard by half, wanting to replace it with trees.

Ania immediately hugged him, her face lighting up the moment she saw him. If she was upset or uncomfortable with the changes he'd made, she certainly was adept at covering up, and he knew her better than that so he assumed she was fine with them.

"Where's Flambé?" Ania asked, sounding disappointed. "Isn't she going to join us?" She reached out a hand to her husband.

Mitya took it and looked at Sevastyan, but there was no condemnation on his face.

"The leopards didn't come back until late morning. She was still asleep so she's showering. She said to tell you she'd be right down." He debated for a moment before telling them. "Remember I told you she has a rare condition that makes it difficult for her to be touched without feeling acute pain? We had no idea that the heat was going to increase the problem to the point she almost didn't make it. In fact, apparently most shifters with this kind of disease commit suicide."

"Sevastyan." Ania gasped and put a defensive hand to her throat, backing up until she was against Mitya. He sank into a chair and pulled her close to him, circling her waist with one arm.

616

"I'm so sorry, Sevastyan. That makes me feel even worse than I already do. I came to apologize to her for my behavior. I should have trusted you to handle your own business and just backed you as you did me." Mitya pressed his fingers to his temples. "That poor girl."

"The doc has been very helpful. She's also a genetic hemophiliac. So, more than one problem. She didn't want me dealing with any of that. It's been a hard sell to convince her that she should let me decide if I want to be with her or not." That was true, and yet not exactly. He tried to gloss over that so neither would catch the partial lie. "Fresh coffee, water, tea, what are you looking for to drink?"

"Coffee," Mitya said.

"Do you have that pineapple juice mix that was so refreshing?" Ania asked. "The last time I was here, you gave me a bottle of it."

He flashed her a smile. "Just for you."

When he returned with their drinks, they were both seated comfortably at the table, waiting expectantly for more of an explanation. "She isn't trusting," Ania said. "At all."

"No, with good reason," Sevastyan agreed, but he wasn't going any further. If Flambé wanted to share — and he hoped she would

617

eventually — then she could do that herself. "It was very difficult to get her leopard to come out without harming her. I wasn't certain it could be done and neither was the doc. I'm very thankful for that man. It will take her a little longer than normal because she has to follow a strict protocol before she can come down."

"Is there still danger to her?" Mitya asked.

Sevastyan sighed and pressed the cool bottle of water to his head. "Unfortunately, I think there's always going to be a little bit of danger. The more we follow the doc's advice, hopefully, the better she'll get. There's a new gene therapy for hemophiliacs. Doc thinks she's a good candidate for that. As for the nerve problem, there is no cure. He's worked on various nerve blockers and lotions to aid in calming the sensations, but they can't completely stop them and certainly not for more than a short while."

"Long enough to allow her leopard out," Mitya said.

Sevastyan nodded. "Yes. She's willing to go through the routine to allow Flamme her freedom. Certainly, during a heat she'll have to use the routine."

"I checked with the elders of Franco Matherson's lair," Mitya said. "He's been

618

cast out completely and he's being hunted. They've sent out their best trackers, two brothers by the names of Luan and Arno. They have quite the reputation, according to Drake Donovan. Once sent out, they never stop. Luan means *lion* and Arno *eagle.* They nearly caught up with Matherson a year ago but he has far more resources than they do. Money counts when you're moving fast. I reached out to them, offered them anything they might need in the way of transportation or information. I told them that he was stalking a young woman here in Texas."

"Do we have any kind of an idea where he is?" Sevastyan asked.

Mitya sighed and shook his head. "I wish I could tell you, but I've called in favors from many of our allies and everyone is looking. He's not going to be able to hide forever. Eventually, he'll make a move. Two of his brothers are back in Africa at their family estate. Another has gone to Switzerland. The family owns a ski resort and the brother spends a lot of time there. I think he goes to the slopes whenever Franco has gotten out of hand and he doesn't want to be associated with him."

"What does one do when you have a crazy, out-of-control brother like that?" Sev-

619

astyan asked.

"I don't know," Mitya answered, his expression droll. "What?"

Ania smacked him. "You think you're so funny."

"I am funny. Most people don't get that I am because they can't tell when I'm smiling. Look, *kotyonok,* take a look at my face."

She framed Mitya's face with both hands and studied his expression and then shook her head. "I'm sorry, love, you look as if you're about to shoot someone."

Sevastyan couldn't help laughing. "He looks like a lovesick donkey." Sobering, he glanced toward the house. "Did Drake find out anything on this woman, Shanty? Or the three employees? Anything about Flambé's father? I know there hasn't been a lot of time, but I asked for all resources to be put on it."

Mitya sobered as well. He brought Ania's hand up to his mouth and nibbled on the ends of her fingers. "Drake said he knew that Leland Carver and, later, Flambé were bringing in shifters legitimately and helping them with education and, eventually, work and even their own businesses. He said when they investigated him, Carver seemed a good man, and he was doing a good service. He only brought in a few shifters at a time. Later, unfortunately, there were rumors about Carver, that he began to bring mostly women and those women lived with him in the biblical sense."

Mitya glanced at the door. "I really hate this, Sevastyan."

"Yeah, so do I. I feel like I'm going behind her back, but I have to know how bad things were and if anyone's betraying her now. Those three employees seemed to think something wasn't right about this woman coming in, and Flambé defended her. She's going to put herself in the line of fire. I have to know how to keep her safe." He reached back to rub at the knots of tension forming in his neck.

"Drake conducted a quiet investigation of Carver and discovered he was sleeping with the women he brought into the country. You have to remember, Drake was very young and his company was fairly new here in the States as well. Carver's sex with the shifter women he brought to the States appeared to be consensual, but still, it was unethical. By that time, his wife was already gone, and he was a widower with a little girl."

"Did he hear about Carver's marriage?"

Mitya nodded. "Drake heard all the rumors, that Carver hadn't stopped having sex with other women, even with his wife

621

pregnant and in the same house. That she was miserable. Drake said there was little he could do since the women Carver was with refused to make any complaints against him."

Sevastyan sighed. That was what Flambé had told him. Carver had kicked his own daughter out of the house in order to have one more room for another woman. She'd been alone. She'd learned to be alone. From the time she was a child she'd learned that shifters were unfaithful. Her father might not have been physically abusive to her, but he was emotionally abusive.

"Damn it, Mitya. I don't know the first thing about how to be right for her. I can protect her. I can give her great sex. But the things she needs to know about, I don't know. I never had those things either." Sevastyan was beginning to sweat. He couldn't sit still. He leapt up and began to pace restlessly.

Ania stood and leaned into her husband. "Sevastyan. Honey. Listen to me. Loving someone isn't terrible like you think it is. It isn't something to be afraid of."

He let his gaze drift over her, dark and savage, banded with red heat. "It is, Ania. I'm not good with emotions, you know that. Look at how I handle you. And what I feel for Flambé . . ." He stumbled, trying to find words, the pressure in his chest so severe that for a moment he was afraid he might have to go to his knees. "It's getting worse. The more I'm with her, it's getting worse. I don't want to be without her."

"Women don't really need grand gestures all the time, Sevastyan," Ania insisted. "You're making things too hard. Tell her you don't want to be without her. Say what you feel." She burst out laughing. "You should see the expression on your face. I haven't told you to lie down in front of a steamroller. Just say what's in your heart once in a while. By that I mean a few times a day. Give her something to hold on to. Then when you're an ass, which you will be, she'll be more inclined to overlook it."

"Is that what you do?" Sevastyan demanded, his focused, leopard's eyes boring into Mitya.

Mitya nodded. "Keeps me out of trouble."

"Not entirely," Ania corrected. "But it goes a long way. Sit down, Sevastyan. You're going to do all right. Admitting to her how you feel isn't the worst thing in the world."

He'd done that. He had told her, and somehow, she had given him so much back. He forced air through his lungs and waited for Ania to sit before taking the chair across from his brother.

"This woman, this Shanty, Drake shares the same concerns as Flambé's three employees. Not because he found anything on her, but because something just didn't add up to him," Mitya said. "She's strawberry. She was caught on camera and her picture was put in just about every newspaper from here to hell and back. Flambé's team did a cursory investigation and filled out the necessary paperwork to bring her and the children to the States. The team has a holding area they take every shifter to before bringing them into the States while the necessary paperwork is being done. They get shots, all the work is done there and they're protected. Shanty's paperwork had to be pushed through quickly and favors had to be called in. She was told ahead of time and yet she still pitched a fit, insisting that Flambé come to meet her personally in South Africa."

Sevastyan's gut tightened the way it did when something felt wrong to him. The woman should have just wanted to get out as fast as possible.

"Could she have been so frightened she just wanted to see Flambé's face? Flambé would have been the most recognizable, right?" Ania asked.

624

"How?" Sevastyan demanded. "She provided an extraction team. They would have sent their photos, not Flambé's. She wouldn't have been involved at that point. She wouldn't be involved until the woman and her children were turned over here in the United States. Flambé had stopped going on runs for a while, especially with her leopard so close to emerging. She has a price on her head. She knew better than to go. So how did this woman know to ask for Flambé personally?"

"Did you ask Flambé?" Mitya said. Surprisingly, his tone was mild. The angrier Sevastyan became, the calmer Mitya became.

"No." Sevastyan shoved both hands through his hair. "I don't want her to think I'm taking over her business. Our relationship is very fragile."

"Her life could be in danger, Sevastyan," Mitya pointed out. "If it was Ania, you'd throw her over your shoulder like a caveman, scowl at me and toss her into the panic room."

"Shut the fuck up," Sevastyan snapped, but his tone was conciliatory. Mitya was right. He would do that. He would expect Mitya to protect Ania and he would be furious if he didn't. He was just so damned afraid of losing ground with Flambé.

"You have to ask her," Mitya pushed. "You don't have a choice."

Sevastyan knew he didn't have a choice in the matter. In a way, Shanty had saved him. He doubted if Flambé would have stuck around if she hadn't been waiting for the woman. But if so many others had a bad feeling about her, then something had to be off.

There was no sound but he turned to look toward the kitchen. Now that Flamme had finally made her appearance and fully integrated with Flambé, she moved even more like a leopard, but there was no covering her scent, not from Sevastyan. Everything around him faded in comparison to her. The colors of the leaves and plants, the clouds drifting across the sky. The way the property rolled and seemed to go on forever.

He inhaled, tasting her on his tongue. Cinnamon and spices, setting up the craving for her the way it always did. Flambé opened the kitchen door and stood framed there, her gaze on his face before she took a breath and looked at their company.

Mitya stood, Ania tucking in quickly beneath his shoulder, giving him her full support. "Flambé," Mitya greeted her first, not waiting. "I had to come to tell you how

626

very sorry I am for the way I've treated you. Please let me explain, although there really is no excuse. I can only throw myself on your mercy and hope you're as compassionate as Sevastyan says you are."

She released her death grip on the edge of the door and stepped onto the porch, a hint of a smile lighting her eyes, turning the green a jeweled emerald. "He says I'm compassionate?"

Mitya nodded. "He does."

Flambé took the chair beside Sevastyan's. "He wishes I was compassionate with all the crap he pulls."

Mitya burst out laughing. "She has your number."

Ania nudged him. "Probably in the same way I have yours. Get on with it."

"Yes, well." Mitya sank back into his seat and pulled Ania down onto his lap. "I've been looking out for Sevastyan since he was a boy. It hasn't been easy either. He's always in some kind of trouble."

"That's easy enough to believe," Flambé said. Sevastyan scowled. "Flambé, I'm the head of security."

"That means nothing." Mitya waved that airily away and then bit lightly on his wife's neck. "Already, you've lived with him. You know how he is. Hot-tempered. But still, a

627

good man. My baby brother, although few know this."

Sevastyan groaned. "Not baby."

"Yes. *Baby.* You were the baby. I had to change your diapers. What a mess that was." Mitya gave a long-suffering sigh.

"You know how to change diapers?" Ania asked, swinging her head around to look at her husband. "You never once mentioned this talent to me. I don't have a clue how to change a baby's little butt. Guess who will be doing that particular chore if we ever get lucky enough to have one of those creatures?"

Mitya wrapped his arm around Ania's shoulders and dragged her even closer. "We'll have a baby someday, *kotyonok.* One way or another we'll have one, although I'm not certain I will remember how to change diapers. You may have to learn."

"Ha!" Sevastyan pounced on that. "He never changed my diapers in the first place. Don't believe a thing he says, Flambé."

"In any case, I was being overprotective of him. I feared he entered into the relationship too fast. He was lonely. I knew this. You are beautiful. Anyone can see that. You both have the same interests but you never looked at him the way I thought a woman who would love him would look at him. I had no right to judge you or the relationship the two of you choose to have together. I wanted so much for him and I put my desires and what I believed was the only right way to love on the two of you. I'm very sorry for that."

"I can't really blame you for thinking I had one foot out the door," Flambé said. "Since I did. I'm not good at relationships, or trusting anyone, especially a male shifter." Sevastyan wrapped his arm around her waist, ignoring the slight stiffening of her body. They had to start somewhere. He pulled her to him. "I didn't make it easy, Flambé. Between visiting the club, my work, and a thousand other things . . ."

She bumped him with her hip. "Don't. You tried way more than I did. I just tried to run. In any case, we're hopefully past that now." She turned to Ania. "Flamme finally made her appearance, thanks to Sevastyan. I don't know how he was able to get her out without it killing me, but he managed."

She smiled up at him and ran her hand up and down his arm. It was just once, but she did it, a small sign of affection she never would have done before. His stomach did a slow, weird flip and he tightened his hold on her.

"Her leopard is gorgeous," he told them.

629

"I've never seen one like her. Her rosettes are actually red, not black, and her fur is definitely ginger, or closer to pink."

"Pink?" Flambé looked outraged. "Definitely not pink. *Red.* My leopard is *red.* I can't believe you even said pink. Strike that word from your vocabulary."

Ania giggled and Mitya coughed behind his hand.

Sevastyan's fingers danced their way up her rib cage, sliding intimately over her thin T-shirt. "I just dyed more rope this morning, various colors, and one of them was a bright pink. I think we'll be using that quite often."

"We will *not* be using that. Not only does it clash with my coloring, but I'm *allergic* to pink," Flambé declared, tossing her head. Several thick sheets of hair dislodged from her ponytail and fell around her face. She tilted her face up toward his, eyes mostly green, looking like twin jewels, high cheekbones flushed with rose.

"Baby," Sevastyan said, his voice very low. "It's impossible to be allergic to a color."

"You don't know. Strawberry leopards have strange maladies. I very well could be allergic to colors."

He bent his head to hers before he could stop himself. There was no resisting her. He wasn't a man who would ever be able to not kiss his woman in public. Or hold her hand. Or put his arm around her. He could refrain from slamming her up against a wall — he was fairly certain he had that much restraint — but he was a shifter and he was oral. He was also tactile. He needed to touch and taste. And claim. The damn truth of it was, he was drowning under her spell.

Sevastyan very gently framed Flambé's face, his thumbs sliding over her chin, her jaw, tracing the delicate lines. He sipped tenderly at her lower lip. Her long lashes swept down as her breath hitched. He kissed the corners of her mouth and then pressed his lips to hers, his tongue sliding along the seam in a silent command for entry.

Flambé obeyed without hesitation. One hand slid around, shaping the back of her skull, pressing into her thick red hair, all that silky brightness. His heart pounded hard in his chest. His thumb stroked over her chin, back and forth in a small caress.

"I need you, *malen'koye plamya,* just to breathe, to live. I've never said that to another human being, but it's the truth. Not for Shturm, but for me." He whispered it to her and then, before she could answer him, or even lift her lashes to look at him and see his intense mortification, he kissed her, this time taking them both into that fiery place that consumed them fast and voraciously.

Flambé kissed him back, her slender arms sliding around his neck, her body pressed tight against his. She gave herself to him the way she did when she was in the ropes. She'd never done that before unless she was tied or in the heat of her leopard. Sevastyan found he could barely stand. As always, his body was completely out of control, his cock diamond hard, ready to shatter at the least little provocation just from having his woman in such close proximity. It wouldn't do to collapse in front of Mitya and Ania or make a fool of himself.

He lifted his head cautiously and glanced around to check how close the nearest chair was. Could he make it without breaking anything important? Keeping his hold on Flambé so she was in front of him, he took a step back and lowered himself gingerly into the chair, sprawling, legs out in front of him.

Mitya snickered. The ass. He glared at him as he gently guided Flambé onto his lap, making certain he positioned her onto his thighs and not his straining cock. She did a little shimmy thing with her body and he had to stifle a groan. Mitya snickered again.

"Do leopard ashes make good compost?"

632

He glared at his brother while he asked his woman the question, biting down on her shoulder as he did so.

A little shiver went through her. "I suppose it would depend on the leopard. If you're talking about Mitya, probably not. In fact, his ashes could be toxic to plants."

Ania burst out laughing. Mitya scowled darkly. "Toxic to plants? You think I'd be toxic to your plants? Woman, you're insane. I'd nurture those plants."

"The way you nurtured little Sevastyan," Ania prompted, and gave in to another fit of giggling.

"*Baby* Sevastyan," Flambé corrected, and laughed with Ania.

Sevastyan put his mouth against her ear and stroked his hand along the cheeks of her bottom. "I have a special tie I can't wait to use on you just to show you what happens to my woman when she teases me like this and I can't retaliate." His teeth bit down on her earlobe, tugged and let go.

He waited, heart pounding, to see if she would recognize that he was teasing her in the same way she was teasing him. He wasn't adept at outward play, but then she wasn't either. They were both feeling their way.

Flambé turned her head and smiled at

633

him, her eyes bright, but she didn't say anything aloud. Like Sevastyan, she was uncertain what to say in front of the others.

"Flambé," Mitya said, sobering, indicating the chair beside Sevastyan's. "I know you've taken over the rescue operation your father started some years ago, which is quite admirable. Drake Donovan is a good friend of mine and he came into contact with your father once or twice. That was how I first came to know of Carver's work."

Flambé sank slowly into the chair beside Sevastyan and drew her legs underneath her, curling up very small. That was never a good sign with her. She definitely didn't want to discuss the rescue operation with Mitya and Ania. She was barely able to discuss it with him.

"Mitya," Sevastyan intervened. "I can talk to Flambé about this later."

"You might not have later, Sevastyan," Mitya said, sounding as if he was striving to keep his voice gentle. He sounded more like a cross between a growling bear and a lethal leopard.

Ania punched his shoulder, which made Flambé, who was trying to look nonchalant while she drank water, spit it out and Sevastyan turn his face away. Ania wasn't in the least intimidated by her husband.

634

"Flambé and I will work it out," Sevastyan insisted, trying not to smirk at the way his sister-in-law got away with everything.

Flambé regarded Mitya steadily and then turned green-gold eyes on Sevastyan. "I think it would be best if you just told me what you're worried about." She pressed the cold water bottle to her head.

"Do you have a headache, baby?" Sevastyan asked.

She nodded. "Big-time. Whatever you're going to tell me is bound to make it worse, so get on with it before Flamme decides to make another appearance."

"Tell us how the protocol worked when you were going to the country to meet with the individual yourself and bring them out," Sevastyan said.

Flambé shrugged. "We contact a lair that's unstable, in trouble, and ask the elders if any of their members are interested in relocating to the United States. If they are, our investigation team takes a look at them to make certain they don't have anything in their background that would in any way detract from them entering the United States, working here and eventually becoming a citizen. While they're doing that, another group works with the attorneys, ensuring all the paperwork is filed properly, and I fly over to meet them. The extraction team is with me and we escort them out."

"How much trouble is there?" Mitya asked.

Flambé made a little face. "In the last couple of years, more often than not, we ran into all kinds of problems, so much so that the extraction team preferred that I didn't accompany them. There was no hiding traveling anymore with the internet. We didn't used to have to hide. It wasn't a big deal when my father was bringing shifters over. No one knew or thought anything about it. All of a sudden in the last two years, no matter if it was a male or female, we ran into people with guns."

"And there is a price on your head," Sevastyan added. "From two different factions."

Flambé nodded. "Yes. My team thought it would be smarter for me to stay out of the mix and meet the shifter here in the US rather than on their home turf. I agreed with them, although I seem to be able to tell when one is not who they say they are even if they slip past the investigation team."

Mitya frowned and stroked his jaw. "Wait, I have to get this straight, Flambé. You don't just go to greet the shifter coming into the country to be welcoming, you are there to serve another purpose."

She nodded. "As a rule, when I talk to them and ask a series of questions, I can usually ascertain whether or not they are legitimately looking to fit into the program we're offering or if they want a handout. We don't give handouts. We expect everyone to pull their own weight. There are too many others waiting in line. That may sound harsh, but it's true. If I can give someone an education and set them up in business and the contract reads they bring someone over to pay it forward, that helps someone else."

"How can you tell if your investigation and your extraction team can't tell?" Sevastyan asked. "Leopards hear lies, it can't be that."

"It has nothing to do with hearing lies," Flambé admitted. "Even as a child, when I went on trips with my father, I could tell. There was something in the way their eyes shifted back and forth. I would tell my father and he would pass on that particular shifter. Not at first, but later, when I had a proven track record."

"What you're saying," Ania mused, "is the shifter really did want to come to the US and was even willing to work for you or your father, but he wasn't going to follow through

637

and hire other shifters. You could tell that even as a child."

She nodded. "They weren't bad people. They just didn't have the same vision as my father — or me. There were other ways for them to leave their lair."

"These last couple of years, when things have changed . . ." Sevastyan continued, pushing his luck, seeing how uncomfortable she was. Flambé didn't squirm or move restlessly. She sat very calmly, but he could tell this was the last conversation she wanted to have. She'd agreed to it, but was still unsure of all of them — him included. She wanted to take that chance with him, but everything about them was so new. This was her business, her passion, and she didn't understand where they were going with it. "Flambé," he persisted, keeping his tone as gentle as possible, using his low, authoritative voice that she responded to the most. "What changed with this particular woman? Shanty Jacobs. Who made the initial contact?"

"We first were contacted by a source at *National Geographic.* They had to run with their story and the photographs they had, but they sent word to us. Our extraction team immediately deployed into the field and were able to make contact fairly quickly

638

with Shanty and the children. Her lair had been destroyed. There were so few left that there hadn't been a way to protect them when they were attacked and those left were scattered and on the run."

"Did your investigation team have time to do a thorough investigation before your extraction team picked her and her children up?" Sevastyan pushed.

Flambé hesitated. She set the water bottle very carefully on the table as if she was afraid of spilling it. Her hand didn't shake. She looked perfectly in control, but that slight pause was unlike her. She was always sure when it came to her business. The hesitation added more knots to Sevastyan's gut.

"No. We had to deploy our extraction team fast. Once we made contact with her and determined she wanted to leave, we realized it wasn't safe for her to stay there. She was being hunted, not only by the government, but by poachers as well."

"If you turned her over to the government, would they have protected her?" Ania asked.

"As a leopard," Flambé said, "she would have been subjected to tests and separated from her children. They wouldn't have

639

known she was a shifter or that her children were."

"But she could have escaped easily," Ania pointed out. "If there was an immediate risk . . ."

"True, but our extraction team was right there and they provided her with an alternative."

"But you told me she didn't want to leave with them," Sevastyan objected. "You told your workers that Shanty refused, at first, to leave unless you came personally to South Africa to escort her back to the United States."

Flambé frowned again and rolled the bottle of water over her forehead. He knew her mind was puzzling out the steps that she normally would take on a rescue. This one had been different from the start. They had been contacted right before the photographs had gone public, putting the remaining strawberry leopards in jeopardy. The shifters had scattered, driven from the lair by poachers and now hunted by the government and tourists as well. They were frightened, not knowing where to turn.

There wasn't time for a thorough investigation, everyone understood that, Sevastyan included. It was also the perfect time for a setup if someone was in a position to get there first. The questions were, how? And why?

"How would she even know your name, or for that matter your face, Flambé?" Sevastyan persisted gently. "It isn't attached in any way to the extraction team. Why would she fixate on you and insist on you coming to South Africa instead of getting her children to safety as fast as she could? You said yourself you haven't been going with the extraction team for close to two years now."

Flambé didn't answer. She closed her eyes, her long lashes, two thick crescents fanning down, making her look more vulnerable than ever.

"Could the extraction team have mentioned her name?" Ania ventured. "She's a woman. If Shanty was frightened, she may have wanted a woman to reassure her."

There was a small silence while the wind tugged at the loose dirt in the yard, whirling it into little eddies, making small dust devils, sending them bouncing and dancing in a wild display.

"That was the exact excuse I used when Etienne and Rory asked me why she had insisted on me meeting her in South Africa. They thought it strange as well. I said that very thing. She was a woman and she was

641

frightened. I never thought to ask how she knew me. No one on the extraction team would ever mention me."

"But you had acquired a reputation," Mitya pointed out, playing the devil's advocate.

"So had Drake Donovan. A much bigger one than mine. His security company is very well known all over the world. Why ask for me? Why not him? It's true he mostly goes after hostages, but he's been known to bring out shifters from troubled areas," Flambé said with a small sigh. "He would have gotten there fast, probably faster than our team."

"Why would this woman want to set you up?" Ania said. "She doesn't know you."

Flambé shook her head.

Knowing she wasn't used to physical comfort, Sevastyan still couldn't help offering it to her. He leaned toward her, sliding his arm around her shoulders. "Come here, baby."

"I'm okay."

"You're not. Come sit on my lap."

She gave a little shake of her head.

He kept the pressure on her shoulder and didn't say anything else. He simply waited. Flambé took time to work it all out. To make up her mind. She had committed to him. She was still in the process of deciding just what that meant to her, what their relationship would be. She did derive comfort from him after being in the ropes. They'd established that over the last few weeks. He had that going for him.

With a soft sigh, Flambé capitulated, sliding from her chair to curl up on his lap, pulling her legs up the way she did, making herself small, cuddling into him. He wrapped his arms around her, giving her firm pressure. His arms were like the ropes, binding her, making her feel safe.

"Most people will betray others for money, power, revenge or if their loved ones are in jeopardy," Mitya supplied into the silence. "This woman could have any of these motives."

"Not power or revenge," Sevastyan ruled out immediately, nuzzling the top of Flambé's head with his chin. "She doesn't know Flambé, and what kind of power would she achieve? So, money. Someone could be paying her a good amount, or her mate is being held hostage. Where is her mate? What's the story on that, *plamya*?"

Flambé had begun to relax into him by slow increments. Her body was used to the feel of his from all the nights they slept together so close, Sevastyan refusing to al-

643

low so much as an inch between their skin. She had been shivering, but even that was slowly dissipating. She rested her head against his chest, her palm pressing into his thigh.

"According to the extraction team, every time they asked about her mate, she became hysterical. She would cry and talk about guns and poachers and everyone being dead."

"Others escaped the massacre because at least nine other strawberry leopards were caught on separate cameras in various areas, isn't that correct?" Ania asked.

"Yes," Flambé said. "As far as I know, the teams are trying to find them. You know as well as I do, shifters are notoriously difficult to find when they don't want to be tracked."

"How does it work on your end?" Sevastyan asked. "You don't use your private cell phone. You said someone at *National Geographic* gave you the heads-up. How?"

"I was working at the club when the call came in. There are only two of us who can answer that phone. Blaise Brodeur, my foreman, or me. He's worked for us for years. My father brought him over years ago, when I was starting into my teens. He went to college, really excelled and came back to work with my father. He loves the landscaping business the way we do. My father gave him enough money to start his own business, but he wanted to stay on as the foreman and has. No one else has been there that long and knows both sides, the rescue and the landscaping."

"So, Blaise took the original call and he set the investigators to work," Sevastyan said.

"Yes, right away. He called me as well. I told him to alert the extraction team and put them in the field as they might have to track the leopards and get to them very fast. We didn't know what was happening. Blaise called me back a few minutes later and told me about Shanty and the children. At that time, we didn't know her name. He just said the contact at *National Geographic* had her picture and a location and she was separated from the others."

Sevastyan exchanged a long look with his brother over Flambé's head. He didn't like the way this was beginning to shape up.

"Sevastyan?" Flambé's voice sounded tired and worn. Hurt and betrayed. "Do you remember the day we were working on the property and I was talking with Rory, Etienne and Blaise? You came up behind me? That was when Flamme was really showing herself."

"I remember." He kept his voice strictly neutral.

"They were all looking at a picture of Shanty. Blaise acted as if he'd never seen her photograph, but he had to have. He was the first one to take the call. There was no way he didn't see the photo and know the location. He had to send it to the investigation and extraction teams."

"Blaise is a strawberry leopard." Mitya made it a statement.

Ania looked at him, clearly puzzled, but she didn't say anything.

"I don't understand."

"You're really quite beautiful, Flambé," Mitya said. "You don't seem to realize that you are. You also own a very successful business. Your father gave Brodeur the start-up money for a new business, but it would be nothing in comparison to what your business makes. In his mind, he paid his dues. He hung in there, worked hard, did what he was supposed to do and he should have gotten it all. You and the business."

Sevastyan was extremely glad he wasn't the one to have to point out to her that Blaise Brodeur was most likely the man who had betrayed her. He knew why Mitya was the one taking that chance. Once again, he was protecting his little brother, risking bringing Flambé's wrath down on him rather than Sevastyan for even suggesting that Blaise might betray her.

She shook her head. "That makes no sense. He asked me out a couple of times, but after I turned him down, he stopped. He's never made a move after that. And this entire thing, the poachers, the setup, all of it, the cost would be prohibitive. No way would it be Blaise."

She didn't want it to be someone she knew. Sevastyan tightened his arms around her, wishing he was alone with her and they were upstairs in their master bedroom where he could tie her with his rope. Arms and rope, more ties to comfort her. She was beginning to shiver again because she already knew the truth. She looked up at Sevastyan and there was despair in her eyes. Hurt. Tears swimming.

"He isn't the one behind it all," Sevastyan said softly. "You know that already, Flambé, but he took the money. He's angry and he took the money."

19

"I don't like this, Flambé," Blaise said, looking around. "It feels too open here. You've always met the clients in a safe house."

"It's the best I could do. You know my leopard's in heat. I can't exactly go out into the public, Blaise," Flambé snapped. She took a deep breath. "I'm sorry. She makes me very moody. This came at such a bad time for everyone. I tried to get out of meeting Shanty. I was going to have you handle it, but she was very insistent. I told you, she would have preferred I meet her in South Africa. There was no way with my leopard so close to emerging."

Blaise nodded his understanding. "Sevastyan wouldn't just leave you, though. Where is he? I can't imagine that with your leopard rising he'd just go work at his cousin's house."

She made an exasperated sound. "I didn't want him where anyone could see him. That would just scare her off. In any case, you know how he is about his cousin. Mitya's house is right next door. It isn't like the time between houses isn't minutes."

Not one word she said was a lie. She'd practiced what she would say when the question of Sevastyan came up. She knew it would. They all knew it would. She'd implied Sevastyan was at Mitya's, she hadn't said he was.

"I don't like any client knowing where you live," Blaise reiterated. "Let alone one we haven't checked out thoroughly."

"She won't know this is my home," Flambé pointed out. "I'll meet briefly with her. The rest of the extraction team will have the children with them and they'll take her to join them at the safe house, where we can decide what to do after I've talked with her."

Blaise nodded. Flambé hadn't stepped off the verandah. She was tucked back in the security of the alcove, which couldn't be seen from any of the trees or rolling hills. Sevastyan and his team of security guards had made certain, looking from every angle, making absolutely sure that no one could get a shot at her if that was the intention. Blaise had left the alcove several times to lean out over the railing, shading his eyes in spite of his sunglasses to peer down the road.

"Why are you so nervous?" Flambé asked curiously. "This isn't that different than any other time."

"I don't know. It just feels off to me."

Flambé tried not to feel hopeful. Or elated. Maybe they were all wrong about Blaise after all. She didn't want him to be working against her. She felt real affection for him. He might not be what she wanted in a life partner, but she felt close to him.

"You realize I don't have any family at all, Blaise. No siblings, no cousins. No one. You're the closest thing to family I have." She meant it. There was an ache in her voice. She couldn't help it. Blaise heard it and he turned around to face her, his back to the railing.

"What's wrong, Flambé?"

"I don't know. Nothing. Everything. I don't think you're happy and I want you to be. Why don't you date anymore? You used to go out all the time."

He hesitated. Like Flambé, he was well aware leopards could hear lies. "I want a life partner, not a one-night stand. I got damn tired of those."

"Can I ask you a personal question? It's really personal," she warned.

650

He shrugged, looking wary, but he nodded. His gaze on her face was very focused, indicating his leopard was close.

"Are your nerve endings in your body close to the surface?"

He frowned. "I don't know what you mean exactly."

"In some strawberry leopards" — Flambé chose her words carefully — "nerve endings are very close to the surface. It can cause real pain if touched the wrong way. It can also develop into a need for sex all the time. I just wondered if that happened to you."

Those eyes didn't blink. Didn't leave hers. He shook his head slowly. "Do you have that problem?"

She had been afraid if she asked, he would retaliate. It was natural that he would. Male strawberry leopards seemed to have a healthy sex drive, like most shifters, but they didn't seem to suffer the genetic affliction some of the women did.

"Are you a hemophiliac?"

He shook his head, frowning now, worry creeping into his eyes. "Flambé, what the hell? Are you? Your father never said a word."

"My mother hemorrhaged in childbirth, Blaise. It was genetic, so yes, I am. I take iron, of course, but I need more than that if

651

I'm going to stay alive. They have a few newer things to try than they did in my mother's time."

Blaise shoved his hand through his hair in agitation. "I wish your father had told me. You shouldn't have been working with all the equipment, Flambé. Too many accidents can happen. One slip of a pruning knife and you've got a dangerous cut."

"I try to take precautions."

"But you didn't tell anyone. You should have at least told me." He swung around, his fingers biting deep into the wooden beams of the railing. "I didn't understand your father. He put you out of the house, left you on your own and then never once reined you in when you needed it. Hell. You could have died."

There was real caring in his voice. Again, she didn't want to believe he had anything to do with betrayal.

"I can't live my entire life shut up in my room, Blaise."

"No, but you could be more careful," he said. "A hell of a lot more careful. What did you mean about nerve endings and needing sex all the time?"

She took a slow drink from her water bottle, placed it carefully on the table and then kept her fingers closed around it.

652

"There's a condition some of the strawberry leopards have — and yes, it's genetic as well — that I suffer from, where nerve endings can make life hell."

Blaise turned back, kept his gaze fixed on her face, but the expression in his eyes had gone predatory. "You need sex all the time? That's what you're saying."

She shrugged. "It's a condition, not something you want to have anyone you care about sharing with you, you know?" That was true as well. She'd been ashamed of it for so long, and truthfully, no matter what Sevastyan said or how she tried to rethink it, she still was. She didn't want to think that her body drove her. She wanted to be in control.

"Damn it, Flambé. You went to the bar and picked up human males and had one-night stands so you wouldn't let anyone you cared about get attached to you." He made it a statement.

Flambé was grateful he had made that a statement. There was no requirement for her one way or another to comment. She just looked at him and shrugged again. He could infer from that that Sevastyan wasn't a man she cared for; she just hoped he didn't ask her any questions. She could see the sudden speculation in his eyes.

653

"Flambé, you should have come to me and told me all of this instead of keeping it to yourself." He heaved a sigh. "I understand why you didn't. Your father has so much to answer for. You spent most of your life alone, trying to figure out everything on your own, but you really need someone to rely on. I've been in your life longer than anyone else and you know you can trust me."

For the first time she could hear that slight discordant note and Flamme scraped hard against her, protesting his declaration. Her heart sank. Blaise. What was left of her family. Unexpected tears burned behind her eyes. Hormones, she told herself. She forced herself to concentrate on the water bottle, lifting it to her mouth and drinking. She didn't taste the cool liquid, but it saved her from crying and giving herself away.

Truck coming up the road, malen'koye plamya. Sevastyan's low voice was in her ear, intimate. Sounding the way he did when he spoke to her with a rope in his hands.

Vehicles moving into position at back of property. I count two, Christophe Tregre reported. He was situated in the control room inside the main house. It was imperative Flambé keep Blaise out of the house.

Can you see how many inside each vehicle? Sevastyan asked.

That's negative at this time, Christophe answered. *Over to you, Ambroise.*

Am looking from above, using heat imaging, Ambroise intoned, sounding distant. He was, in fact, at Mitya's. *In all but the first vehicle going to front of house, there are five-man teams. First vehicle holds three people.*

"I have to text Sevastyan that all is well, Blaise. Give me a minute. I don't want him charging in and ruining everything. He likes to take over."

A look of annoyance slid over Blaise's face, hastily gone as he turned away. He walked down the stairs and bent down to examine the newly planted shrubs.

That should be right, Sevastyan. Two of my extraction team members would escort Shanty to me. They would then take her to the safe house from here, she texted to him.

Don't leave that alcove for any reason. When you're going to talk to Shanty, have them bring her there and make everyone else leave. You have access to the house and you can get her inside and lock both of you in if necessary. Again, his voice was like liquid velvet in her ear, stroking her nerves when Blaise had unsettled her.

655

If they do have her husband, she won't come with me unless we've gotten him back. Do you have any idea where he is? Who has him?

He has to be close. If it isn't the money and it is her mate, she will continue to ask for reassurance that he's alive. That means she has to ask for constant contact. Have her do that. When she does, we can get his location and go after him.

Blaise is coming back.

Knowing Sevastyan was close, that he had eyes on her, comforted her to some degree, but there was this underlying hurt and feeling of betrayal that just wouldn't let go. She had grown up feeling that male shifters were not trustworthy. They didn't care about females. Females had to rely on themselves. She wasn't going to miraculously get over years of conditioning because Sevastyan had called the doctor and tried to find ways to help her. She knew she would question his integrity even when she didn't want to.

"What's wrong, Flambé? Is Sevastyan giving you trouble?" Blaise asked, perching on the railing, looking confident, as if he owned the property. There was something almost proprietorial in the way he acted, both over

656

the land and over her.

She shrugged. "I don't know. I'm just out of sorts. Moody, I guess. I wish this was over and I could just be myself again."

"Did you say just be yourself again? Do you think you made a mistake with Sevastyan, Flambé?" Blaise asked.

Flambé hesitated. She had made her choice to be with Sevastyan, made that commitment to him. Was she sure of him? Absolutely not. She was still very much terrified. How did anyone, man or woman, know they weren't making a terrible mistake when they entered into a life partnership? Sevastyan wasn't an easy partner. He wasn't ever going to be easy, but then, if she was honest, neither was she.

SUV turning up driveway. Sevastyan's voice was in her ear.

Gratefully, Flambé turned to look at the vehicle proceeding toward them. She recognized the 4Runner used by the extraction team in the United States to transport the shifters they brought in. They already had received all their shots, had their papers and were ready to go to their assigned home, usually the confines of a safe house for a week until they were brought onto the main property. The men slept in the barracks and

657

the women usually had rooms in the main house.

"They're here, Blaise."

"Flambé," Blaise began. "You don't have to stay with this man. You know that, don't you? It's your leopard's first cycle and they often make mistakes the first time around."

"She was terrified." Flambé kept her eyes on the 4Runner in the distance. "I was as well. Franco Matherson had been stalking me for a while. He ran me off the road when I was coming out here to talk to Sevastyan about working on his property. He threw me up against his car, punched me when I fought him, and I hit my head really hard on the ground when I went down. I fought him and barely managed to get away."

Flambé had turned back to watch the expressions chasing across Blaise's face. There was genuine outrage. Fury. He was leopard and he had a leopard's temper. "What the hell? Why didn't you say anything to me?"

She shrugged and kept going with her explanation. "I was very disoriented and I ran into the woods. I knew the property because I'd been here with my father. I ran up to the house and unfortunately, my leopard was able to break free enough to call to Sevastyan's male. I was too out of it

658

to know what was happening until it was too late for both of us. I have to take full responsibility for that. It wasn't his fault. My leopard was very seductive. She thought she was protecting us from that creeper."

"Franco Matherson?" Blaise echoed.

She nodded. "Yes." Deliberately she ran her hands up and down her arms, shivering. "He's never going to leave me alone. He's sent several of his men to kidnap me even after that. At least three different tries."

Blaise stood up, his back to her, watching the 4Runner as it came closer to the house. "Are you absolutely certain it was Matherson, Flambé?" His voice was very quiet.

"Yes." She remained seated. "When she gets out of the car, will you have them bring her up here into the alcove, Blaise? I always interview each person alone. That's imperative. If I don't have access to them alone, where I feel they can be completely candid with me, I can't get a feel if they're right for our program. If she isn't, we can ask Drake Donovan to help her and her children. We're very full and there's more of these shifters out there, displaced from their lair."

"She's going to insist that you accompany her and the children to the safe house, Flambé," Blaise said.

"Why would you think that? Her children

659

are already there."

"She was so nervous she was insisting you go to South Africa."

Flambé nodded. "You're right. Well, maybe this one time I might have to make an exception, as long as I don't think my leopard is too close to rising. If so, I'd have to let Sevastyan know." She let her voice trail off.

Blaise shook his head decisively. "I don't think it's a good idea, Flambé. You should just tell her no. She can be like everyone else."

There was a hardness in his voice she'd never heard before. Whatever Blaise was up to, whatever the original plan was, and she was certain it involved getting into the 4Runner with Shanty, Blaise had suddenly changed his mind.

Flambé recognized two members of the extraction team. They regularly moved back and forth between the United States and any country where they retrieved shifters and brought them to work in the landscaping business until they could decide where they wanted to go to school and what they were interested in as a business.

Terry Orsan was a tall, dark-skinned man with a ready smile and the roped muscles of the shifters. He wore his hair longer and it

660

tended to curl around his head in ringlets, although the only one who could get away with calling the long dark curls ringlets was his daughter. She was ten now and adored her father. Jet Vicks was short in contrast to Terry, but equally as muscular, with a thick lion's mane of graying hair that was wildly out of control, tamed only by a loose tie. It was clear the two men had worked together for a long time. Jet helped the young woman out of the 4Runner while Terry watched their backtrail. In spite of being on private property, they were both wary, very cognizant of being responsible for their client.

"Blaise, this is Shanty Jacobs. She's come to speak with Flambé," Jet said.

Terry and Jet both scanned all around them, looking up on the rooftops and over to the trees as if they were nervous.

"Are you expecting trouble?" Flambé asked, standing, drawing their attention. She didn't come out of the alcove, very conscious of Sevastyan's orders. "I'm Flambé, Shanty. I'm so sorry I couldn't meet you in South Africa, but my female was rising. Her first heat."

"I understand," Shanty said. Her eyes were a delicate blue, but she looked as if she'd been crying for days. Her eyes were swollen, her face puffy. She looked at

Flambé once and then down at the ground. A tremor went through her body.

"I don't know about trouble, Flambé," Terry answered. "I've got this feeling in my gut. I've had it for a while now. When I get it, it's not a good thing to ignore."

Jet nodded. "He's never been wrong yet."

"Shanty and I are going to sit here for a few minutes and talk," Flambé said. "If you gentlemen would give us space. A good deal of it, please. Leopards have excellent hearing and I would prefer that you get out of range. We'll put on some music to help mute what we say to each other as well, but this conversation is strictly between us. Blaise, in the cooler there are two ice-cold water bottles. Would you mind?" She gave him one of her sweetest smiles.

Blaise immediately handed the two women a bottle of water each and then stepped off the porch. "I don't like getting too far from you."

"It's not like anyone can get to us," Flambé pointed out. She made certain she didn't look at the front door, which was only a few steps away. Inside that house was a team of Sevastyan's men ready to surround her and Shanty with safety if she could just get Shanty to make a call to the men holding her husband hostage.

662

Blaise nodded and the three men left them. Flambé waved Shanty to a chair. "This must have been a very long, scary trip for you and the children. How are they?"

Shanty nodded. "I think they're good," she mumbled.

"Where are they?"

"They were taken to the safe house by the other members of the team."

Shanty was speaking so low, in spite of the fact that Flambé was leopard, she could barely hear her. Flambé looked her over. The woman was thin. She looked utterly miserable. Her skin was red, her face blotchy. Flambé took a deep breath. It was now or never. She pushed a sheet of paper across the table at Shanty. Flambe turned on a small fountain set sitting on the table and leaned close to it allowing them to whisper, the water interfering if Shanty was wired.

"They'll have toys for them. Jack and Lyndon are really great guys, they'll watch out for them. And both men believe in ice cream treats. The kids will be spoiled rotten." She poured enthusiasm into her voice as Shanty read the note.

Both brows came together. Her face flooded with color. It was a simple enough question. *Was there a bug planted on her so*

663

someone could overhear their conversation? Shanty stared down at the note for a long time. She shook her head several times and her eyes filled with tears. Her hands trembled.

She pressed her fingers over her mouth and nodded.

"You'd usually stay at the safe house for a week before being taken to the main property where you're housed. Because you have children, I'm hoping we can put you up in one of the little houses." Flambé poured enthusiasm into her voice as she pushed the second note at her. "We're trying to make one available as quickly as possible."

Shanty read it.

Betrayal for money? Or what?

"I'm sorry. I'm so sorry. They have my mate. My Reiner." She whispered it leaning into the fountain.

"I suspected as much." Flambé spoke softly. The others may have moved away, but she didn't trust that leopards might not overhear.

Can you insist on contacting him? Hearing his voice so you know he's alive? Answer in a whisper but keep very close to the fountain. She wrote it out carefully, showed it to Shanty and when the woman nodded, tore it off, crumpled the paper and put it care-

664

fully in the pocket of her jeans.

Flambé flashed her an encouraging smile and indicated the water bottle. "Do you know who is behind this?"

"A man named Matherson. He wanted me to say I was beaten and my husband was following me. That I couldn't get away from him. I was supposed to say I was afraid to tell that to the men. I was to tell you that he threatened to kill me and take my children." She put the water bottle to her mouth but didn't drink. Tears were falling and she tried to keep her face covered if anyone could see her. "I didn't want to hurt you. I really didn't. He said he would kill Reiner."

"The most important thing is to find your mate and get him free before we do anything else. Can you insist on a call, demanding to hear his voice before you go any further? Just step onto the porch away from me. Say you think I'm really nice and you want to know your husband is safe before you betray me. Something that will convince them you need encouragement. You need to hear his physical voice. Make them let you talk to him. If they let you, stay on with him as long as you can."

Shanty took a deep breath and then she nodded. She stood up and walked away from Flambé. Flambé hadn't heard a lie in

665

her voice. Either the woman was very, very good at deception, or her husband really had been taken prisoner. Matherson wanted Karisa, Basil Andino's mate, back. It had become a matter of pride with him. She also had the feeling that he was just as determined to claim her. He wouldn't keep her long, but he'd claim her.

A little shiver went down her spine. She wished she knew more good shifter males. Ania insisted there were many and that she'd introduce Flambé to them as soon as they took care of her problems and Flamme was no longer in heat. That was another thing that was a little worrisome. Her skin was beginning to feel a little prickly. It was very early in the morning, although the sun was out. They'd deliberately scheduled the meeting for early morning, when Flamme should be worn out from the night before from her run with Shturm.

Ambroise is getting a lock on the position. Sevastyan kept her informed through the small earpiece. *Gorya, Logan, Kyanite, Trey and Jeremiah are on the move and as soon as they have an actual address will hit the place and secure him. Will let you know. Hopefully, she stays on the phone long enough to give us an address.*

Flambé silently willed Shanty to do so.

666

Shanty glanced at her once and Flambé mouthed for her to keep talking and then took a hasty drink of water, grateful she was farther back in the shadows, because Blaise was looking at the two women. He paced back and forth, ignoring Terry and Jet, who paid more attention to security, watching for any sign of danger. They faced away from Blaise.

Flambé's heart began to pound. She pulled out her phone, unable to help herself, and texted Sevastyan. Worried Blaise might harm Terry or Jet.

Under control, baby, Sevastyan's soft voice whispered in her ear.

She had to have faith that he did. Why was she so nervous? Why was she suddenly having doubts all over again? She pushed both hands through her hair, finding she was shaking. She didn't want Blaise to be the one betraying her. All along she kept hoping they were all wrong.

Blaise had never really shown any signs of being a typical male shifter, arrogant and controlling — like Sevastyan. Like Mitya. Like so many of the others she saw take advantage of the women. He'd been sweet and friendly and always accommodating. When she'd turned him down after he'd asked her out, he'd never gotten weird with her, or upset. He took her refusal in stride. She'd made it clear she didn't mix work with pleasure and she never had. If Blaise could turn on her after years of acting so caring, what did that mean for her future with a man like Sevastyan?

You're crying, baby. What's wrong? What's going through your head? I'll come to you right now if you need me. The hell with the plan. I'll figure something out. The words whispered in her ear via the tiny radio.

She heard the anxiety in Sevastyan's voice. He would come to her. He would blow the entire operation just because she was in tears. She wiped her face with her palms and shook her head. Nothing. Being silly. I get things in my head, she texted him.

She kept her eyes on Shanty, knowing just texting Sevestyan that much was enough for him to figure out what she was thinking. He knew her that well. It was their connection through the ropes. The way he read her.

Ambroise has an address. The boys are close. Tell Shanty to end the call.

Triumph burst through her. Flambé immediately signaled Shanty, who reluctantly allowed whoever was talking to her to dictate to her what she had to do. She kept nodding her head and sobbing. Abruptly she ended the call and returned to the table.

668

"They're on their way to rescue him," Flambé whispered to Shanty and indicated the water bottle. "Are the children okay?" she asked aloud for the sake of anyone listening.

"Yes. They're very happy. Playing." Shanty gave a little sniff. "I wanted you to meet me in South Africa for a reason. I wasn't being silly. It's my husband." She lowered her voice even more. "He's very abusive. When the poachers came, I took the opportunity to run with the children to try to get away from him. Most of the lair went in one direction, but I hid in all the chaos and he was fighting back with the men and I was able to get out with the children without him seeing us."

Flambé frowned and leaned forward, dropping her chin onto the heel of her hand, her gaze on Shanty as if entirely riveted. Whoever was listening and watching would definitely think that Flambé was taking the bait. They needed to give the rescue team as much time as possible to get to her husband.

"Your mate's name is Reiner?" Flambé interjected just for something to say, to slow time down.

Shanty got the hint and took another drink of water, nodding. "Yes. He's horrible.

669

He likes to beat me. It excites him. That's what he does before he . . ." She broke off and looked down at the wooden beams running under her feet. "He's very violent when he touches me after he beats me."

Flambé would have known she was lying even if she couldn't hear lies. Shanty sounded as if she'd rehearsed a written script. Someone had made her repeat the words over and over until they were memorized verbatim.

"I'm sorry, what did you say?" she asked, sitting up straight as if she couldn't believe her ears.

"He's horrible. He likes to beat me. It excites him. That's what he does before he . . ." She broke off, but this time she looked down at her hands, fingers twisted together in her lap. "He's very violent when he touches me after he beats me."

Definitely scripted and memorized. She'd repeated it verbatim down to the exact way she had acted. No one did that unless they were lying. Shanty put her hands back on the table and looked up at Flambé, almost afraid to breathe.

Flambé reached across the table sympathetically and laid her hand over Shanty's. "I'm so sorry. That must be so awful for you. The extraction team got you out fast.

He couldn't have followed you here."

"No, but he'll know. He'll find me. You know it's impossible to hide from a leopard. No one can do it. No one. He said if I ever ran from him, he'd beat me to death. He promised me he would do it." Shanty put her head down on the table and cried like her heart was breaking. The sobbing was genuine, a reaction to the terror of knowing men were trying to get her husband free of those holding him hostage.

"There are agencies in the United States that protect women," Flambé said gently.

In her mind she was urging the rescue team to hurry. Every time she looked up, she could see that Blaise was inching closer to them. He couldn't get too close. The moment the rescue team signaled they had Reiner, she was to make a break for the front door with Shanty. It was unlocked. She had only to fling the door open, get inside and slam it closed. Once inside, Blaise and Matherson couldn't get to them. Unfortunately, that would leave Jet and Terry to the enemy, and that didn't sit well with her.

"How are those agencies going to protect me against a shifter?" Shanty demanded, sitting up straight and dashing at her tears. "I watch enough news to know that your

671

protection orders didn't stop stalkers if they wanted to really hurt someone or kill them. It happens all the time. Judges throw out cases due to lack of evidence and cops don't listen."

Flambé sighed. "Well, that much is true. I have a man stalking me and I called the cops. I even own a very respected business and that hasn't helped at all. They told me he hadn't really done anything to warrant them arresting him. I felt threatened by him. He showed up everywhere I was, but until he ran me off the road and assaulted me, which I didn't have proof of because it took place where no one was around, he hadn't really done anything the cops considered to be dangerous."

She rubbed her hairline where the swelling had been. "We can move you out of state, Shanty. We've got other businesses set up where you can work and make money. I can have my people watch the airports to see if he enters the country. There's a man named Drake Donovan who owns a security company. I'm sure you've heard of him. He might be able to help. I can reach out to him on your behalf as well."

She wanted to text Sevastyan that the team had to hurry. What if something was going wrong? She could see panic beginning to gather in Shanty's eyes. She was beginning to feel it in the pit of her stomach. How long did a rescue take? How many men were holding Shanty's husband hostage? Did Ambroise have that information? She should have asked. She had to keep calm so Shanty would.

She lifted the water bottle to her mouth and took a long, deliberate drink, giving herself time to mark Blaise's position. He was a few feet closer to them, but still several yards away. He was certain Shanty was doing her job, convincing Flambé she was an abused woman.

Shanty shook her head with a little moan of fear. "He'll find me. You know he will. You have to help me, Flambé. I know you can. I heard that you can."

Flambé drummed her fingers on the tabletop. It would be risky to capitulate this soon. She wouldn't do that. "I'm trying to help you, Shanty. You're not willing to take any of the avenues I've got open for you. I will admit, running from a shifter isn't the easiest thing, especially with three little ones in tow, but if he's as bad as you say, I don't think you have a choice. If it was me, I'd opt to make a run for it. I'd go to Donovan for help. He's got an entire security force and he knows all kinds of places he can put

673

you where your husband would have a difficult time finding you."

Shanty was silent for a long time. "Have you sent other women to Donovan before?" she finally asked, her voice very low, but she made certain the sound carried enough that Blaise, the way he'd inched closer, couldn't fail to hear, nor could anyone else who was listening through the bug that had been planted on her.

Flambé shrugged. "Once or twice it was necessary. He's very good at making people disappear. I had considered availing myself of his services at one point. I was waiting for you."

Technically, there was no lie there either. Blaise would hear the ring of truth. Matherson was on the other end of Shanty's wire. He would hear it as well. Both men would think that Basil Andino's mate, Karisa, had gone to Drake Donovan and he'd protected her by sending her to some undisclosed location. In truth, Karisa was very safe, long gone in the route Flambé had established and used very sparingly and only when absolutely necessary. Only four women aided her with that route and she used a special scent blocker perfected just for her by Charisse Mercier from New Orleans.

For the first time, Flambé felt just a little

674

amused. She could see a hint of frustration on Blaise's face. He believed her. He wanted the entire mess over with, almost more than she did. Terry was casting little warning glances over his shoulder, which meant his gut was telling him something wasn't right. He'd always had good instincts. He wanted them finished so he could get Shanty out of there.

"Will Donovan be able to hide me from Reiner?" There was real desperation in Shanty's voice. Real panic welling up in her eyes. On her face. She was going to lose it in another minute.

Flambé instinctively took a deep breath to try to breathe for both of them.

They've got Reiner Jacobs safe. He is with the rescue team. He is safe and unharmed. Sevastyan's voice was calm and oh-so-welcoming in her ear. *I repeat, Jacobs is safe and with the rescue team. Get inside with Shanty now, Flambé.*

That was a clear order and one she would have no trouble obeying. A smile broke out on her face. She leaned close to Shanty, caught her hand and squeezed hard. "Safe. Unharmed. They have him." She stood up and tugged Shanty to her feet. *"Run."*

Flambé was already in motion, running for the front door. It was already wide open,

675

Kirill and Matvei stepping outside with automatic weapons to protect them as the two women sprinted across the porch.

Blaise flung himself down on the ground, using the corner of the verandah column as cover, aiming his gun at Shanty. Flambé paused just long enough to allow Shanty to get in front of her, her body blocking the woman from Blaise's aim just as Kirill and Matvei laid down covering fire.

Terry and Jet had no idea what was going on or who the enemy was. Both men had weapons out, but as exposed as they were, they had the presence of mind to go down to the ground with their hands out in a sign of surrender.

Blaise rolled under the corner of the verandah, kicked off his shoes, stripped fast, and shifted. His leopard crawled under the house to the other side and ran full out to where two SUVs with Matherson and the crews of ten shifters waited on an old little-used dirt back road behind the property.

All of the shifters were out of the vehicles, weapons ready, prowling around, looking as if they were in a high state of awareness. Blaise shifted, uncaring of his nudity. "We've got to get out of here."

"Where is she?" Matherson demanded. "What happened?"

"She ran. She and that fucking woman ran into the house. It was some kind of setup. I thought you had it covered," Blaise snapped.

Matherson immediately whipped out his phone and texted. "They can kill her husband now, that lying, double-crossing bitch." He stared down at his phone. Blinked. Stared. Texted repeatedly. Swore.

"We gotta go now," Blaise repeated. "Right now."

Matherson shot him between the eyes and watched the body drop to the ground. "Let's go get that little bitch. Both of them," he shouted, waving his gun. He signaled his crew toward the house in the distance.

Like wraiths emerging from shadows high up in the trees, ghostly men dressed in combat gear appeared, guns aimed at those on the ground. "Drop your weapons." Sevastyan gave the order in his usual calm, very quiet manner.

"Fuck you," Matherson yelled and lifted his automatic, spraying the trees.

Immediately chaos broke out as for the next three minutes hell reigned. There was nowhere for those on the ground to hide from the barrage of return bullets coming at them and Matherson had made it impossible to surrender. Within three minutes it was once again quiet and those on the ground were either dead or dying.

Sevastyan leapt from the tree, Zinoviy and Vikenti flanking him, while Zakhar stayed close, making it clear he was acting as a bodyguard. Sevastyan gave him an annoyed warning look, but as usual, Zakhar ignored him.

The other team members came out of the trees as well, checking the downed shifters for any signs of life while Sevastyan went straight to Matherson.

"You really could be the devil, Matherson," Sevastyan greeted, seeing he was alive.

Franco Matherson had been shot in both his shoulder and leg. The shoulder was shattered, but the leg wound looked no more than superficial. No one could be that lucky. His weapon had been flung some distance from him and he'd lain as if dead among the bodies, probably hoping no one would notice he was alive so he could slink off.

Matherson groaned but didn't respond.

"Sevastyan," Zakhar warned.

Sevastyan had scented the two strange shifters coming up behind them. In spite of many guns trained on them, they kept walking toward the group with easy, ground-covering strides. Both men were tall and dark-skinned. They had the roped muscles

678

and easy fluid, flowing movements of the shifters. They were very much at ease as they walked right up to Sevastyan and bowed slightly to him.

"I am Luan. This is my brother, Arno. We've come a long way to find this man and bring him to justice. He has committed many crimes against our people. He has brought disgrace to our lair. I ask that you allow us to administer the final justice to him. We have to answer to the elders and our lair."

Matherson shook his head. "I stayed away from the lair. I didn't go near any of the women."

Sevastyan ignored him. Luan and Arno ignored him.

"It is important for the honor of our lair," Arno continued, as if Matherson hadn't interrupted his brother.

"Of course. I understand completely. We have plenty of cleanup to do, but the man has to go. He's been stalking my woman," Sevastyan said.

Luan nodded. "I am aware of his crimes." For the first time he looked down at Matherson, his dark eyes settling on the man. There was no malice. No personal animosity. "You betrayed every sacred law of the lair, Franco Matherson."

679

"I have money. So much," Matherson cried, thinking to bribe them.

"You failed to protect and hold sacred our women or protect and treasure our children," Arno intoned.

"You committed crimes against the outside world and humanity," Luan continued.

"You hunted and killed others of our species knowing they were near extinction," Arno added to the list of crimes.

"You risked exposing all of us to outsiders," Luan said.

"You hunted and murdered other shifters, men and women, for the sole purpose of your pleasure. You have been sentenced by the elders of the lair to die as an abomination," Arno pronounced.

There was no waiting. No hesitation. Luan plunged a sharp blade directly through Matherson's throat while simultaneously Arno's blade went through the man's heart. Sevastyan regarded the open, shocked eyes as they stared, horrified and unbelieving that anyone would dare take his life. He had too much money. Too much power. People did what he ordered. He bought and sold people. No one would dare kill him.

"I heard his good friend Basil Andino disappeared recently," Luan said matter-of-factly. He pulled his knife free and casually

680

wiped blood from the ceremonial knife onto Matherson's shirt. "He was last seen drinking in a bar with a young Russian woman. They left together and no one has seen either of them since."

Sevastyan raised an eyebrow. "I thought Andino was a married man. What would he be doing in a bar with a woman?"

Luan nodded. "That is so. Perhaps the rumor is not true." He bowed. "Thank you again. My lair owes you a favor."

20

Sevastyan woke in the middle of the night the way he often did. The moon was high, a silver ball shining through the wall of glass, and stars scattered like diamonds across a dark sky. It was a perfect night. He turned his head to look down at the woman lying so still beside him.

Flambé rarely moved in her sleep. She always curled up, her bright red hair a splash of crimson against the black sheets. The artist in him loved that picture, the contrast of red and black. It was why he often used those colors of ropes on her.

She slept nude, the way he liked, and he was tempted to wake her. He would, but not yet. It was rare that he got the chance to touch her so gently, when her nerve endings allowed it, and he had taken full advantage. He'd made love to her as tenderly as possible the night before. Slowly. Making them both wait. His fingers threaded through hers. Looking into her eyes. Seeing into her heart. Her soul. Giving her his. God, but he loved her.

He began to untangle his body slowly from Flambé's. He liked to sleep with his arm locked around her waist. One thigh over hers. Sometimes her breast cupped in his palm. His cheek on top of her head. He wrapped himself around her. He knew it was because oftentimes it still felt as if she had one foot out the door. She would suddenly, inexplicably withdraw from him, and he knew she was second-guessing herself, becoming fearful again. He had a fear that she might try to run and instinctively, he held her closer.

At first, whenever Flambé became afraid, Sevastyan would try to step up his tenderness, being thoughtful, making certain he spent more time with her and being more attentive. Over time, he realized those things backfired. She associated the niceties that shifters did for their women with setting them up for the bigger fall later. Once he realized she didn't respond well to his sweetness, he would fall back on his rope art and the connection they had through that. Eventually, she would talk to him and after, when he held her, she would relax into him and be able to let go of her insecurities.

The fact that she had those trust issues upset her more than it did him. He reached down and caught at her silky hair, letting it slide through his fingers the way he always slid the ropes through his fingers, feeling protective of her. She had worked hard on their property, more so on the outside than the inside of their home. She'd made few changes to the interior, but the outside was already so transformed he barely recognized the property. Ania had been shocked, admitting the landscaping was unbelievably beautiful and should be written up in a magazine.

Very slowly, so as not to disturb his woman, Sevastyan slid from the bed and padded across the room to the long, thick glass wall. Ordinarily, he would have lowered the privacy screens so Flambé could sleep in going into the weekend, but he liked full moons, and so did she. Most full moons, he kept the screens up so when he woke, he spent time absorbing the beauty of the night.

Opening the door, he slipped out onto the balcony and wandered around to face the large two-story indoor garden. The two garages had fit seamlessly together. They had their own version of a lush garden of paradise in that giant glass rectangle housing trees, waterfalls and luscious plants of all kinds. Small stone pathways wandered through the garden where chairs or a couch invited one to sit and rest or read or play depending on the mood.

Small lockers were hidden, housing his ropes in different areas as well as other toys and weapons they might need in an emergency. Sevastyan believed in being prepared for anything. For the leopards there were climbing routes as well as places for them to curl up and lie together up high in the loft concealed among the plants.

In one corner of either end were bathrooms, thankfully already built in. Flambé had remodeled them to fit with the theme and they were artfully draped with plants on the outside. The doors were an archway with flowering vines crawling up. There was a small kitchen off either of the bathrooms where refrigerators housed their very cold water, something he always insisted on for both of them. He ran hot and she needed to stay hydrated.

There was something very special about the indoor garden. He couldn't quite decide if it was because the two of them had made the plans together and worked side by side doing quite a lot of the planting once her crew had gotten all the big items in. She'd showed him how to plant the smaller shrubs and flowers and he'd gotten good at it.

They laughed a lot together while they worked. He took orders from her and she talked a lot about things that mattered to her. She'd been a little shy at first, but in the end, because he clearly was interested in anything Flambé, she talked more and more to him. He found that because she gave up little things about herself, he was more willing to answer questions about himself and give her things about him no one else really knew. That garden was the place they shared the most of themselves while they worked. It was still young, and there was still so much more work to do, but both looked forward to it.

Sevastyan scented Flambé before he felt her hand move up the back of his thigh to his left buttock. It was an intimacy she would never have shown a few short weeks earlier and it set his heart tripping. Her hair slid over his skin, following the path of her fingers and he closed his eyes, absorbing the feel of the silky strands as they moved over his left cheek. Then he felt her lips, soft and warm, kissing him, shaping his firm muscles right before her teeth nipped daringly.

He laughed softly and caught her arm,

bringing her around to the front of him, locking her there, her back to his front so they were both looking out over their property. "It's so beautiful, Flambé. The difference you've made not only to our land, but to me, to our home, defies all logic. I had no idea one woman could change my life the way you have."

"I haven't done much in the house, Sevastyan," she admitted, rubbing her chin on his forearm. "I just am not the best interior designer. I've been considering bringing various plants into the house. We've got the room. The ceilings are extremely high and the lighting is perfect. It's good for the air. You've already got a few, but I think we could use more."

There was a little anxious note in her voice that surprised him. She still wasn't sure of herself when it came to ascertaining ownership with him.

"Babe, I told you to do whatever makes you happy. This is your home too. I put a ring on your finger. That's what I cared about and you let me. I get all the sex I want, when I want, how I want. Our outdoor property is amazing. My woman is gorgeous and she indulges me."

"She can't cook."

"You cook."

687

She burst out laughing. "Is that what you call it? Honey, your cooking is a million times better than mine."

"I heat up what the chef leaves us."

"I burned up what the chef left us the last three times."

He kissed the top of her head, wrapping his arms more securely around her. "That may have had something to do with you being tied up in ropes."

"But I forgot to tell you I had something in the oven. I was a little too enthusiastic. What if I'd burned down the house?"

"The smoke alarms did their job." Amusement burst through him the way it did most of the time now when he was with her. Or maybe it was pure joy. He couldn't remember wanting to laugh before; now, it seemed, he was happy more often than not, and he attributed that to the woman who had taught him how to have fun.

"I suppose they did."

"And you haven't made the same mistake again since I tied you so beautifully in the corner of the kitchen, facing the stove . . ."

"And the window," she groused, "telling me I was to learn my lesson."

"Red rope again," he pointed out. "Beautiful diamond pattern, the harness framed your incredible breasts. I'm very fond of

688

your breasts."

"As I recall, you spent time playing when you were supposed to be working," she pointed out, pretending to be pouting.

"That's only because you're such a temptation." There was no remorse. "I want to tie you in the garden tonight with the full moon shining down on your red hair." He swept his hand through it. "It might take a little time for what I've got in mind, but it will be beautiful. It will leave marks on your skin, but nowhere you can't cover up and only for a couple of days. It's the kind of tie that will make me wild and very out of control for you. I'm just going to warn you, baby. I'm going to play for a while and tease you until you catch up with me and then I'm fucking you hard. You up for that?"

Her hand went up to his wrist and then rubbed up his arm. "I'm always up for that, Sevastyan."

He could practically hear her purr.

"After, we'll have to let the leopards out. Shturm can't go without Flamme any longer than I can go without you. If I deprive him, he gets edgy and moody."

She burst out laughing. "Believe me, Sevastyan, I'm well aware."

He turned her in his arms and found her mouth with his. Gently. Tenderly. Loving

689

her. Giving her that because once they walked out to their garden of paradise, he knew it was going to be hot, wild and savage, the way they both could get when they showed each other their feral side.

He lifted his head and cupped the side of her face, looking down into her eyes. "You know I love you. No matter how we come together, Flambé, you know I love you, right? You're my world."

She leaned into him, tilting her head back, her gaze meeting his steadily. "I know you love me, Sevastyan. I love you more than you could possibly know. I love when we're wild and crazy and I love when we're gentle now. Before, that was what scared me, because I could feel the emotion. Now I feel the love no matter how we come together."

He bent his head and took her mouth again. This time he wasn't quite as gentle.

690

ABOUT THE AUTHOR

Christine Feehan is the #1 *New York Times* bestselling author of the Carpathian series, the GhostWalker series, the Leopard series, the Shadow Riders series, and the Sea Haven novels, including the Drake Sisters series and the Sisters of the Heart series.

The employees of Thorndike Press hope you have enjoyed this Large Print book. All our Thorndike, Wheeler, and Kennebec Large Print titles are designed for easy reading, and all our books are made to last. Other Thorndike Press Large Print books are available at your library, through selected bookstores, or directly from us.

For information about titles, please call:
(800) 223-1244

or visit our website at:
gale.com/thorndike

To share your comments, please write:
Publisher
Thorndike Press
10 Water St., Suite 310
Waterville, ME 04901